Water *is* Wider

Also by Marie Green McKeon

A BALM IN GILEAD

Water
is
Wider

Marie Green McKeon

WATER IS WIDER

White Bird Publishing
Email: whitebirdpub@gmail.com

Cover design: Rachel Caldwell

ISBN: 978-0-9904338-4-2

First Edition

For the ghosts of those gone before us,
And for those with us now. All connected by love.

Blood is thicker than water.

—COMMON PROVERB

For Blood, as all men know, than Water's thicker,
But water's wider, thank the Lord, than Blood.

—ALDOUS HUXLEY,
"Ninth Philosopher's Song," *Leda*

One

It could have been a prison cell, this room in the attic. From her vantage point on the floor, she surveyed her surroundings and imagined: this was what it was like to be jailed like a prisoner. No, not *like* a prisoner. She *was* a prisoner. Locked up alone in this dusty room.

She ran a finger through the grime next to her in a straight line, adding a loop to make a "P," and finishing her name with a flourish. *Phoebe.*

Okay, she thought as she considered the word. So the dust had been accumulating for years while she had been there only a few hours. Yet every minute felt like an eternity since the argument, the one that had broken out during breakfast, when her stepmother Adele had taken the startled Phoebe by the arm, marched her upstairs, and shoved her into the attic room. In retrospect, the few moments of stunned silence that had followed had offered Phoebe's sole opportunity to escape. Instead, she had stood still, bewildered and then alarmed as she heard a key scrape in the lock and Adele's footsteps retreat.

Phoebe groaned and rested her head against the wall. "I have to get out!" she cried. A slight echo responded, which only made her feel more isolated and panicky.

She lightly pummeled her forehead with her fists, beating back the fear that she really was abandoned, that this was no joke. She had to reel back in that thought, that *belief,* that had strengthened her for the hours so far—the certainty that her stepmother Adele was simply acting on impulse when she shoved Phoebe through the door, pulled it shut, and locked it. Of course, Adele would come to her senses. She would feel bad, she would drive back home, and release her, Phoebe told herself. But the day wore on, and no Adele.

The more she thought about it, the more Phoebe became convinced that there was only one solution. That was to escape. She grew desperate for some kind of brainstorm or any idea at all. She ran through endless mental plans and dismissed them all as silly and childish.

"Think, think," she muttered, clutching her head. What chance did her eleven-year-old brain have of coming up with some way out of here? A genius probably couldn't do it.

In near despair, she looked around the empty room. No tools, no equipment, no furniture. Nothing but dust, the horrid, green paint peeling off the walls, and a rough, wooden floor someone had once started to paint dark brown. But the project had been abandoned, so only about a third of the expanse was covered with haphazard brush strokes.

At least there was a window, Phoebe thought, glancing at it again. Graceful tree branches brushed the glass, but unfortunately they didn't offer a means of escape. She had realized that right away. As soon as she spotted the window, she had run over and started tugging on it, thinking that she would jump, third floor or no third floor, only to discover that the wooden frame around the glass was painted shut. After the long hours, she supposed she should appreciate the fact that the window allowed light to come in despite its layers of filmy dirt.

Judging from the light, it had to be afternoon. Someone was bound to come home soon and rescue her. *Or maybe they won't*, she thought, again pushing down panic. Her eyes landed on the blank, unforgiving door that stared back. Maybe that still offered some way of escaping? It was the most obvious way out.

The door was obviously also a dead end. Duh. She had not only heard the key turning in the lock, but she had also rattled the doorknob countless times since just to check. Nonetheless, she scrutinized the door as if it held a secret latch if only she could locate it. She studied the cut-glass, crystal-like doorknob and the small, old-fashioned metal plate beneath it. She peered through the keyhole where barely a scrap of the empty hallway was visible. She pressed her face against the floor and looked through a gap below the door. Not much more to see.

Phoebe straightened. Why should a forgotten room up in the attic have a lock and key anyway? There were no keys to any other room in the house, except the front door. It might make sense to the grownups, but to her, it was a mystery.

She rubbed her eyes. She had nothing to show for all this mental exercise but a headache. Maybe because she was hungry. She had had nothing to eat since breakfast, and even that was interrupted by the fight with Adele. Once she was free, Phoebe thought, one of the first things she would do would be to eat. Second, she would run away from home.

So many kids talked about running away from home, Phoebe knew. Her friend Alicia threatened it about once a week. But Phoebe had been seriously thinking about it, and not because Adele was mean to her. Well, locking her in a room all day wasn't good, even if Phoebe did have to consider what a brat she had been, especially that morning. It wasn't because Adele didn't want her anymore, which might be true. Phoebe was pretty sure Adele hadn't been so crazy about her lately.

No, the real reason Phoebe needed to run away from home was that she had to find her father. He had disappeared. And

Phoebe felt—no, she *knew* with all her being—that he needed her help.

But the very, very first thing I'll do once I get out of here is go to the bathroom. The thought popped in her head and, instantly, she regretted giving form to it. After so many hours, the sudden urgency threatened to overwhelm her. She started pacing. *Clear your brain*, she told herself. *Think of nothing.*

That was the moment, when she stopped concentrating so hard, that she came up with the solution, the escape route, like remembering a name after you quit groping for it. She could conjure up a mental image of the key that would unlock this door.

She had seen the little, silver key hanging on a paper clip that served as a makeshift key chain on Adele's dresser amid tubes of makeup and hair goo. At least, that was where it had been a few days before when Phoebe was searching her parents' bedroom.

Adele would have been angry about the snooping, but Phoebe convinced herself there was a very good reason for it. Her father had gone missing with no warning, no note, no phone call, nothing, and Adele seemed curiously uninterested in finding him despite Phoebe's frequent questions. Searching for clues seemed like a first step.

One afternoon when she got home from school and before Adele returned from work, Phoebe combed through the house for anything that might shed light on her father's disappearance. Maybe she could find some kind of clue, she thought, something that would tell whether he was in some sort of trouble.

She focused most of her search on her parents' bedroom. She hunted through his closet, flipping through hangers of jackets, crisp shirts, and neatly pressed trousers. Maybe some clothes were missing, but it looked to Phoebe that most of them were undisturbed. This scared her. If this was a planned trip, like Adele was saying it was, why didn't he pack?

Phoebe turned to the dresser, where she spotted the key. She plucked it from the clutter and examined it closely, wondering whether it could possibly be connected with her father. She decided that it was just a key and probably had been there forever. She tossed it back and continued her search, opening and shutting drawers. Her father's drawers were somewhat sparse, but she wasn't sure if that was because he had taken some clothes, or because he didn't have overflowing drawers like Adele. Hers were filled to capacity, and most wouldn't shut properly.

Phoebe was about to close one drawer when she spotted it—stuck in but not completely hidden by a small, neatly stacked pile of her father's t-shirts. It was a postcard.

One side, the photograph side, showed a montage of scenes, mostly trees in colorful fall foliage, swept over by large lettering: *Greetings from Connecticut.* On the reverse side, in the blank, white space for penning a message, was a terse note in small block printing: "I'm OK. In Orange, Conn." There was no signature.

Phoebe studied the postcard for a long time, turning it over and re-reading the brief message. She first thought, *This has to be from Dad.* He had grown up in Connecticut, and every now and then he talked about his childhood there, especially the summers he spent with his grandparents. Once or twice, her father had said that one day they might visit his brother who still lived there, but they never had.

The more she looked at the card, the more doubtful she became. Why printing? Her father always wrote in cursive script, never print. Why not call? Anyone could have sent this postcard, especially if they didn't want her father to be in touch. Maybe it was a kidnapper. Phoebe tucked the card back in the pile of shirts and slowly slid the drawer shut.

She wanted to pull out the shirts and hold them close to breathe in a whiff of him. "Where are you, Dad?" she whispered to the mirror over the dresser. She blinked, hoping that her father would suddenly appear behind her, imagining that he would tell her that he was back, and this had all been a big mistake.

In that moment, she jumped. She could have sworn that something moved in the corner of the mirror. She blinked again but saw only her own reflection, standing alone. It was probably a breeze—Adele had left the window open—moving the curtains a little. But somehow she could imagine that small movement was a ghost, and that ghost was her mother.

Now, sitting in the attic and remembering that moment, Phoebe could scoff at the idea of anything being in the mirror. But even if it was silly, she couldn't help but wonder if this whole series of events, whatever had happened to her father had some connection to her mother. Maybe it all began with her mother.

Phoebe had been only two years old when her mother died of cancer. He met and married Adele only months after the death of Phoebe's mother, but he was always careful to keep alive the sacred memory of her mother for Phoebe. These were memories Phoebe didn't have but thought she did. She had heard the descriptions and stories so often that they became real. Although Adele was the only mother Phoebe had known, it was as if a giant portrait of her birth mother hovered over them.

Adele didn't seem to mind. She was a no-nonsense person, the type who hated putting on airs, she always said. Everything about her relationship with Phoebe signaled: *I'm not Phoebe's real mother, so why pretend?* She taught Phoebe to call her by her given name. Even after Phoebe's younger brother Bobby was born, and he learned to call her "Mommy," Phoebe was not permitted to do the same. She remembered the time in kindergarten, when trying to model the other children, she tentatively addressed her step-mother as "Mom." The correction was firm and immediate: "You call me Adele, okay?"

It had been okay, Phoebe thought. She knew Adele took care of her like a mother would her own child. Anyway, there had always been Dad. The special bond with him couldn't be broken.

Phoebe stared at the locked door and began to wonder if maybe her father's disappearance had something to do with Adele. Thoughts wandered in her head. *Maybe he doesn't want to be married to her anymore. Maybe he doesn't love her.*

"No!" Her outcry was a rejection of this idea. It wasn't possible that her father would leave them. He might leave Adele but he wouldn't leave *her,* his daughter. Every day, he told Phoebe he loved her. No. The answer was that he must be hurt or the victim of bad guys. Otherwise, he would have contacted her.

Still, the way her stepmother was acting was weird, Phoebe thought. If Adele was convinced her husband was leaving them, she was awfully calm about it. Phoebe's brother Bobby didn't seem fazed either, but he was only six, too young to understand anything.

Adele had told them both that their dad was away on an unexpected trip. She didn't give this excuse the first night he was gone, but it had been her answer since then. Bobby accepted this unquestioning, but Phoebe didn't buy it. Her father never did anything unexpectedly. He was very precise about his schedule, his eating habits, his clothing. "Fussy," Adele called it. He came home from work at the same time every evening and had the same routine. He headed upstairs to change into comfortable clothes and then stopped at Phoebe's room to ask about her day. There was never a break in the routine. That was what made her father's not coming home so strange.

During dinner, Phoebe kept throwing pointed looks at his empty chair, at the plate and silverware set out for him as usual, and then at her stepmother. Adele avoided eye contact.

They ate in silence until Adele cleared her throat and said brightly, "I'm sure your father will be home any minute." Phoebe dropped her fork in disgust. When Adele glared, Phoebe mumbled her request to be excused from the table. Later, as she finished her homework, she noted that her father's place setting remained untouched. Adele cleaned the kitchen and packed lunches, and Bobby watched television, both seemingly oblivious.

Over the following days, her father's absence weighed heavier and heavier on Phoebe. She peppered Adele with questions.

"I told you, he had to go on a business trip." Adele didn't look up from the pot of chili she was stirring at the stove.

"Why didn't he tell us about it?" Phoebe demanded. She waited. "Aren't you going to call the police?" she shouted into Adele's silence. "My dad is missing!"

"Calm down, Phoebe. He's fine. He'll come back soon."

"No, he is not fine!" Phoebe stood in the middle of the kitchen, jaw clenched. She turned and ran upstairs.

After that, Phoebe took on what she thought, resentfully, should have been Adele's role. She lay awake at night worrying. She kept watch at the windows, hoping to see her father striding up the walk to tell her it was all a big mistake. She tried to think of ways to find him. But all she landed on were far-fetched ideas or ones that she, as a young girl, had no hope of accomplishing, such as gathering the entire neighborhood into a search party. She could try to wear down Adele, though. She harped at her stepmother every day until Adele's stoicism, and her patience, wore thin.

When Adele came home from work looking spent, Phoebe noticed but didn't care. "We're wasting time," she told Adele. "We have to look for him. Let's go now!" She followed her stepmother from the living room to the kitchen to the dining room, like a dog nipping at her heels.

On this particular evening, Adele leaned against the ladder back of the dining room chair, lit a cigarette, and snapped her lighter shut. She twisted her jaw to blow the smoke away, but Phoebe waved her hand pointedly and coughed. Her father had been adamant about not smoking and had never allowed it in the house. Yet here was Adele, who had quit smoking more than two years ago, brazenly lighting up at the dining-room table and using a saucer as an ashtray.

"I think there was foul play," Phoebe announced. She had heard about foul play on TV.

A smile played around Adele's mouth. Then, she looked down and unnecessarily tapped the ashes of the cigarette.

"I'm afraid you have to face it, Phoebe. He's gone."

"No, something happened to him. He wouldn't just go away like this." Phoebe wanted to cry, wanted to add, "He wouldn't leave me," but something about Adele's exhausted, sad voice stopped her.

"It's very difficult to understand. It's hard for me to understand sometimes." Adele bit her lip as she looked sorrowfully at Phoebe. "But it's a grownup thing. You're still a kid."

Phoebe, once more pacing the attic room while recalling this exchange, stubbornly thought, *I might be just a kid, but I still have to deal with this. It's my dad who's missing.* But she felt guilty at the same time. Maybe she went too far that morning. Maybe she shouldn't have made that threat at breakfast.

Phoebe had awoken feeling quarrelsome and achy after another restless night. She splashed cold water on her bleary eyes, but that didn't stop them from burning. She felt like she was moving underwater as she stumbled around her room getting dressed for school. Adele called upstairs twice, telling her to hurry.

When Phoebe finally entered the kitchen, chaos reigned. Adele apparently had awoken in a terrible mood herself. She rushed back and forth between the refrigerator and the kitchen table to check the homework Bobby was finishing.

"How many times do I have to ask you, Bobby, whether you've done your homework?" Adele demanded. "As a matter of fact, I did ask you last night, and you told me yes! You are going to be punished, mister." She glanced up at the clock. "Look at the time! You're going to make me late. Phoebe, please hurry. Can't you move faster than that?"

Phoebe, who had poured dry cereal into a bowl and was methodically crunching it as she studied the back of the cereal box, said, "I'll move faster if you start moving faster to find Dad."

"What did you say?"

Phoebe looked up. Bobby was staring at her, and Adele was standing over her. Phoebe shrank back.

"What did you say?" Adele repeated. "And you're talking with your mouth full."

Phoebe swallowed and tried to be defiant. "Why won't you find Dad? Can't you answer that?"

For a moment, Phoebe thought Adele might cry. Then, her expression reset into anger. "Hey! I'm the one asking the questions, not you." She wheeled around and returned to slathering bread with peanut butter and jelly for lunch sandwiches.

That was the moment that Phoebe remembered something else she had seen on TV, about a couple arrested for hurting their little kid. Child abuse, they called it. The newscast talked about how some sort of government group was supposed to watch over children. With no reason except that she was as angry at Adele as Adele was at her, Phoebe pulled out this bit of information she had tucked away.

"I'll call Child Protection Services and turn you in," she told her stepmother.

Adele turned to her, the knife sticky with peanut butter poised in midair. "Turn me in for what?"

Phoebe couldn't speak. She watched a wave of shifting emotions alter her stepmother's features, from shock to anger and then outrage. That was when the chain reaction occurred: Adele dropped the knife on the kitchen counter, grabbed Phoebe by the arm, wrenched her up from the table, and marched her upstairs. Phoebe tried squirming, but Adele's grip was too strong, and before she knew it, there she was. Locked in.

How many hours had passed? She didn't know. She finally gave up trying to distract herself from going to the bathroom and peed on a dirty rag she found in the closet. She threw it back in the corner of the closet.

She spent a long time looking out the window through the dancing branches of the elm tree. She pressed her forehead against the windowpane. She couldn't see much. A bit of the house next door, which belonged to deaf, old Mrs. Oliver. Even if she could get the window open—heck, even if Phoebe was yelling directly into the old lady's ear—Mrs. Oliver would never hear a thing, let alone calls for help.

Dejected, Phoebe slid again to the floor. She was thinking, *I'll never get out of here,* when she heard the voices.

"It's my goldfish, and I'm telling you, he had a heart attack! That's what he died of."

"He did not!"

The conversation was coming from a metal pipe in the corner. Phoebe thought it might be part of the heating system, but it had seemed useless for her purposes until now. She scrambled over and pressed her ear to the pipe. She could hear the voices three stories below in the living room, as clearly as if they were next to her.

It was her brother Bobby, home from school. Normally, Phoebe watched Bobby until Adele returned from work. Phoebe guessed that her stepmother had either forgotten or figured Bobby would survive a few hours on his own. The other voice Phoebe heard most likely was Andrew, one of her brother's friends from school. Bobby wasn't supposed to bring friends over when Adele wasn't home, but he broke this rule practically every day.

"Bobby!"

Phoebe put her mouth close to the pipe and yelled as loudly as she could. There was no response, but the voices stopped. That meant they had heard her, she thought, heartened. Phoebe yelled again. She tried banging on the pipe. But the thick metal was unyielding, and she barely produced a slapping sound.

"Bobby, it's me. Come upstairs to the attic. The room in the back." Her voice cracked from the effort. "Please," she shouted.

She put her ear to the pipe but could hear nothing. She gave one last scream that hurt her throat. "Bobby!"

"What do you want?" Bobby's voice came, not from the living room but from the other side of the door. He sounded equal parts curious and disbelieving. Relieved, Phoebe ran to the door and again tried to peer through the keyhole.

"Bobby, you've got to help me. The door is locked. I think the key is on your mom's dresser—"

"What are you doing in there?" he interrupted. "Is that why you didn't come with us this morning?"

"It was a mistake. An accident." Phoebe swallowed. "Come on, the key is right there in your mom's room. A little, silver key. All you have to do is bring it here and push it under the door."

"I'll get in trouble."

"No, you won't." She knew that at any moment, Bobby could bolt. It would be just like him to go back to watching cartoons as if nothing happened, and her chance of escape would be lost.

But as she bit her lip and listened intently, she realized that he hadn't run away. He didn't seem to be heading toward Adele's room either. Phoebe switched tactics.

"How's your goldfish?" she asked.

Bobby snorted. "Why?"

She heard Andrew pipe up in a helpful manner. "His fish saw a cat looking in the window, and the fish had heart failure."

"You're an idiot!" Bobby yelled, apparently at Andrew. Phoebe heard a commotion. Somebody hit the wall, hard.

"Hey! I know how to help your fish." Phoebe thought she wouldn't be heard over the scuffle, but to her surprise, there was a sudden silence.

"How could you help Merlin?" Bobby asked in a small voice.

"Merlin?"

"My goldfish, stupid!" Bobby was annoyed. "Forget it. You don't know how to help."

"Yes, I do," Phoebe said. "I know about a special kind of medicine that will help him, but I have to get it fast." He was wavering, she could tell. She spoke urgently. "The key. It's right on the dresser, Bobby."

Bobby let out a burst of air. "Fine!" He stomped off. Minutes later, a tiny edge of silver began sliding slowly onto the scarred, wooden floor on Phoebe's side of the door. She crouched, ready to grab it once enough of the key came into view. But no sooner did the bit of silver appear than it was pulled back.

"Ha, ha!" Bobby yelled.

Phoebe stifled her cry and kept her eyes on the lower edge of the door. The key reappeared, moving a millimeter at a time. This time, she was ready. As soon as a large enough piece appeared, she quickly pressed her thumb down on the bit of silver and dragged it toward her. To her great relief, the key worked to unlock it from her side of the door.

"Don't worry," she said, ignoring Bobby's outstretched hand as she passed. "I'll put this back." She raced downstairs. The boys listened to her running about on the second floor and hadn't moved from the hallway before she bounded back up the staircase. "I'll be back with that medicine as soon as I can," she reassured them and again disappeared.

Fifteen minutes later, the boys were sprawled across the living room floor, watching television. They barely reacted to the slamming of the front door.

Just then, the show they were watching ended with a flourish of music. The spell broken, Andrew climbed onto the sofa and pulled back the gauzy curtain on the front window. He could still see Phoebe, although she was already a distant figure running up the street.

Andrew let the curtain fall and looked at Bobby, lying with his crossed feet resting on the seat of an armchair, his body twisted around to watch the screen. "Do you think your sister is really going to save your fish?" Andrew asked.

Bobby didn't take his eyes off the television. "I don't care," he said. "My mom will buy me a new one anyway."

~

Phoebe had been running for what seemed many hours. Her legs had grown heavy, and it was becoming harder to lift them. A couple of times, cramps forced her to stop. She tried to rub her legs briskly, gritting her teeth, and started running again as soon as the pain subsided a little.

After running for blocks and blocks, she passed through neighborhoods she no longer recognized, not even from the windows on the bus she took to school. She hoped that she was either already far from home or at least on streets her stepmother wouldn't be likely to search for her.

Phoebe's body was starting to protest, screaming like it had its own voice. In gym class, they were forced to run short sprints but nothing like this kind of long-distance running. Not only was she not used to it, she also found it hard to manage the knapsack strapped to her back. Still, she didn't regret taking it. She needed to pack a few things for this journey. The small, pink backpack with the Hello Kitty insignia, which had served as her schoolbag back in the third grade, might be childish but it was perfect for this adventure—or so she had thought. She had filled it with a few items of clothing, her toothbrush, and some things she found in the kitchen: some cheese, a small package of potato chips, and a bottle of water that was in the back of the fridge. That was all, but the backpack was starting to feel heavy, bouncing against her with every step, which she felt keenly despite the padding of the heavy jacket and extra layers of clothes she was wearing.

She allowed herself to slow a little from a run to a quick walk. Her breathing was still labored. Her lungs actually hurt. As frightening as that was, she knew she had to start running again. She had to put as much distance as possible between herself and the house before her stepmother returned home and discovered she was missing. Despite Phoebe's intentions, her feet slowed on their own accord until finally she halted and bent over. Somehow that made it feel less like sharp pins going into her.

Her breathing grew less harsh and she straightened. *Don't sit down. Don't even think about sitting down*, she warned herself.

The weather was chilly for early April. The wind sometimes kicked up in sharp gusts, but between running and the layers of clothing, Phoebe hadn't felt the cold. Now that she stopped, though, she became aware of sweat dripping from the ends of her hair and running down her spine. The shirt closest to her skin clung to her back. Phoebe debated whether to shed the coat or maybe some of her layers. But it would be dark soon. She would probably end up cold and shivering.

She took a quick look around the deserted street and set off again.

Almost immediately, she began to worry that she was heading in the wrong direction. Maybe any direction that was the opposite of home was right, she reminded herself. But she should probably be heading toward Connecticut. Wherever that was. She had become disoriented. It also didn't help that the neighborhoods all looked the same.

She hesitated. Had she seen this same block of houses already?

She soldiered on. After a while, she was rewarded with unfamiliar scenery. Soon, twilight set in, and the birds noisily twittered their bedtime rituals. Phoebe was drawn by the lights flicking on in one house after another. As she passed, she caught glimpses of scenes of evening family life playing out in homes where the shades were not yet drawn: mothers making dinner, kids playing and doing homework, fathers resting in recliners in front of flickering television screens. It was all so normal.

What was she doing anyway? It was getting to be nighttime, and she should be inside like these kids, doing normal kid things. Instead, she was out on the street, running away. *But I have to do this. I have to find Dad.* She blinked back tears.

It was soon very dark, as she imagined what midnight was like, although she wasn't allowed out that late and never experienced it. She trudged block after block, the adrenaline long gone. In its absence, her body felt weak and rubbery. She entered another neighborhood. This one was seedier, with smaller homes. Some had mildewed roofs and front lawns with weeds poking through even though it was spring.

Phoebe began to wonder how long she could go on before she dropped from exhaustion. She needed to find a place to sleep. She also began to fret about how she would find Connecticut. She hadn't paid much attention to geography in school, so she wasn't sure where Connecticut was. She had the vague idea it was north.

Not north like the North Pole but something between her home state of Pennsylvania and Canada. That was about it. It might take months to walk there. She could be like the pioneers and wagon trains that went west, she told herself. If they could walk all the way to California… She could use the sun as her guide. But wait, what about cloudy days? Why hadn't she thought to borrow a compass from her friend Eliza, who was a Girl Scout? Too late for that.

Phoebe sighed. She had bigger problems at the moment, like figuring out where she would sleep. And what if Adele called the police? Phoebe glanced involuntarily over her shoulder. No cruising patrol cars followed her, which was good.

Despite the streetlamps, she nearly tripped on the uneven sidewalk. She decided to walk in the street, but then, she saw a car's headlights moving slowly toward her. She slipped behind one of the large trees lining the street until it passed.

She came to a small development, with houses grouped close together. It seemed a sort of promising place to spend the night. Good thing, Phoebe thought. She was so tired she could barely walk a straight line.

The first back yard had a locked gate. As she approached a second yard, a dog and then a whole series of dogs went into a barking frenzy that sent her into a hasty retreat. She spotted another house with only a dim upstairs light showing. Cautiously, she moved into the shadows on the side of the house. No animals, at least not the barking kind. She crept further. As her eyes adjusted to the moonlight and the light from other houses, she spotted a shed. When she reached it, she found it even more miraculous that it was unlocked. She breathed a quick little prayer of thanks and slipped inside.

There was a small window of louvered glass slats that gave some relief from the darkness, and that she could also crank open for fresh air. That was good, she thought, because the place reeked of fertilizer and other stuff people put on their grass. It was already making her feel a little sick.

She slid off the backpack and tried to clear a spot on the wooden floor. Wrapping her coat tightly around her, she rested her head on a bag that didn't smell so bad. Grass seed, maybe? It would do for a pillow. Her last conscious thought was the hope that bugs wouldn't crawl into the shed. But she had hardly given form to it when she fell into an exhausted sleep.

Dawn seeped through the glass slats, growing into golden shafts of sunlight that struck Phoebe's closed eyelids. She struggled to sit, stiff but as tired as if she hadn't slept at all. Yawning, she looked around at the rough, wooden walls adorned with rakes and shovels hung neatly on hooks, a lawn mower in the corner, along with a wheelbarrow. It was amazing that she hadn't created an awful racket when she had crawled in the shed in the darkness.

That was when she recalled the thought she had, just as she was curling up on the shed floor, that she should wake very early. She would leave at dawn, she had thought, before anyone saw her. She squinted at the bright sunshine. Okay, she had missed her chance. That meant she had to be extra careful sneaking away. At this point, she would be happy if she could just figure out a way to escape and get some food. She was starving. There was still some of the block of cheese she had brought from home but she wanted to save that, although it was getting harder to stop herself from devouring it.

She pulled herself up to peek through the window. The sun passed through the tree branches at a sharp angle and encased the house in light. It seemed miles away across the expanse of a large yard. There were a few trees but not much that would make for good cover if she dashed across the lawn.

Even while peering through the dirty glass slats of the shed all the way from the other end of the yard, Phoebe could see that on the small deck at the back of the house, there was a wrought-iron table, and on that table was breakfast. Phoebe's stomach rumbled.

Just then the screen door opened, and a woman appeared, carrying plates. Instinctively, Phoebe dropped her head, then raised it again to peek through a corner of the window. The woman was talking to someone in the house. "It's not cold this morning," she informed the unseen person.

Phoebe already had the shed door opened and somehow timed it perfectly, running across the lawn and stealing onto the deck as the woman disappeared into the house. Phoebe frantically stuffed bacon and toast into her pockets until she heard a noise from the house. In an instant, she was running back down the deck steps and around the side of the house, trying to keep her footsteps as light as possible.

The screen door creaked open again, and the woman gave a startled cry.

"See? Now, that's why we can't eat outside," Phoebe heard a man's voice say as she hid behind the shrubbery on the side of the house. "You can't leave anything out here for one minute before the Wilsons' dog makes off with it."

Two

Sidney counted herself lucky. She had a job. She was gainfully employed as a proofreader, which, granted, was not a highly valued occupation these days anywhere, let alone at the printing company where she worked. But at least she had a job.

Several times a day, she reminded herself that she was very lucky to have any position at all, considering the state of affairs at Poppy Press. Even the slowest, most dense employee—who, of course, was poor Sammy in the mailroom, who had been hit on the head with a baseball bat at age nine and had never been quite the same since—was aware that the company stood on the brink of ruin, this time for good.

What staff that was left, skeletal compared with the bustling crew of only five or six years earlier, knew perfectly well what was happening. The company had a few months at most before it went bust. Then, they would all be out on the street.

Sidney seemed to be the only one left at Poppy Press stubbornly clinging to optimism. She was hoping for the best. If her coworkers knew that, they would undoubtedly ridicule her. But they didn't know. They were too busy complaining, trading rumors, and sniping at each other. All of them, even those with sunny personalities, had sunk into perpetually bad moods. Each work day, Sidney moved among them, trying to ward off the negativity and thanking God for another day of employment.

I have more to be sad about than they do. She couldn't resist the bitter thought as she sat through yet another lecture from a coworker who was unnecessarily chewing her out for a supposed infraction. *I just buried my mother.*

The rational part of Sidney knew that this was a juvenile reaction. Everyone at the company was afraid that they would be thrown out of work. Plenty had many more serious problems and responsibilities than she, a fifty-one-year-old spinster whose elderly mother had just passed away.

It was ironic, maybe even a little weird, how Poppy Press's deterioration had coincided with her mother's downward slide. The only difference was that Agatha's end had come much quicker, within weeks, while the Press's demise seemed interminable. Sidney had returned to work from her leave of absence to find things at Poppy Press had not improved. If anything, they had gone from bad to grim.

"We've got three, four weeks left, tops," Carla said at lunch one day. She looked disapproving. But then, her expression was one of permanent disapproval. "I'm telling you, girls, that's it. Pink slips. Layoffs."

Carla was the self-appointed leader of the Lunch Ladies, the group of women who ate at the same table every day. Not just anyone could join the Lunch Ladies. You had to be chosen, supposedly elected by the group, although everyone knew that it was Carla who hand-picked the participants, discarding some and reaching out to others. Sidney, not known for extreme opinions, disliked Carla from the first moment they met. That feeling only intensified when Sidney was asked to join the lunch group and witnessed how cruel and demeaning Carla could be. Sidney sometimes considered quitting, picturing herself in a corner with a book for the duration of lunch. But she knew she would never have the courage to do that. Sometimes she wondered why she had been invited to the Lunch Ladies in the first place. She wasn't much of a talker. Maybe that was the answer. Carla was most definitely a talker.

A natural storyteller, Carla could spend the entire lunch hour in a nonstop monologue. The others grunted in agreement or gave sympathetic headshakes. At the same time, Carla managed to consume a great deal of food, presumably to replenish her massive, nearly three-hundred-pound frame, all while barely taking a breath. The food went in and words came out in effortless rhythm. By the end of lunch, her tray, once packed with items, was stripped clean.

"Good luck finding work before your unemployment checks run out," Carla was saying. "And good luck getting unemployment. I wouldn't put it past them to somehow cheat us out of that."

"You don't know what's going to happen." As one, the lunch table crew turned toward the corner, where the small voice had come from. It was Sidney, who appeared just as surprised as the rest that she had spoken.

"Maybe it will work out…" Sidney's voice faltered.

"Don't be an idiot," Carla snapped.

The next instant, Sidney recoiled. She could have sworn that Carla spat at her, shooting saliva the length of the table. Shocked, Sidney looked around at the Lunch Ladies. But they were eating, and Carla was droning on as if nothing had happened. Maybe nothing had happened, Sidney thought, confused.

Carla was busy finishing up her stem-winder of a sermon. "We all have to face facts. And let me tell you something: those facts aren't looking good. Even the union guys are worried. Think about this," she leaned forward so far over the table that her girth pushed aside her tray. "*We* don't got no union."

Sidney picked up her sandwich, still unbitten on its neatly turned-down plastic wrap. She put it down again. One woman, Josie, caught Sidney's eye, then busied herself with her plastic container. But Sidney had seen what crossed Josie's sad, ordinarily passive face. It was unmistakable panic.

Everyone should be used to this by now, Sidney thought. An undercurrent of panic had become pervasive. It was a cloud that did not so much hang over the old warehouse building that the founder Charlie Post had purchased and renovated years earlier. Rather, the cloud was *in* the building. It permeated every floor, every cubicle, even the cavernous printing press area.

It wasn't like Poppy Press had reached some sort of business pinnacle and then tumbled from grace. It was always a lower-tier printer. There were those who contended that Charlie Post was satisfied with mediocrity, but perhaps he simply knew the limitations of his company. In any case, for a long time, Charlie Post had been getting enough business to keep his approximately one hundred employees busy and make a decent profit each year. His top salesman, Harry Corcoran, was the key. Harry reeled in new accounts, kept the jobs flowing, and quickly became Charlie's protégé. Poppy Press employees were lulled into thinking that it would all go on forever.

According to Carla, they were being killed by computers and, more specifically, the Internet. "I mean, it's the new millennium. How do you compete with the World Wide Web?" Carla would ask ruefully, shaking her head. Even Sidney, normally myopic about any trend, saw that the computerized world was changing the print world. At first, people made light of it: print was dead. Ha! Print was like the dead letter office in the postal service. Then, one by one, small printers, such as Poppy Press, saw their business dry up. It was no joke.

"Our sales guys didn't realize what was happening until it was too late," Carla intoned. The ladies chewed and listened. "They would try to get the same business they always got, knock on the same doors they always did. But poof! All gone. No one wants old-fashioned printing anymore."

When Sidney returned after her mother's funeral, she found the place in turmoil. Some staff had begun searching for new jobs, scarce in the bad economy, and even worse for many Poppy Press employees whose skills weren't exactly marketable. Those not hunting for employment were secretly terrified, but they criticized the job-seekers for jumping ship. Nearly everyone gossiped about the impending layoffs—when they would occur and who might be on the chopping block. The rumors grew wilder and more virulent until word leaked out. Charlie Post had sold Poppy Press.

Given the desperate circumstances, the sale shouldn't have been a shock to the employees, but it was. They revered the ebullient Charlie Post, who responded with unabashed love for the company and the workers. With the sale, Charlie seemed to betray both. It split Poppy Press into two camps: those still loyal to Charlie Post and those who loathed him.

"Come on, this was an act of desperation. He had no choice," the Charlie-adoring Carla exhorted the nodding Lunch Ladies. "If you think about it, he was saving us from going out of business."

"Yeah, right." Josie found the courage to speak up. "Charlie got his big payday, and we're hanging on by our fingernails. We're stuck with the New York people."

Maybe it was because Josie had brought up the hated new owners, a parent company based in New York City, but Carla's response was surprisingly sympathetic. "I know. Darn carpetbaggers from New York sticking their noses in our business. Do you believe it?" She popped a half-sandwich in her mouth.

Everyone knew that Carla was referring to the executives whom the parent company had dispatched to restore order to Poppy Press. To clean house, some said. None had bothered to settle in Pennsylvania but instead lived out of suitcases during the work week and headed back to New York for weekends. It couldn't have been clearer that they did not view Poppy Press as a long-term commitment.

After this lunch conversation, Sidney returned to her desk feeling slightly ill. She reminded herself that most of this was just talk. Still, if she let herself think of the prospect of her paychecks vanishing, with no other means of support, no family to lean on, she started to feel faint.

So don't think about it. That was the kind of thing her mother would say. It was good advice, Sidney thought as she pulled her work from her desk drawer and began proofreading. In a way, her job as the company's proofreader helped her go on as if nothing whatsoever was wrong. It was one of the things she liked about her job: working alone and shutting out the noise and speculation. Now that there wasn't much business and consequently few projects to proofread, it could sometimes be hard to keep busy. She had taken to digging up and redoing old proofreading tasks that had long been printed and completed.

Sidney enjoyed proofreading, especially the printed words themselves, the typography, even the big, chunky blocks of sans serif type. She preferred the physicality of proofing on paper to scanning a computer screen. It was a pleasure to feel the paper and go through the long columns of printed text, running her red pen lightly over the paper, not quite touching it, searching for errors, and silently rejoicing when she found one.

Mostly, she loved the solitary nature of the work. If she could work in a cave, she had thought many times, she would.

These hermit-like tendencies had worsened since Agatha's death. Sidney found herself minimizing contact with others as much as possible. She left the house early, often when it was still dark. On her return home, she kept her head bowed as she quickly pulled circulars and bills from the mailbox, then hurried up the walk to the front porch. Once, she caught sight of Mrs. Hammond, her neighbor who had been her mother's best friend. Mrs. Hammond stood on her porch, gesturing. Sidney pretended not to see her and rushed into the house. Later, she felt guilty. Maybe she should pay a visit, make amends, and see if Mrs. Hammond was okay. But what excuse could she possibly give?

For the few groceries she needed, she took to venturing out late at night to shop at the twenty-four-hour mini-mart at the gas station on the edge of town. It was a location where there was little chance of running into anyone she knew. Who went out for gas at midnight in their small town? The older man who owned the gas station, Mr. Ahmazhetti, had long witnessed Sidney fueling her car every Saturday morning whether it needed it or not. But he was either too polite or too uncaring to question the sudden onset of her late-night shopping trips. He bagged her groceries, made change, and bid her a good night, all mercifully without comment.

While she went to great lengths to avoid the neighbors (she couldn't say why; they were like family after all these years), Sidney still suffered through the purgatory of her time with the Lunch Ladies. It was the only sensible thing to do. Her absence would have been conspicuous. Carla would send someone to hound her for an explanation. It was far better to show up and fade into the background.

Other than that, Sidney managed to get through most work days relatively people-free, so it was especially disconcerting when she found herself making her way through Poppy Press's rambling, old structure on what was likely a fool's errand. She had been minding her own business, doing her own work, when she was dispatched for a mission that she knew nothing about. But she couldn't decline the assignment because it came directly from Harry Corcoran.

Harry was in charge of sales and had been Charlie Post's star employee. With the number of printing jobs and sales opportunities dwindling, Harry's star had fallen. That's what everyone said, Carla related to the Lunch Ladies. In Harry's defense, she added that he was still closing some deals. "There just aren't as many as there used to be," Carla said, clucking sympathetically.

When Harry arrived in the office that morning, something—perhaps a scribbled reminder on his desk—had gotten him fretting about one of the few printing jobs he had in progress. Sidney, whose desk was close to Harry's office, could tell he was agitated. She could hear him rustling papers and muttering. Although she could often tune out his reverberating baritone, it was unavoidable that when Harry was in the office, his presence overwhelmed the entire area. He conducted business in a very vocal manner, holding all phone conversations in speaker mode and barking commands to the dark-haired, bright-lipped secretary who sat directly outside his open door. Some of those interactions filtered to Sidney no matter how hard she tried to block them out. She often thought herself as fortunate that she was not Harry's assistant. However, the assistant—whose name was Antoinette, although Harry called her Toni—took him in stride. Actually, she delighted in his every action, no matter how rude.

"Toni, I need you to compile a list of every telephone call I made in the last month," Harry might shout, startling everyone in the vicinity. "Toni, what was the name of that prospect from Jersey? You know, the one with the annoying cackle of a laugh?" "Did you pick up an anniversary gift for my wife, Toni?" Antoinette took care of it all. She was in love with Harry. That meant she would not tolerate so much as the implication of a negative view. Harry, for his part, accepted the fawning responses from his assistant as his due and ignored everyone else. Generally speaking, any other employee didn't exist for him because they weren't instantly jumping at his command.

That was why when that booming voice sounded in her ear, Sidney nearly jumped out of her skin.

"Well? Will you help me or not?"

Sidney looked up at Harry Corcoran. At six-feet, five-inches, he seemed a giant of a man and, from her seated position, even more intimidating. Despite middle age, Harry still had the bright, carrot-colored, straw-like hair and freckled face of an adolescent. Yet he somehow managed to carry an air of something. Nobility, maybe. His manner conveyed that he knew his place in the world, and it was a place at least one notch higher than the rest of humanity.

"I didn't expect to see you here, um, ah…" Harry was searching for her name. Sidney was convinced that he had no idea who she was even though she had worked in the same spot adjacent to his office for the past seven years. If their paths happened to cross, he never gave a flicker of recognition.

"No matter," he continued with a small, dismissive wave when Sidney failed to introduce herself. "Go check on the Unilex project for me, would you? Ask them to speed it up. The client is in a hurry. We have to make sure that the few clients we have are happy. Sidney," he added as an afterthought. He smiled, pleased with himself for having remembered.

Sidney hesitated. What Unilex job? This would undoubtedly require a great deal of wandering about and asking a lot of questions of random people to try to pin it down, with those same people not reacting well, probably haranguing her for her trouble. "What about Antoinette—err, Toni?" she mumbled.

"She has the day off." Harry said it mildly enough, but there was a trace of annoyance. When he spoke again, it was impatiently. "Look, do I need to impress upon you the importance of meeting client expectations? How crucial it is that every single project is absolutely on time?" Chastened, Sidney kept her eyes at Harry's neck level, watching as it flushed a splotchy red. He stopped speaking, and she automatically looked up. His expression had become calculating.

"Say, didn't you used to be on Denise's team? You must be at loose ends, organizationally, that is, since she's left the company."

Sidney froze. Harry indeed knew who Sidney was. He also saw her, opportunistically, as an employee available for his own purposes.

It was true that Sidney lacked a boss. Hers had been fired the previous month. Denise had taken on more and more responsibility without complaint and was equally stoic when informed that her services would no longer be required. No replacement was named nor was any effort made to provide Sidney and the others who had worked for Denise a new chain of command. In the chaos reigning at the Press, they remained silent and hoped no one noticed.

Moving to another team was likely inevitable. But Harry? Sidney looked up at his frame bent over her, casting a long shadow over her and her desk. She shrank in her chair.

Even without the regular chronicles from Carla, Harry's exploits were well known, first as a protégé and then as a trusted advisor to Charlie Post. People said that Harry was the one behind Charlie's schemes to build up the company, the brazen attempts to put Poppy Press on the publishing map that eventually, and inevitably, fell apart. Had Harry counseled Charlie to go ahead with the desperate move to sell Poppy Press to the New York company? No one was quite sure. That didn't stop people like Carla from speculating.

"It was just like Charlie," Carla would say, a common refrain for her. "No doubt he believed that he could sell the company and then swoop back in and save the day. But Harry? I don't know. But he always has something up his sleeve."

Whatever Harry had up his sleeve, Sidney didn't want any part of it, she thought as she set out on the mission he mandated, a mission that would likely be a big waste of time. Well, what else did she have to do? she asked herself as she plodded along the corridors. *At least you have a job*, she reminded herself. It was more than poor Denise had.

Sidney had been heading toward the press area, but at the main stairwell, she changed her mind and decided to visit the shop they still called by the antiquated label, *typesetting*. There, they handled all the pre-print services, such as design and layout. It was worth a detour to see if they were working on Harry's job.

She darted up the cinderblock stairwell that reminded her of a dungeon. The exterior of the old, converted factory had a medieval look, incongruous with the main floors where many employees worked in standard office configurations. Sidney pushed open the heavy, metal door to the second floor, where several departments were housed in the typical offices and rows of cubicles of corporate America.

It was a good distance from the printing equipment, so it was quiet. Very quiet. For a moment, Sidney thought that maybe the fabric-covered cubicles and carpeting were deadening any sound. Then it hit her. The area was noiseless simply because it was empty. There were no phones, no undercurrent of chatter, no keyboards tapping. She walked down the main aisle amid the cubicle ghost-town.

She stopped and peered over the top of a wall. Filing drawers stood open with a few limp manila folders hanging out. The desk was bare, with none of the usual personal mementos. Sidney imagined the occupant hurriedly packing like an evacuating refugee.

Here was something left, Sidney thought, and she entered the cubicle to extract a slip of paper tacked to the gray fabric wall. It was a comic strip, one that was popular a few years earlier because it depicted the humor in office life. Maybe the person left it because it no longer seemed funny, she thought as she examined the yellowing paper.

Something in her peripheral vision caught her attention, and she hopped backwards, stifling a scream. A cockroach scurried past her.

Even without the unnerving sight of an insect, the voice sounding in her ear would have been enough to make her jump out of her skin.

"Disgusting creatures. Somebody ought to get rid of them. Oh, sorry. That somebody would be me."

Grabbing the edge of the desk to regain her footing and her composure, she turned. It was J.T., the Poppy Press maintenance man, materializing inches from her.

"I thought no one was around," she admitted, flushing. "What are you doing here?"

J.T. shrugged. He was uncomfortably close but made no attempt to give her any space. Sidney tilted her head back and looked at him as if she didn't know him, as if he didn't stop by her desk at least once a week to talk, complain, and rant about the foibles of the Press. It was like seeing him for the first time. What she saw was a pudgy, pasty, balding, middle-aged man with a remarkably baby face. His lips were especially like a little boy's, except they were twisted, as they often were, into a sneer.

Despite the sardonic persona he conveyed, J.T. was the type of person who was compelled to share his thoughts with someone, anyone. Recently, he gravitated to the reticent Sidney, probably because she listened without interruption and so was the perfect audience. "You're part of my inner circle," he once told her. Sidney suspected that she was the only member of that circle. He had no friends that she could tell.

At first, she was mortified by the attention J.T. paid her. As a rule, men ignored Sidney. That had always been the case, but as she grew older, she became even less visible. She hadn't minded, but it had been to the lasting disappointment of her mother Agatha that Sidney never married and, in fact, never had a suitor or any man the least bit interested in her. Her mother would have been overjoyed if she had seen the times that J.T. appeared at Sidney's desk or how he would launch into one of his lectures. Agatha would have been convinced, Sidney knew, that J.T. was courting her despite Sidney's advanced, long-past-marriageable age.

At first, it alarmed Sidney that for some crazy reason, J.T. might in fact be interested in her, but she soon realized he was far more interested in being heard. She grew used to their one-sided conversations. Sometimes, she even enjoyed them. J.T. had an entertaining way of telling stories and presenting his ideas, which were sometimes plausible but at other times nothing more than wild conspiracy theories. Curiously, he never talked about himself. Never even mentioned something as prosaic as his likes or dislikes. Every now and then, Sidney found herself wondering whether he might be holding something back or hiding a secret past. Or maybe that was her own conspiracy theory, she thought.

Everyone, including Sidney, was aware that J.T. had gotten his job as the building janitor because his brother, who worked in the pressroom, had been able to pull strings. J.T. freely shared his opinions about the Press (one of his favorite topics) and occasionally made sarcastic comments about his janitorial role. But his brother, who no longer worked there, was another forbidden topic. J.T. never mentioned him.

"We have our pick of locations to work from, don't we?" J.T. said sorrowfully, drawing circles on the dusty desktop with his forefinger. He grabbed a handful of file folders and began looking through them, occasionally pausing to read. Soon he was simply pulling out papers and tossing them on the floor without a glance. Trapped, Sidney watched a pile of papers grow around their feet.

"Nothing of interest here," J.T. announced. He dusted off his hands and shut the desk drawers.

"What did you expect to find?" It wasn't often that Sidney made any comment, but she was curious. He didn't answer her question, though.

"These New York people"—J.T. always referred to the new management with the same tone of disgust—"they're something else. Even if they're trying to put the company back on its feet, they're doing all the wrong things. Look." He waved, nearly hitting Sidney's head. "Cutting staff, getting rid of people. They *say* it's all early retirement and people leaving for other jobs and such. We know better."

J.T. kicked the pile of papers. "I predict a massive layoff. Everyone gone, like that." He snapped his fingers and scanned the vacant surroundings, as if amazed to see his prediction come true. Then, his gaze refocused past Sidney's shoulder. She turned. A group of men headed purposefully in their direction.

The man leading the way strode with authority. Despite his small stature, the others looked like they were having difficulty keeping up. Sidney recognized the leader as Vincent Ayers, the recently installed president from New York.

The group sailed down the corridor. One bony, young man with longish hair slicked straight back shot a glance in her direction. Sidney reddened with embarrassment. They must look like peasants, overwhelmed at the sight of the king.

When the entourage had passed, Sidney turned to J.T., prepared to hear a torrent of scornful comments. But he, too, was gone.

The abandoned section of the old building again assumed its eerie feeling. She had to get out of here, she thought, feeling suddenly cold. In any case, she needed to finish Harry's errand before he blew a gasket.

Three

Phoebe had been walking for nearly two full days. She figured that she must have gone at least a hundred miles, but even as she told herself this, another thought came to her. *Now, that's a big whopper, isn't it? Stop exaggerating*. That was what her stepmother would say automatically in response to Phoebe's often dramatic statements: "Phoebe, stop exaggerating." Anyway, it was true that she had gone a very long way, she thought, defiant. She just didn't know if she had gotten any closer to Connecticut.

Probably not. She kicked a stone in disgust and it pinged against a car. She didn't care. Still, she glanced furtively behind her. Good. No one was following her, not even the people whose breakfast she had stolen. After helping herself to the food on the deck, she had hidden on the side of the house, her heart knocking in her chest. The couple took their time eating the remains of the breakfast and carrying the dishes back indoors. It took many trips, the screen door banging shut and unnerving Phoebe, who remained curled up behind a large, scratchy shrub. Even after all was quiet, she waited another ten minutes, then slipped away.

Long after she had continued her journey, she kept casting sidelong looks at the passing cars, expecting the couple to track her down. Phoebe imagined the woman, her head sticking out the car window, yelling, "Stop, breakfast thief!" She smiled but quickly sobered. She had taken food that didn't belong to her. She was a thief after all.

The thing was, she might have to steal food again. She was still very hungry. It was like she couldn't remember a time when she wasn't hungry.

As she walked, she saw that her shadow had shrunk. She remembered her science teacher Mrs. Goya saying that shadows were longest when the sun was starting to set and shortest at noon when the sun was high in the sky. No wonder she was hungry. It was lunchtime.

She thought of the small piece of cheese, all that remained in the backpack. *Guess I'll skip lunch*, she told herself with regret.

Phoebe trudged down street after street, through many different neighborhoods, but she stopped paying attention to them or even what direction she was heading. Twice, she saw garden hoses within easy access, so after a quick look around, she turned on the water and drank from the end of the hose. The second time made her stomach cramp up. Maybe it was the cold water, she thought. Or hunger.

Whatever it was, it all made her walk slower, almost a shuffle. She raised her head and tried to focus on something else, but it only disoriented her. The landscape had changed without her noticing. The houses were gone, and she had wandered into some kind of industrial area. There were no factories, only a few scraggly trees trying to hide the long, low warehouse buildings and wide parking lots. After a few more minutes of walking, the businesses also disappeared, and there was nothing but fields of weeds and some woods, with more trash and debris on the side of the road.

It grew quieter the further she traveled. Few cars passed by (a good thing because they made her nervous). She came upon an intersection where a green, wooden bench with large, concrete sides was installed on a small concrete platform. She looked up at the sign next to the bench. It announced that this was a bus stop for the number 184 bus.

As she was reading the sign, she started swaying and almost lost her footing. Suddenly all she wanted to do was to curl up in a ball and sleep. She pictured herself on the bus, letting its rocking motion soothe her. Public transportation probably wasn't such a good idea. Who knew where the number 184 bus would take her? She rubbed her eyes. At the same time, she was just so tired.

Without removing her backpack, she sank down on the bench and let her eyes close. The sun warmed her. *This is nice*, she thought.

Her thoughts drifted to her father. She could see him in her mind's eye, not hurt, not in danger, just like he always was. Always there. She could imagine him driving up, right there at the bus stop, rolling down the window and saying, "Get in, Phoebe, I've been looking for you."

Maybe I'm wrong, she thought suddenly, her eyelids twitching. *Maybe he's the one searching for me.* What if she had messed everything up by running away?

Her eyes opened and focused on her dirty sneakers before tears blurred her vision. She couldn't go back even if she wanted to. It was useless to try to retrace her steps. She was lost.

Blinking, she looked down the street and saw a large bus turning a corner. As it rumbled up to the bus stop, she could read the digital numbers on the front that said "184." The bus gave an ear-splitting squeal as it stopped in front of her. The doors collapsed open. Phoebe looked up at the heavy-set woman driver, who looked back expectantly at her.

"Well?" the driver called out finally. "Are you getting on or not, honey? I've got a lotta stops to make."

The decision seemed to be made for her. Phoebe rose and climbed the steps of the bus.

—

The driver was right. There were many stops, although there was rarely anyone getting on or off. The driver apparently was required to stop at each designated area regardless. The bus heaved and bucked at each one, like a bull at a rodeo. Phoebe, after using two of her precious dollars for bus fare, had taken a seat near the front, a few seats behind the little wall separating the driver from the scattered passengers. She stared out the window and tried not to draw attention to herself.

"Where you headed, honey?" the driver said loudly, craning her neck to catch sight of Phoebe in her rearview mirror.

Phoebe fumbled for an answer. One option was to truthfully respond, "Connecticut," but that was too scary.

"Um…I'm meeting up with my sister." Phoebe winced. The lady driver was sure to know that she was lying.

The driver gave a sharp look in the mirror. "I don't know," she said doubtfully. "You seem pretty young to be traveling around by yourself." She paused as she negotiated a turn. "How old are you again?"

Phoebe froze. The driver hadn't asked her age before, she was sure of it. Turning toward the window, Phoebe studied the scenery and hoped that she would quit asking questions. The driver seemed to understand, and returned to focusing on her driving with no further attempt at conversation. Phoebe slowly exhaled.

Looking out the window, she realized that none of the passing landscape seemed familiar. At least she didn't seem to be heading back home, but she began to worry about where they were going. It felt like she was on a boat, drifting at sea. But the drifting was soon replaced by the feeling that the bus was out of control as it picked up speed. The landscape swirled by and Phoebe began to feel panicky as the bus rocketed down a highway.

Ten minutes later, the bus creaked and groaned its way downhill, narrowly avoiding tipping over on a sharp bend before coming to a halt.

Phoebe jumped up. As soon as the doors hissed open, she ran down the bus steps. Without looking back at the driver, who called after her, she started walking as if she knew where she was going.

Phoebe marched down a nondescript road, passing a few seedy shopping centers, then just trees and tall brush.

Traffic thickened. She tried to keep on the shoulder of the road, but tangled bushes got in her way. Sometimes, she had to walk on the roadway itself. She tried to keep as far over as possible. She didn't need an adult to tell her that this was dangerous, that she might be hit by a car. Once or twice, she could almost feel metal brushing her. Some cars honked as they passed. Each time, it left her heart pounding.

She was close to breaking down when she finally spotted a blacktop path curving away from the road. She turned along with it, but after a short distance, she stopped and looked back. It was surprising how far away the traffic seemed, how the noise was muted. Through a gap in the trees, she could see the cars and trucks looking like toys on the same road she had been walking on. Turning, she continued up the hill. Whatever this was, a park or a rest stop, she wasn't sure, but it was quiet and empty. This was what she needed, a place of peace. She looked up. Ancient trees bent down from the sky, beckoning to her, *Come. Come home.*

Phoebe imagined the branches picking her up and placing her on their tops, still mostly leafless even though it was spring. She would perch on their bristly ends, much like sitting on a hairbrush. Craning her neck, she could see bird's nests among the branches. They looked strangely secure so high up, swaying in the tips of the trees. She wished a bird would swoop down and carry her up. There, she would be safe.

She walked on, not in a hurry, taking deep breaths and catching the scent of pine trees. She was actually enjoying herself. There was something familiar and comforting about the whole place. She kept going, unable to shake the feeling that she had been there before.

Rounding a bend, she came to a clearing with two small, log cabins. She moved closer to read the sign near the cabins and laughed. No wonder this place was familiar. She was in Valley Forge Park, the same place, of course, where George Washington and his army had stayed, but it also was where her family had once visited. Her father had always promised they would go back, but he never seemed to get around to it.

Phoebe looked about. The family had spent most of their day right in this spot, she thought. She tried to piece together memories of that summer day—the steamy air, their lunch at a picnic table under a giant tree, Phoebe and Bobby climbing atop the cannons and posing for photos.

The park seemed very different on this chilly spring day that was nearing evening. It was desolate. Her foot crunched a twig, and a flock of small birds flew up out of the grass, frightened and noisy. "Sorry," she whispered.

Eventually, she came upon a water fountain and public restrooms. Just in time. She used both, filling up her water bottle, and resumed her hike. The landscape shifted again, she noticed. It was more thickly wooded, but with the sun sinking behind the hills, she could see a rocky trail not far in the distance. She stopped and considered this path, which headed uphill and into the woods. No way. It was scary enough that she would have to spend the night in the park. Spending it in the middle of the woods terrified her. There were probably wild animals there.

She needed to keep going while it was still light, Phoebe thought. Maybe she would be lucky enough to find a house or some shelter. She hesitated a moment longer, wondering if she should try to make her way back to the restroom. At least that was a building. No turning back, she thought with a bravado she didn't feel and moved forward along the blacktop path.

Before long, the path turned into a road, one that was fairly wide, smooth, and empty. The ribbon of roadway curved before her, with no one, not a car in sight. Better than someone stopping and questioning why a kid her age was out alone, she thought. But the place felt endlessly large and frighteningly empty.

She walked, feeling more tired than ever. When she swallowed, it hurt. On top of everything, her throat was getting sore. She wasn't sick. She couldn't be sick. It was just because she was thirsty, she told herself. Taking out the water bottle she had filled at the water fountain, she tilted it back to drain what was left. *I'll find another water fountain soon*, she thought. But as she picked her way in the dimming light, her hopes flagged.

Phoebe kept moving mostly because she was afraid to stop. Little halos of fear circled around inside her head. Unconsciously, she picked up speed, thinking she could somehow escape them or make them go away. Soon, she was practically running, the blacktop disappearing under her feet, until a blister that had rubbed raw on her heel forced her to slow. She struggled up an incline. She reached the crest of the hill as the last bits of daylight clung to the edges of the hills in the distance.

She stopped, bending to rub the calves of her legs, then straightened. The wind had kicked up and was whipping to the point that it almost knocked her over, but as she contemplated the expanse, a smile spread across her face. She had made it to the other side of the woods. Just then the moon appeared, bright and round, seemingly out of nowhere.

In the moonlight, she spotted a log cabin in the valley below. It was hard to tell, her eyes might be playing tricks, she thought, but it looked like water was making an indentation in the ground next to the cabin. A stream, maybe?

"I *do* have some luck," Phoebe cried, forgetting her sore throat. She was ready to run down the hill toward the cabin but stopped short. The hill was steep, and as clouds shifted over the moon, it was difficult to see. She would have to go down very carefully.

She was making some progress despite the rough ground when her short-lived luck ran out. In an instant, the wind had whipped into a fury. Fat raindrops splashed her face as she raised it to the sky, at the same moment that she heard a clap of thunder. It was a storm and she was outside in an open field, exactly what her parents always warned her not to do.

She bent her head and crept down the hill. The rain started beating down, soaking her and the ground and making the grass slippery. She had managed to descend about halfway when her body unexpectedly spasmed. Her foot had caught a small hole in the ground. She tried to regain her balance but clutched at air. She felt herself falling in slow motion.

Somehow, her body turned itself so that she was rolling on her side. She rolled and rolled for many frightening minutes, all while she was unable to catch her breath. At last, the ground leveled out, and she flung out an arm, which brought her to a jarring halt in mid-roll.

Pain from her arm sent lights shooting in front of her eyes. At least, her arm didn't snap off. Or maybe it did. She didn't want to open her eyes to look.

Phoebe lay on the ground, letting the rain pound her. Then as suddenly as it started, it let up, just as the pain started to subside. She opened her eyes and saw a stone wall inches from her face. With a shaky breath, she tried wiggling her fingers and toes, and then gingerly tested her arms. Everything worked. Getting hold of the stone wall, she grunted and pulled herself up on it.

While her body didn't seem damaged, her head throbbed. She tentatively touched her scalp with her fingers and drew back her wet hand. Even in the moonlight, she knew it was blood. What did that mean? Her skull was split open, her brains would spill out, and she would die? After a few moments, she again cautiously patted her head and realized with relief that there wasn't much blood after all. Just a tiny bit and a big lump. She had probably banged her head bumping down the hill. In fact, she was beginning to feel the sting of many scratches and bruises.

The storm was over. The moon emerged in full force, throwing a sharp, white light. Phoebe felt exposed here. She needed to get inside. Twisting around carefully, she took in what lay on the other side of the stone wall. And there, so close that she would have rolled right into it if the wall hadn't stopped her, was the wooden cabin.

Phoebe rose and was overcome with a sudden dizziness and a powerful thirst. Her throat felt raw. She first had to see if there really was a stream next to the cabin.

She went to the side of the cabin. Kneeling, she reached down, expecting to feel water. There was nothing but wet dirt, soggy leaves, and pebbles. No water. Even the brief rainstorm that had soaked her had only made a little mud in the stream bed.

Phoebe sat back, so thirsty and shaking so hard that it was difficult to think. To pull herself up, she grabbed hold of the branch of a tree growing along the bank. Water sprayed over her. Water had collected in the big leaves, she realized, and she started reaching for leaves and putting them to her mouth. She found another tree and was able to collect a small amount in her water bottle before raindrops began to fall again.

"It's raining!" she exclaimed. Gleeful, she held her open water bottle under the drops that were fast becoming a steady rain and then tilted her head to catch some in her open mouth. It was the answer to her prayer. Maybe it was proof, she thought, that God wanted her to find her father.

~

Adele sat, staring out of the living room window at a dark, rain-swept street, though she couldn't see much: her car in the driveway and a slice of the empty street. That was about it. She sighed and lit another cigarette. Nearly two full days had passed since Phoebe had run away. The panic and anxiety that had overwhelmed Adele the previous day when she discovered Phoebe was missing had devolved into a low-grade, never-ending sense of horror. Adele had grown calmer, she supposed. *Do you get used to such a thing?* she wondered. The fear that this was all her doing had driven her into a worse condition, a horribly depressed state. All kinds of black thoughts about what could befall an eleven-year-old filled her head. A young girl out there all alone in the rain and cold. Better Phoebe was alone, Adele told herself grimly, than picked up by some awful predator who would do who-knows-what to her. *Would Phoebe actually get in a car with a stranger?* she wondered. They had drilled stranger danger into Phoebe's and Bobby's heads, but if Phoebe were desperate…

Adele sucked on the cigarette nervously. If Robert were here, he would undoubtedly blame her. Hell, he'd kill her for not taking proper care of Phoebe. That would be just like Robert—protective of Phoebe but not taking responsibility. He left the responsibility to Adele.

But blaming her for Phoebe running away would take a lot of nerve, Adele thought, flicking ashes angrily toward the ashtray perched on the back of the sofa and succeeding only in scattering them over the cushions. The fact was that Robert wasn't here. He had left her high and dry with two kids. All of this was his fault. Phoebe was excessively attached to her father. Those two were thick as thieves—everyone knew that. And, as a result, Phoebe was obsessed with finding him. From the moment Phoebe went missing, Adele knew that was what the girl had set out to do.

The previous day, Adele had returned home from work in a state of utter exhaustion. All day, she had carried horrible guilt about her impulsive, angry reaction that led her to lock Phoebe in the upstairs room. Why had she done that? It wasn't something you could rationalize. Adele had felt even worse when she called the school and lied, telling them that Phoebe was sick. Over and over throughout the day, she considered running back home to free Phoebe. But she couldn't risk being absent from work, not even for a second. If her supervisor caught her skipping out, he would fire her, and she desperately needed this job. So, she reluctantly stayed put until the end of the day and then drove home as fast as she could, cursing the traffic.

Tossing her bag on the living room recliner, she saw Bobby parked in front of the TV watching cartoons as usual. He didn't acknowledge her entrance, which ordinarily would both annoy and hurt Adele, but she let it pass. There had already been too much drama for one day.

The sullen teenager, whom Adele had called and recruited at the last minute to watch Bobby, was sprawled out on the sofa, twisting a lock of her hair with one hand and texting on her phone with the other. The babysitter didn't acknowledge her either. But just as Adele turned to run upstairs to Phoebe, she found her way blocked by the babysitter, who materialized with her hand outstretched for payment.

Sighing, Adele reached for her purse and dug in it for some bills. She handed them to the girl, who stuffed them in the pocket of her jeans and ambled to the door, still without a word.

"You can see yourself out, right?" Adele called after her as the door slammed shut. *Undoubtedly the worst babysitter ever*, she thought. Phoebe had been watching Bobby after school, and even if eleven years old seemed young, Phoebe had done a much better job.

Adele climbed the stairs. At the top floor, she stopped and stared in disbelief. The door that she had locked that morning was standing wide open. "What in God's name…" Her voice trailed off as she entered the room and confirmed the obvious. It was empty.

She returned to the top of the stairs. "Bobby!" she bellowed. "Get up here!"

Later that night—after she wrested the story from Bobby, who grew quiet and sullen with his mother's anxious questioning—they went searching for Phoebe. They drove around the neighborhood, Bobby uncharacteristically quiet in the back seat. Eventually, he fell asleep, slumping over as far as the seat belt restraint allowed.

Adele continued to cruise the streets, knuckles white on the steering wheel, trying to peer between the dark houses. Finally, she gave up and returned home, hoping that Phoebe might be sitting on the front porch, waiting for them. A fresh stab of panic overcame Adele when she saw the vacant porch awash in the light from the outside lamp.

Carrying the sleeping Bobby into the house and upstairs to bed, she fretted about whether to call the police. *It certainly wouldn't look good*, she thought, pacing around the living room and dining room. She could guess the reaction. *First, your husband takes off, and then your daughter disappears? Oh, sorry, stepdaughter. Hmmm, a stepdaughter. How did you two get along?*

Adele gave a low moan. The parents were always the first ones the police suspect, she thought. What would they think of a stepmother? Especially if it came out that she had locked her stepdaughter in a room all day instead of sending her to school.

Adele stopped in front of the bookcase that held more framed family photos than books. She picked up the most recent school photo of Phoebe, the one with her hair captured in two neat braids. Adele had been the one to show Phoebe how to braid her hair and still often helped her fix her hair in the morning. Adele studied the photograph for a full two minutes.

"This is ridiculous," she said aloud. "Of course, I have to call. I can't *not* call." She carefully replaced the picture frame on the shelf and retrieved her phone.

Her call to the police proved distressing but not for the reasons Adele expected. Instead of being on the defensive, Adele found herself trying to convince them that this was a genuine case of a missing child.

"I understand how you must feel, Mrs. Locke, but we try to be judicious about our use of Amber Alerts," the woman from the police headquarters said. She conveyed, even over the phone, a condescension barely concealed by a thin layer of politeness. Adele found the woman insufferable but didn't dare react.

"We conduct full-blown searches only in cases of evidence that a child has been abducted," the policewoman said in a stiff, formal voice. "We certainly can't do this in every case, given the resources it requires. And with what you're telling me about the child and your recent separation from your husband, it's very possible—I'd say highly likely—that her father took her. Unfortunately, that's what happens in a large majority of these circumstances. It's rarely an abduction with intent to do harm."

The woman did say the last part gently. Adele also had to admit that she had responded promptly to her 911 call and briskly set about asking appropriate questions and getting relevant background. But it didn't take long for the woman to make up her mind. This was a run-of-the-mill case of a couple splitting up, with one parent snatching the child. Adele tried to convince her otherwise. "Why didn't he take his son then? Why take one child and not the other?" she had demanded. "Mmm," the woman murmured.

That was when Adele decided to switch tactics. She suggested a search party or maybe an Amber Alert to notify surrounding regions to be on the lookout. Even as she said it, she knew how demanding and pathetic she sounded. In response, it sparked another lecture about feuding divorcing parents.

Undeterred, Adele jumped in as soon as the woman took a breath.

"Can't the police at least *look* for her? When they're out on patrol or something? Just in case her father hasn't taken her. There can't be too many eleven-year-old girls walking around at this time of night."

"We'll send a patrol car to search the vicinity in the morning," the woman responded without a trace of irritation, which Adele found irritating in itself. "And, of course, we'll work to get in touch with your husband. I know it's difficult, but try not to worry, Mrs. Locke. Chances are that Phoebe is with her dad."

Chances are? Fat chance was more like it. Adele pressed the button to end the call. Phoebe's father had abandoned all of them, including Phoebe. Robert had moved onto his new life that didn't include any of them. But Adele couldn't explain that to the police.

Replaying it all in her mind as she sat at the living room window the next day, Adele thought, *Once again, it's left up to me.* She felt isolated, and furious at being isolated. She was angrier than when Robert announced his intention to leave. Then, an instant later, the fury was gone and she was deflated. She had Bobby to take care of, after all. If she looked at it through an entirely pragmatic lens—hell, if one looked at it that way, Phoebe was Robert's kid and his responsibility. Not hers.

She climbed the stairs to get ready for bed, telling herself she had done all she could do. But that was a lie. It added more fuel to the guilt bonfire she was stoking. There were so many layers to her guilt about Phoebe—for not considering how Robert leaving would affect Phoebe, for losing patience with her, for the unforgiveable sin of locking her up, for not being able to find her.

Adele plucked a notebook from the crowded dresser top and began making a list of things she could do, places she could look, actions she could take. She had to get past the guilt, but it nagged at her that she might have prevented this if she had told Phoebe the truth about her father. On the other hand, was that her place? She had raised Phoebe and was extremely fond of her, but the fact was that Phoebe wasn't her flesh and blood. She was not Phoebe's mother. Just the stepmother.

Adele picked up the phone to dial Robert's cell phone number again but hesitated. It was very late. *So what?* she thought, punching the numbers. *He's not going to answer anyway.* Sure enough, just like all the other times she had tried to call, the phone rang precisely five times and then switched to a recorded voice informing her that the mobile phone subscriber she was trying to reach wasn't available. Did that mean the phone was turned off? Or had he thrown the phone away? Would the police—to whom she had provided Robert's cell phone number—have some other means of reaching him? Adele had no clue but thought it was unbelievably rude that the guy didn't even have a voicemail account to take messages.

Sighing, she went to the window and watched the raindrops beading on the car under the street light. *If Phoebe comes back, or I find her, I promise to tell her. I'll tell her everything. She deserves to know.* But as Adele leaned her head against the glass, she knew that she probably wouldn't follow through on that promise.

Keeping the truth from Phoebe was a way to protect her. Or her father. Or both.

Damn him, Adele thought, angry again. *Robert does have some kind of colossal selfishness.* He always showed favoritism, always so protective of his precious Phoebe while practically ignoring Bobby. But in the end, Robert walked out on all of them.

It was raining again and harder. Adele watched the raindrops until they were indistinguishable from her tears. Tomorrow would have to do, she thought. She would give one more pitch to the police to see if she could get them to be more proactive. She tried to picture a happy ending to all of this. If they found Phoebe, she would be so relieved at first, and then, she would give that girl a big piece of her mind. But what a blessing it would be to put this worrisome stunt behind them. They could move on as a family. She had to hope that was how things would turn out.

Maybe after work, she thought, she and Bobby would go searching again. She would see about that. Tomorrow.

~

Phoebe's eyes flew open. It was still nighttime, but she had no idea how long she had been asleep. It could have been seconds or hours.

After setting her water bottle on the ground to try to catch more rainwater, she had stumbled into the darkness of the cabin. She was confronted by an odd smell—rotting wood and leaves, maybe animals, or even humans. Still, the cabin was protection. She felt her way to the rude bunks of wooden planks built into the wall, and in her exhaustion, she dropped onto the lower one, falling asleep instantly. It felt like she had awoken just as abruptly.

She lay there, eyes wide open in the darkness. It wasn't as quiet as before…there was a noise like a low rumble. Was that thunder? She rolled over and propped herself up on her elbows, trying to peer out the doorway. She couldn't hear any more rain, but water dripped from the eaves. There was the rumble again, low and steady.

Phoebe crawled out of the bunk, wincing. She was still sore from her long downhill fall. She shuffled to the doorway and managed to retrieve the water bottle so that she wouldn't knock it over. Outside, the air was fresher and cooler after the storm. The moon had traveled high in the now clear sky and was once again very bright.

The rumble grew louder. Phoebe watched as a herd of deer burst out of the woods, further down the little valley. They headed across the meadow, staggeringly beautiful in the moonlight, led by a buck with majestic antlers. He was the king of the herd. Hundreds of deer, far too many to count, ran on and on, deer after deer, following their king deep into the woods. Phoebe stood for a long time, shivering in the chill, looking at the spot where they disappeared, and thinking, *They're running with light hearts. They're running free.*

Four

It was lunchtime. Sidney sat in her usual spot among the Lunch Ladies, at the furthest reaches of the table. She twisted in her seat so that she was almost entirely turned away from the group. She kept her back to them as she occasionally reached around to pull off a bit of her sandwich, turning away again to chew and swallow with difficulty. She was being rude to her coworkers, but they didn't seem to notice. Instead, they were focused on their new lunch companion, who was center stage.

J.T. had invited himself to lunch. That he was permitted to attend was extraordinary in itself, let alone that he was welcomed. The Lunch Ladies generally went to great lengths to keep their group isolated, as if they were a secret society. Hardly a secret, Sidney thought. They gathered every day in the middle of the lunchroom. Whether or not he sensed these barriers, J.T. set to work from the first moments of his appearance to employ his charm, and it appeared to be working. He had squeezed into a spot at middle of the table and had managed to smoothly commandeer the conversation away from Carla, all by simply bringing up his favorite topic: what would become of Poppy Press now that the New York crowd had taken over?

Carla didn't even seem put out at being displaced. Each time Sidney shot a glance in her direction, she saw Carla listening with rapt attention.

To Sidney, J.T. was a horrible embarrassment. It was as if she had forgotten all the times that she had fallen under the spell of J.T.'s storytelling. In front of the women, she found herself feeling responsible for his behavior, like a parent held accountable for an unruly child. No matter how many times she had heard his wild conspiracy theories, hearing him tell them to the group with great flourish made her cringe. Even more discomfiting was the prospect of the unmerciful teasing she would have to endure about J.T.'s oddities and, no doubt, him being her "beau." Sidney picked up her sandwich and angrily ripped off a piece of bread with her teeth. She would have greatly preferred that the others had remained unaware of any of her interactions with J.T. or even that she knew who he was. But he had appeared in the cafeteria without warning, and walked right up to the table, inviting himself to join them.

Sidney fixed her gaze on the blank wall and tried not to listen to J.T. As usual, she found him impossible to ignore. He could be talking nonsense (and generally was), but he had a mesmerizing way about him.

"You think it was Charlie Post's idea to give up control of the company? No way," J.T. was saying. He was speaking fast, as he always did. But his eyes shone, and his voice, normally a nasal drone, boomed the length of the table. He wasn't just relishing the spotlight. He was a missionary preaching the gospel of the old Poppy Press.

"I'll tell you what happened. While you folks were busy with your lives and your jobs, Charlie was wheeling and dealing, trying to keep the Press afloat. He got investors, angel investors they call them, silent partners. He talked them into sinking money into the company. That gave Charlie the cash he needed. We always seemed to get the printing jobs, sooner or later. And then we'd make enough to buy out the investors."

"And how do you know all of this?" Carla demanded, suddenly doubtful. "Who's your source?"

J.T. held up a hand but spoke soothingly. "Sorry, sister, I'm afraid I can't divulge my sources."

Sister? Sidney was horrified. No one spoke that way to Carla. It was mystifying, but Carla appeared mollified instead of angry.

"Anyhow," J.T. continued, "this angel investor thing was working for Charlie Post. It worked for a long time. The Press got more business, and we were okay. That is, until the bottom fell out, and no one was interested in printing anymore. Print is dead, they say. Charlie was stuck, you see. No investor money, no printing jobs. What was he going to do?"

J.T. paused to take a sip of water from his Styrofoam cup. It was likely for dramatic effect, but apparently, water was all he was consuming for lunch. The Lunch Ladies watched, riveted. Along with the rest of the Poppy Press population, they had spent weeks speculating about how events might have played out in the front offices. Now they were getting the inside story, and it had a ring of truth. Even Carla was no longer questioning the authenticity of his narrative.

"I'll tell you what Charlie does," J.T. said when no one answered his rhetorical question. "He looks for another source of capital. He searches and searches and eventually lands on this New York outfit. They're in the printing business, but they've diversified in other things, too. They seem to know what they're doing. Problem solved. Charlie makes the deal.

"But because he can't afford fancy lawyers like New York, he overlooks a big loophole in the agreement. In the end, Charlie is booted out as president of Poppy Press. He even gets kicked out of the building. Charlie had sold the company, this time for real."

In the silence, Lydia from Fulfillment, a well-known Charlie Post loyalist, emitted a loud sniff. The others glared at her. "Well, it's very sad," she said defensively.

"Don't worry, ladies. This isn't the end of the line for Charlie Post. I believe that." J.T. swept his arm over the table. "He's way too smart to give up that easy. He'll be back to save the company. And us."

"How exactly will he do that?" Carla spoke up. "He's not even allowed in the building."

"I can't say *exactly* how," J.T. said. "But I'll bet it will be with the help of Harry Corcoran. You know Harry. He's in the middle of everything." J.T. looked down the table at Sidney. "In fact, Harry is now Sidney's boss. Maybe our girl Sidney will let us know what she hears."

All eyes swung to Sidney. She flushed an unattractive shade of red. "Harry is not my boss," she mumbled.

"Hey, buddy, I'm on to you." Carla confronted J.T. and everyone shifted back to their leader. Grateful for the distraction, Sidney sunk further in her seat.

"You must have gotten these ridiculous ideas from your brother," Carla was saying. "Hal always seemed to have an inside track. But that doesn't mean the stories aren't embellished, you know what I'm saying? Anyway, who cares what happened to Charlie? Bottom line is, we're here, and he's not."

Both triumphant and angry, Carla began crumpling cellophane and trash, crunching them in her hand as she eyed J.T. "And let's not forget," she said, "your brother's not around either, so what does he know? He got fired too."

It was now J.T. who flushed. Sidney flipped from irritation to feeling sorry for him. Carla had a mean streak, especially when she found someone's hot button. *I should say something*, Sidney thought but knew she wouldn't have the courage. Just then words burst from J.T. "That's not true!" The entire lunchroom fell silent.

J.T. jumped up. He was shaking. "My brother didn't get fired. He left for other reasons. Perfectly good reasons." He looked as if he might cry. Sidney held her breath, waiting for a further outburst, but J.T. turned and ran.

In the silence that followed, Carla said, amused, "Well, Sidney, I'm not sure we can stand the excitement of having your boyfriend join us for lunch every day."

"He's not my boyfriend," Sidney muttered, but no one heard her in the ensuing chatter.

It was much later, well after she had gotten home and sat, sagging into the faded slip-covered armchair, that Sidney suddenly took it into her head to go outside and garden. For someone who rigidly maintained a daily routine, this activity was certainly out of the norm. Still, she thought, as she knelt on the wet grass, it was therapeutic after the events of the day. Her headache, which had been threatening to bloom into a migraine, seemed to ease as she yanked crabgrass from the front lawn.

It was difficult to see despite the rising moon and the outside lights she had switched on. She had brought a flashlight, but it proved impossible to train it on the ground as she weeded, so she set it aside. The lights threw everything into sharp shadows so that the familiar surroundings, every inch of which she had known since birth, seemed surreal. Also, the air had grown chilly and damp, and her thin jacket wasn't much protection. Despite all this, she persevered, crawling about on the grass, feeling for errant weeds, getting the knees of her work slacks soaked and likely grass-stained.

If Agatha were alive, Sidney thought, she would be standing at the door, reminding Sidney that she had no business out there in the middle of the night. To her mother, weeding the lawn at seven-thirty in the evening would be as bad as gallivanting on the streets at two o'clock in the morning. Sidney smiled. That was Agatha for you. "What in the world are you doing out there, Sidney?" she could imagine Agatha saying. "If you had any sense, you would get inside where you belong."

Sidney had to stop herself from looking up to see if her mother's figure were silhouetted in the doorway. She would give the weeding just another ten minutes or so, she decided. It was a tiny act of defiance. Maybe it was time she finally established her independence from her dead mother.

I'm far too old to start acting like a rebellious teenager, she thought, yanking at the grass and dirt. *And who am I proving this to? No one is left. Just me, in this old house.* Shivering from the chill, she stubbornly remained crouched over the damp grass.

Minutes later, she sat back on her heels with a handful of soggy weeds. As she thrust the mess into a plastic bag, a small stick dug into her finger. She winced. It was further proof that she should call it a night. Still, she remained, shaking her hand until the stinging stopped. She wanted to savor one more moment of normalcy.

This did feel like a normal, familiar thing. She had always enjoyed outdoor work, taking care of the yard and the garden year after year, like old friends. Even as a child, she had gravitated toward it, tagging along with her grandfather as he performed the outside chores. Despite his stature in the community as a respected attorney, and the long hours he put in at his law firm, her grandfather loved to putter about in the yard. It was more than puttering, though; his landscaping helped make their house something of a showcase in the neighborhood. Sidney, who idolized her grandfather, had wanted to be just as much of an expert in gardening. By the time she was eight, her grandfather was showing her how to use the push mower, instructing her on the importance of keeping the garden tools clean and dry to avoid rust, and helping her stow everything neatly in the shed. Sidney thought about all the years they worked side by side, sharing gardening and conversations. It had been so long since her grandfather's death, but she still felt an aching loss every time she worked in the garden.

Everyone was dead and gone. If nothing else, she ought to feel a sense of ownership for the whole house, indoors and out. But she didn't. She felt like an imposter homeowner.

Maybe it was too soon after Agatha's death to switch her thinking. No, she told herself, she needed to get used to it. After that disturbing phone conversation with her mother's attorney earlier in the day, what she needed to do was to mentally detach herself from the place entirely. She had to steel herself and start thinking the unthinkable—leaving this beautiful Victorian house, the only home she had ever known.

That was ridiculous, crazy talk. It couldn't happen. She pulled her jacket tighter and looked about the yard. Maybe she should change things up, she thought suddenly. It was still early enough in the spring to plant something different. She would shock the neighborhood and skip the same boring annuals she planted every year. She would rip out the old stand-bys and make the tiny front lawn a sea of new blooms. She closed her eyes, visualizing tall wildflowers, riotous colors, an explosion of daylilies and cone-flowers sprouting from every corner. She could even lay a little brick walkway that would let her swim waist-deep through flora back and forth from the house.

She opened her eyes and immediately felt deflated. That sort of garden would be too bold. Too bold for the house, for the neighborhood, for "our kind of people," as Agatha used to put it. Sidney never was exactly certain what kind of people they were supposed to be.

It didn't matter, after hearing what Mr. Smithson, the lawyer, had to say. It was too late to make changes to the property anyway. She might very well lose the house.

Tears blurred her vision and slipped down her cheeks. She wiped her face, smearing it with mud in the process, and hoisted herself from the ground with some effort. As she turned to go back into the house, she instinctively glanced across the street at the Hammonds' residence, one half of a hulking, three-story twin. The place was mostly dark as usual, with one small lamp on and the blue screen of the television barely visible through the lace curtains in the front room. What would her mother's dear friend Mrs. Hammond think if Sidney's little lawn became a horticultural showcase? She imagined Mrs. Hammond's scolding. "What would your mother say? My goodness, she's barely cold in the ground!"

Although Mrs. Hammond was no relation—and Sidney had probably spoken fewer than ten words to the woman in the previous decade—her neighbor still managed to hold a certain sway.

Simply the threat of what Mrs. Hammond might say kept Sidney in line, a part of her mother's legacy. Agatha always had pointed to Mrs. Hammond as the neighborhood barometer, the what-will-people-think gauge. *I wouldn't be surprised if Mrs. Hammond swore to my mother that she would keep an eye on me,* Sidney thought. As if Sidney were a loose cannon who would do something crazy at a moment's notice.

Sidney knotted the plastic strips that served as handles on the bag of weeds and slowly walked to the side of the house to place it into a trash can. She was taking her time, delaying her re-entry into the desolate house.

At last, there was nothing else to do but climb the porch steps. She locked the door and double checked the deadbolt as had become her custom, and then started wandering through the rooms, flipping on light switches. Keeping the lights lit had also become habitual since Agatha's death. With all the lamps blazing, the place felt more lived-in, even if it was an appalling waste of electricity.

She halted her tour in the kitchen, where she stood blinking under the blinding overhead lights. She should probably eat, she thought, and pulled open the refrigerator door. There was a half-gallon of milk with an expiration date that had passed two weeks earlier. She poured the curdled mess into the sink.

Okay, so your mother died. It happens to most people, she lectured herself as she ran hot water to clear the drain of the sour odor. She needed to get on with the new phase of her life, but she had no clue how to start. There were no rules left to follow, no one to discuss things with. Just her alone in this empty house. If it were merely a matter of money, she could probably figure out how to make ends meet with her meager paycheck. A lonelier existence maybe, but not an insurmountable problem. The real issue was the growing number of problems she faced.

With a burst of energy, Sidney pulled a tablet of paper from a drawer and sat at the scarred, wooden kitchen table. It was time to do something practical. She would make a list of her problems and try to figure out solutions.

First, she thought, chewing the end of the pen, there was the alarming prospect that her employer was failing. NO JOB, she scribbled. If Poppy Press went under she could be out of a job sooner rather than later, with not even that meager paycheck to count on.

Second, and perhaps more pressing, there was the news she had received in the phone call with the lawyer, Mr. Smithson, that afternoon.

It appeared, the stiff-sounding Mr. Smithson admitted in a roundabout way, that Agatha did not have the large nest egg Sidney may have been counting on. This alone was a jolt to Sidney, whose mother had often brought up the comfortable amount of money from Sidney's grandfather that she would inherit when Agatha passed on. That money was nonexistent, according to Mr. Smithson. Agatha was nearly destitute at her death.

There was another complicating factor involving the house, the lawyer said, lowering his voice so that Sidney had to strain to hear. Instead of inheriting the house as the sole survivor, as one might logically assume, Sidney instead might legally be required to forfeit it. More specifically, he said, his monotone dropping in volume with every word, she might not be the only person with ownership rights to the property.

Despite the lawyer's near whisper, the last part came through clearly. Sidney sat, stunned, the phone heavy in her hand. After a lengthy silence, she heard Mr. Smithson's quiet voice asking, "Are you still there, Sidney?"

"Yes," she answered dutifully. "I'm still here."

She might have been on the other end of the phone line, but she hadn't been taking it in. She had been blissfully ignorant. At the very least, she had failed to pay attention to these matters when her mother was alive. As her mother's only child and caregiver, Sidney was embarrassed that she knew nothing of her own financial situation and that Agatha may have actually misled her. It was especially humiliating to hear it from Mr. Smithson, an attorney in the law firm where Sidney's grandfather had built a fortune. What had happened to all the money? And what was Mr. Smithson talking about—someone else inheriting the house?

Sidney gripped the phone and swallowed. She reminded herself that Mr. Smithson was giving her special treatment as the granddaughter of one of the firm's founding partners. Mr. Smithson had long been the family's personal lawyer. She had seen him treat her mother like royalty during various office visits over the years. She thought of the final time she brought Agatha there, about six months before her passing. As usual, Sidney was not invited to the meeting. She had waited in the parlor-like anteroom, glancing through magazines while her mother disappeared inside to discuss unknown topics. As usual, there was no discussion afterward.

She should have pressed Agatha, Sidney thought during the interminable phone call while Mr. Smithson explained everything, clearly and slowly as if to a child.

"I'm afraid that your mother did not leave a last will and testament, at least not to our knowledge," Mr. Smithson was saying. "It pains me to say that. Your grandfather would be horrified. Spinning in his grave, if you'll forgive the expression. Many times, we strongly advised her to create a will. There are multiple problems with dying intestate, which is the term for dying without a will. But she always refused to allow our office to draw one up for her. It's rather shocking behavior for the daughter of an attorney, but I believe she was under the misconception that the lack of a will would somehow make it better for you. Exactly how, I'm not quite certain.

"I'm not sure if you realize this, Ms. O'Neill, but if one dies without a will in the Commonwealth of Pennsylvania, the state will essentially create one for you based on certain rules of succession." He paused again. "Do you understand?"

"Yes." Sidney just wanted him to get to the point.

"For example," he continued, "if you have children surviving you and no one else, your children inherit."

"Okay, I'm Agatha's surviving child, so…"

"If you'll bear with me. Let's say you have no surviving children or parents, but you're married at the time of death. Your surviving spouse would then receive the entire estate. If, for instance, you have a spouse *and* surviving children, the spouse gets a certain amount plus half the balance of the estate, and the child or children get the remainder." He sighed. "It's all a little technical, I know."

Sidney was confused. "I'm following you, but my mother had no surviving spouse. My father left when I was a baby."

"I don't know how to tell you this, so I'm just going to say it. Someone who claims to be your father has contacted our office with a claim to the estate."

Sidney nearly dropped the phone. Her father! That was impossible.

"Are you sure?" She wet her lips. "We never heard from him all these years. We assumed…but they divorced." She hesitated. "Weren't they divorced?"

"Apparently not," he said. "I was aware of that from your mother. She said because she never heard from him again, she didn't see any benefit in pursuing a divorce. Even a legal separation was a waste of time and money in her view." He cleared his throat. "It is my understanding that she believed that he had already passed away."

"So did I," Sidney said faintly. She didn't know what questions to ask or what this might mean. Mr. Smithson must have read her mind.

"I'm afraid what all this means is that if this person turns out to be your father, then he has a valid claim to more than half the estate—of which the main asset is your house." He paused to gauge Sidney's reaction, but she was silent. "Your home would have to be sold, and the proceeds split." He hesitated again. "It's a bit of a mess, I'm afraid."

Sidney felt as if she had been punched in the gut. "Didn't my grandfather leave a significant amount of money? What happened?"

"Your grandfather had a good amount of net wealth in his time, I'm sure. But I never was in a position to know the exact nature of his finances or how much he may have left to your mother. By the time I was brought into the picture, there didn't seem to be much money. Don't worry, though," he added quickly. "The firm will continue to represent you on this issue pro bono."

Sidney held the phone so tightly that her arm ached with the effort to hold it.

"Let me offer my sincere sympathies, Ms. O'Neill. But might I also suggest something?" Mr. Smithson cleared his throat. "I don't want to give false hope, but it might be worth searching for a will. As I said, I begged your mother on numerous occasions to draw one up, and one time I think I almost convinced her. At least, she conceded that it wasn't such a bad idea. For your mother, that was a big step, wouldn't you agree?"

Sidney murmured agreement.

"Good. Let's entertain the notion that your mother did write out something. Any written statement of one's intentions, even on a brown paper bag, can be a legally valid will. It doesn't have to be drawn up by a lawyer, although lawyers generally don't like to tell people that." He chuckled at his own joke but stopped when Sidney didn't respond.

"Anyway, it's worth checking. If you find a piece of paper signed and dated by your mother that simply states that she wanted to leave everything to you upon her death, that could help. We could use it as leverage in resolving this claim.

"Meanwhile, I need to move forward in the proceedings, but the bureaucracy moves slowly in these matters, especially when someone shows up out of the blue after fifty years. He's going to have to offer some proof of his own. That should give you some time."

At the kitchen table that night, Sidney stared at the list of challenges she had made. So far, there were only two items, but they were big ones: she was facing no job and no home. Homeless.

It seemed worse than death. It made her actually jealous of her mother.

She rose and resumed her aimless wandering from room to room. She couldn't bring herself to search for a will yet. She wasn't even searching for answers. She was simply rattling around in emptiness.

She picked up a little blue ceramic elephant with a raised tusk that her mother had kept on the coffee table. Every week, Sidney had dusted the elephant without thinking about what it meant to Agatha, or why she had chosen to display it. Maybe there was no reason. Sidney frowned at the grime that had collected in its crevices, and carefully replaced it on the table.

She should start looking for the will. But she didn't have the heart to start tearing the place apart for a document that in all likelihood didn't exist.

The clock on the shelf ticked loudly, a reminder of how quiet the house had become. Without Agatha, it was as if a noisy radio had been switched off.

Really, the quiet had started before Agatha's death when a stroke abruptly silenced her. In her last weeks, in those times when she was awake, Agatha seemed as surprised as Sidney by her inability to speak. She would look at Sidney with confusion and wonderment, soundlessly moving her mouth and jaw. Before long, she seemed to accept her fate. She lay in bed staring at nothing, before slipping into a slumber that eventually made the silence permanent.

It was odd and maybe profane that the sacred moment of remembering the sad shell of her mother dying would be violated by the thought of Sidney's father. She had no memory of him. Over the years, she had never given him much thought, even on the rare occasions when his name had been brought up. As she indicated to Mr. Smithson, she had long ago concluded that he must be dead.

The circumstances under which her father had left them were a mystery. Or maybe they weren't mysterious at all: some portion of men, ill-fitted for family life, have walked out on their wives and families since the beginning of time. Sidney never knew. But what difference did it make? She had had a family, a home, and security, thanks to her grandparents. That they never heard from her father seemed a relief to Agatha, who did little to hide her distaste when she spoke of him, which wasn't often.

Ironically, Agatha mentioned Sidney's father more in the last years of her life than ever before. She spoke disparagingly, of course, still nursing old wounds. "That man was no good. I don't know what possessed me to have anything to do with him," she would say. Then, she would add the worst insult she could hurl: "He didn't even come from a good family."

Beyond that, there were only vague complaints and bits of stories. Sidney had never heard how her father had done her mother wrong, other than walking out on them. Perhaps that was all it was, probably more than enough humiliation for Agatha. This no doubt reinforced Sidney's assumption—based on no facts, really—that her father was dead.

People get old, and then they die, Sidney told herself. Still, she knew that was glib. It was much easier to be philosophical about a father she had never met, than about the death of her mother. Despite her quirks, Agatha doted on Sidney, and considered her daughter the center of her universe.

For her part, Sidney was floundering without Agatha. Her mother's death was, in a strange way, a shock. Not because an elderly woman wasn't expected to die, but because her mother had been so protective, had so sheltered Sidney, that here she was, well into middle age and still not prepared to be a grownup.

It was her own fault. She had put blinders on and assumed that things would never change. Of course, things change.

Sidney dropped to the floor, sitting on the thin, rough carpeting that Agatha had insisted on covering the hardwood floors. Clutching her knees, Sidney rocked back and forth. For a moment, it was comforting. It was also blatant self-pity, but no one was there to tell her to stop it. No Agatha, for example, to say, *Stop this nonsense*. Sidney barked out a strangled laugh, and then gave into the grief, letting it wash over her.

She sat there, rocking and weeping, what Agatha surely would have called carrying on. At last, spent and exhausted, she lay on the serviceable carpeting, a big, orphaned baby, age fifty-one.

~

Harry Corcoran never liked to be kept waiting. He was always very prompt, so he disliked tardiness in others, just as he disdained sloppiness and bad hygiene. But his job was in sales, so if a client chose to turn up hours late for an appointment, there wasn't much he could do about it. He accepted this with clients, but he didn't have to put up with it at the office, with the person purported to be his boss.

Harry, seated on an uncomfortable chair in the reception area of the Poppy Press executive offices, picked imaginary lint from his immaculately pressed trousers. He checked his wristwatch again. It was the eighth or ninth time he had checked in the past twenty minutes.

He sighed loudly for the benefit of Sondra, Vincent Ayers's administrative assistant. She ignored him. In fact, Sondra was doing a pretty good job of pretending she had no idea who Harry was, although she had been Charlie Post's assistant, and in that capacity had seen Harry in Charlie's office almost daily. Since Charlie was deposed, Sondra's loyalties had conveniently landed with the parent company in New York, and she chose not to associate with anyone from Charlie's era.

Harry watched as Sondra fussed with the papers on her desk and examined her fingernails with concern. With an unnecessary amount of flourish, she rummaged in her purse before drawing out a small bottle of nail polish. She bent over her repair work.

Harry grew tired of watching the manicure. His leg bobbed nervously. He had many things to do and little time to get them done, yet he was stuck in this nail salon. Meanwhile, the recently installed president of Poppy Press was seriously late for the meeting that he had called himself. This wasn't Harry's idea.

He was on the verge of leaving when Ayers arrived. More than simply entering the area, Ayers swept in. He went directly to his office door and extracted a set of keys, trying several before he found the one to unlock it. Harry thought this was unusual. No one went to the trouble of locking their office doors at the Press.

Ayers entered his office, still not acknowledging Harry's presence. The secretary cleared her throat twice, then finally, reluctantly, rose and slouched against the office doorway. When Ayers finally looked up, she pointed in Harry's direction.

"Oh, yes, of course. Come in, come in." With no visible embarrassment, Ayers ushered Harry in and shut the door.

They settled on opposite sides of a large executive desk. Harry had promised himself, as a strategic move, that he would let Ayers speak first. Ayers hadn't been at the Press long but he already had a reputation for volatility. He could blow up at a moment's notice. Harry wasn't sure when the best time to tip his hand to Ayers might be—but he suspected that this particular meeting was probably not right.

Harry arranged himself as best he could in the uncomfortable guest chair and waited. Ayers played absently with a large, rather dangerous-looking silver letter opener. A little ironic, Harry thought, considering that everyone was all about digital, not old-fashioned letters.

"So what can I do for you?" Ayers asked.

Harry couldn't resist a smile. He had been told his smile was part of his charm. "I believe you called this meeting."

"Ah, so I did." Ayers remained unflustered. "I did want to talk with you, Corcoran." His manner turned brisk and businesslike. "We've decided to take Poppy Press into bankruptcy. Chapter Eleven bankruptcy." Ayers glanced at Harry, as if to gauge his reaction, then resumed studying the letter opener. "What does that mean? It means the company can continue to operate, assuming you do your job and bring in a sufficient number of printing projects."

Ayers dropped the opener on the desk and shoved his chair back. "Thought it would be sporting to give you a heads up. Of course, all of this is confidential. We'll announce it to the staff after the papers are filed in court, probably in a couple of weeks."

In the time it took Ayers to make this speech, Harry felt himself shriveling up until he was nothing but a deflated balloon. It was a feeling he hadn't had in a very long time. He looked out the window behind Ayers's massive desk. Bankruptcy! He hadn't seen this coming. Charlie Post, ever the chess player, hadn't either. They should have thought of this, Harry thought, panicking.

Buy some time, he told himself. *Keep calm.* Yet he could feel sweat pooling in his armpits, dampening his crisp, white shirt. This was going to seriously ruin their plans, his and Charlie's.

"Of course, won't breathe a word," Harry murmured. "However..." he paused. "I'm wondering," he continued with regained assurance, "if you would entertain the notion of holding off on this action. Just for a bit longer. Mr. Post and I were going to make a business proposal that I think you'll find has merit. But we need time to put the package together."

"Mr. Post? Charlie?" Ayers barked out a laugh. "He sold us the company. He's not involved anymore."

"Yes. I mean, I know. But we're exploring some options, some investors. The idea is—well, we want to buy the Press back from you." Harry was losing control of the situation. Charlie would kill him.

Harry leaned forward and looked at Ayers earnestly. "Look, if the New York office believes that it's bad enough to file for bankruptcy, then this could be a way out. You could sell the Press back. Your headaches go away."

Ayers picked up the letter opener again and tapped it on his desk. He stared at Harry. Ayers's eyes tended to protrude anyway. Now they were all but popping out of his head.

Finally, Ayers gave a snort. "I don't know what kind of games you and Charlie Post played with this company in the past and, frankly, I don't care. But it's a different game now. Let me tell you the facts. Fact one. No printing shop is doing well. Fact two. Because of fact one, you won't find investors willing to sink big bucks into this place. Fact three. Poppy Press can't meet its financial obligations. Ergo, bankruptcy."

Blood roared in Harry's head, and he couldn't, for the life of him, think of anything to say. No answer, no quick retort. It didn't matter, though, because Ayers was prattling on.

"Anyway," Ayers was saying cheerfully, "bankruptcy isn't necessarily the end. Don't you know how Chapter Eleven works? It allows the company to operate without the pressure of the company's creditors threatening to put it out of business. Everything is like normal, only under the protection of the bankruptcy court."

Harry pursed his lips. "But we're the subsidiary company, right? Can we file for bankruptcy? Doesn't the parent company have to absorb the loss, so to speak?"

"Not quite," Ayers said. He wasn't fazed. Harry knew that meant that they had probably had endless discussions about this point with New York. "It isn't common, I'll grant you that, but we appear to have the court's approval."

Ayers looked far too smug, Harry thought with annoyance, but he nodded and forced a smile.

"I suppose bankruptcy would kill any kind of deal to get the Press back on its feet. Selling the company, for example."

Ayers shot him a look but responded calmly enough. "Not necessarily. The court obviously would have to approve a sale. It would all have to be part of a bankruptcy plan— "

Harry felt revived. This still might work. "Look, you're a good businessman. If it's a possibility as you say, then we would just need a little more time to pull this deal together." He gave his most earnest look. "You can get out of this with a profit. Wouldn't a profit be nice?"

Harry held Ayers's stare. Surprisingly, Ayers gave in first, but when he spoke, there was warning in his voice.

"You said you need more time. Don't take too much. See if you can do this deal, and then we'll see."

"I would need assurances—"

"This is all you're getting at the moment." Ayers turned his back and looked out the large window behind his desk. After a long moment, he swiveled back. "Don't you have work to do?" he said to Harry and reached to pick up his phone.

~

The table where the Lunch Ladies sat every day was the only one in the Poppy Press cafeteria with a view. Considering that the old factory building offered very little natural light, any sort of window seating was sought after. The Lunch Ladies might have to strain to take in the view from the small, square window set high in the wall, but it nonetheless was a view, showing a patch of sky and the corner of the next building. That, and Carla's mesmerizing voice, felt soothing.

Sidney had to admit that Carla also made lunch interesting. She could talk easily and at length about anything. Once, she had spent twenty-five minutes talking about the differences in the produce, bananas in particular, at the three supermarkets in her neighborhood. She never lacked for opinions and, of course, was the Ladies' primary source of Press gossip.

Carla knew everything that was going on in the shop. She refused to reveal her sources. Sidney suspected there weren't many of them, some probably outright inventions of Carla's imagination. True or false, it was all delivered seamlessly, often in a single, long story. One moment Carla would be expounding on the sad case of someone in the Fulfillment Department who was splitting from her cheating husband from Pre-Press, and in the next minute the story would glide into intrigue and deception. Sometimes this would startle everyone until they realized Carla was retelling the plot to one of her favorite television soaps.

During this particular lunch hour, Carla was discussing the possibility—the distinct possibility, in her view—that two co-workers were brazenly conducting an affair, even though the man's wife also worked at the Press. The Lunch Ladies had heard this adulterous story before. Carla retold it as if it had just happened, and as if she hadn't previously spoken of it. The women didn't care. They listened, munching potato chips nearly in unison.

Sidney looked around, seeing the others as if for the first time. They were middle-aged women, all remarkably similar; that is to say, they had given up caring about appearances. Their hair was wispy and flyaway, and their backsides were encased in taut, ugly pants, hanging over the edges of the plastic chairs. Funny that she had never noticed how worn and tired they were. She glanced down at her own electric-blue, nylon-blend slacks, which were at least twenty years old and far too short.

She wouldn't have guessed that it would be an ugly old pair of pants that would overwhelm her with sadness. But she felt suddenly and immeasurably closer to the edge of a precipice, the abyss of depression that she had been tiptoeing around for some time. But that would be just plain silly, she told herself, to succumb to clinical depression because she was dressed badly.

"I have it on very good authority," Carla was saying, in a conspiratorial stage whisper, "that when his wife brought in a cake to celebrate his birthday, and practically the whole department was gathered to sing 'Happy Birthday,' well, what do you know? They couldn't find the birthday boy. Funny thing—his girlfriend couldn't be found either. They waited and waited and then ate the cake without him. A chocolate cake, too, really good."

Carla, reflecting on the cake, dabbed her mouth with the edge of a paper napkin. Sidney thought, not for the first time, that Carla had a pretty face, but it reminded Sidney of a bird. In the folds of fat were bright black eyes, a little finch's eyes. Even Carla's small sharp nose was like a beak. Sidney found herself enthralled by the jerky, bird-like movements of Carla's head. If nothing else, Carla served as a distraction, Sidney thought.

Then Carla resumed her story, and Sidney lost interest. She had too much on her mind. Her eyes slid back to the window and she daydreamed until she heard Carla pronounce J.T.'s name.

"Of course, his brother J.T. still works here. You ladies remember J.T., right? He joined us for lunch the other week? It seems our own Sidney knows him well." Carla threw a dark grin in Sidney's direction. "And exactly how well do you know him, dear?"

Sidney stared, uncomprehending, before stuttering, "I'm not, I mean J.T. and I—"

"Pffft, no matter," Carla interrupted. "Let's just jump into what happened with J.T. and Hal."

Even in her flustered state, Sidney wondered why Carla would dredge up the topic of J.T.'s brother Hal. Unless it was because J.T. had reacted so badly when Carla mentioned his brother at lunch, which was what seemed to have provoked J.T. to run from the room. In a way, Sidney was curious. She didn't know much about Hal other than that he had once worked at Poppy Press and had moved out of state. Sidney remembered hearing at the time something about Hal getting married, getting fired, or perhaps both. Now, Carla was filling them in.

"It was your classic love triangle. A tragedy, really," Carla was saying. "Well, a bit of a twist. It kind of reminded me of what happened with Allison and Brent and Brent's brother. You know, in *Parkwood Terrace.*" Imperceptibly, she began taking tiny bites of a cream-filled cupcake.

"Anyway," Carla swallowed, "Hal worked here first as a pressman. After a while, he got them to hire his little brother J.T. Those two were pretty much inseparable. They commuted to work, ate lunch, went fishing, to the movies, you name it, together. They were best buddies." She took another bite.

"Then one day, Hal got it in his head to go to North Carolina on vacation. Maybe they had people down there, who knows? Naturally, J.T. went along.

"They're on vacation, having a good old time, drinking at a bar. Hal starts talking to this woman, a floozy, I have it on good authority. Plus, she was married *three times before*." Carla waited for the requisite clucking sounds of disapproval from the ladies. "Hal should have known better, but he just fell head over heels. To him, she was the ideal woman. Unfortunately, J.T. thought the same thing. *He* fell head over heels for this woman, too. When it came to J.T., though, the lady didn't feel the same way. Just picture it: J.T., totally in love, a third wheel. The happy couple, shooing him away."

Carla leaned forward and whispered loudly to Sidney, "Sorry, I know he's your boyfriend." Sidney flushed but kept her lips pressed shut.

"Anyhow, you can just imagine the heartache, the tragedy that followed," Carla said in a dramatic tone. She stopped suddenly and pulled up her sleeve to examine her wristwatch and winced. Only a few minutes remained of their lunch hour. That meant she would have to rush through the rest of the story, which she hated to do.

"Hal brings his girlfriend back north," she said hurriedly. "They end up getting married. Like, immediately. Hal did not look like he was enjoying marital bliss, I'll tell you. He was downright miserable. He also started treating J.T. like garbage. People said that was because his wife detested J.T. But it was also true that Hal started acting mean to everyone. He picked fights for no reason. I heard that he got into a fistfight right here on the premises, and that was why he got fired. They picked up and moved to North Carolina, which was probably his floozy wife's idea all along.

"And J.T.? Well, he's not welcome there, not even for a visit. So he lost his brother and his best friend. He's not been quite right since then. Very sad."

That final summation, expressed quite cheerfully, was the signal for the Lunch Ladies to return to work. In less than a minute, the group scattered.

Sidney headed to her cubicle, musing about J.T. and thinking that it *was* sad. As annoying as he could be, no one deserved that kind of treatment from his own brother.

But maybe she wasn't as magnanimous as she pretended, she thought uncomfortably. Maybe she felt empathy for J.T. only because his circumstances were so familiar. They pretty much reflected her own life—bereft and alone.

Five

When Phoebe awoke, she had been dreaming deeply and had to recall why she was lying on rough planks. Then she remembered. She was in the cabin in the park.

The leaden, gray light of dawn was seeping through the cracks in the cabin walls. Even in the dim light, she could see it was a proper log cabin. It probably was one of the original huts built by the Revolutionary War soldiers, she thought. It had to be because the place smelled so musty and old.

Phoebe shifted on the uncomfortable bunk. Her clothes were damp and made her feel clammy and chilly. Her fever had set her throat on fire, and her whole body ached. She couldn't rise from this wooden bed even if General George Washington himself walked in.

The rain, which had been a light patter on the roof, became a downpour. Phoebe turned her head to the doorway and watched rain streaming down from the eaves. Despite the curtain of water, she could see a gnarled tree whose branches looked like arms and elbows. The tree seemed to be watching over the cabin.

It was the last thought she had before she fell back to sleep.

The next morning was so much like the first in the little soldier's hut that Phoebe thought she might be dreaming. It was the same gray light coming through the chinks in the logs and through the wide-open space that was a doorway with no door. It was the same damp air. The same wooden slats of the upper bunk staring back at her.

Phoebe sneezed, so violently that her head came up off the bunk and banged down again. Wiping her nose on her sleeve, she realized that one thing was different from the previous day: she was feeling much better.

She felt her head. It was no longer warm. The fever must have gone away. She sat up, and except for a bit of dizziness that she managed to shake off, she felt a lot more like her normal self. Stepping to the open doorway, she looked out.

Water still dripped from the trees, but the rain had stopped. It all looked very wet, which only made her aware of how thirsty she was. It was time to leave and find something to drink.

Back on the road, she soon came upon public restrooms that had, mercifully, a water fountain nearby. She drank, filled up her water bottle, and drank some more. In the restroom, she did her best to clean some of the grime from herself with the trickle of cold water from the faucet.

When she emerged, a weak sun was breaking through the clouds, sparkling on the wet blacktop of the path. This should have cheered her, but she suddenly felt overwhelmed by her predicament. She looked about, not sure which way to go. Worse, she was completely uncertain whether anything she had done since she ran away made any sense. "I want to go home!" she called out to the trees. There was no response, not even birds chirping.

Her tears made the path's surface sparkle more. She sniffed, then wiped her nose on her sleeve. She might have been completely stupid, but now she had no choice but to keep going.

She started walking in the direction her feet were pointed.

The park seemed to go on forever. She no longer felt sick, but she was famished. Hunger was making her weak. "I'm so hungry,

I'm so hungry," she found herself repeating like a mantra. She searched for something else to think of, anything else—school, home, her dad. If this were an ordinary day, what would she be doing? At this time of day, she guessed she would be in history class. She wondered how Jessie and her other friends had reacted to her disappearance. They were probably really worried about her, no matter what the adults said. The thought made her sad again.

She stopped at the peak of a steep hill to catch her breath. Looking down, she could see a road, a regular one with cars crawling along. She saw a few houses, too. She pictured herself running up and knocking on a door to beg for food. But she knew that wouldn't happen. She wouldn't dare. In any case, she was nearly out of the park. Maybe she could find some food somehow. She started walking faster.

There was much more traffic on this road. Cars whizzed by, and she was forced to cling to the road's shoulder, which was not much more than a narrow strip, littered with trash. She was struggling to pick her way forward when she felt a rush of air and heard a roaring engine. The sudden blare of the truck's horn directly behind her startled her and caused her to tumble into some sharp branches.

Tears stung her eyes, but she struggled to pull herself upright. She set off again, using more care to keep inside the white line marking the edge of the road. After a few miles she felt relieved as the road widened and she could walk more easily.

She was plodding along more confidently when a car veered onto the shoulder and came to a halt in front of her.

Phoebe also stopped. She was close enough that she could see the driver's eyes in the rearview mirror. He was watching her.

Part of her wanted to run past the car and down the road. But then what would happen? Would he run her down? Would he jump out and grab her and then throw her into the car?

Phoebe cast a desperate look around. There was a driveway just to her right, nearly hidden by underbrush. Through the foliage, she spotted a church. At least, it looked like there was a steeple. *Run there*, she commanded herself. *You'll be safe there*. But she was too frightened to move.

The car door opened, and the man began to climb out. At that movement, Phoebe turned and nearly flew up the steep driveway.

"Don't you want a ride? That's all I'm asking!"

She didn't stop running, not daring to glance back at the sound of the man's voice, not even to see if he was following her. She reached the top of the hill and saw that the structure there was in fact a small, white church, partially nestled in the woods, with the front opening to a small, paved parking lot. She darted to the rear of the building.

Somehow, she found an entrance and, by some miracle, it was unlocked. She pushed open the heavy, metal door and slipped inside, immediately stumbling over something in the dim light. As her eyes adjusted, she saw that she was in a sort of storage closet, stuffed with dusty boxes and stacks of straight-backed, wooden chairs. The good thing was, she thought, this all offered hiding places. She checked the door. There was no lock, so she wedged a chair under the doorknob. Considering her handiwork, she decided that wasn't enough. Pulling out more chairs, she jammed them around the doorknob until it was a tangle of seats and chair legs. Then, she crawled into a small space in a corner. In the pale light filtering through the narrow slit of glass in the door, she waited.

After long minutes watching the dust under the chairs, she felt her eyelids droop. Just as she was thinking that it was probably safe to leave, that she should probably make her way outside and get back on the road, she heard the doorknob rattle.

It rattled again, insistent, followed by a series of thuds, the awful sound of someone pushing hard on the door. Phoebe couldn't breathe.

Just as suddenly, it fell silent. She waited, not daring to breathe, then finally allowing herself a sharp intake of breath. She knew she should continue to hide, to curl up into an even smaller, tighter ball. But she couldn't stand it anymore. She had to get out of there.

Panic rising into her throat, she crawled from under the chairs as fast as she could, her hands slapping on the linoleum floor. She started pulling the chairs away from the door, banging them against her legs and arms as she desperately tossed them aside.

Finally, she was outside, gulping air and racing down the driveway. Relief made her legs rubbery, but still she ran. When she reached the road, the man and his car were gone.

She ran at least a mile before she slowed, panting, her heart pounding.

I want to go home, she thought. She was sorry, really, really sorry that she had ever tried such a stupid thing as running away. But the truly horrible thing was that she didn't know how to get home. Even if she knew how to, there probably was no going back. She just couldn't face Adele and all the punishment she would get. Feeling lower than ever, she knew she had to keep going.

The sun was starting to set. For once, she at least knew the direction she was headed. West. It might not be the right way to Connecticut, but it was the way the road was going. And, she was convinced, it was going away from home.

~

It was nearly midnight when Adele, exhausted, retrieved the sleeping Bobby from the back seat of the car and carried him up the porch steps. She had forgotten to turn on the outside light before she left, so she was forced to fumble in the dark for the lock while clutching Bobby, who weighed a ton. She cursed softly when she dropped her keys. Finally, she got Bobby upstairs and deposited him, fully dressed, in bed. She stood for a moment looking at him in the moonlight.

Thank God he wasn't the one who went missing, she thought. Immediately, a wave of guilt, and then defensiveness, swept over her. Was it so terrible to think that? After all, Bobby was a little kid. He was her son, all she had.

That was it, wasn't it? As sick with worry about Phoebe as she was, she knew that if Bobby had gone missing, she would have been frantic, out of her mind, unable to exist until she found him. It wasn't that she didn't love Phoebe. She had cared for Phoebe since she was tiny. But it was also true that she had been more impatient with Phoebe since Robert left. She felt bad about that. She really felt horrible about locking Phoebe in the attic, but the kid had pushed all her buttons.

No excuses, Adele told herself firmly. Phoebe was distraught about her father. Even if Adele was experiencing her own devastation from Robert's abrupt announcement and departure, she should never have taken it out on Phoebe.

Adele went to the kitchen to clean up their hastily made dinner. She needed to accept some basic facts, she thought. Like that no one seemed to care that a young girl was wandering the streets on her own. Robert didn't care. He was in Connecticut, caring only about himself. The police didn't care. They clearly wanted to believe that Robert had taken Phoebe in a custody dispute. Also, Adele needed to quit worrying that the authorities would hold her responsible. There was no point. They weren't the least bit suspicious of her.

"Mrs. Locke, it would be wise to look at this objectively," the child welfare agency representative had said in one of their interminable phone calls, mostly calls that Adele had initiated. The woman spoke slowly, enunciating syllables as if English were Adele's second language. The woman's tone was smug, making her even more annoying than the police.

"You've stated that the child and her father—he is her natural father, no?—are very close. Your marriage to Robert appears to be over, but you have to realize that perhaps your husband couldn't end his relationship with his daughter so easily. That may be hard for you to accept."

Adele felt the unreasonable anger bubbling up again. "Well, if you're so sure that it was Robert, then why don't you check with him? I haven't been able to reach him. I've called a million times. He must have thrown his cell phone away." She took a deep breath. "Look, I'm doing what I can, calling everyone I know, but I'm getting nowhere. Robert used to have a lot of folks up in Connecticut, but very few are left. I gave the police all the information I have, but I don't know if they followed up on any of it."

"We're trying to find him, Mrs. Locke." The woman sounded offended. Adele must have struck a nerve. "Connecticut is not a huge state, but a postcard you received isn't a lot to go on. And if he came back for Phoebe, how do we know he returned to Connecticut with her?"

Adele felt her anger drain away. The woman was right, of course. It wasn't the fault of any of the authorities that this was such a mess, that her life had become a wreck, or that she had chosen the wrong person to marry.

Exhausted, Adele moved slowly to clean up the kitchen. Maybe Robert had arranged to pick up Phoebe. Maybe she was with her father, and maybe she was fine. Adele had already called the school and said that Phoebe would be staying with her father for a while. It seemed easier that way as that was what everyone wanted to believe. Maybe she too needed to believe it.

Hand on the light switch, Adele took a last look around the kitchen. Her eyes fell on the chair where Phoebe always sat. She could picture Phoebe talking nonstop as she always did, about school, about kids she knew, about any subject. How she would try to get her father laughing and generally succeeded, although he would also counsel or lecture her. Adele thought about how she would remind Phoebe to eat her broccoli, and Phoebe would respond, "I am eating it!" just as Adele would catch her draping a crumpled paper napkin over the uneaten food.

Tears blurred Adele's view of the empty table and chairs. She flicked off the lights and slowly climbed the stairs to bed.

Phoebe felt as if she had been walking for miles when she finally, thankfully, reached a small town. It wasn't much of a town, but at least it was more than roadway and trees. She walked past a gas station and a car dealership and then she stopped and peered down a side street. It was more of an alley than a street and seemed to lead to the back of a shopping center. She could see a couple of large dumpsters. They would have trash in them, but in that trash might also be food.

She ran, eyes focused on the dumpsters, and nearly bumped into the boy. He was a teenager, angular, with a shock of dark curls, and he burst from an unmarked door just as she was passing. He staggered under the weight of bulging trash bags, his momentum moving him directly toward Phoebe. She leaped out of the way and fell into a prickly hedge.

She scrambled to her feet, ready to fight, but the teenager didn't so much as glance at her. Phoebe watched as he hoisted one bag and then the other, shoving them into the bin. Wiping his hands on his long apron, he headed back into the building, still without acknowledging her, although she was only a few feet away.

As he opened the door, she caught a glimpse inside, where a man was pulling something out of the wall with a long-handled tool. A pizza. It was a pizza shop. Phoebe could smell it, and she was so hungry that her mouth was watering before the door fell shut.

Phoebe stood blinking in the now-empty alley. She turned and surveyed the dumpster. With no tree or fence close enough for a foothold, it wouldn't be easy to climb in, but she had to try. She dragged over some discarded cardboard boxes to give herself a boost, but they were soft from sitting out in the rain. She went back and poked among the debris, finding a wooden crate to pull herself to the rim of the chipped, blue metal.

The odor of rotting garbage was overpowering and almost knocked her off her perch. She readjusted, and clinging to the side of the dumpster with one arm, she used her fingers to poke holes in plastic bags until she struck pay dirt. Sitting directly on top of the muck of one of the bags was an entire pizza, blackened on the edges but edible.

She had hardly jumped to the ground before she was chewing. She was trying to convince herself to save part of the pizza for later when a long, narrow shadow fell over her. She looked up and squinted at a woman framed by the afternoon sun.

Phoebe took another bite. She couldn't stop eating. "Hi," she said, her mouth full.

Something flickered across the woman's face. "Are you hungry?" she asked.

Phoebe swallowed and nodded guiltily. "I'm sorry I took it, but it was in the trash."

The woman nodded. "Wait here," she said and ran back to the same scarred door where the boy had gone. She returned moments later with an oil-stained paper bag so wrinkled it must have been used and reused many times, along with a large paper cup with a cap and straw.

"Here." She roughly shoved the items at Phoebe.

Phoebe removed the lid to gulp directly from the cup.

"Hey, take it easy," the woman said. She looked at Phoebe more closely. "What are you doing out here on your own? Not that it's any of my business, but you do look a mess."

Phoebe stopped chewing. For the first time in days, she considered how she must look: streaks of dirt on her face, her jacket filthy, her pants torn. She touched a hand to her matted hair.

"I'm on my way to my dad's," she said, carefully tucking the bag in her knapsack. "I'm trying to get to the, um, bus station. I just have to get to my aunt's house first, and she'll take me to the bus station." Phoebe glanced at the woman, who looked skeptical.

"Why doesn't your father just come and get you?"

The woman was nice, but Phoebe was starting to wish that she wouldn't ask so many questions. "He was supposed to, but it got messed up."

The woman persisted. "What about your mom?"

"She died."

At that, the woman's mouth shut into a thin line that was neither a smile nor a frown. She started to say something when a man's voice, harsh-sounding but muffled, sounded from inside the building. The woman threw an anxious look down the alleyway.

Shoving some crumpled bills into Phoebe's hand, she whispered, "I hope you get to your father." Then she was gone.

Phoebe looked down at the money. "Thank you," she said quietly to the empty alley.

Retracing her steps, she was soon back on the main road. It was amazing how much better she felt, how a little food left her feeling stronger and her heart lighter. It was really all because of the kind lady, she knew. She could keep going, and her journey didn't seem quite so impossible.

Six

Ayers was in rare form, the assistant thought, his heart sinking, as he watched his boss launch into one of his infamous tirades. Even on a good day (was there ever a good day with Ayers?), any action considered to be inept or stupid, any failure to take action for fear that it would be considered inept or stupid, anything less than total assent to whatever came from the churlish mouth of the president and CEO of Poppy Press—any of that, the assistant knew, could bring a tongue lashing or a tirade. Which was why, during his tenure as special assistant to Ayers, he had perfected the art of remaining perfectly still while his boss ranted. The trick was to look interested and alert, yet not move a muscle. The assistant found that the merest nod or inadvertent raise of an eyebrow would be enough to set Ayers off. You did not want to set him off. He could transform from polished, silver-haired executive to screaming, raving lunatic in no time flat.

Once, early in the assistant's relatively brief career, when members of Ayers's management team were being treated to one of his performances, the assistant, seated behind the executive, had spontaneously rolled his eyes, flapped his fingers together, and mouthed, "Blah, blah, blah." It was his attempt to regain a few shreds of self-respect amid the venom raining down. Or so he thought. Later, one of the inner circle, a burly guy with a kindly face, had taken him aside to warn him. "Just a piece of advice," the man had said. "With Ayers, if you get caught making a fool of him, you'll regret it. You're better off doing what you're told and keeping your mouth shut."

The assistant had been smart enough to heed that advice. He hadn't been so smart a few months later when he made the fateful and brainless decision to leave New York and follow Ayers to this backwater Pennsylvanian town on a fruitless mission to save this failing printing company. Still, he had learned an important lesson. Never bat an eye.

The assistant balanced a legal pad on his knee as Ayers paced, further matting down a worn path in the shag carpeting of the shabby presidential office. Back and forth he went, a caged lion, between the oversized, executive-style, fake mahogany desk and the mocha-colored and equally fake leather sofa. Despite his short legs, Ayers managed to complete the laps so quickly that the assistant was developing a headache from the effort of watching without moving his head. But he didn't need to witness the rage building in his boss. He could feel it. When he dared a quick glance, he saw that Ayers's thick black eyebrows were drawn together into a solid line, which was not a good sign. An explosion was imminent.

"I don't know what the hell they think they're doing, but if NYC thinks for one lousy minute"—he pronounced New York City's initials as a sarcastic en-why-see—"that I'm going to be left here high and dry and have my career languish in this place, this WASTELAND"— the assistant couldn't help recoiling as Ayers swept by and stuck a forefinger millimeters from his face—"they can just think again."

Ayers resumed pacing. "I re-FUSE to allow this to happen." Ayers was jabbing the air, but his bellow was starting to disintegrate into a mutter. The assistant began to hope that the storm was passing.

"You!" Ayers wheeled around, suddenly close again. The assistant wasn't always sure if Ayers was actually addressing him or merely venting. It was also disconcerting that Ayers never used his given name. More than disconcerting, it was offensive, the assistant thought. He had a given name, of course. He was Nicholas Baker. He should remind Ayers of this fact once again, but something always stopped him. Maybe it was because he felt so isolated in this job that sometimes he would almost forget that he wasn't nameless.

"Yes, sir," Nicholas said with mild politeness.

Ayers looked down at his assistant, which meant that he was looking at him at eye level because Nicholas was tall, and Ayers was just five-foot-five in his shoes. Nicholas watched Ayers's face form a grimace with unmistakable contempt. The assistant was aware, hyper-aware in fact, that Ayers preferred military-style responses. An immediate, shouted "Yes, sir!" was best. Ayers considered anything less the sign of a wimp. Nicholas, who could not bring himself to pretend to be a Marine or anything remotely resembling one, continued to resist, his one final act of rebellion. Now, he suppressed a sigh and looked impassively at the wall, waiting for the inevitable lecture (or worse), but was surprised by Ayers's comment.

"Why do they call the company by this ridiculous name, Poppy Press? Why don't we just change it?"

It wasn't an unreasonable request, but Ayers's look kept his assistant from responding. *He probably doesn't want an answer anyway*, Nicholas thought.

He was spared by the phone buzzing on Ayers's desk. Ayers depressed a button, and the voice of the administrative assistant, Sondra, floated into the office.

"I have Mr. Thornton from New York on the line, sir. Shall I put him through?"

From the expression on Ayers's face, he had not been expecting this call, but he told Sondra to go ahead in an authoritative, if subdued, tone.

Nicholas started to rise and gestured toward the door. He usually was evicted from conference calls with the New York brass. But Ayers surprised his assistant by waving him back. Nicholas, uncertain, slowly sank back into his seat.

"Allen!" Ayers shouted into the phone. "How goes it?"

A snort could be heard on the speaker phone. "Knock it off, Vince. I don't have time for small talk. We need to discuss this harebrained bankruptcy plan of yours."

Ayers's eyes flicked briefly in Nicholas's direction.

"What do you mean, Allen? We talked about this at length last week. Everything is in order." Ayers leaned so far over the phone console that he almost hugged it.

"No, everything is not in order." The disembodied voice was annoyed. "I just came out of a very difficult meeting with the legal department. Let's just say they're questioning everything, including the need to go this bankruptcy route to begin with. They don't want to do it. One attorney kept saying, 'This is an extreme action.' They believe there are other measures to take first. Have you taken those measures?"

Ayers, silent, stared at the phone.

"Look," Allen continued, exasperated, "I mentored you. I supported you. I went out on a limb for you with this Poppy Press gig. I had to convince the entire board to let you run it. So don't mess this up, Vince. Don't mess it up."

Ayers clutched the desk as if he would crumple to the floor otherwise. Finally, he pulled himself together enough for a response. Nicholas listened, his head down and studying the carpet. Ayers was clearly attempting to be both reassuring and cajoling, but to Nicholas, it sounded like groveling.

After an eternity, the call ended and the office fell quiet. After what seemed a long pause, Nicholas ventured a glance at his boss. There was no telling how the volatile Ayers would react. Instead, Ayers was only staring at the phone, lost in thought.

Suddenly, Ayers threw himself in his chair. "So what do you think?" he asked.

Nicholas was startled. "Me? You want to know what I think?"

"Yes, I really want to know."

There was none of Ayers's typical sarcasm. *The guy actually wants my advice. But it could be a trap*, Nicholas thought.

"That was bad, wasn't it?" Ayers's eyes were haunted. "I just came across as so weak…I can't be seen as weak. I've worked too hard for this. Look, you've got to help me."

Nicholas recoiled slightly. He didn't know whether he felt sorry for Ayers or found him embarrassing. He cleared his throat. "Sir, why don't you consider talking to Harry? That proposal Harry had, the one to have investors buy the Press? Maybe it's not such a bad idea after all."

Ayers sat back and thought, tapping his steepled fingers together. "Yeah. Not a bad idea. Except I really hate dealing with that big know-it-all." He spoke so softly, he might have been talking to himself.

"All right, good idea," he said and clapped his hands. "Get Harry in here."

Nicholas couldn't help feeling a little surge of pride. *Maybe I can add some value after all*, he thought, and was nearly out of the office when Ayers followed, snapping his fingers.

"Wait, uh…" He unsuccessfully searched for Nicholas's name. "Listen, I also need you to make arrangements for a visitor. My place here in town, four-thirty. The usual services. And ask for someone better looking this time, will you?" Ayers fell on the sofa that Nicholas had abandoned.

A wave of disgust passed over Nicholas's face before he could restrain himself. He turned away before saying what he was thinking: *Just when I thought you were human.*

Back at his desk, Nicholas dialed Harry's office number. At ten o'clock on a Tuesday morning, it was doubtful that Harry, ever the salesman, would be in the building. More than likely, he would be on the road, in meetings, visiting clients, the usual sales stuff. But Nicholas had to start somewhere, he thought as he listened to the phone ring.

He was caught off guard when Harry answered. With a brief, stumbling preamble, Nicholas repeated the directive from Ayers. It was met with silence.

"Who did you say this was again?" Harry sounded mildly curious.

"Nicholas Baker, Mr. Ayers's assistant." He paused and repeated, "He wants to see you right away."

"Well, you see, Nick—may I call you Nick?—I'm running late for a meeting as it is." When Nicholas didn't respond, Harry added, "It's a very important meeting."

"This is important."

"In my experience, you guys think everything is important." Harry made a sound that might have been a chuckle. "Can you give me a hint what this is about?"

Nicholas hesitated, then turning toward the wall and speaking in a near whisper, he gave a brief summary of the conference call.

Harry listened and then said quietly, "Thank you, Nick. I'm heading up now. Tell him to keep his pants on."

True to his word, Harry was standing at Nicholas's desk within five minutes. Wordlessly, Nicholas went to Ayers's office and gave a sharp rap on the door. Pushing it open without waiting for permission, he stood back to let Harry pass. Then Nicholas hurried back to his desk before Ayers could suggest that he stay. He had had enough drama for one morning.

Nicholas tried to focus on his work, but no matter how hard he tried to concentrate, he kept replaying in his head the humiliating scene of Ayers on the phone. That was a whole side of his boss that he hadn't witnessed before. Maybe it showed that Ayers was as trapped as everyone else at Poppy Press.

I'm not trapped. I can quit and go back to New York anytime I want, Nicolas reminded himself. A voice inside responded, *Yeah? Then, why don't you?*

Why he didn't quit the job that he detested was a question he asked every day. He was a glorified coffee boy, so it wasn't like he carried the weight of responsibility for the company, whether it survived or crashed and burned. His best explanation or rationale or whatever you wanted to call it, was that he was curious. The place, the mercurial boss, people's jobs hanging in the balance—it was like a tragedy in three acts, and he had to see how it all came out.

Nicholas's thoughts were interrupted by raised voices. The door burst open and a sputtering Ayers ushered Harry out.

"You couldn't leave well enough alone, could you?" Ayers's face was red and sweating. "You just had to talk to New York on your own, behind my back." Ayers was shouting in Harry's ear as he retreated from the office, but Harry didn't flinch.

"Now you've done it." Ayers continued at a slightly lower decibel level but still sounded irrational. "New York is committed to this bankruptcy plan. They want it done now, never mind your crazy deals. They're not happy with you, they're not happy with me, and most of all—I'm not happy!" Ayers was breathing hard, but Harry appeared unruffled.

Nicholas considered Harry with more than a little admiration. With his carrot-red hair and ruddy complexion, he was a man few would have called handsome. But he was definitely cool, as self-assured as a Hollywood actor. Maybe it was all an act, Nicholas thought.

Harry was looking at Ayers with something between amusement and pity. Then, a crooked smile transformed his face.

"I'm not trying to tell you what to do," Harry said, "but here are two suggestions. One, perhaps you might calm down a bit before you have a heart attack. Second, think about giving us some breathing room on our deal. If it goes through, then it's a win-win. Especially for you. Okay?" Harry winked at Ayers and turned to leave.

"See you around, Nick." Harry gave a little salute as he pulled the executive suite door shut behind him.

Uncomfortable minutes passed as Ayers stood, weaving slightly from side to side, and Nicholas wondered if he should be prepared to catch him. Then Ayers looked at his assistant.

"Who the hell is Nick?" he demanded.

It was Harry's whistling on his way back to his office that tipped off Sidney that something was different. Not necessarily wrong but different.

Absorbed in her work, Sidney had shut out the normal background noises, as usual. They generally never bothered her. She had learned to tune it all out, even when Harry, sitting at his desk, conducted booming conversations with Antoinette at her station just outside his office. But she had never heard Harry whistle before.

At first, she wasn't sure who it was, and didn't guess it was Harry. She was distracted by the tune. The haunting melody, echoing down the hallway and growing increasingly louder, had caused her to stop and lift her head. *What is that song?* she wondered just as Harry appeared. He stopped at Antoinette's desk.

"Toni, I need you in my office right away." As he turned away, he added, "And be prepared to work late for the next week or so. We've got a lot to do!"

Harry was excited, Sidney realized with a start. He never conveyed emotion as far as she knew, she thought as she bowed her head again over the document she was proofreading. *He was whistling and now he sounds like a kid on Christmas Eve.*

"You, too. In my office." The booming voice rang over her. Sidney's head jerked up, but Harry was gone. Slowly, she recapped her red pen and followed him, filled with trepidation. She had never been asked to Harry's office before.

Her heart hammering, Sidney stood about six inches from the door—the better to escape, she thought. Antoinette had already arranged herself in one of the chairs in front of Harry's desk. She looked completely at ease.

Harry stood at his desk, going through some papers and ignoring them both. Sidney began to wonder if she had misunderstood him. Perhaps he hadn't intended that she actually join him in his office or be part of whatever scheme he was cooking up. She was thinking about slipping out, when he spoke in an offhanded way.

"What progress have you made on that project? The one I asked you to take care of?"

Sidney, panicky, glanced at Antoinette. She didn't know what he was talking about, but something told her that she had better not claim ignorance. She tried to think. There was that printing job he had asked her to look into that day Antoinette wasn't around. Was that what he meant? She couldn't remember the name of the project.

"What project?" she said finally and felt herself redden.

"You know perfectly well what project," Harry said. He no longer sounded excited, Sidney thought. Just annoyed.

"The white paper," he snapped. "The one that's vitally important for the continued survival of this company. We're going to publish a white paper as a business case, to convince certain key investors to put their money in Poppy Press. Have you let us down on this?"

The awful, accusatory voice reverberated against the office walls. Then, as blood rushed through her head, the sound of his voice grew muffled, as if she were underwater. She began to sway.

Without moving from her chair, and seemingly with no effort, Antoinette tilted her heart-shaped face confidently toward Harry, and with an upturn of her perfect scarlet bow of a mouth, she saved Sidney.

"Harry, don't you remember? You haven't given this project to Sidney yet. Last night you said there was still more work to do on the draft."

Harry looked at his assistant dispassionately for a long moment and then, to Sidney's relief, decided he was appeased. "Ah, yes," he said mildly. "I suppose that's why I keep you girls around—to keep me in line," he added lightly. "At this point, though, we're going to close the book, so to speak, on the writing part. Let's declare it finished. We're pressed for time."

He pointed at Antoinette. "Toni, get the latest draft to Sidney here. While Sidney gives it a fast proofread, Toni, I'll need you to give a heads up to that gal, you know, the one who does the design?" He arched his brows.

"Betty," Antoinette supplied.

"Yes, Betty. Tell her we need something very basic. Just make it look professional. There's no time for something fancy. As for you, Sidney, I want you to get this printed and produced the quickest, easiest way possible, with a nice, simple cover." Sidney couldn't help cringing. She was a proofreader, and getting things printed was not part of her job, so she saw herself fumbling these unfamiliar tasks. Harry was oblivious. "Toni! What am I missing?"

But Antoinette was already heading back to her desk, ready to fulfill her mission. Harry was back in command, Sidney thought. Still, it was unusual for Harry to order Sidney about. Mostly, he ignored her because she wasn't part of his staff. But who knew what her job was anymore or who she worked for? She wasn't even sure whether she had been officially dismissed from Harry's office. She remained rooted to the spot near the door.

Harry may have read her thoughts, because without looking up, he said, "Why are you still here? I said, we're in a hurry."

Sidney nearly tripped as she rushed out the door.

Once Sidney was back at her desk, she saw that Antoinette had already sent the file with the white paper, so she printed a copy to set to proofreading right away. It was best to follow Antoinette's example and act swiftly. Harry would probably ask for a status report in about fifteen minutes.

Pulling her chair close to the desk, she began to read, her red pen hovering. After a few minutes, she turned back to the first page. Curious, she reread the first paragraphs. It was odd. What did this paper have to do with saving the Press?

As a proofreader and technically not part of the actual printing operations, she was on the lower rungs of the Poppy Press enterprise. She was also a woman in a male-dominated company, but it was true that she knew nothing about the business side of running the company. Nor, she had to admit, did she know the first thing about investors or convincing them of anything. But even she could tell that this white paper was a huge gamble. She was fairly sure that most business cases were boring and fact-filled, but this was different. It was an emotional essay and a history lesson rolled into one. It certainly showed a different side of Harry, his fascination with printing and its inventor.

The Rationale Behind Printing
By Harry Corcoran

This business case seeking investment in the printing company known as Poppy Press is admittedly an unusual one. We could present numbers and forecasts of future profitability in a logical argument. However, there's something about printing, about the printed word that defies logic. Something ingrained in us that can't be dismissed simply because some say, "Print is dead." Even if we now do some of our reading on computer screens or smartphones, there will still always be a place for printing, for the real, printed word. Not that computers, the Internet, or electronic forms of communication are bad. They've changed things tremendously and for the better. Maybe they're revolutionary. But it's hard to say that they've revolutionized things on the same scale as Gutenberg did. With the invention of his printing press 600 years ago, he changed everything. He literally took the world out of the Dark Ages because his invention created printed words on the page, real words that could outlive people.

And for that reason, print will never die. There's still a need, and there will be a need in the future. Demand may go down, and the number of printing companies may contract. But that simply calls for investors with the vision to identify the right printing company, one that will not only survive but thrive.

Sidney flipped through several more pages and returned to the beginning. Maybe this was acceptable among Harry's cigar-smoking, golf-playing circle. But detailing the life and times of an inventor from the Middle Ages to persuade investment in a sinking, twenty-first-century enterprise? That seemed far worse than a gamble. It seemed delusional.

She rifled through the rest of the document. Should she try to revise it? Maybe she should share her concerns with Harry, even if the idea made her shudder. She rose and peered over the cubicle wall. The office door was shut. *This is insane,* she chided herself. *If I raised any objection, I'd be lucky if the worst he would say was, "Shut up, and do your job."*

She sat and resumed proofreading. She needed to take the imagined advice: keep your head down and do your job.

Seven

At some point during Phoebe's journey, spring had burst without her noticing, even though she had been outdoors the entire time. She squinted at the sun as it glittered on suddenly emerald lawns and gawked at trees and bushes covered in delicate blooms. She began to stop just to breathe in the fragrant air.

It had been the birds' noisy chirping that awakened Phoebe to the onset of the season, jolting her from what had become near sleepwalking. She had been marching, bleary-eyed, for days, and each night tried to find some sort of sheltered place to curl up for a few hours of fitful sleep. In her exhaustion, she had taken little notice of anything else, including the weather.

Did it happen overnight, like magic? she wondered. She slowed and tilted her face to the sun. It should have made her happy, even joyous. But it somehow was having the opposite effect. She could feel the sun's warmth turning into a sadness that traveled down through her body, reminding her of her lonely journey.

Is it fair? Is it fair that my mother is dead, and my father is gone, too? Phoebe wiped her eyes. It did no good to feel sorry for herself, she told herself. That was what her father always said when she would say how much she wanted to have a mom, her real mom. "You're far from the only kid who's lost their mother," her father would say. "Besides, you have Adele. She loves you like her own. Not to mention, you have me. You'll always have me."

He said that so many times, she remembered, that it was easy to believe him. She would always have her dad. Then, just like that, she didn't. He was gone, and it wasn't fair.

She kicked a pebble, and it pinged harmlessly away. She tried kicking a bigger rock. It didn't make her feel any better; in fact, it hurt her foot. She looked about, suddenly, violently angry at the beautiful day, wishing she could tear it apart.

What she really wished, she thought as she limped along, was that she could remember her mother. She always wanted that. She often pored over the old snapshots that her father had preserved, turning the pages of the photo albums until they were ready to fall out. The young woman in the pictures seemed always to be captured laughing at the camera. That was her mother. Phoebe was expected to believe this—she wanted to believe this—because she had been told it was true. But it never seemed quite real. No matter how many times she looked at the photos, she couldn't recall anything about her mother. Not the sound of her voice, not even her presence. They were just pictures of a dead person.

But her father—that was a different story. Until he disappeared, he was, as promised, always there, the most important person in her life. With his glasses, his shock of dark hair, and his thin frame, he looked young. That was what everyone said. "You don't look old enough to be out of high school," was the common refrain. Her father would just smile in response.

Not long before he vanished, he suddenly seemed to age. Even Phoebe noticed. Deep lines appeared around his mouth. His dark hair, still thick, became streaked with gray one day, nearly all silver the next. The silver hair was impossible to ignore. One morning, Adele stared at him across the breakfast table. "Robert," she said, her voice shaking slightly. "What is it? Are you sick?" Phoebe's father looked away without responding.

Phoebe had another stone in her shoe. How these tiny pebbles managed to work their way under the sole, she had no idea. At the edge of a well-kept lawn, Phoebe sat on a small brick wall and pulled off her tennis shoe. Tiny bits of gravel fell out. She turned the shoe over and saw a hole worn in the bottom. "Well, no wonder," she said aloud.

The air felt so cool on her stockinged foot that she pulled off the other shoe and wriggled her toes. She could take a little rest. Probably not a good idea to linger, though. She was always worried that if she stayed too long in the open, someone might notice her.

Amazingly, considering she was a kid traveling on her own, most people ignored her. Maybe it was because there weren't very many people about, she thought. She also tried to keep out of sight when people were coming home from work. She was still skittish after that car had pulled over, forcing her to hide in the church. She recalled that with a shiver. It would be much better if no one paid her any mind.

Once, a carload of smart-aleck, teenage boys yelled something rude. One startled her by stretching out his head from the passenger window like a crowing rooster. At first she was upset until she considered that kids like that would say any old stuff to anyone—to grownups, to other kids, to whoever. They weren't acting that way because she was a girl—not that she even looked much like a girl anymore, but more like the matted, skinny dog she had seen the other day staggering down the road. She had felt bad because the dog looked to be starving. But then, she, too, was starving.

She was constantly hungry. Even when she was able to get food and wolf it down, she immediately felt more hunger pangs. Her stomach never got full. No wonder, she thought. She was hardly eating at all. At this point of her journey, she was about to run out of everything—food, money, energy. She had been pushing on, despite her rubbery legs, but weakness often took over. She found herself resting more. She was definitely not getting as far in a day as she had early on, not covering nearly as much ground.

She had been purposely limiting her food because she was trying very hard to save most of the money that the woman in the alley had given her. Phoebe had made only a few purchases, chips at a convenience store, a hamburger at a fast food restaurant, and some crackers at a dollar store. But as careful as she had been, she didn't have much left. Automatically, she felt in her pocket to assure herself that the money was still there and caught her breath as the pocket felt empty. She dug further and sighed with relief as she pulled out some flattened cash.

Phoebe carefully laid the money in her lap and counted it. Five wrinkled dollar bills and some change remained. That wasn't much. Not enough. She could spend that at McDonald's in one shot. "Guess it's back to dumpster diving," she whispered grimly.

She stared at the bills, so lost in thought that she never saw the cop until he was hovering over her.

"You know you can't be sitting here all day. There are laws against loitering."

Phoebe's eyes moved up the police officer's uniform to his face, a silhouette against the sun. His voice was deep, gruff, and scary. She wanted to ask what "loitering" meant but didn't dare. Instead, she slipped her money back in her pocket and shoved her feet into her shoes. "I'm just resting a minute," she mumbled.

The police officer watched Phoebe as she shouldered her backpack. "Okay, thanks," she said and gave a small wave as she started to walk away.

"Hang on," the cop called before Phoebe had advanced more than a step. She froze. "Do you live far from here?" he asked mildly. "Want a ride?"

Phoebe gave him a bright smile. "Thank you, but it's really close. I shouldn't have stopped because, well, I'm almost home."

He looked doubtful. "You're sure, now?"

"Yes, yes. My house is so close you can see it. In fact, it's…" Phoebe waved her arm, pointing haphazardly, "right over there."

"Where?" The cop craned his neck.

"Um, there. Right there." She tried to sound confident, but as she glanced over to where she was pointing, she wondered if she should have chosen a house that stood out less. Slowly, she dropped her arm, and they both looked down the block at the remarkable house.

The windows—and there were many of them, up to little dormer windows near the roof—looked back blankly. It could be haunted, Phoebe thought. Yet something told her it was a good place. She could even see herself living in that house, and in her existence there, everything that had been going so wrong would suddenly be all right.

"I guess I better be going," she said to the cop. And that was how, in broad daylight and with a police officer as her witness, Phoebe boldly crossed the street and entered the garden gate to the house, as if she had done it a thousand times before.

~~~

When Sidney arrived at Poppy Press at her usual early hour, the firings were already under way. At first, she didn't know what was going on. She knew, though, as soon as she stepped inside the building, that something was terribly wrong. Sidney headed down the long hallway to her desk, walking slowly past knots of people who were hoarsely whispering, and tried to get a sense of what was happening from the snatches of conversation. One man's comment, floating by with a mocking laugh, confirmed it for her. "So much for, 'Don't fear the pink slip,'" he said.

Before she had gotten far, she gathered that Human Resources had selected a small group of workers to fire. Exactly how many was unclear, but Sidney heard someone say confidently that it was fewer than ten people. She lingered near that group, hoping to hear more, and sucked in her breath when she heard a name she knew, a sad-looking single mother who was trying to raise two children.
~~~

Sidney pretended to search through her purse as she listened to a description of how the unlucky workers were brought to a conference room and abruptly informed of their fate. "They're going to be escorted from the building as soon as they gather up their stuff," the man whispered.

In her entire life, Sidney had never acted on a whim. Yet in that moment, she turned and ran without thinking. Down the corridor she went, then down the stairs to the main lobby. She suddenly felt that it was important to witness this event, the layoff victims leaving the building. What good it would do, she didn't know, but she had the fuzzy notion of showing a sign of support.

When she reached the lobby, a small clutch of stunned-looking employees had just disembarked from the elevator. They were shepherded by Allen, the evening shift supervisor. He looked like he was trying to protect them from paparazzi about to jump out and snap their pictures. The white-haired, crotchety security guard, who ordinarily worked nights, followed closely.

The group were shuffling across the lobby when one of the women stopped. "Wait—the pictures on my desk. I forgot the picture of my kids," she said breathlessly.

"We'll pack up any personal items and send it to you," Allen said to the woman. "Come on, Cynthia. You've got to go now."

"I just need to run upstairs and get it. Please." Her face began to crumble. Allen hesitated and seemed about to relent when the security guard intervened.

"Let's go," the security guard said loudly. Brushing past Allen, the guard grabbed the woman's arm and began marching her toward the door. Cynthia acquiesced, and the rest followed, the shamefaced Allen bringing up the rear.

At the entrance, the guard started hustling each one through the revolving door. The last in the group, a man with hairy arms exposed by his short-sleeved shirt, stopped short of the swishing door. Suddenly, he turned and bolted back across the lobby. Sidney caught her breath as she watched the man dart away, then skid on the shiny floor, allowing Allen to reach out and grab his shirt.

In the tussle that followed, with the man flailing and yelling, the security guard showed surprising agility, grabbing the man's wrist and twisting his arm behind his back.

"Hey!" the man howled, but he had gone limp. Unceremoniously, the guard shoved him into the revolving door and gave him a mighty push. The man went straight through, landing in a humiliating heap on the sidewalk, the door catching on him and standing ajar. Sidney could hear the man sobbing.

"Jeez, take it like a man," the security guard said in disgust. He turned to Allen, who looked shaken. "Come on, you're all right. Let's go."

The security guard jerked his head in the direction of the elevators and stalked off. Allen followed slowly.

Sidney remained in the shadowy corner, feeling as spent as if she had been one of the subjects in this emotional scene. After a few deep breaths, she crossed over to the elevators and, shaking, pushed the button.

What was the point of coming down here? She hadn't even had the courage to offer to get Cynthia's photos. The only lesson from that display was that she now knew what to expect if she were included in a future wave of layoffs.

Who was she kidding? she thought as she waited for the elevator doors to open. *It wasn't a matter of "if," but "when."*

She became aware of a presence of someone standing beside her. The doors slid open and she hung back to allow the person, a young man carrying a briefcase, to enter first. In the elevator, Sidney threw him another glance. Something about him was familiar. Then she remembered: he was part of Ayers's entourage the day she and J.T. were looking through files in the empty cubicles. She flushed and looked down. Now, he had caught her standing around the lobby as the fired employees were escorted from the building. He probably thought she was a snoop who had nothing better to do. This probably would ensure that she would be among the next to be fired.

The young man cleared his throat. "Pretty tough day, huh?"

Sidney looked up, surprised. He sounded wistful. She managed a nod and the two returned to gazing at the floor numbers lighting up the panel.

The doors opened at her floor, and she stepped out. "Have a good day," he called after her, and his tone seemed to confirm Sidney's suspicion. He was racked with guilt.

"Yeah, good day," Sidney mumbled just as the doors began to close.

Suddenly, the young man thrust in his arm to block the doors' shutting.

"You know, in Japan they think nothing of killing themselves if they lose their job. No, it's not that they think nothing of it," he corrected himself. "They consider it an *honor.* It's the honorable thing to do, to turn their violence and rage inward. But here? Here, everyone gets angry and points fingers. They want to kill the messenger. I guess I can't blame them." He dropped his arm and stepped back, watching Sidney's puzzled expression as the doors slid shut.

At last, Sidney reached the sanctuary of her cubicle. It wasn't even nine in the morning, and yet she was exhausted. Her head pounded. She sat very still, eyes closed, trying to regain her composure. She was about to look for some aspirin when a rumble of voices distracted her.

She opened her eyes. The voices were coming from Antoinette's desk. None seemed to be Harry's, which was a blessing. Occasionally someone would sound agitated, though, which made Sidney's stomach twist.

A long period of silence made Sidney think that the visitors had drifted away. Then Sidney was jolted by an outburst from Antoinette.

"Look," Antoinette said firmly and quite loudly, "Harry is doing everything he possibly can to save this place. He's *committed* to saving all of you. Your jobs. You don't get it…" Antoinette's voice broke into sobs.

Sidney stood, distressed. Antoinette never looked so much as remotely troubled, let alone gloomy. If she was sobbing at her desk, then the situation had to be God-awful.

"Is she crying?"

The question—said in loud, exasperated tones—was directed right into Sidney's ear. J.T. had once again materialized out of nowhere. She frowned and gestured to him to keep quiet. His voice was as bad as Harry's, booming all over the place. "It's about the layoffs," Sidney mouthed to him.

Ordinarily, J.T. didn't care who heard his bold opinions, but even he seemed to grasp the gravity of the situation. He motioned her to follow him, and the two crept away.

Sidney followed J.T. to the lunchroom, which was well populated although it was too late for breakfast and too early for lunch. But no one was eating. They just sat in small, despondent groups.

"No one is getting work done today," Sidney remarked as J.T. led her to an alcove in the corner.

"What difference does it make?" J.T. growled. "This isn't a normal day. What's normal about people losing their jobs? Being kicked out on the street?"

"So you heard about that."

"I saw it. I was in the lobby."

Sidney nodded but gave him a sharp look. She didn't remember seeing him there. Once again, she found herself wondering why J.T. seemed always free to come and go as he pleased. But then, there were few rules anymore at Poppy Press.

As J.T. launched into one of his tirades, Sidney kept an eye on the entrance, watching for supervisors. The place was emptying as the others headed back to work. It made her nervous, like she was playing hooky.

Then J.T.'s comment popped back into her head, striking her as eminently logical. *He's right. What difference does it make whether anyone works or not? The company will probably get rid of us all anyway.*

She felt she was able to think about the situation rationally, perhaps for the first time. There was nothing she could do to erase her name from a layoff list if it was already there. It wasn't any of her business if J.T. was or wasn't doing his job. Who cared if he was in the lobby? After all, she had been there too.

From the upheaval of the morning had emerged—no, whooshed in—a whole, new world at the Press, one that felt entirely alien but, at the same time, freeing. They were no longer bound to the old ways. They were free to do as they pleased.

With confidence from this sudden revelation, she interrupted J.T.'s babbling. "It's kind of exciting, isn't it?"

"What?" He was mystified. "Exciting? I guess you could call it that."

"I mean, usually nothing goes on around here. But this morning, it was…kind of exciting." His expression made her uncertain. "Wasn't it?"

As J.T. stared, she reddened. Not only had her little speech been ten times more than he had ever heard her say, but he must have thought her callous and uncaring. Ashamed, she realized she had sounded that way.

J.T., however, ignored her comment and began to repeat his latest theory, slowly as if she were five years old.

"Now, here's the thing. Harry has been trying to work a deal, most likely with Charlie Post. This has Charlie written all over it. I'll bet Harry is close to completing whatever he's doing, and it sounds like he just needs more time. But Ayers isn't helping at all. He's trying to stop him." He looked at her. "You're listening, right?"

Sidney was confused.

"Time!" J.T. was exasperated. "Harry needs more time! Then, he can work out his plan to save the company, but Ayers wants to lay off everyone." J.T. leaned forward and whispered, "Ayers wants to put us right out of business."

"How do you know this?" she asked curiously.

"I hacked their emails." The statement contained a certain amount of pride, although he avoided looking directly at her.

How much did J.T. know about technology? Sidney wondered, quickly forgetting her vow not to question him. Her next words surprised even her. "You can do that? Break into their email?" Her tone was skeptical, even challenging.

J.T. was unruffled. "Okay, so I didn't exactly hack into it. I saw a print-out of the emails."

"So you saw something at the copier."

"Sort of." He looked uncomfortable. "All right, I saw it in the trash, in the locked bin where all the sensitive stuff is supposed to be shredded."

Sidney nodded hesitantly.

J.T. sighed. "It's okay. I'm the janitor. And it's a job, right?" he mused. "I used to be a pressman like my brother, in the union and everything. An honorable trade. It wasn't like I was doing a bad job. It was just that Hal—that's my brother, you know—he left the Press. It wasn't his fault that he left. He should be able to move on with his life. But without him around to stick up for me, they could do whatever they felt like. And they felt like giving me a new job as a janitor."

Sidney waited to see if he would continue. But he apparently was finished spilling secrets and sat fiddling with an empty paper cup. She searched for something to say.

"Carla mentioned your brother. I didn't realize that he was let go. That must have been difficult."

"No, no," he sputtered. "Nothing like that. Like I told you all before, Hal wasn't fired. He just decided to leave." J.T. took a deep breath, but Sidney could see the anger building. Then, he exploded. She recoiled as he pounded the table with his fist.

"I hate that people think he was fired, saying that he did a bad job. That's not true!" He made an effort to control himself and shook his head. "Firing is the worst thing that can happen to you. The worst."

He then related a different version of the events involving Hal. The basic thread of J.T.'s tale matched Carla's story. The brothers had gone to North Carolina on vacation, where Hal had met his future bride. Only they met while standing in line at McDonald's instead of in a bar. J.T. didn't disparage his sister-in-law. He was quite matter of fact, but from his telling, it was clear that she was the cause of the rift between Hal and J.T. "It was all a big misunderstanding," J.T. was quick to say.

J.T. haltingly described how he tried to keep up a relationship with Hal after the marriage. But it was never the same, he said, roughly. J.T. would call his brother every Sunday night, and each time, the phone would switch to the answering machine, so he knew they were screening his calls. He would stop by, but no one would open the door. He was certain they were pretending not to be home. Then came the terrible day when Hal finally called him, only to let him know that they were moving to North Carolina. At a loss, J.T. had responded, "Maybe I could come and visit."

"I don't think that's a good idea, J.T. You shouldn't ever come and see us." Without another word, Hal had hung up the phone.

Silence hung over the table when J.T. finished. Pain etched his face. Sidney was embarrassed to find that she was close to tears herself. She turned to blink them away, wondering why his story affected her so much. After all, she barely knew him.

She looked up and saw J.T. watching her. He seemed to be waiting for something. A response perhaps? She shifted. "Um, about those emails between Ayers and Harry. What did they say?"

"I told you." J.T. was impatient but seemed relieved to change the subject.

"Okay, Ayers asked Harry for an 'update.' There's some arrangement Harry's working on, and he's close to a deal, but Ayers is still talking about layoffs. He says they're necessary for the bankruptcy proceedings—"

"Bankruptcy!" Sidney said. "You didn't tell me that before."

"I might have skipped that part," J.T. said. "I think they're trying to make it look like they're somehow saving money and saving the company. It's an act. If they go into bankruptcy, it's over. Forget about layoffs. We're all out of work."

Remarkably, J.T. seemed to have run out of words. Maybe the idea of dismantling the company was too much for him to bear. Sidney ran a finger over the cracked, stained tabletop.

"What should we do?" she asked finally.

He shrugged. "What *can* we do?" At Sidney's look, he added, "Don't worry, I have a few ideas. Something to get everyone's attention. It might even buy Harry some of the time he needs."

Sidney was worried. "What do you mean, get everyone's attention? How?" But instead of J.T., another voice responded.

"What are you two doing?"

Sidney's head swiveled. It was Sondra, the president's secretary. Sidney didn't know her well, but, over the course of many lunches, she had heard plenty from Carla, who detested the woman. Meanwhile, J.T., although a self-proclaimed expert on everyone at the Press, was acting as if he had never seen Sondra before, as if she had just landed from the moon.

A tall woman who intentionally wore four-inch heels to intimidate others, Sondra towered over their table. She was scarecrow-thin with a face that had settled into deep frown lines, and she had long, bright-red fingernails. Sidney found her terrifying in an average encounter, but in this situation, Sondra was particularly alarming.

J.T. was braver. "Whassup?" he grunted.

"I said, what are you doing?" Sondra glared.

"What does it look like we're doing?" he said defiantly.

Sidney stirred. It was probably best to rein in J.T. before they were both fired on the spot. "Just taking a break," she mumbled, rising so quickly that she knocked her chair over. "Come on, J.T., let's go," she said. She set the chair upright and was at the exit before she dared look back. Relieved, she saw that J.T. was following her, muttering. The door banged shut behind them, leaving Sondra still scowling.

Sidney had barely returned to her desk when Antoinette appeared. She was glad to see Harry's assistant. Despite the flap that Sidney had overheard earlier that ended in Antoinette shedding tears, there was something calming about her. Maybe it was her unassailable belief in Harry. Sidney searched Antoinette's face for answers to the fate of the Press, but her Greek goddess features were perfectly composed.

"There you are." Antoinette sounded annoyed. She dropped a file on Sidney's desk. "Here. The next section of Harry's white paper, ready for you to proof."

Sidney studied the papers a moment, then looked up. "You know what I heard?" she blurted. "I heard that the company is going bankrupt, but Harry's trying to save us." She looked intently at Antoinette. "Is that true?"

Antoinette gave a blank stare. "If I were you," she said, "I wouldn't repeat that. You just do what you're supposed to do, and let Harry do what he…well, what he does. Now, maybe you should get busy proofreading."

Antoinette turned on her heels and was gone.

It wasn't exactly a rebuke, but Sidney shriveled in her seat. This wasn't her. It wasn't her personality to get involved in other people's sad stories. She wasn't pushy, and she didn't engage in rumor mongering. Antoinette was saying that she needed to mind her own business. Yes, she needed to listen to that advice, and crawl back into her shell where it was safe.

She opened the folder and began to read the next installment of Harry's paper.

> *Gutenberg's earliest printed works were likely small brochures. The first true book was a small book of prayers. However, his big project—what he hoped would prove a bestseller—was the Bible.*
>
> *It was, indeed, a mammoth project. Gutenberg found an investor to fund the capital he needed. He spent years working on it. Finally, he was on the brink of completing a masterpiece of book design, one of the most beautifully typeset, well-balanced books ever printed by any standard. Known as the 42-Line Bible, or, simply, the Gutenberg Bible, it was near completion in 1455, ready to roll off the press. That was when disaster struck.*

Eight

Upon entering the crazy-looking house that Phoebe had told the policeman was her home, she stood blinking in the cool darkness of the mudroom. Getting in had been easy, as if she entered it as a matter of course every day, even though she had never before set foot in this town, let alone in this house. Yet she had confidently opened the gate, giving another little wave to the cop who was still watching her before going around to the back. Somehow, she had *known* that the enclosed porch in the rear of the house would have an open screen door and that inside the porch she would find an unlocked window. Sure enough, there it was, and after the simple matter of climbing through the window, she was inside.

The mudroom led to a kitchen. A clock in the shape of a rooster ticked quietly on the wall. Otherwise the house was perfectly still.

It didn't occur to her to worry that someone might be home and could wander in and discover her at any moment. The house didn't feel like anyone was home. But at least one person lived there, she thought, because a teacup and saucer were neatly stacked in the dish drainer by the sink. The counters were worn and scarred but tidy. Everything looked old but clean, and it was sparingly furnished.

Whoever lived here must be poor, Phoebe decided. They didn't have much.

She opened the refrigerator. There wasn't much food, either. A container of yogurt, a small bowl of peas and pearl onions covered in plastic wrap, jars of pickles and mayonnaise, and a bottle of ketchup. Phoebe was tempted to eat everything, including the condiments, but she hesitated. If it all disappeared it would be noticed for sure. She stared into the refrigerator. She had to, she decided. She was starving. She began pulling out the contents.

After she had devoured as much as she dared and was regretfully replacing the jar with one remaining pickle, she caught sight of something sticking out of a small drawer marked "deli." Inside were plastic bags with sliced ham and turkey.

"Lunch meat! Praise and thanks be to the Lord," she exclaimed, repeating her stepmother's oft-used phrase, and started searching for a loaf of bread.

After Phoebe had eaten two sandwiches, she cleaned up, carefully sweeping up the crumbs. When she couldn't find paper towels, she used the edge of her shirt to wipe up the counters, then looked about to see if she had erased all traces of herself, as they did on television. Even to her untrained eye, she thought she hadn't done a great job covering her tracks. She wished she had paid more attention to where things were when she had entered the kitchen.

She set out to explore the house. Outside the kitchen there was a small hallway leading to two rooms, one with cheery wallpaper and a table and chairs of honey-colored maple. The other was a dark, formal dining room, with thick draperies and furniture that was almost black. In the front of the house were two more matching rooms, both like living rooms. In one room was a television, an older model, and in the other room was an old-fashioned desk and some armchairs near a fireplace. *Two dining rooms and two living rooms*, Phoebe thought. *Weird.*

Yet for some reason, she felt completely comfortable, as if she were enveloped in warm, loving arms. Even if the homeowner ended up catching her, Phoebe had the feeling that she would be forgiven her trespasses—and she was definitely trespassing. She might even be invited to stay awhile, Phoebe thought hopefully. As much as she missed her dad, the effort of being on her own was overwhelming, always looking for food and a place to sleep that wasn't too scary. It was wearing her down, she thought, as a fresh wave of exhaustion came over her.

She had to stop herself from climbing the stairs, finding a real bed, and curling up to sleep. She knew that whoever lived in this house, no matter how nice they might be, would probably freak out if they found a real-life Goldilocks in their bed. She sat on the sofa to collect her thoughts.

After only a few moments of reflection, she decided that getting cleaned up would probably make her feel almost as good as eating had. Maybe then she could find somewhere in this rambling house to hide and get some sleep. After she got some real sleep, she could probably think more clearly about the next steps to take.

First, she went to the front window and carefully lifted the edge of the curtain. Huge shrubs blocked most of her view, but she could see a bit of a small front garden, a section of brick sidewalk, and the street beyond. All seemed quiet. It was still early afternoon, so she probably had time before people started coming home from work.

Just then, an old car with peeling paint crawled into view. It slowed to a halt directly in front of the house. Phoebe's heart jumped. This could be the owner returning home. She should hide—but where? A closet? Could she find her way to the basement? She wanted to run but was unable to move, compelled to watch the scene unfold.

The passenger door swung open, and a skinny pair of legs emerged. An old woman pulled herself out of the car with great effort and the help of a cane. Phoebe held her breath, but the old woman and her driver, who also looked ancient, both hobbled to a house across the street. Once the driver saw the woman safely to her front door, she slowly retraced her steps and got back into the car. With agonizing slowness, the car pulled away from the curb.

Phoebe drew a long breath and put the drapery back in place very carefully, not wanting the old lady across the street or anyone else to notice any movement in a house that was supposed to be empty. She continued to huddle by the window. *That was a close call*, she told herself. She desperately wanted that hot shower, but she wondered if the homeowner might return any minute. Maybe that woman she had seen drive away really was the homeowner. Maybe she just went on a quick errand and would be back. Phoebe scratched herself absently. The thing was, she felt so dirty after so many days on the road.

The shower won out. It wouldn't take long, she promised herself.

In the end, it all took much longer than she had expected, in part because there was no shower. She took a hot bath in the old-fashioned tub, one with curved feet. There was a neatly coiled pink rubber hose that she finally figured out could be used to wash and rinse her hair. She soaked for a long while, letting her fears drift away with the dirt.

Afterward she meticulously scrubbed the tub and wiped down the bathroom. Not bad, she thought as she inspected it with satisfaction. No one would guess that a very dirty person had just bathed there. She glanced down at the damp towel that she had dried herself with and had used to clean the tub. A wet towel appearing in the laundry wasn't a good idea. She would bring it with her to her hiding spot.

She entered the largest bedroom, the one that, strangely, didn't look lived in. The bed was made, and the bare dresser and nightstand didn't have a speck of dust. The hardwood floor gleamed in the trace of light seeping around the edges of the bay window. It should have brought in plenty of daylight, but the heavy window shades kept the room dark.

Phoebe explored the other rooms on the second floor. Only one smaller bedroom showed any signs of occupancy. *If I owned this place, I'd take turns sleeping in all the rooms*, she thought. But it was the master bedroom that she decided to use to get dressed. It felt special.

The clothes she had been wearing were so dirty, she couldn't bear to put them back on after her bath. She found some neatly folded clothes in the dresser. She laid them carefully on the immaculate bedspread and put her hair bands on the dresser alongside a pretty hairbrush-and-comb set that she had also discovered in a drawer. As she brushed out the tangles in her hair, she pretended she was a guest in a hotel room, preparing for a night on the town. *I'll be picked up in a limo and taken to a restaurant,* she thought, brushing and smiling. *My dad will be there, waiting for me.* Her smile faded.

After dressing, she looked at herself in the wavy mirror and, as she expected, the threadbare sweatshirt and knit pants were miles too big. She searched the closet and found an old belt. At least she didn't have to walk around with the waistband bunched in her fist.

She suddenly realized how much time she had been spending upstairs. She needed to hurry. She gathered up the wet towel with her things and headed to the basement, which, she had already decided, would make the best hideout.

As she had discovered in the quick exploration she had made before bathing, the basement was accessed by a door just off the kitchen. She hadn't investigated very far, taking only a few steps down the stairs and peering into the dimness. She had noticed a bit of daylight struggling through a small casement window. Now, as she stood at the top of the steps with her hand hovering over the wall switch, she hesitated. Would flipping on the light be seen from the outside? Better not take the chance.

She crept down the stairs slowly, holding her things with one hand and clinging to the rough wooden handrail with the other. Despite the window, it was almost impossible to see. *That was dumb not turn on the light*, Phoebe scolded herself. Well, maybe not so dumb, she reconsidered as she cautiously slid a foot over each step. Once she reached the bottom, there might not be any way to turn the light off.

When she felt the concrete floor, she made her way even more cautiously. Using the wall for support, she came upon smooth painted wood, and realized it was a door. A closet? She felt for the doorknob and opened it to even more unrelenting blackness. Phoebe waved her arm around wildly, finally banging it on a wall and locating a light switch. She hesitated but knew she had to take a chance and turn it on.

Light flooded the space. She quickly shut the door and blinked as she looked about. It did in fact seem like a large closet. Or maybe it had been a tiny room that had been transformed into a closet. At any rate, it was as ship-shape as the kitchen and the rest of the house. Boxes of clothing and Christmas decorations were marked and stored on shelves, along with some neatly folded blankets. There were also shelves with a few canned goods, but it didn't seem the sort of storage place a person would enter very often. *Except maybe to clean.* Phoebe eyed the spotless shelves and floor. *This person sure is clean.*

Even if the homeowner came down regularly to dust, it was the perfect place to conceal herself, she thought. She would remain hidden but would be able to hear footsteps upstairs to judge comings and goings.

Maybe because she was hidden in the closet, but Phoebe was suddenly very tired, so tired that she could barely make herself move. Somehow she managed to summon the energy to throw her belongings in a corner, pull down some blankets from the shelf, and spread one out. With a deep sigh, she switched off the light and settled down on the floor.

She didn't really mind the darkness. She didn't even mind being in a closet. She felt safe, maybe for the first time since she had left home. She had discovered that sleeping in a back yard where dogs or animals might be wandering about, or outside alone, was not fun. It was not like camping, as she had tried to convince herself many times. She needed to take a break from her journey. She wasn't giving up—she had to find her father—but it was just that she was so very, very tired.

As she was falling asleep, she saw herself brushing her hair in the bedroom after her bath. Her eyes flew open. She could envision it: the brush-and-comb set, left on the dresser that had had nothing on it before. What if the homeowner saw it? Would the person check the unused bedrooms? Had she left the door ajar? Phoebe didn't know, but it seemed too late to risk going back upstairs. *I'll go tomorrow*. The thought had barely formed before she was asleep.

~

It didn't seem so long ago, Sidney mused as she made the long, disheartening commute to work, that life at Poppy Press was so routine that it could be considered boring. She had never minded the routine, though. In fact, all the recent turmoil made her nostalgic for it. The sameness of it all had given her a sense of security. The expectations of her job never changed over the many years she worked there. She knew that she could leave at the end of each day and that the following day would be similar, if not identical.

But ever since Charlie Post had sold the company this last time, the atmosphere had become tense. Press employees continued to argue about his motives for selling. Some said that Charlie was doing what was best for the Press. No, Charlie was in it for himself, said others. The cynical ones argued that Charlie was simply trying to make a fast buck.

The fact of the matter was that Charlie was gone, and the tension had become unbearable. Since the recent, unexpected layoffs, any pretense of normalcy was gone. Poppy Press was broken, a shattered place. Friendships fragmented as coworkers brought complaints, real and imagined, against each other. Supervisors, fearful that any slip-ups would reflect badly, were harshly critical of their staffs. Everyone looked for ways to get rid of someone else, lest they be gotten rid of themselves.

Naturally, the gossip was nonstop. People whispered all manner of rumors, from the latest word from New York about whether a reorganization was in the works, to what the lawyers were working on behind the scenes. *How could they possibly know this stuff?* Sidney thought. The answer, she knew, was that they probably didn't.

Except J.T. He was always supremely confident in his insider knowledge, even if it amounted to tidbits of information or nothing more than conspiracy theories. Even his crazier notions seemed to contain kernels of truth. Other than his admission about the email exchanges, it generally wasn't clear where he got his information. Anyway, Sidney didn't want to know. Yet J.T. was often in possession of the facts, not conjecture, which made some of his pronouncements—the bankruptcy plan, for instance—believable.

It was funny, Sidney mused. In all the gossiping and speculation that had been circulating around the Press, no one else had brought up one word about bankruptcy.

She reached her desk at 8:03, a few minutes past her usual start time. Throughout her many years at Poppy Press, Sidney reliably reported a half hour early. Now it was all she could do to drag herself into the building.

Fortunately, everyone was too absorbed in their own problems to notice her tardiness. The morning passed quietly, with Sidney sorting through old projects. At noon she decided to be bold and abandon the Lunch Ladies. She needed some air, so she would spend her lunch hour taking a walk.

As she squinted in the brilliant sunshine, she could feel her spirits lift. It had been a long time since she had gone outside the building during work hours. She should do this more often, she told herself.

But as she walked several blocks, she began to grow uncomfortable, realizing that she was wandering into a seedier neighborhood. She moved on nervously and tried to ignore the graffiti-scrawled walls and trash-strewn empty lots. Then at the end of one block, she could see a few men loitering outside a small group of storefronts shuttered by thick grates. She hesitated. It seemed foolish to try to pass by without incident, but if she turned and ran, she couldn't be sure what would happen. Would they chase her? Hurt her? Sidney swallowed. She should never have ventured out.

Just then she thought she saw one of the men rising from his seat on the curb. She didn't delay any further, but turned and walked away swiftly. Before long she broke into a run, not caring who saw her jogging like a fool into Poppy Press.

Back at her desk, she sat fanning herself with a piece of paper and tried to control her still rapid breathing.

"You know that law firm downtown—Perry, Bayer & Fillard?" Harry boomed. Once again he had come out of nowhere and was towering over her cubicle wall. Sidney stifled a tiny scream and automatically looked for Antoinette, thinking that he must be conversing with her and just happened to pass by Sidney's cubicle as he was speaking. Instead, he was looking directly at her.

"I have a feeling those cheapskates are on the verge of finally spending a few bucks on a real printing job. Maybe even a big job," Harry was saying, "*if*, that is, we do right by them with our special little project." He winked at Sidney and let a slip of pink paper drift over the wall onto her desk.

"Do me a favor and check with Al on this job." Harry's ruddy face disappeared then popped back again a second later. "Oh, and make sure you have them expedite it. We don't want to risk losing this piece of business. I'm counting on you."

He was gone, but Sidney continued to sit very still. *Not again. I'm not good at this stuff.* She looked down and saw that the paper was a purchase order. Harry had scrawled something in his slapdash hand. "Probable order" was the only part Sidney could make out.

Antoinette next appeared at the top of the cubicle wall. "It would be a good idea to check if Al could schedule press time as soon as possible." She started to leave and then turned back. "If I were you, I would do what he says. Like now."

It was with some effort that Sidney extricated herself from her desk. Her limbs didn't seem to want to move, but before she knew it she was standing in front of the press foreman's desk.

With as much courage as she could muster, she started to plead her case, which was, of course, Harry's case. Al, the shift foreman, was not in the mood to listen. He refused to look at her as she stumbled through her little speech before cutting her off. "We have real, live jobs right now, so I don't have time for this. A white paper? I don't even know what that is." His dismissive manner sent Sidney into a cold sweat.

She looked at Al leaning back in his worn swivel chair, arms crossed over a protruding belly, his deep-set eyes in tiny slits. She hated this. She was not someone who could persuade people, but she was too afraid to go back and admit defeat to Harry. She took another breath.

"Al, please, Harry needs this paper on the schedule."

A few other pressmen, who had moved closer to eavesdrop, laughed out loud. "What schedule?" one jeered.

Sidney flushed. "I thought…I mean, we aren't that busy anyway…"

"Speak for yourself." Al stood, an annoyed Buddha rising from the lotus position to his full six-and-a-half-foot frame. The pressmen scurried back to their posts. Sidney knew that her audience was over. As if to prove this point, Al sat back down and swiveled his chair to his desk, his back to her.

Sidney slowly turned away. The thought occurred to her that it was not only time to leave the pressroom but was probably also time to walk out of the building. Time to quit. This job had become unbearable. If nothing else, it would let her avoid the inevitable trauma of a layoff or the humiliation of being fired.

She headed for the exit, thinking how horrified her mother would be that she was entertaining the notion of quitting her job without another one lined up. Just as she put her hand on the door, pondering what chance she might have of finding employment, the fire alarm sounded.

Sidney clapped her hands over her ears. Despite the din, she heard Al screaming like a madman.

"Turn them off! Shut the damn presses down! The sprinklers are going to start!"

On cue, the sprinkler system kicked in, sending enormous sprays over the equipment, wetting the paper, causing ink to run along the painted, concrete floor. The water soon soaked everyone in the vicinity, including Sidney, Al, and the pressmen, but only Al reacted. He became a madman, literally hopping mad, dancing on the wet floor among already forming puddles and yelling obscenities as he picked up soggy papers from his desk and threw them at the presses.

His antics sent Sidney darting out the double doors that led to the building's main section. There she joined clusters of people flowing slowly like syrup toward the building's exits. No one was taking it seriously, she realized. They were acting as if they had been let out of school early.

The giddy group funneled into the main corridor. Sidney was standing on her toes, trying to peer over the crowd, when someone grabbed her arm.

"Come this way," J.T. said into her ear. He steered her down a side corridor.

With his strong grip, Sidney had no choice. But when he let go, as they reached a stairwell, she followed him upstairs despite her doubts. *It's just J.T.*, she told herself, even if he was acting odd—authoritative but not quite in control of himself.

"Who goes upstairs in a fire?" Sidney had to yell over the fire alarm. J.T. ignored her.

"We should get out of the building," she tried again.

"How do you know it's a fire?" he shouted. "Don't worry."

The awful alarm continued its assault on their eardrums. She had yet to see or smell smoke. Perhaps that didn't mean anything, she thought as she followed J.T., but she wondered if she should turn and run downstairs.

He stopped before an unmarked door. "Are you sure about this?" Sidney started to say as he pushed open the door.

"Don't worry. I've saved all these other people too. We'll be safe here."

A shaft of light was momentarily blinding. Blinking, Sidney stumbled over the threshold and joined a group crowding a concrete balcony. It was a fairly large balcony and a familiar feature on the exterior of the building, but Sidney had never before seen anyone on it and had always assumed it was merely ornamental. Was it even meant to be used? she wondered. It seemed an unlikely place during an emergency, but apparently quite a few people had been persuaded to crowd onto it. Sidney suspected that it was J.T. who had done the convincing.

J.T. stepped out and squeezed into a small, vacant space near her. She heard the door click shut behind him. That silenced the deafening alarm, but instead of relief Sidney felt a certain dread. She had a sudden urge to escape. She looked at J.T., who appeared quite calm.

For that matter, the other balcony occupants were surprisingly carefree. A small tangle of people near one section of the pitted railing gave a low-key roar as they watched a chunk of concrete fall away under a man's arm and drop to the pavement three stories down. "Look out below!" the man yelled belatedly.

"Isn't this just like the Press? Evacuate us from a burning building and then stick us out on this ledge where there's no escape?" another male voice said cheerfully.

"Whose idea was it to come out here anyway?" the first man said.

"And why does the building have balconies?" a woman asked rhetorically.

"Fire escapes would be a lot more practical," another grumbled.

A woman, leaning against another part of the railing, screamed as more concrete pinged on the pavement below. She wasn't in danger of falling, but hands reached out to grab her.

As they crowded around the woman, something triggered in J.T.

"Keep calm, keep calm!" J.T. began shouting, his voice higher-pitched and more piercing than usual. "This is exactly what the New York people want to happen. They want us to panic and lose our cool. Then they'll swoop in and keep us under their thumbs! Permanently!" He looked wild-eyed and panicky, despite his admonitions. "What you need to do is keep calm. Keep calm and act normal."

He abruptly began to wade through the crowd, cutting through as if he were swimming. He reached the railing and tried to climb onto it, starting to shout, anxious to be heard. Others grabbed him, snatching pieces of his clothing, pulling him down. "Watch out, buddy, you're going to get hurt," one man said soothingly.

By turns, Sidney was horrified and burned with embarrassment. For no good reason, she felt somehow responsible for J.T.'s erratic behavior. He seemed to be growing increasingly unhinged. All she wanted to do was escape.

Turning back to the metal door, she tugged on the handle. It was stuck. She leveraged herself with her free hand, pushing against the wall, and pulled on the door again. And again. No, she needed to push it, she thought, trying to keep calm. She pushed. Then pulled and pushed again. The realization swept over her. The door was locked.

"We're trapped."

It was little more than a mumble from Sidney, but it was heard by a nearby man, who didn't appear to be paying her any mind until that moment. His outcry caused a near riot.

"The door's locked! We're trapped! We're stuck here and the building's on fire!" the man's voice resonated insistently.

He might as well have dropped a match on a gasoline spill. Sidney felt herself pressed against the door as the crowd surged forward. A woman sobbed. "Let us out!" yelled a man, pounding his fist on the metal door.

Sidney was shoved aside. She felt her cheek scrape on the rough wall. She was going to be crushed; the thought came to her with complete clarity.

"Knock it off!"

The voice spoke so authoritatively that the crowd drew back on instinct. It was J.T. again. Somehow he had managed to push his way back through the crowd to return to his original spot between the mob and the door.

"Keep your heads! They'll come and get us."

Sidney gaped. Not only was J.T. defusing a near riot, but he was making sense.

Still, J.T., his face glistening with sweat, wouldn't be able to hold them off for long. He pleaded for order, even as the crowd again started pulsing forward. Then the door opened a crack.

The person on the other side must have been surprised that the door could open only an inch before it hit a wall of people. It immediately clicked shut.

The same man who had initiated the panic noticed it and once again called out to the group. "Hey! The door just opened!"

As the crowd obligingly made room, the door opened again slowly.

A firefighter in full gear stood in the entrance. "What are you folks doing out here?" He stepped to the side and beckoned impatiently. "Come on, fire drill's over. Back to school."

Sheepishly, the group filed back into the building. Sidney followed along, noting how quiet everyone had become. She heard mostly feet on the stairs, echoing off the cinderblock walls.

"What's wrong with J.T.?" Startled, Sidney turned to see Sondra, bracelets jangling, standing next to her on the second flight of stairs. Sidney didn't respond, not sure if the question was directed to her. She focused on the slow-moving man in front of her, trying not to jostle him.

"Why did he want us all to go out on that balcony?" Sondra asked. This time there was no mistaking that Sondra was speaking to her. "I should have known better than to listen to him."

"By the way, you two are as thick as thieves," Sondra pressed. "I think you're up to something."

Sidney wished the plodding man in front would go faster.

"Well?" Sondra reached out and gave Sidney a little back-hand slap on her arm.

"Well, what?" Sidney snapped, stopping short. This was too much, even for her passive personality.

"Please keep moving," whined the woman behind them. "You can't just stop like that on the stairs."

Sidney resumed her march with as much dignity as she could gather. She was grateful that the next landing was her floor. She slipped through the door but heard the bracelets jangling behind her as she strode quickly down the corridor.

Despite her spiky heels, Sondra managed to overtake Sidney. They walked, side by side, in silence for a few moments before Sondra glided ahead of her, moving swiftly.

"He didn't have anything to do with the fire alarm," Sidney called out after her.

"Who said he did?" Sondra said over her shoulder, waggling her red-tipped fingers.

~

When Phoebe awoke, the pitch black of the closet disoriented her. After she had lain there for a while, blinking in the darkness, she became convinced that it was morning, even though she couldn't see any daylight. Maybe she had even overslept. It might be lunchtime for all she knew.

Still, she didn't want to take a chance by switching on the light in the closet. She felt for the doorknob and opened the door a crack. She was wrong. It was nighttime, not morning. The basement was dark, although not as deep black as the closet. No daylight came through the small, high window in the corner, only the weak light of a distant streetlamp.

Phoebe wondered just how late it was. It felt like the middle of the night. Surely the homeowner had returned from work and was already in bed. She again began to worry about the hairbrush-and-comb set she had accidentally left on the dresser. She fought the impulse to run upstairs and grab it, just slipping upstairs and back in a flash. *No, that would be stupid. I would be caught for sure*, she told herself. *Just wait for morning.*

She sat on the blankets and thought, arguing with herself. In the end, though, she couldn't resist the opportunity to catch a glimpse of the owner of the house. The middle of the night would be the safest time to do this, she rationalized.

Her decision made, she cocked her head and listened for sounds on the floors above her. All was quiet. No footsteps.

She took a deep breath and switched on the bare light bulb in the closet. She would need it to guide her way back down the cellar steps.

Tiptoeing up the stairs, she listened at the kitchen door for a long time and then opened it with agonizing slowness.

She was back in the same kitchen where she had been only hours earlier, but it looked entirely different in the dim light. The clock ticked gently, and the house made soft, settling noises, the comforting sounds of an old home.

Phoebe made her way to the front rooms. It was so quiet that she began to wonder if perhaps she was alone. She thought for a moment. Was the homeowner away on a trip? Or just hadn't come home yet for the night? She pictured the front door opening and an outraged person confronting her right there in the living room.

She bit her lip and decided to chance it. She had come this far.

As she started up the staircase, the second step gave a loud creak and froze her in place. Her eyes darted upstairs, expecting to see a figure rushing down.

No one appeared. She started moving with even more care, placing her feet near the corners of each step. She hoped the old, wooden stairs would be stronger there and not groan under her weight.

On the second floor she began creeping down the long hallway to the master bedroom, the one she had used after her bath. As she passed the smaller bedroom, she saw the door standing partially open. She peeked around the door. In the bed was a form, more like a lump, covered in blankets. Phoebe squinted. She could see it was a woman, an older woman but not an old lady. She looked tired, even in sleep.

Phoebe stepped back, squeaking the floor even louder than the creak on the step. She flew back behind the door and held her breath.

She counted to ten. No sound.

Breathing again, she tiptoed to the master bedroom and managed to open the door silently. The brush and comb sat undisturbed on the dresser.

She had her hands on the dresser drawer, ready to put the set back where she had found it, when she thought better of it. Opening the drawer was bound to make a racket. She would take the set with her and replace it when she was alone in the house.

It seemed to take far less time to get back to the cellar and the safety of the closet, with the door shut and the light off. At this point she welcomed the darkness. It was protecting her.

She curled up on the blankets and tried to go back to sleep. She thought again about the still figure in the bed upstairs and how quietly the woman slept. Phoebe, though, always sprawled out in her sleep. Come morning, she would probably wake up, spread out as much as the small space would allow, arms and legs at all angles. *What a difference from that lady upstairs*, was Phoebe's last thought before she fell asleep.

—

Sidney's eyes opened. A shaft of moonlight fell through the gap in the curtains. It wasn't yet morning, but something had woken her. Some kind of noise? She lay still, listening. Well, there was no longer any noise. Maybe she had dreamed it.

Moving the blankets aside, she swung her legs over the side of the bed and felt for her bedroom slippers with her feet. She padded toward the bathroom, pausing in the hallway to cock her head and listen again. Was that a rustle and a click? She couldn't be sure. Perhaps just her overactive imagination, as her mother would have said.

It could be Agatha's ghost, came the sudden thought as she entered the bathroom and switched on the light. Sidney clucked to herself. That was ridiculous. Her mother, even in spirit form, would probably have been horrified at the suggestion. Agatha considered the supernatural to be absurd, if not abhorrent. "It's the devil's work," she would say at any mention of the paranormal. Her mother held the opinion that once you were dead, that was it. There would be nothing but blackness.

Not for the first time, Sidney wondered if her mother had discovered an afterlife and found that she had been wrong about death. *Well, she's not coming back to tell me*, Sidney told herself and turned on the tap to wash her hands. Although…every now and then since her mother's passing there had been some indefinable quality to the house, like a fleeting bit of a dream. Once in a while she swore she could feel Agatha's presence.

As Sidney returned to her room, she threw a glance down the stairwell. It was that same feeling again—like someone else was in the house.

If it was Agatha, she thought resolutely as she climbed back into bed, there was nothing to worry about. Her mother may not have been the easiest person to live with, but she would never do anything to harm Sidney, in life or in death.

Nine

From Harry Corcoran's white paper:

Legacy Despite Betrayal

Gutenberg spent years working on his special invention, developing and perfecting the art of movable type, setting up his workshop, and hiding his big idea from the world. It may have been a brilliant idea, but there were practical aspects to consider. For example, he needed capital. He borrowed money from Johann Fust, a merchant who dealt in manuscripts and books made from block printing methods. Fust's adopted son and later his son-in-law, Peter Schoffer, became Gutenberg's chief apprentice, probably as part of the investment deal.

Fust himself had to borrow to invest in Gutenberg's printing venture, and he demanded compound interest from Gutenberg to cover what he had to pay. But Gutenberg couldn't meet his financial obligations. With everything tied up in the business, he was broke.

Several years later, around 1455, things were looking up. The Gutenberg Bible was pre-sold. Gutenberg only needed to add the finishing touches to the volumes. He was close to success, and he was sure that the Bible would show the beauty of the printing press and the brilliance of movable type.

It was precisely at that moment that disaster struck. Fust sued, alleging that Gutenberg had misappropriated funds for his own private venture instead of the "work of the books." As collateral, Fust claimed Gutenberg's masterpiece, the Bible.

The drama came down to a hearing at the Convent of the Barefoot Friars in 1455. Gutenberg couldn't bear to hear the judgment, which predictably went against him, so he sent his house servant. He was permitted to keep one workshop with a single press, but he lost the Bible. Fust and the assistant, Peter Schoffer, went on to try to claim the Bible as their own.

Gutenberg never fully recovered from this betrayal. He went on printing, but nothing carried his imprint. Yet his legacy, his genius behind movable type and printing, has lived on through the centuries.

Readers of this white paper may be curious. Why point to occurrences of more than five hundred years ago to make a point about a printing company today? It has relevance, of course. Just as Gutenberg had his vision of a world of printed books and needed capital to make it happen, we at this small press have our own vision of a world where print lives on, where we can explore new, digital opportunities at which Gutenberg would have marveled. Just like Gutenberg long ago, we require the assistance of investors who share that vision and can see that print is not dead after all. It's simply evolving.

~

They were all there, hastily assembled in a rarely used conference room. Vincent Ayers had called them together, this group he insisted on referring to as the "leadership," even though none of them wielded any power, constantly had their decisions second-guessed or countermanded, and generally were not even consulted.

No wonder they don't look like a happy bunch, Harry Corcoran thought as he looked at the group squeezed between the conference table and the scuffed walls. There was Oliver, the pressroom superintendent; Al, one of the more senior press foremen; and Candace, the accounting team head who was often referred to as the Ice Queen. She clearly relished the nickname. At the head of the table was Ayers. His lapdog assistant was wedged into a corner to Ayers's right. *What's his name again?* Harry tried to remember. Nick something. Oh, yes, Nicholas Baker. The kid was trying to look noncommittal, but it seemed to Harry that the assistant would have preferred to have been anywhere but in this room.

Harry hoped that this meeting might be about something innocuous, perhaps an update on the company's finances. At worst, maybe a reprimand for the events of the previous day, when a fire alarm emptied the building and ruined a print run. The incident was disruptive but not the end of the world. Harry watched the assistant's face and thought, *This is something else altogether and it isn't going to be good.*

Ayers wasted no time in getting to the bad news.

"Today we're publicly announcing that we're taking Poppy Press into Chapter Eleven bankruptcy. Papers are being filed in bankruptcy court. There should be little or no impact on the company in the short term. We will discuss cuts in staff, changes in budget, and so forth once we reach some clarity on the rehabilitation plan."

That son of a bitch! He said he would hold off on the bankruptcy. Harry felt the familiar knot in his gut coming alive, expanding, and pressing his organs. It threatened to constrict his breathing if he didn't get control of it. Harry looked at the others around the table. They looked stunned—even Candace, who prided herself on never showing emotion. They hadn't had a clue that the parent company would take this course, Harry realized. That helped him regain his balance. He still had his plan with Charlie Post, and that was something, at least. Some kind of leverage.

"It's a shame we couldn't have held off." Harry's voice as smooth as ever. "We were making progress, and we're in the midst of some promising discussions. All the result of our white paper, which clearly is working."

"What kind of joke is that?" Ayers interrupted, shifting suddenly from the calm, regal tone he had used only a moment earlier. "White paper? When I read that piece of trash, I couldn't believe it." He appealed to the group, his face twisted into a grimace. "Hey, can you believe it? The place is going down the tubes, and Mr. Brilliant here writes a white paper about the Middle Ages and the dawn of printing. He can't own up to the fact that printing is dead. Dead! Nobody will give us money based on some kind of history lesson."

Ayers stopped, breathing hard. Most were studying the table or the ceiling, anything to avoid making eye contact with him or each other. The exception was Harry, who met Ayers's stare with a calm look. *Charlie warned me about the white paper*, Harry thought. *Tough. I think it was what we needed to make our case. Anyway, I'm never admitting defeat to this guy.*

Harry allowed the uncomfortable silence to continue in the room for a few minutes before speaking.

"I must say I'm a bit surprised by your reaction. Perhaps you haven't had an opportunity to review the entire paper," he said. "It's a complete business case, everything potential investors need to make a fully-informed decision. I merely began the paper with some background, if you will, to help make the point.

"I suppose a question for you, sir, is," Harry drew out his words to Ayers, "if print is so 'dead,' then what are you president of?"

Harry rose, made his way to the door, and pulled it open sharply, aiming to hit the back of Ayers's chair. It did, jolting him.

"See you all at the announcement meeting." Harry winked at the group as he quietly pulled the door shut behind him.

The false fire alarm was still the topic of conversation the next day. As commonplace as fire drills were, this was not planned, and many saw it as something more than a prank. It was a sign of anger, people said, a warning to management.

Sidney tried to ignore the chatter, but she was worried. Would others think, as she did, that J.T. had something to do with it? If so, would she be implicated? Everyone saw them together frequently. Sidney listened to the buzz of conversation ebbing and flowing near her workstation, her heart sinking.

By mid-morning, she couldn't take it any longer. She had to find out more. She passed Antoinette's desk, muttering that she had an errand to run, and headed down the hall. Her plan was to stroll along and try to catch what people were saying and whether J.T. was considered a suspect.

A few small groups still stood together talking, much as they did on the day of the first round of layoffs. Sidney considered it a senseless waste of time to rehash an incident as trivial as a faulty fire alarm, but she understood that the workers were desperate for any distraction. *Better than talking about layoffs*, she thought with bravado as she walked past. What she really hoped, though, was that she, someone who would much rather die than be in the spot-light, wasn't popping up in these conversations. She suspected, however, that if J.T. were around, he would take pride in the fact that people were talking about him.

As if on cue, drifting from one small knot of workers came the clear reference of a single name: J.T.

Sidney hurried away, certain that their eyes followed her. She was sure that they knew that she and J.T. were friends. Well, not friends, exactly. She was just his sounding board. She wanted to turn and tell them this, that she really didn't know J.T. all that well, but that would make her look even more suspicious. What she had to do was to put her foot down with J.T. She vowed that the next time he wanted to confide in her, she would tell him to take his crazy ideas and get lost.

The news later in the day was that there had indeed been a reason for the fire alarm, that it wasn't a false alarm after all. This should have been vindicating, but it didn't make Sidney feel much better. It wasn't even a fire exactly, just some smoke coming from machinery in the pressroom, which would account for the sprinkler system activating there. Unfortunately for the company, a great deal of paper was ruined, and two jobs had to be rerun.

So maybe J.T. had nothing to do with it after all, Sidney thought. It was hard to know. While it made her soften her decision to have nothing more to do with him, she was still determined not to get drawn into his web of conspiracy theories. And it was probably best to distance herself a bit, considering how quickly the incident seemed to become part of Poppy Press lore.

"Let's take this supposed fire or smoke or whatever it was," Carla said at lunch, still obsessed with the incident a few days later. "Are we to believe that smoke suddenly materializes from the presses? Mind you, it's not like they've been overused lately. I, for one, am not buying it. This was a deliberate act, like sabotage."

Sidney looked away, waiting with some anxiety for Carla to hint about J.T.'s role. Instead, Carla began to focus on her own spin on the fire, which involved New York, theorizing that management planned to burn the place down, collect the insurance money, and be done with it. When someone pointed out that it would be unusual to set an arson fire in the middle of the day when the building was most crowded, Carla blithely dismissed it.

"Evildoers don't worry about things like collateral damage," she responded with a wave of her hand. Recently, Carla had begun referring to upper management as "evildoers." She neatly licked her fingers, sucking a trifle longer on the end of her thumb. "I'm sure their idea was to knock a few of us off while they were burning the building to the ground."

Later, back in the solitude of her desk, Sidney thought about the exchange and felt some of her anxiety drain away. She had been concerned over nothing. No one suspected J.T., and for that matter, she had no knowledge either that he had anything to do with it. She felt a little guilty for suspecting him, even if he did behave strangely.

"Psst."

Sidney jumped. The top half of J.T.'s head, up to his nose, bobbed at the top of her cubicle wall.

"Sidney, get your head down. We have to take precautions."

She looked at him wearily.

"Get down!"

At the urgency in his voice, she reflexively rested her head on the desktop. J.T. crawled around to her side of the cubicle and sat cross-legged on the floor. For a long moment, they looked at each other.

"Well?" Sidney was impatient with herself. Despite her intentions not to get caught up in J.T.'s intrigues, here she was, complying as she always did, even when he was acting more foolish than usual.

"Well, it's their biggest scheme yet." He spoke loudly considering his proximity and despite his persistent motioning for her to keep quiet. She rolled her eyes, which he ignored.

"I don't know all the details yet, but they're planning to get us, one at a time, as each person enters the lunchroom. That's where they'll fire everyone. Today. It will happen today."

She looked at him more closely. His eyes were wild and hollow, and he seemed genuinely frightened. Sidney wasn't sure how to calm him, and uncertain about what might further agitate him. Finally, she tried reasoning with him.

"It doesn't seem like it would be today, does it? Lunchtime is over. People wouldn't be heading to the lunchroom." She winced at the weak argument.

J.T. was considering the logic of this when Antoinette appeared. She stopped short at the sight of him sitting on the floor.

"What do you think you're doing?" Antoinette's tone conveyed a resigned curiosity.

He scrambled to his feet, but Antoinette ignored him and addressed Sidney. "There's a special all-staff meeting this afternoon. It starts at two o'clock sharp, so you best get to the lunchroom."

"See?" came J.T.'s strangled cry. He barreled past Antoinette, nearly knocking her over.

Antoinette recovered her footing and watched him run away. "I would ask, what's his problem, but I think I know," she said to Sidney, rubbing her arm where J.T. had shoved her. "He's just plain crazy."

If Sidney had been anxious earlier, she was a nervous wreck as she waited for the hastily called meeting to start. With minutes left before the appointed time, there were only a few employees present—perhaps twenty scattered among the haphazardly arranged metal folding chairs. Some of the long cafeteria-style tables had been removed to make the room more spacious. The meeting attendees watched dolefully as a pressman struggled to drag a heavy wooden podium across the linoleum and set it to face the audience. He disappeared and returned with a huge, potted fern that obscured his face, dropping it unceremoniously next to the podium. *Why bother with these niceties?* Sidney wondered.

The low buzz that had been filling the room subsided as Ayers strode into the room. He took a position behind the podium, and an entourage of managers and supervisors filled the space behind him. They looked singularly uncomfortable. Harry was absent, but Sidney recognized the young man with slicked-back hair.

Ayers was imposing despite his short stature. His head and shoulders barely emerged above the podium, but he managed to look the part of executive with his wavy, silver-flecked hair and excellent tan. In contrast, the Poppy Press audience seemed even more drab and rag-tag than usual.

Ayers pulled some notes from the inner pocket of his jacket. Frowning, he reached in again for reading glasses. Very deliberately, he adjusted the glasses on his nose before reviewing the papers as if seeing them for the first time.

"Here's the situation." He sounded so angry that Sidney unconsciously flinched.

"The company is entering into Chapter Eleven of the bankruptcy law," he continued. "We're currently involved in court proceedings to reorganize the company. This does not mean Poppy Press is out of business. I repeat, we are not out of business. We will continue to operate as usual, and I expect each of you will do the same." He looked around and scowled as he refolded the paper and slipped it back into his pocket.

"That is all," Ayers said. He strode out of the room, his managers in tow.

No one in the audience moved. They were stunned into silence. *Bankruptcy*—the word seemed to ricochet against the walls. A moment later, the room reacted as if on delay, at first with murmurs, then raised voices. They rose, nearly jumping out of their seats, scraping their chairs on the floor, and heading toward the exits.

Sidney kept seated, eyes cast down, and waited for the group to clear out. As the door closed after the last person, the room became quiet. She bent to pick up the notepad she had slid beneath her seat—why she thought it would be necessary to take notes, she had no idea—and let out a long breath.

This drama was exhausting, she thought as she left the lunchroom. It was all she could do to keep her eyelids open. She longed to go home and sleep. *Sleep, and just forget everything*, she thought. As tempting as that was, it wouldn't change anything, she knew. Not the problems at work, not the problems at home. It was high time she just learned to face them.

Ten

In her dreams, Sidney began to hear noises. Floorboards creaking, doors closing, water running. Everyday noises, but in her sleep they became the stuff of nightmares.

In spite of all her intentions to plan and strategize following the big Poppy Press bankruptcy announcement, as soon as she arrived home she climbed the stairs, fell into bed with her clothes on (which would have horrified her mother), and was asleep almost instantly. But some time during the night the noises erupted. She tried to climb out of her deep sleep, but other dreams took over, pushing her back into slumber.

Just as dawn was breaking, she woke. She lay very still, watching the gray light seep into the room and listening for the sounds, but heard nothing but the twittering of birds outside the window.

It was simply her dreams, Sidney told herself, her brain on overdrive even in sleep. Either that, or Agatha was haunting her. If it was her mother…then, there was nothing to be afraid of, she thought firmly. She sat up with some effort, swinging her legs over the edge of the bed. She studied the large, braided rug under her feet. It was the same handmade rug with the familiar blue and gray colors that had covered the hardwood floor for as long as she could remember. She had the sudden mental image of the many times Agatha had stood on the rug in Sidney's childhood, to wish her good night or wake her for school. Now it was like Agatha's ghost might be standing on the same spot.

c. But she wasn't imagining the strange feeling in the pit of her stomach. As she stood she felt a wave of nausea. She started to walk to the bathroom, somewhat shakily, but promptly had to retreat to bed. She suddenly was feverish and shivering at the same time. She lay back on the pillow.

After a length of time she roused herself. She had to get herself into work somehow. With the uproar at the Press, it wouldn't be smart to call in sick. Besides, she never missed work. She had been raised to think of sick days as cheating. Her grandfather had believed in perfect attendance at school, work, and church regardless of how ill one was.

Was there really any honor in going to work when you're sick? Sidney thought, feeling disloyal as she staggered to the bathroom. Nonetheless, the old rule took charge, propelling her to try to prepare for work. She put a tiny amount of toothpaste on the brush and immediately rinsed it off because the smell made her queasier. As she settled for a swish of mouthwash, she glanced in the mirror. Her reflection was deathly pale. *You can make it,* she told herself.

In the end, she made it only as far as the front door. She stood, weaving slightly, her rumpled raincoat falling off her shoulders, and frowned at the front walkway. It seemed much longer than usual.

If she didn't show up at work, would anyone even notice?

Weakly, Sidney pushed the door shut and, clutching the banister, made the trek back upstairs to her room. Throwing her coat in a heap in the corner, she climbed into bed fully dressed for a second day in a row and slept.

~

"Adele? Anyone home?"

It was Liz's knuckles rapping on the desk rather than her insistent voice that roused Adele from her fog. Adele tried to smile but it was more a stretching of her jaw. She hoped her friend wouldn't notice. Or would pretend not to notice.

"Sorry, I was a million miles away," Adele said.

"Obviously. You look hypnotized."

Uninvited, Liz squeezed into the narrow chair next to Adele's desk. "Is everything okay? It's a stupid question, I know. It must be horrible, suddenly a single mom to two kids now that Robert's gone." Her voice trailed off as she cocked her head at Adele and squinted. "This is going to sound bad, but I've got to say it. You look dreadful."

"Gee, thanks." Adele tucked some of her dank hair behind her ears. It was true. She looked a fright. Since Robert left, she didn't even bother to look in the mirror when getting ready for work. She didn't want to see the dark circles, the lines of worry, the gray starting to salt her hair. It had only grown worse since Phoebe ran away. Adele touched her hair again and wondered if she had remembered to comb it.

"Is something else bothering you?" Liz was still sitting at eye level, but to Adele she seemed to be looming, a large shadow threatening to swallow her.

Adele looked down and shuffled some papers. She had already made the mistake of confiding in Liz when things were getting bad with Robert and then felt compelled to tell her that he had left. But Adele couldn't bring herself to talk about Phoebe. Robert made her look like a woman scorned. Phoebe made her look like a bad mother at best, and a criminal at worst.

Still avoiding Liz's gaze, Adele stumbled in her response. "I'm fine. I'm just tired…a single mom, like you said." She managed a smile that she hoped appeared genuine. Liz hesitated and then, to Adele's relief, launched into more office gossip. Adele settled back in her chair, knowing that it would be mostly a one-sided conversation.

At first, Adele tried to appear interested. Soon, though, her mind wandered, as it usually did these days, to Phoebe. It didn't help to dwell on the events—finding Phoebe gone, the frantic searching, and the frustration with the police—but they all circled in her mind like water around a drain. She had a sudden urge to interrupt Liz and tell her that Phoebe had run away, and no one, not even the police, would listen because they all believed Robert had taken her.

But she didn't dare risk the inevitable suspicions. Adele could picture Liz's reaction. *She's been gone for weeks? What do they say at her school? What do you mean, you haven't told them!*

There would be the inevitable gossip. Her coworkers would, at minimum, hold her responsible. She would be the bad guy. *None of them could possibly understand what I'm going through,* she thought defiantly.

Adele had been keeping Phoebe's disappearance secret from most people, even though it probably only made matters worse. Why didn't she come clean? she wondered. She couldn't say why. Possibly it was embarrassment—God knew how humiliated she was about Robert. No one, absolutely no one, knew the real reason he had left her.

As a result, she had become deceptive. How she handled it with Phoebe's school was just one example. She initially told them that Phoebe was visiting relatives out of state. After a week, she called again to inform them that Phoebe's stay had been extended and that she most likely would not be returning for the remainder of the school year. She hung up the phone, feeling somehow comforted by her own lie. Acting as if Phoebe were safe made it easier to pretend for a moment that it was true. At work, Adele had said nothing to her supervisor. Nor did she say a word to the neighbors. The only person she discussed Phoebe's disappearance with, other than the police and officials, was her mother. Their long-distance phone calls had become more frequent. Adele found some solace with her mother as a sounding board.

Adele certainly didn't find any comfort in talking to the authorities. Well, she wasn't so much communicating with them as she was hounding them. Their reaction continued to amaze her. It was so far from what she expected—suspicion, accusation—that their laid-back attitude played games with her head. She would steel herself every time she spoke to the police, fearing that their apathy would eventually turn to interrogation. She worried that she would slip and bring up how she had left her stepdaughter locked in an empty room all day until Phoebe managed to escape and run away. They would definitely look at her differently then, Adele thought. She managed to keep still and, short of that kind of confession, apparently nothing else could dissuade the police from their opinion that this was a case of parental kidnapping.

Adele could understand, in her more rational moments, why it made sense to assume that Phoebe was with her biological father and only living parent. Unfortunately, this theory led the police to focus more on Adele's and Robert's rocky marital situation rather than finding Phoebe. Though her conversations with the police weren't interrogations, they still often turned awkward and painful.

"Why exactly did your husband leave you, Mrs. Locke?" was the one question she was asked the most and the one she least wanted to answer.

She needed to stop worrying about it, play along, and act as if Robert had spirited Phoebe away. He had somehow contacted Phoebe and had picked her up. Phoebe was fine.

It would also be easier, she thought, if she could believe it was true.

Even if she wanted to believe it, it didn't make sense, the nagging voice in Adele's head said. When would Robert have contacted Phoebe? It certainly didn't explain Phoebe's behavior the morning she ran away, when she had been nearly hysterical. Would Phoebe act that way if she had heard from her father? Instead, she had been genuinely distraught, as if it had just dawned on her that he wasn't coming back.

To Phoebe, the ultimate betrayal was that Adele failed to try to find her father. But what Phoebe didn't know was that Robert didn't want to be found. Not by anyone, including Phoebe.

She looked up. Liz's words were a distant buzz, but for some reason, they were helping her think clearly. Where would Phoebe go to search for her father? Connecticut, maybe? Robert had always talked to Phoebe about growing up there. He made it sound like the best place on earth, a kind of Disneyland. But would Phoebe set out for a place so far away with no means of getting there? It seemed so far-fetched. Why would Phoebe even think of Connecticut as a potential destination?

Wait. The postcard. Adele pictured the card Robert had sent. She had kept it in her dresser, the cryptic message from Connecticut, the only correspondence she had received from him since he left. She didn't know why she had kept it. She had been spitting-nails angry with him, even more so since she had been forced to deal with his daughter's disappearance, the same daughter he once claimed was the only one he ever loved.

In any case, it had been silly to hang onto this card that told Adele nothing except that Robert had apparently been in Connecticut when he mailed it. It was especially thoughtless to risk having Phoebe find it. Adele should have known that Phoebe would be looking for clues, desperate to learn anything about her dad's whereabouts.

Stupid, stupid, Adele chided herself. What it all added up to was that the girl had set out alone on some kind of crazy adventure to Connecticut to find Robert.

Refocusing, Adele looked at Liz. She was *still* talking. "Do you know what I mean?" she was asking.

Adele had long since stopped responding to this phrase because she no longer cared to know what Liz meant. She watched Liz's lips moving and wondered for a second how Liz's expression would change if she suddenly spilled her own secrets. Would Liz know what *she* meant? Adele had the sudden, desperate wish to call her mother.

It took a couple of weeks after Phoebe went missing for Adele to break down at last and tell her mother. The only reason she had been able to hold off that long was because her mother lived in California. Distance made it easier to keep silent for longer. But when Adele did confess she wondered why she had waited. Her mother was someone who listened and never judged or scolded. It was no different when she told her mother all about Robert and Phoebe.

The only thing she omitted was the reason why Robert had left. It was still too raw. Her mother didn't ask questions, for which Adele was grateful. Better that everyone assume that their marriage simply fell apart. At the same time, the lack of information made her mother a proponent of the theory that Robert had taken Phoebe. "It does make sense, dear," her mother said in her mild tone. Adele found it exasperating but had to admit she would likely reach the same conclusion if she were in her mother's place.

"It's something to consider," her mother had said. "Maybe Phoebe was able to get in touch with Robert. She seems pretty resourceful for a young girl."

"Maybe." Adele said, trying to keep the doubt out of her voice. Maybe but not likely, she wanted to say, considering how selfish Robert turned out to be.

Remembering the conversation with her mother as she half-listened to Liz, Adele had a sudden inspiration. She had been looking at this all wrong, she thought, her head jerking up. Perhaps she had been the selfish one, viewing it only from her own perspective.

She needed to consider how special Phoebe had been to Robert. It was true he cared about Phoebe more than he ever did about Adele or their son. Those were the facts, and they had to be accepted. If she could accept that, maybe she should admit that the police's theory was right after all. Robert had come back for Phoebe. Just because he had rejected Adele didn't necessarily mean that he had rejected his daughter as well.

It was conceivable that Phoebe had gotten in touch with Robert, perhaps after she ran away. As Adele's mother had said, Phoebe was resourceful. Still, it was important—critical, even—to learn whether Phoebe was safe. She had to get in touch with Robert somehow. If Phoebe could do it, she could too.

Adele had told the investigators about the postcard and had given them contact information for Robert's aunt and uncle, the family members she knew still lived in Connecticut after the death of Robert's parents. She believed that Robert's brother, his only sibling, might also still live in the state, although the brothers apparently hadn't spoken in years. She gave them his name nonetheless. The lack of close family would make Connecticut an odd destination for Robert, Adele had told the police, but the officer taking the information had only asked for any additional names. She gave him the names of the few coworkers and acquaintances she had heard Robert speak of.

"What about, um, the love interest? You mentioned he left you for someone?" the officer had stuttered, flushing with embarrassment.

"I don't have that information," she had answered coldly.

Now Adele wondered if the police had made headway contacting anyone from that brief list she had provided. Her guess was that they had not.

Instead, she would try. At a minimum she could work the phone, and maybe she would have luck tracking Robert down. Although his contact list was in his phone, which was with him, Adele suddenly remembered him jotting something into a small address book and then slipping it into a drawer in their bedroom. *You never know when you might need paper as a backup*, he had said casually.

He could have taken the address book with him, but chances were that he had not, considering the haste with which he had left. As soon as she got home, she would search for it. Even without it, there was always the Internet. She would find Robert or someone who knew where he was.

"You're not even listening!" Liz's accusation startled Adele. "Do I have to start all over again?"

~~~
~~~

"What in heaven's name is the matter with you?" Agatha was asking Sidney. She looked distressed, her face wavy, moving in and out of focus. Agatha was on the other side of something, some kind of surface. A mirror? No. Her mother was underwater. That was odd, Sidney thought, because she was talking so normally.

"Sidney, get out of there. What's wrong with you?" Agatha's concern was turning into panic. Sidney realized that she was the one underwater. Desperately, she tried to swim to the surface, so her lungs could fill with air, so she could reach Agatha and safety. Sidney struggled, but she couldn't move. Clammy fear paralyzed her, but then she realized that she was having no trouble breathing. She was breathing in the water.

"Sidney, please, help me." Her mother was begging. Were those tears rolling down Agatha's face? It was hard to tell from Sidney's watery vantage point. Yes, they were definitely tears. Sidney was confused why her mother needed help. Sidney was the one drowning.

Then, the wavy Agatha lifted a large rock. Sidney knew that her mother, looking tortured, intended to strike her with it. Sidney flinched, readying herself for the blow, but it didn't come. The rock missed her face, but it made a loud noise, striking something.

With that, Sidney was awake, kicking away the blankets, and reminding herself: she was alive, and Agatha was dead.

Sidney sat up amid the damp tangle of sheets. She was starting to get her bearings, recalling that she had been too ill to go to work and had gone back to bed. She glanced at the clock, then thrust her face closer, disbelieving. It was after three o'clock. *Did I really sleep away the entire day?* Probably she needed the rest. She was no longer nauseated or feverish. She was actually better, immeasurably better.

There was that sound again, she thought, lifting her head. Not a bang but more like a muffled thud. Definitely not a dream.

Sidney stiffened as it dawned on her. Someone was downstairs.

She looked around the bedroom as if it hadn't been her room her entire life, as if she might miraculously find a weapon, which would be the last thing she would ever possess. She should call the police. No, she couldn't call the police. Agatha had never allowed a phone upstairs.

Suddenly Sidney was shivering. She tiptoed to the corner where she had tossed her raincoat. With shaking fingers, she wrapped it closely around her and tried to think. Maybe she should wait it out. The robber probably didn't know she was home. It was possible, she told herself, that he would take what he wanted downstairs and leave. Her stomach began to feel unsettled again as she thought how naïve that was. Any burglar would go to the second floor where jewelry and valuables were likely to be.

The best she could do, she thought with an uncharacteristic decisiveness born of fear, was to get out of the house, immediately and silently.

Carrying her shoes, Sidney crept down the rear staircase. She hugged the wall to avoid the squeaky areas. Sidney, Agatha, and her grandparents had always used this set of back stairs more frequently than the front staircase, especially in the mornings, because it led down to the kitchen. Once down these steps, it was a straight shot to the back door.

She had padded most of the way down the steps when she heard another sound. It was the unmistakable clink of silverware against dinnerware, the sound of someone eating off a plate.

At the bottom of the stairs, Sidney cautiously peeked around the corner of the wall. What she saw caused her to both slump with relief and nearly laugh out loud.

One of the kitchen chairs was pushed close to the tall cupboards. The heavy oak chair must have accounted for the noises Sidney had heard in her sleep. A cabinet door stood wide open. Seated at the table, intently studying the back of a box of corn flakes, was a girl.

The girl held a spoon that seemed to move on its own volition, clinking against one of Sidney's ceramic bowls, traveling automatically from bowl to mouth, all while her eyes remained riveted on the cereal box.

Sidney was equally fascinated. The girl was a frail-looking thing who appeared no more than nine years old, Sidney guessed. She was not quite conventionally pretty but had a face that perhaps would grow to be beautiful. She was skinny, painfully so. Her clothes were far too large. Sidney's eyes traveled over the saggy, brown cardigan and floral-print blouse that seemed wrong for a young person but oddly familiar. They looked like the kind of clothes that an old lady would wear. There was something else in the girl's face, she thought. A kind of sadness that seemed as out of place as the clothes for someone so young.

After watching for another minute, Sidney decided to break the spell. She slid into the kitchen until she was in full view. The girl remained absorbed, as the spoon, dripping milk, continued its arc from bowl to mouth.

"Excuse me." Sidney's voice was timid, but the effect was dramatic.

The girl shot to her feet as if she had been poked with a pin. The spoon ricocheted out of her hand. Milk and soggy flakes splattered the table and wall.

"I'm sorry, I'm sorry," the girl stammered. "I was just eating…" She glanced at the table to check. "Cereal." She looked at Sidney as if that explained everything.

"Who are you?" Sidney didn't say it unkindly. "How long have you been here?"

"Three days. No, four days."

"You're kidding." Sidney suddenly recalled a few other noises that she had heard, or thought she imagined. "No, you're not kidding." How could she have missed someone being in the house for the better part of a week? She looked again at the girl and then around the kitchen.

"Were you in the basement?"

The girl looked miserable. "I'm sorry," she said again. Sidney waited for more, but the girl stood silent, her head hanging.

Suddenly out of breath, Sidney sat heavily in the chair the girl had just vacated. All the stress of Agatha's death, the house, work, it was all bad enough. But this? A child showing up in the kitchen? This was too much.

She didn't know what to do, so she decided to start with the basics.

"What's your name?"

"Phoebe."

"And how old are you, Phoebe?"

"Eleven."

Sidney was surprised because her waif-like appearance made her seem younger. In any case, Sidney thought, eleven years old was far too young to be wandering about and hiding in people's basements.

Sidney tried to think of another question but was stumped. *What do I know about kids?* she thought. She rubbed her hands over her face as if Phoebe might be a strange vision that would disappear. But when she dropped her hands Phoebe was still there, looking beseechingly at her.

It was foolish not to simply pick up the phone and call the police. Something, she wasn't sure what, held her back. She sighed and waved a hand.

"Why don't you start at the beginning and tell me what's going on?"

Phoebe swallowed and nodded but was silent for another moment. Then she said simply, "Your mother passed away, didn't she?"

Sidney was confused. "What?"

Phoebe started again patiently. "Your mother—"

"Okay, I heard you." Sidney jumped up, went to the sink, wet a dish cloth, and compulsively began mopping up the cereal and milk. It stood to reason, she told herself, that some evidence of Agatha and her recent death would be apparent, and even a child hanging around the house for four days would be able to figure it out. But it was unnerving all the same.

"How did you know about that?"

The girl looked ashamed. "There was a letter from a lawyer on the table."

Sidney resumed wiping the cloth over an area that was already clean.

"It's okay, you know. My mom died when I was little."

"I'm very sorry." Sidney straightened. "All right, where were we?"

"I ran away."

"All right."

"I ran away to find my father."

Slowly at first, then in a rush, Phoebe told Sidney everything, about her mother's death from cancer, about how her father married her stepmother, and then they had Bobby. He wasn't bad for a brother, Phoebe said. "Most of the time, neither is my mom, my stepmom, I mean," she said. But things had gotten worse in recent months. Her parents kept fighting and the fights kept getting worse.

"Do you mean physically fighting, like hitting?" Sidney interrupted, alarmed.

"No, they just yelled at each other. I could hear them at night. After a while, it would be so much yelling that it would wake me up. I don't know what they were fighting about, but they were really mad at each other."

Sidney nodded as Phoebe continued. "Then, one day, my stepmom told Bobby and me that my dad was gone. At first, she said he would come back soon, but he didn't. I couldn't believe that my dad would leave like that without saying anything. Without saying goodbye." Phoebe's eyes welled up. "I thought something happened to him. I begged my stepmother to look for him. Or call the police. She wouldn't even do that. She was mad at him, I guess. It made me mad at her that she wouldn't do anything. I got madder and madder because she wouldn't try to find him."

Phoebe wiped at the tears rolling down her face. Sidney, as she silently reached for a box of tissues and handed a wad to Phoebe, wondered if the tears were real or if this was all playacting.

"My dad is from Connecticut," Phoebe continued. "After he left, I found a postcard from him from Connecticut. My stepmom got it and didn't tell me. I just happened to find it. So that's where I'm going. I'll find him myself."

"Connecticut? You're a long way from there."

"I am? I was walking such a long time. I thought I might be close." Phoebe looked so crestfallen that Sidney tried to soften her statement.

"Oh, I mean you probably are closer. You must have come a long way already." Sidney watched with distress as Phoebe's face crumpled. Worse, the girl then sank right to the floor. Hiding her face in the crook of her arm, her shoulders shook with silent sobs. *This had to be real,* Sidney thought.

"Don't cry. Please don't cry," Sidney said helplessly. Her eyes darted around the kitchen. "Hey, how about ice cream? Everyone likes ice cream." She pulled open the freezer door. "I think I have some in here somewhere," she said, rooting among the bags of frozen vegetables.

"Um, I ate it all." The voice was muffled as Phoebe's head was still tucked in her arms.

"Oh." Sidney shut the freezer and looked toward the sink for inspiration.

"I'm still kind of hungry, though." Phoebe raised her head. "I'm really sorry about eating all your food. It's just that I've been so hungry. Most of the time when I was on the road, I was eating stuff out of garbage cans."

As Sidney tried to stifle her look of horror, she found herself filled with sudden resolve. It didn't matter that she really should be calling the police to turn in a runaway, or, at minimum, minding her own business. She needed to protect this girl. She would help her figure out what to do. Stripping off her raincoat, Sidney draped it on the back of the chair.

"Well, let's see if we can't fatten you up a bit," she said brightly and returned to the refrigerator. "I do have bacon and eggs. It will be like breakfast in the afternoon. After that, I can run to the store to get a few more supplies. How does that sound?"

She thought Phoebe, still sitting on the floor, appeared a little more hopeful. She started bustling about the kitchen. "Now while I cook, why don't you have a seat?"

Phoebe obediently scrambled back onto the chair and watched Sidney set bacon strips in a skillet and light the flame on the stove. They were both quiet until Sidney set the plate of food in front of Phoebe and sat across from her.

"Maybe you could get hot dogs at the store," Phoebe offered. "I mean, I'll eat anything, but I love hot dogs. I think because my little brother likes them so much, so it reminds me of him. He could eat hot dogs for breakfast, lunch, and dinner. That's what my dad always said."

Sidney's mouth twitched into a smile. "We'll see. Right now, let's talk about what we should do."

"What do you mean?" Phoebe was shoveling food into her mouth and protecting the dish with her other arm, as if Sidney might take it away.

"Well, shouldn't we contact your stepmother? She must be worried sick."

Phoebe's fork clattered on her plate. She looked at Sidney with panic. "No, no, no! You can't do that! Please don't do that. Please."

"Why in the world…" Sidney found Phoebe's sudden vehemence confusing. "Are you afraid of her? Did she hurt you?"

"No. Well, she did lock me in a room, but I got away."

This time Sidney couldn't stop herself from looking horrified. "Good God." She grabbed a napkin and patted her face. With jerky movements, she rose and went to the sink to fill the teakettle.

Out of politeness more than anything else, Sidney turned to ask Phoebe if she would like some tea but was taken aback by the sight of the girl reaching out to grab her hand in supplication.

"I'm begging you," Phoebe pleaded. "You have to help me."

Sidney reluctantly let Phoebe take her hand. She didn't know what to make of this. Finally, she said, "Shouldn't we at least let your stepmother know where you are?"

"You don't understand. She doesn't care. She's probably glad to be rid of me. She's been mad ever since my father left. She said I'm just another mouth to feed."

Sidney bit her lip. This was truly terrible, she thought. "What about school? They must have noticed that you're gone."

Phoebe looked away. "My stepmother probably told the school that I went with my dad." She hesitated. "I haven't been to school in a while."

"For how long?"

"Um, Christmas." It was a whisper.

Sidney leaned against the sink, gaping. This might be a case of child abuse, she told herself. She looked at the girl with new eyes, but it was hard for her to assess. She knew nothing about children—another reason she should contact the authorities.

"Did your stepmother ever hurt you?"

"No, not really, but I need to be with my dad." Phoebe's tone was stubborn as she inched away from Sidney.

Sidney mentally shuffled through possible options. Calling the police was what any normal person would do. The girl was a runaway. But they would be sure to return the girl to her stepmother. Would the woman have legal custody? Would they track down the father? Sidney had no idea nor experience in such matters.

Sidney pressed her palms against her head. This was too much responsibility. Then, with sudden clarity, she knew what to do.

"The best thing is not to rush to judgment," Sidney pronounced.

Phoebe looked puzzled.

"We'll take a few days and think about it." All Sidney was doing was delaying taking action, but she was relieved that she had found a reasonable answer. She was spared the unpleasantness of dragging this girl back to a home she clearly didn't want to return to, but she didn't entirely close the door on going to the authorities. In the meantime, what was the harm in giving her some food and shelter?

"You can stay here a couple of days. Then we'll decide from there," Sidney said firmly, as if this wishy-washy response was the ideal solution.

Phoebe was humbled. "Thank you," she said in a small voice.

In the awkward silence that followed, Sidney started to clear the table and stack the dishes in the sink.

"I can do that. It was one of my chores at home." Phoebe was again shy.

"Oh, of course. That's very nice of you." But Sidney felt a nagging worry as she watched Phoebe dig into the sink full of dirty dishes and pans. Should she leave Phoebe to her own devices with scalding hot water? The girl wasn't a toddler. But still. Agatha wouldn't have approved. *Then again, Agatha wouldn't have approved of a girl breaking in and hiding in the basement, or of my inviting her to stay on as a guest.*

Sidney put on her jacket and looked at Phoebe. "Will you be okay here until I get back? I guess that's a silly question." As she went out the back door, Sidney was rewarded with a smile and a nod.

Well, this certainly is an unexpected turn of events, Sidney thought as she clicked the seat belt into place and pulled the car out onto the street. A young girl in the kitchen. That was something she would never have imagined in a million years.

Surprisingly, this odd incident made her feel optimistic. Everything that had rained down on her in recent months had been dark, negative, and dire. But this—this left her feeling weirdly upbeat and hopeful.

The positive feeling didn't last. By the time she reached the supermarket she had sunk back into paranoia. She was certain the other shoppers could tell that she was harboring a child back at her house. Harboring…that sounded illegal. Did that make her a kidnapper?

She threw items into her cart and was relieved when she was finally on her way home. She pulled in the driveway with far less care than she normally did. As she lifted the trunk lid, she stopped short at the sight of all the plastic grocery bags. There was a rather alarming number. Maybe she had gone overboard trying to guess what an eleven-year-old would like. *What difference does it make?* she thought and began pulling out bags.

A voice in her ear made her jerk, nearly causing her to bang her head.

"Can I give you a hand, Miss Sidney?" It was Franny, the son of her neighbor, Mrs. Hammond. He didn't wait for a response but started dragging out bags.

"That's okay, I can manage," Sidney said quickly. She tried to position herself between him and the groceries. That was all she needed, she thought, Franny reporting back to Mrs. Hammond, who would speculate endlessly why she was buying so much food.

"Oh, don't worry. It's my pleasure," Franny insisted.

Sidney reluctantly acquiesced, deciding that there was no stopping him. The two were silent as they made several trips carrying the bags to the back of the house. Sidney motioned to him to line up the bags on the porch steps, mumbling that she would get them inside. She could imagine Franny's shock if he should march inside and discover Phoebe.

By the time they had everything neatly stacked, twilight had settled in. Sidney fumbled in her purse for her key. Franny lingered. "Needed a lot of stuff, huh?"

Sidney paused. He was only making small talk, she thought, as she pulled out her house key. "Okay, thank you, Franny," she said, looking back at him. "You can go now," she added lamely when he failed to move.

"I can help bring the bags in. I don't mind."

"No, I'm fine. Really." Sidney's voice rose, her edginess noticeable. She studied him in the dim light, and saw that he wasn't even looking at her. He was eyeing her handbag.

It finally dawned on her. He wasn't searching for information or gossip for his mother. He was looking for a tip. She shoved her hand back into her purse, pulled out a crumpled five-dollar bill, and held it out. Franny grabbed it and headed off, calling out a polite, "Goodbye, Miss Sidney." She watched until he was gone.

Only when she had everything stowed indoors and the door locked, did she feel calm. Drawn by a light, she headed to the living room. There was Phoebe, curled up on the sofa in a pool of lamplight, her face reflecting the flickering blue of the television. Phoebe was also in plain sight for the neighborhood to see through the large front windows.

Thank goodness she had gotten rid of Franny, was Sidney's first thought, followed by regret. Why hadn't she simply introduced Phoebe to Franny as a distant cousin who was visiting? That could have been the story he would have taken back to his mother. Sidney was irritated about the entire dilemma, one not of her making. Why did she have to resolve it?

Phoebe must have felt Sidney watching her because she first glanced up and then stood, putting herself in even clearer view of Mrs. Hammond and all the world to see.

"I can help you put the food away," Phoebe offered.

Sidney rushed to the windows to draw the blinds, making sure they were tightly closed. It gave her a moment to control the unexpected surge of anger. This girl was young, but it was hard to believe that she could be that ignorant of the risk that Sidney was taking by letting her stay and not calling the police. Phoebe was savvy enough to get so far from home without getting caught. *Look how she talked me into believing her,* Sidney mused. *Maybe she's smarter than I thought? Maybe none of her story is true?*

"What's wrong?"

At the sound of Phoebe's small voice, something clicked inside Sidney. Of course, what Phoebe told her was true. No child would make up something like that.

Sidney stepped away from the window. "It's just that after dark, it's easy to see in here." Tentatively, her arm started to reach out on its own accord as if she might pull Phoebe to her but then she pulled her arm to her side and headed to the kitchen. Phoebe trailed behind.

"Let me put these things away, and I'll fix us some dinner," Sidney said briskly.

"Can I help?"

Sidney looked at Phoebe, who appeared both eager and embarrassed. *She's perceptive enough to know I was upset,* Sidney thought as she nodded toward a kitchen chair. "Actually, I would appreciate some company." Phoebe brightened again.

As she stowed the groceries away and pulled out pots and pans for dinner, Phoebe chattered, all concern forgotten. Sidney, listening, realized with surprise that she was enjoying herself. It was both the company and the cooking, neither of which had been in great supply recently. She hadn't spent much time in the kitchen since Agatha had died; it didn't seem worth it to prepare meals for herself. If nothing else, it felt good to move in the familiar circuit from refrigerator to sink to stove, preparing the meal and setting the table. She listened to Phoebe's description of her journey, how she had traveled through different neighborhoods, on the bus, and through the park, relying on not much more than her wits.

How did a child that young, Sidney thought as she opened the oven door to check on the chicken, manage to get so far without help?

"I didn't try to get into any house other than this," Phoebe was saying. "One night, I stayed in a shed, but that's not the same. And it really stunk." She wrinkled her nose. "But your house—I don't know, I just had this feeling it was the right place to go. It looks so cool. Kind of like it was inviting me in."

"It's a Victorian," Sidney said automatically as she and her family had often responded to comments on the house. She glanced at Phoebe, who looked confused, and realized that the house's architectural style was meaningless to her. "Never mind," Sidney said. "It just was terrible that no one helped you."

"The pizza lady did. She came out of the pizza shop and brought me some food. She was really nice. She even gave me some money." Phoebe stopped for a second. Sidney cast a quick look, wondering if Phoebe would be expecting a similar contribution from her, but Phoebe was looking away pensively.

"That money helped me to keep going," Phoebe said, rousing herself. "A couple of days later, I got to this town."

Sidney set a dinner plate in front of Phoebe, who immediately dug in as if she hadn't eaten in a week. Agatha would definitely not have been pleased with this child's lack of etiquette, Sidney thought as she spread a napkin on her lap. She wanted to remind the girl about table manners, but it seemed presumptuous. Not yet, she told herself.

Phoebe not only ate quickly but also with gusto, continuing to talk as she chewed. Sidney's mother wouldn't have hesitated to observe that one should eat with one's mouth closed, but Sidney was stopped by something other than her natural reticence. *That's not my place. She's not my daughter*, she told herself. She looked down and picked at her meal with her fork.

Phoebe must have sensed Sidney's reaction, or maybe was suddenly struck by the gravity of it all. Her nervous chatter halted, and she looked at Sidney, shamefaced. "I just want to say, I'm sorry. I came in here without permission. I feel really bad about that."

"Well . . ." Sidney poured a small pool of ketchup on her plate and swirled a chicken tender in it carefully as she considered a response. Phoebe watched intently, as if she expected Sidney to mete out some punishment. "I guess you did what you had to do," Sidney said finally.

Phoebe looked relieved, apparently taking this weak statement as absolution. "Do you always put ketchup on your chicken?"

Sidney laughed in spite of herself and regarded Phoebe as she took a long drink from her glass of milk. Her tale was strange and wild, one that most people would probably dismiss, Sidney knew. But then, she thought, people always assume that children lie. She never understood why children were automatically thought to be fibbing, while adults, known to spit out whopping lies on a regular basis, were trusted without question.

Sidney wanted to believe Phoebe's story. In fact, she *did* believe it, most of it. The part she had trouble with was the stepmother refusing to let her go to school for months, and maybe the part about locking her up in a room. It wasn't that Sidney didn't think some people could do awful things, but she was skeptical because Phoebe seemed nervous when describing her stepmother's behavior. *She might be scared of her stepmother. She certainly was agitated when I wanted to call,* Sidney rationalized.

"When your stepmother wouldn't let you go to school," Sidney said carefully, "no one saw you all that time?"

Phoebe looked uncomfortable and fidgeted. "Well, my brother Bobby did. But he's little. He doesn't understand."

Maybe Phoebe was exaggerating certain parts of the tale? Maybe most of it? Sidney wasn't sure. She pushed her plate away decisively. For once in her life, she was not going to be afraid or cautious. Whether the girl's story was fact or fiction, she would do something crazy, and come to the aid of someone who needed help. *Her* help, Sidney's.

"How about some tea? Do you like tea?" Sidney rose from the table to get the kettle.

"I never had it. But I'll try some." Phoebe's expression was trusting. *How can I turn my back on her?* Sidney thought.

Once the teakettle whistled, Sidney poured and showed Phoebe how to dip the tea bag and then cradle it in her spoon. Phoebe awkwardly spilled milk onto the saucer.

"Is this like a tea party?" Phoebe asked, taking a sip from the teacup. "I always wanted to go to one."

Sidney couldn't help smiling. "Yes," she answered. "It's exactly like a tea party."

Eleven

Sidney was tempted to call in sick for a second day, but that would have been unprecedented and also probably unwise. She had already taken a big risk by failing to show up the previous day after the big bankruptcy announcement. Management would be looking for any excuse to get rid of people.

I definitely need my job, Sidney thought. *It appears I have another mouth to feed.*

Sidney bathed and dressed quickly and stood outside Agatha's bedroom door, closed for the first time in the months since her mother's death. She realized that her anxiety had less to do with what she was facing at work and more to do with Phoebe, who was sleeping in Agatha's bed.

Gingerly, Sidney opened the door a crack and saw Phoebe sleeping peacefully. Dark, coarse hair was all that showed at the edge of the blanket, but Sidney could see the up-and-down movement of her even breathing under the little mound of bedcovers. Sidney thought that this was likely the first time Phoebe had slept in a bed for who knew how long. The idea of leaving this child—even for a work day, even knowing that Phoebe had been wandering around creation for quite some time—seemed irresponsible on her part.

Sidney considered leaving a note of detailed instructions. No, that was preposterous. Phoebe had spent days in the house before Sidney had learned that she was there and she had managed to take perfectly good care of herself.

But at the last moment before she left the house, Sidney scribbled a note with her office phone number and propped it up on the kitchen table. There. That made her feel more like a responsible adult, she thought as she shut the door firmly, rattling the knob to make sure it was locked.

The further Sidney drove from home, however, the looser her bond with Phoebe became. Her anxiety about the girl diminished with each block, and she again began to fret whether she was making a mistake in not calling the authorities. Once again, she was torn. She would tell herself that she would call the police as soon as she got to work, but then she would remember the look of terror on Phoebe's face.

At a traffic light, she slumped in the driver's seat. Why couldn't she just stick to a plan? She could hear Agatha's voice in her head saying, *Don't be a ninny.*

Sidney watched the cars passing in the intersection and considered how "ninny" was the right word for her. She was too scared to live life, and always had been.

She had never been one to reflect on the direction her life had taken or to wonder if she should have chosen another path. It simply never occurred to her that there might be another path. She went through her days, fulfilling the expectations of her roles, those of diligent employee and dutiful daughter. Of course, now she was no longer a daughter. She missed that. She had never minded that role, not a bit. Perhaps it was because her mother was now gone that Sidney was suddenly questioning her purpose in life. Going to work, coming home, from one void to another. Maybe, the thought struck her, maybe this was why she found herself leaping at the opportunity to help Phoebe. It gave a purpose to everything.

The driver behind her had had enough and leaned angrily on the horn. Sidney jumped and looked up. The light was green.

She resumed her usual below-the-speed-limit pace. As she pulled into the Press parking lot, she knew there could be no more second-guessing about Phoebe. She simply had to let her stay, even if it meant that Sidney had officially taken leave of her senses. If her mother were around, she would offer one of her pithy sayings at this point. Sidney knew which one it would be: *Mind your own business.*

All the indecision and false starts of the morning had thrown Sidney off schedule. She had once again missed her usual early arrival time, the golden hour before the office bustle began, when the other workers started to trickle in. She didn't like to upset her routine, but it couldn't be helped.

Sidney stood at her desk with her coat on, listening to the buzz already building and looking through the small pile of notes and papers thrown carelessly on her chair during her absence. Apparently, life at Poppy Press had continued just fine since the shattering announcement that it was going under. It was surprising, though, to have accumulated enough work to create a pile on her chair after just one day out of the office. Business must be picking up.

Harry appeared, looking both relieved and annoyed.

"I'm certainly glad to see you've decided to grace us with your presence. Come to my office. Toni's not in today, and I have a lot of things that have to get done, so you're going to have to do them. What is it with you girls, anyway?" He was throwing the words over his shoulder as he went, not bothering to check whether Sidney was following or even listening.

Thirty minutes later, she was back at her desk, squinting at the scrawled notes she had taken during their meeting. They made no sense to her, even though she had created them. But Harry's instructions, which he had snarled and barked as she furiously tried to write them down, hadn't made much sense either. There were references to people, systems, and procedures that might have been completely clear to Antoinette but were a mystery to Sidney, who was unfamiliar with Harry's ways.

Sidney sighed and tossed the notebook on her desk. She would be better off relying on her memory. One thing she clearly remembered Harry saying was that she needed to mail copies of the completed white paper to a list of people—people presumably familiar to Harry and Antoinette, but strangers to Sidney. She wondered how she could accomplish that.

But all the confusing instructions paled in comparison with Harry's main assignment. He wanted Sidney to set up a conference call. "Immediately," he had said.

Sidney took another look at her notes. Sure enough, she had printed the word "TODAY" and heavily underlined it. Near the word were the names of those who were to participate in the call, including C. Post. That would be Charlie Post. Not only was she stumped on the rest, but she had never arranged a conference call before, and had no idea where to start.

Sidney went to Antoinette's empty desk and stared at it. With any luck, the assistant would be back the next day. She would save Sidney by handling most of the assigned tasks. Except the conference call, of course. Sidney was on her own for that.

Sitting in Antoinette's chair, she tentatively opened a few drawers. She hoped the information she needed wasn't somewhere on the computer, where there was no chance of accessing it. Just then she spotted an old Rolodex tucked in a corner. God bless Antoinette for using an antiquated paper system, she thought. She set to work, flipping through the tabs and trying to match up names with her scribbled notes, pausing only to say a small prayer. *Please let Antoinette come back tomorrow. I don't think I can survive Harry for more than a day.*

It was a mammoth struggle, requiring a crash course in teleconferencing from Angie, another administrative assistant, who was not enthusiastic about helping, but Sidney was able to schedule and initiate the conference call for that very afternoon. In a nervous, wavering voice, she announced the parties in a roll call.

"All right, thank you, Sidney," Harry said in a loud, dismissive tone. He was telling her to get off the line, Sidney realized. She was all too glad to comply.

Her finger was on the button, ready to depress it, when she had a dreadful thought: if she hung up, would the call end for everyone? She had failed to ask about that. Imagining the fury if the men were left with a dead phone line, she tried to think back if Angie had told her how to disengage herself from the call. She couldn't remember. She decided that the safest thing to do was to sit quietly and wait out the call.

She probably should have put the phone receiver on the desk so that she wouldn't hear the conversation, but she couldn't help herself. It wasn't much more than banter, complete with expletives and crude jokes. *Is this what men do in business meetings?* she thought. This would make it even more embarrassing if she were discovered. She looked in vain for a "mute" button on her telephone console, and finally settled for remaining as quiet as possible and hoping that the call would be brief.

In fact, the mood of the call had already shifted, with talk turning to business. Holding the phone gently and trying not to breathe, Sidney listened to Harry leaning hard on the others with his pitch, imploring them to invest in Poppy Press.

No one seemed especially keen on the idea. One man, whom the others deferentially called Mr. Heppelwhite, was blunt in his distinctive, gravelly voice.

"Save your breath, Harry," Mr. Heppelwhite interrupted midway through Harry's speech. "We've heard it all before. Bottom line, we just want to know how this can be a good deal? The word on the street is that New York is giving up on the Press, maybe wants to dump it. Taking it into Chapter Eleven bankruptcy. Sounds like you want us to sink dollars into a failing enterprise."

"Think of it as value investing." Harry was undeterred. "Look, nothing, including the bankruptcy thing, is a done deal. New York has been exploring options, it's true, but it's not necessarily going to happen. They're making some smart moves, so it will be a more efficient operation. Cuts, that sort of thing. In the end, good for the company."

It was quiet for a moment, and then several voices started speaking at once, some shouting to be heard. Sidney was starting to wonder if order would ever be restored when Mr. Heppelwhite took command.

"I, for one," he boomed, "am not going to invest a dime until we have an understanding—or at least a conversation—with that fellow who's representing the parent company. What's his name again?"

"Ayers." It was Harry, sounding subdued.

"Well, whatever his name is, we've got to talk to him. Now, I'm not making any promises, but set up a meeting with this guy Ayers, and we'll see how it goes."

There was another hubbub, interrupted this time by Harry.

"Hang on a minute. Just hang on. It might be wise to consider that…I mean, you should have all the information in hand before you go talk with Ayers. He might not be dealing in good faith." Harry seemed nervous, which wasn't like him.

"What the heck are you talking about, boy?" Mr. Heppelwhite demanded. "He's in charge, right? We can't make a deal without speaking with him. Are we all in agreement on that?" he addressed the group. There were murmurs of assent.

"Good, let's get the ball rolling," Mr. Heppelwhite said.

Sidney listened to clicks as they said their goodbyes and exited the call one by one. Her hand hovered over the telephone set, again ready to end the call, when she heard Charlie Post speak. "Harry, are you still on the line?"

"Yeah—anyone else here?"

Sidney held her breath but Charlie had already resumed speaking.

"Listen, Harry, get that wild man Ayers on board with this before the group talks to him. Once they start quizzing him, it will take about thirty seconds before they catch on that New York has every intention of going through with Chapter Eleven."

"I know, I know. I've got a plan, trust me."

"Do you?" Charlie waited, but Harry was silent.

Charlie gave a deep sigh that turned into a coughing fit. When it subsided, Harry asked, "Are you okay?"

Charlie gave one last cough. "I wasn't going to tell you this just yet, not until we settled all this nonsense." His voice regained its strength. "I've got cancer. It's not good."

"Oh, no." There was a long pause. "What—I mean, how long?"

"The doc says maybe a few months. Who knows? You take what you can get. I'm going to live each day I have left the best I can. Until I can't anymore."

Harry didn't seem sympathetic to this view. "You might have told me before we started all this," he said. He sounded testy. "There are the employees to consider. They're looking for you to come back and save the Press. They're counting on you."

"Pffft, come on," Charlie said. "As if you're suddenly concerned about the employees. It's true that the Press is my baby, and I would like nothing more than to come back to work. But you and I both want the same thing, and that's to get the Press back on track. In the end, you can run the place. You don't need me."

Harry was silent a moment.

"What about treatment? There's so much they can do—"

"Stop. I've chosen not to go through all that. I have my reasons. No need to worry about that. Instead, here's what I worry about." Charlie paused, and Sidney heard him trying to catch his breath. "I worry that this last-ditch effort won't work. I just don't know…"

"Don't know what?" Harry urged as Charlie's voice drifted away. *Can't you see that the man is exhausted?* Sidney thought, wanting to shout this at Harrry.

"I don't know," Charlie finally continued, "that we can convince these investors to bail out a company that clearly doesn't want to be bailed out."

"So you're saying to give up?"

Sidney didn't hear Charlie's response.

"What is it? What's going on?" Another voice, urgent, panicky, and loud, interrupted.

Sidney cringed. Harry and Charlie must have heard this voice, too. She pushed the button to end the call and looked up to see J.T.'s head bobbing above the cubicle wall. "Thanks a lot," she whispered.

"What was that about?" His voice was so loud that he seemed to be shouting, which, to Sidney, made things worse and was pointless. Why shout when he was a few inches from her ear?

"Please, keep your voice down," she hissed. She stood to look for Harry and, not seeing him, turned back to J.T., ready to give him a lecture and send him on his way. But the unexpected innocence of his expression made her relent.

"I was on Harry's conference call," she whispered. "Actually, I was only supposed to set up the call and not listen in, but—"

"You were eavesdropping?" J.T. looked at her with respect. "I didn't think you had it in you."

"I had to—oh, never mind. Here's the important thing. Harry wanted the call to convince a bunch of people—investors, I think—to put money into the Press. It's his plan to save the company, so we can get back on our feet. But the men aren't too sure about it. You want to know why?"

J.T. shook his head.

"Because they don't trust Ayers, that's why. They think he'll shut the Press down."

J.T. continued to stare, uncomprehending.

"Don't you see?" she pleaded. "Those emails you saw and the conclusions you reached? You were right. Ayers and New York are not committed to this place. They're not going to reorganize and get on track under the bankruptcy plan. We're just going to go bankrupt."

She took off her glasses to rub her eyes. "And another thing," she dropped her voice even lower. "I'm afraid poor Charlie Post can't help us out of this jam. He has cancer."

"Jeez." J.T. looked as if he had been struck. Within a few seconds, he appeared to be undergoing a full-blown panic attack. His breathing became raspy. As sweat beaded on his upper lip, he wiped it off with odd, mechanical movements.

"For heaven's sake, what's the matter?" She was growing alarmed.

"What do you mean, what's the matter?" he said, raising his voice again. "This is bad, very bad. Much worse than I thought."

"But this pretty much confirms what you thought, right? About the emails between Harry and Ayers?" Sidney said.

"Yeah, but what it really confirms is that things are much worse than I realized. We have no choice but to do something about it."

"Do something about it? What do you mean? And what do you mean, 'we'?" she added guardedly.

But J.T. was staring at her computer screen, lost in thought. "It's all becoming clear. The IRS. Yes! They must have been involved from the beginning."

"The IRS," Sidney repeated. She wanted to add, "You're kidding," but the look in his eyes stopped her.

"Okay, what about the IRS?" Sidney pressed after a moment.

J.T. sighed. "Do I have to repeat myself? They're here, undercover. The New York people brought them to spy on us. It's more information, ammunition if you will, for the bankruptcy. I found out about it because of the buttons."

Now, he's really starting to scare me, Sidney thought. She looked at him with as blank an expression as she could manage, and started to consider how she could get him to leave. At the same time, she was reluctant to speak. Anything she might say could set him off.

"The buttons on Ayers's jacket! I saw them," J.T. was saying. "They have a design on them that's probably some kind of code. I saw the letters, 'I-R-S.' Clear as day."

It suddenly occurred to her how fatigued J.T. looked. The circles under his eyes were so exaggerated, they could have been smudged ashes. His skin was paler than usual, with an unhealthy sheen. She eyed his white knuckles as he gripped the top of the cubicle wall. He was not acting normal. Or, she thought, maybe she was finally seeing the "normal" J.T.

Without any prompting, he turned to go. "If I were you, I wouldn't drive home. Too many terrorist threats. Take the bus. Yes, the bus. Public transportation is the safest."

After J.T. left, Sidney stayed in her cubicle for a few minutes. All was quiet, but still she hesitantly rose and peeked around the wall. It seemed too much to hope that no one overheard that crazy conversation, but the area was empty. Harry wasn't descending upon her with recriminations for listening to the conference call or with a set of new, impossible orders. Thank goodness, Sidney thought, returning to her desk. *I don't know how much more drama I can take.*

The new version of J.T. was more than dramatic, she thought. It was unnerving. Thus far she had put up with J.T. out of simple politeness, not friendship. It was how Agatha raised her. That, and the fact that he had no one to talk to. She felt sorry for him. But what if J.T. were spiraling into some form of madness? He might even be dangerous.

Sidney shook her head. Despite what she had just witnessed, she couldn't believe that J.T. had mental issues. She had had a bad day and was overreacting. He was just upset. Everyone at the Press was upset. That was it, she told herself—but it probably didn't hurt to follow her earlier decision about steering clear of J.T. The problem was, he always just seemed to pop up.

Sidney looked at the mess on her desk, normally so tidy. Papers and notes were strewn everywhere, the big Rolodex taking up a large portion of her desktop. She picked up a sheaf of papers, weighing them in her hand before tossing them back on the desk. There was only so much a person could handle, she thought. Resentment flashed through her and just as quickly receded. She leaned back into her chair, exhausted.

J.T., she told herself, was just going to have to deal with his demons on his own.

Twelve

At home, Sidney fell with remarkable swiftness into a comfortable routine with Phoebe. After a week, Phoebe might have always been part of her life. After two weeks, Sidney felt that she had slipped easily into the role of surrogate mother.

They talked each night as they cleared the supper dishes together, Sidney washing and Phoebe drying. The discussions spilled over long into the evening, the two of them at either end of the living-room sofa, lasting well past when Sidney ordinarily retired and what should have been Phoebe's bedtime, and made it harder in the mornings for Sidney to struggle out of bed with the alarm. But each evening as Phoebe started asking questions, Sidney found herself once again reminiscing about her family or telling long stories of past events. It was baffling that an eleven-year-old was the least bit interested in an old spinster's boring life. But Phoebe listened, entranced as Sidney inevitably got caught up relating her family history and telling old stories she hadn't thought about in years, about her grandparents, aunts, cousins, picnics, and holidays, funny incidents, family lore, and everyday occurrences. To her amazement, the stories spilled out of Sidney, as if a tap had been turned on.

Talking to Phoebe felt curiously natural, as if she were catching up with a relative about family goings-on. Sidney often had to remind herself that the girl was a stranger. Once or twice, the thought struck her that Phoebe was perhaps only looking for a family. The poor thing had been discarded by her own family, Sidney thought, sadly watching Phoebe eagerly latch onto the old stories. But then, Sidney had to admit, she was in desperate need of a family herself.

Although the evenings were filled with camaraderie and a growing affection for Phoebe, each morning Sidney opened her eyes to a mental debate. Should she keep up this façade or do what most reasonable adults would do—call the authorities? No matter how many times she pushed the thought aside and reminded herself that she was only helping Phoebe, the nagging questions would surface. Wouldn't the authorities make the proper determination about Phoebe? It wasn't up to her to decide, was it? She even practiced making the phone call. Then every day she found another reason to talk herself out of it. She repeatedly gave Phoebe and herself another twenty-four hours, then another, and another.

She had to admit that she liked having Phoebe there, but she wasn't sure that this was entirely fair to Phoebe. As a matter of child welfare, if one were looking at it objectively, it would likely be better to let the authorities handle it. But the fact was that Sidney had fallen in love with Phoebe. She loved her with the same intensity she would have felt had Phoebe been her own child. It became easy, far easier than Sidney would have guessed, to brush aside any concerns.

But even Sidney couldn't quite dismiss one development. As the weeks wore on, Phoebe grew less and less anxious to resume the search for her father. Soon she didn't even bring up his name. This was a development that Sidney found unsettling. She wanted to ask about it but didn't want to seem to be pushing Phoebe away. She could imagine Phoebe reaction—she might run away again, interpreting the question as an indication that Sidney didn't want her there. Sidney couldn't risk that. Just the thought of losing Phoebe was enough to make her go cold.

Harboring Phoebe (although she preferred to think of it as "sheltering") was the most disreputable, unethical thing Sidney had ever done, yet she was fully participating in it, even embracing it. She only had to look at the way she was lying to her neighbors. Sidney never dreamed that she would intentionally mislead others or find it easy to cover her tracks, but she had done both. And done them effectively.

It had started when Franny had helped her with the groceries. If he had discovered Phoebe, he would surely have told his mother. Sidney decided that a story was needed to keep Mrs. Hammond from learning the truth about Phoebe, one that would put a halt to any rumors before they could start. A few days later, Sidney stopped by to see Mrs. Hammond under the pretext of returning a Tupperware container that Agatha had long ago borrowed. Over a second cup of tea, and as Mrs. Hammond began to steal glances at the clock, Sidney casually mentioned that her second cousin's youngest daughter was visiting because the cousin had taken ill.

"The poor thing is recovering from pneumonia and just needs some rest. The family also thought the girl would make good company since, you know, Mother's passing," Sidney said. Mrs. Hammond looked at her sharply but didn't ask any questions about these cousins, about whom she had probably never heard one word from Agatha.

The lies emerged with a glibness that astonished Sidney, but she couldn't stop prattling.

"My cousin's daughter has a kind of chronic illness herself, um, very bad asthma. Or something very similar." She swallowed. "I might home-school her or get a tutor or something while she's here."

Sidney had to force herself to stop talking. She was really piling it on, which would be noticeable to a child, let alone to Mrs. Hammond, who missed nothing. Yet to her amazement, Mrs. Hammond seemed to be interested in this development, even approving of it, nodding sagely at Sidney's babble. Sidney gulped the rest of the contents of her teacup and found an excuse to make her exit.

As she hurried across the street, she hoped that Mrs. Hammond wouldn't reconsider about how odd a visit it had been and grow suspicious. Instead, as the weeks went on and Sidney had the courage to take Phoebe with her wherever she went, Mrs. Hammond fell into the role of doting grandmother. Soon all the neighbors were following Mrs. Hammond's lead. They called hellos to Sidney and Phoebe, usually stopping to chat, as accepting as if Phoebe had been in the neighborhood since birth.

As easy as it was for Sidney to rationalize everything, she still worried about Phoebe not attending school. It wasn't just the lie she had told Mrs. Hammond about planning Phoebe's education. Every day that she allowed Phoebe to play hooky seemed to drill home the fact that Sidney was not being a good guardian. It seemed worse, in some strange way, than pretending that Phoebe was a visiting relative, or even hiding her as a runaway.

Even so, Sidney did nothing about school, mostly because she didn't know what to do. She toyed with the idea of enrolling Phoebe locally but rejected it as far too risky. Hiring a tutor, as she mentioned to Mrs. Hammond, seemed daunting. Where would she find one? Teaching Phoebe herself also seemed impossible. Without knowing how to begin, inertia won out. She continued to allow Phoebe to stay home and watch TV while she was at work.

She had enough to deal with, Sidney rationalized. Instead of looking for new problems, she should tackle some current ones, such as finding the will that Agatha may or may not have hidden somewhere, or perhaps devising a plan in case her long-lost father showed up to claim the house as his own.

It didn't matter how many stern lectures Sidney gave herself. At the end of each day, she found herself rushing home to dive into the sheer indulgence of talking, talking, talking with Phoebe well into the night.

—

One evening, after Sidney and Phoebe had cleaned up the dinner dishes, they retired to the living room, as had become their routine. As usual, they began with the pretense of watching television, which soon developed into a lengthy tête-à-tête.

"What kind of friends did you have when you were about my age?" Phoebe believed in throwing out random questions as conversation starters. Sidney found it irresistible.

"Oh, I suppose I never had that many friends. I was the type of person who only had one or two good friends."

"Tell me about your good friends. Did you do everything together?"

Sidney thought this comment sounded wistful, but Phoebe looked as she always did—interested in what Sidney had to say. "All right," Sidney nodded. "I'll tell you about Elizabeth Humphries. I was best friends with her until Elizabeth decided another girl in our fifth-grade class was her best friend.

"So I was relegated to second best. I didn't mind at first. Then Elizabeth always seemed to be busy, and we spent less and less time together. We were still friends but not best friends, until her family moved away when we were in high school. But that period of our best friendship was great. You might even say glorious. Anyway, I thought it was the most glorious thing. We spent hours playing board games, riding bikes, that sort of thing. And talking. Especially talking." Sidney looked at Phoebe. "A little like you and me."

"What kinds of things did you talk about?" Phoebe asked.

"Oh, school, the kids in the neighborhood, what we wanted to be when we grew up. Elizabeth wanted to be a fashion model. I said I wanted to be a Supreme Court justice." Sidney smiled. "I guess that was a little too ambitious for Elizabeth because she said I needed a backup plan, a second choice if the Supreme Court didn't work out. She wouldn't leave me alone about it, so finally I said I wanted to be a famous artist on a ranch in the desert, like Georgia O'Keefe. Honestly, I had no intention of becoming anything like those big dreams. I suppose I had no ambition at all."

Sidney chuckled and looked at Phoebe, who seemed mystified. *Okay, I'm single-handedly destroying any dreams she might have*, Sidney thought, stricken.

"What about you?" she asked quickly. "How about your friends? They must be wondering why you haven't been around."

Phoebe turned her gaze abruptly back to the television.

"I don't have any friends," she said. "Not real friends. Most days I sit with a group of girls at lunchtime, but that's just so I don't have to sit by myself. The rest of the time, I mind my own business. You know how it is. You're not part of *them*, but you don't want them to pick on you."

"That's funny. At lunch I sit with a bunch of women just so I don't have to sit alone. I don't even like them."

They both laughed.

"It's okay, I guess," Phoebe said, serious again. "But now, you and I are friends, right?"

Sidney felt her heart catch. "Who wants to be best friends with Elizabeth Humphries anyway?"

Maybe it was friendship, or maybe they were just playing mother and daughter. Whatever it was, Sidney felt that their bond was undeniable. *What an unlikely pair we make,* she would think. *I'm old enough to be her grandmother.*

Once again, it began to worry Sidney that Phoebe would avoid the topic of her family and what had brought her to Sidney's house in the first place. It was nothing short of a quest, wasn't it? Shouldn't Phoebe be anxious, even desperate to find her father? But Sidney always came back to the explanation that the experiences Phoebe had gone through before finding her way to Sidney's basement had been traumatic. It stood to reason. Who would want to discuss it?

In a way, Sidney didn't even want to hear about Phoebe's father. She was angry with him. What kind of parent was he, to leave his family? How could he leave his daughter in the hands of a second wife who clearly mistreated her? Where was his sense of responsibility?

It got to the point that Sidney distrusted everything Phoebe said about the man in the increasingly rare moments she spoke of him. Those mentions usually amounted to Phoebe reverently repeating her father's opinions on a topic. Sidney, for her part, found it irksome, which she tried to hide.

"You know what my dad always says about flea collars for dogs?" Phoebe offered suddenly, spurred by a TV commercial. "He would say those things never work and aren't worth two cents." Phoebe waved a hand at the screen. "He said he had a lot of dogs growing up, and he would know. They got lots of fleas, I guess. Anyway, that's why he never wanted us to get a dog. They're dirty and a lot of work, he said." Phoebe looked at the TV screen longingly. "I always wanted a dog, though."

Into the silence that followed, Phoebe spoke in a small voice.

"You know what I would really, really like?"

"Please don't say a dog," Sidney said.

"What? No. It's just that I really need to get to Connecticut to find my dad. I was wondering...maybe you could drive me there?"

Sidney choked back an involuntary gasp of air. She shouldn't have been taken aback. After all, she had been the one fretting that Phoebe had stopped talking about finding her father. And something in Sidney had wondered if this request would come sooner or later. Sidney was the adult. Sidney had a car. Phoebe would see her as holding the power to reunite her with her father.

Yet, Sidney was stunned. She might have suspected this was coming, but she wasn't prepared. She had fooled herself into believing that this idyllic existence with Phoebe would continue without end.

"I..." Sidney started, then stopped. *How do I explain that I'm not that kind of person? I could no sooner drive to Connecticut than I could fly to the moon.*

With Phoebe's eyes pleading for an answer, Sidney impulsively decided to distract her. "Listen, I have something important to tell you. I need your help."

Phoebe blinked away her disappointment.

Sidney took a breath. Now that she had brought up the topic, she was at a loss to explain it. She hadn't discussed it with anyone other than Mr. Smithson. She had gotten yet another polite but anxious message from the lawyer again that afternoon. There was no question that this was a serious problem that Sidney had somehow managed to push away and ignore in the bubble world she shared with Phoebe. She had to do something, though, and if she didn't address it soon—Mr. Smithson, in his gentle way of delivering bad news, had implied—it could mean eviction. That would leave her and, therefore, Phoebe without a home.

In a halting voice, Sidney began telling Phoebe about Agatha's refusal to let Mr. Smithson draft a last will and testament for her. Here was her mother, Sidney told Phoebe, the daughter of a prominent attorney and founding partner of the law firm where Mr. Smithson practiced, so stubborn about such matters. Sidney was in the midst of explaining estate planning rules when she was stopped by the bewilderment on Phoebe's face.

"I'm sorry. This isn't easy for most adults to understand, and here I am going on to an eleven-year-old. Let me try again." Sidney shut her eyes a moment. "Basically, it comes down to this scenario. A person shows up at the law office after my mother's death. He says he's my father. How he heard that she passed or what he's been doing all these years, I don't know. All I know is that now he's claiming that he's the owner of this house. He was married to my mother, so he's got first rights. Or so he says." Sidney couldn't keep the bitterness from her voice.

"You told me about your dad leaving. Do you remember what he looks like?" Phoebe asked.

"He left when I was a baby. He never came back, not even for a visit. If he walked in here now, I wouldn't know him. I never saw so much as a photo."

"If you don't know what your father looks like, how do the people at the lawyer place know?" Phoebe's eyes were wide.

Sidney reached over and ruffled Phoebe's hair. "You are smart, aren't you? A very good question and exactly what I wanted to know." She smoothed the hair back into place. "Mr. Smithson has been looking into this man's credentials. He claims to have proof that he is my father."

Phoebe's look turned anxious, and Sidney thought that it was a mistake to unfairly pile her problems on top of Phoebe's own.

"All is not lost." Sidney gave a bright smile. "You see, we might take this to court. I don't believe any judge is going to turn over an entire estate to a man who disappears for fifty years and then shows up with his hand out."

"Is that what the lawyer said?"

"Well, not exactly, but he did say that it would help a lot if Agatha had left some kind of document that showed her intent to have everything go to me, especially the house. Sort of a makeshift will. That's what I wanted to ask your help with. Mr. Smithson thinks it's possible that Agatha wrote down her intentions on a piece of paper. That would count legally. She could have done something like that, and it would have been just like her to hide it. That was the way her mind worked. I started looking, but I think I'm going to need help."

Sidney glanced away, embarrassed by her sudden emotion. "Would you help me search for this will? I don't know if it exists, but I have to look. I can't lose this house." She reached in her pocket for a tissue and, finding none, used the heel of her hand to wipe her face.

Phoebe grasped Sidney's free hand. "Don't worry." She paused. "You know my dad always said, 'If there's a will, there's a way.' Funny now, huh?"

Sidney laughed as she found a box of tissues and blew her nose. "That was one of my mother's favorite sayings too. Maybe it's a good sign."

They agreed that there was no time to waste and began their search that evening. Sidney said she would try to think like Agatha, although, she warned, that was a task easier said than done. She closed her eyes and, after just a few moments, announced that they should start with the closet in Agatha's bedroom.

"Who knows what's in there?" Sidney said, leading the way upstairs. Throwing open the closet door, they looked up at a shelf loaded with cardboard boxes, the sort that could contain photos, memorabilia, and documents. They were neatly stacked, reaching almost to the high ceiling. "Maybe we'll get lucky," Sidney said. She was more than hopeful. For the first time in a long time, she was excited.

They stayed up late that night and for the two nights following, going through box after box. Sidney's hopes had at first risen when she saw that many of the boxes held paperwork, but most of it dated to her grandfather's time. There were tax returns and paid invoices from forty years earlier and a few innocuous documents related to the house, such as minor repairs. Other boxes contained more personal items, such as greeting cards and even Sidney's school report cards. But nothing of significance, such as a birth certificate or property deed. Or a will.

"This is getting us nowhere," Sidney said grimly on the third evening of searching. Phoebe was sitting on the bed, sorting through the contents of yet another box. Her hands full, she turned her head and sneezed violently three times in quick succession.

"Dust," Phoebe said and resumed pawing through the papers. "This one is pretty boring."

"You know what?" Sidney looked at Phoebe turning over the papers. "This is exactly why we're going about this the wrong way. If we're disturbing the dust, then obviously this stuff hasn't been touched in decades." Sidney stood before the open closet door and studied it again.

"And how in the world did an old lady get these boxes down on her own?" Sidney muttered.

Sidney turned and scanned the bedroom, tapping a finger against her lips. "Practically speaking, she would hide it in a place she could get to pretty easily, right? It wasn't in her dresser drawers because I went through them and got rid of most of her clothes." Her gaze fell on an old jewelry box. "Why didn't I think of this before?" she said.

The jewelry box stood in the same spot where Sidney always remembered it, on top of the high chest of drawers in the corner. It likely had been there for much longer. Agatha had received it as a birthday gift when she was a girl. One of Sidney's favorite childhood pastimes was when her mother took the jewelry box down from its perch and allowed Sidney to play dress-up with costume jewelry. Sidney had loved playing with the jewelry box and its many small compartments, even more than with its contents.

"I used to think of this as a treasure chest," Sidney said as she carried the jewelry box to the bed and set it gently on the comforter. They admired the dark wood and the fading, hand-painted flowers. "It's pretty," Phoebe said.

Sidney nodded and lifted the lid. She searched through it, including the drawers along the bottom, but there was no envelope or paper of any kind. She couldn't help feeling disappointed. "It was a long shot," she told Phoebe.

"Maybe there's a hidden compartment?"

Sidney looked doubtful, but she fetched a nail file from the dresser. Using the tip of the file, she pried up an edge of the felt lining of the box. She did the same with two other edges until she could easily lift the whole lining out and lay it gently on the bed.

"Well, what do you know." Sidney pulled out a white envelope. It was folded in half, and as she unfolded it, a small key dropped out. Phoebe clapped her hands.

"Let's not get too excited yet. We don't know that it's a will." But Sidney couldn't suppress her own exhilaration as she brought the envelope closer to the boudoir lamp. "I'm afraid to open it," she told Phoebe as she carefully peeled the paper back with shaking hands.

Inside the envelope was a single sheet of paper covered with handwriting. Sidney held it near the light and began to read.

"Well?" Phoebe asked impatiently.

"It's not a will. At least, I don't think so. It appears to be a letter, addressed to me."

"Okay, but what does she *say*?"

"She says ..." Sidney paused. "It does say that she wanted me to be okay financially, so maybe this is her attempt at a will in way. But mainly it says that there is an inheritance in addition to the house. My grandfather had a life insurance policy. Let's see...it paid out a lot of money when he died. My mother had the money all these years. Apparently, she was saving it for me."

"That's good news, right?" Phoebe asked cautiously.

Sidney wiped her eyes and turned back to the letter. "Yes, good news. Really good news. God bless her, Agatha was taking care of me to the end." She read more. "But some not-so-good news. She hid the money somewhere in the back yard. It's not giving many clues, but I don't know—it sounds like she might have buried it."

Phoebe whistled. "Wow, buried treasure!"

"Yes, but how would she have the strength to do that? Although," Sidney answered her own question, "my grandfather died over thirty years ago. My mother would have been younger and stronger then. Not to mention resourceful. The letter only says the money is somewhere in the back yard. It doesn't say where." Sidney consulted the paper once more. "We might have to dig up the entire yard to find it."

Late that night, as Sidney padded down the dark hallway to the bathroom, she thought she heard a noise coming from Phoebe's room. She stood outside the door, which was slightly ajar, and listened, then peeked in. In the moonlight angling in from the windows, Sidney could see a little lump of blankets on the bed and realized that Phoebe was huddled under them. The sounds were muffled sobs.

Sidney felt actual pain in her chest. *I want more than anything to help her, but I'm too much of a coward to help her find her father. If I were her mother, though, her real flesh and blood, I probably wouldn't think twice.*

The next morning, Sidney called out sick again. She was probably ensuring the end of her employment, she thought as she hung up after leaving a brief message for Antoinette. But it couldn't be helped. She picked up her coffee cup and returned to her contemplation of her view of the back yard through the kitchen window.

Sidney had risen early after a fitful night's sleep and strange dreams of Agatha digging up yards and parks across town and burying many pirate-like treasure chests with padlocks. In her dream, Sidney dug up all of them and managed to pry them open, only to find them empty.

I can't go crazy over this money. But, she thought as she started to fix breakfast, the money would resolve a lot. First, she had to find the money.

When she climbed into bed the night before, still in shock that her mother had managed to keep five hundred thousand dollars a secret (and had Agatha somehow managed to keep all that money in cash? Sidney wondered), she resolved that her very first step should be paying Mr. Smithson a visit. She would show him the letter, which he could review and determine if it could serve as Agatha's will, maybe enough to fight the claim from that horrid man who purported to be her father.

By dawn, she had started to rethink the plan.

What if Mr. Smithson says that the insurance money must be shared with my father? Sidney felt a surge of anger at the idea of giving this mystery man anything. Although he was spending a lot of time insisting to the law firm that he was her father, he hadn't shown the decency to contact the daughter he had abandoned so many years before. It was wrong. She didn't want him to get the house or force a sale of the house. She certainly didn't want him to get a dime of the insurance money. Assuming she found it.

Absently sipping the coffee that had grown cold, Sidney studied the small back yard. There was the tall fence that she painted every year, and the rhododendrons, the lilacs, and other greenery lining much of the perimeter. She had lovingly tended to it all for more seasons than she cared to count. Wouldn't she have noticed a hole in the ground if her mother had decided to start digging one? There was also a large shed taking up part of the back corner. Maybe Agatha had hid it behind the shed? There were many places to search, but they would all have to wait until she returned from the lawyer's office.

No, she thought with sudden vehemence. She would *not* go to Mr. Smithson's. She wouldn't even return his phone call. Better to delay. For one thing, how did she know whose side Mr. Smithson was really on? He might really be representing her father, for all she knew.

"Good morning," a sleepy voice sounded behind her.

Sidney jumped, and coffee sloshed over the rim of her cup. "Good morning, Phoebe." She smiled at the girl. "Let's make you some breakfast because we have a big day ahead of us. We're going on a treasure hunt."

By late afternoon, Sidney and Phoebe were both exhausted, and the back lawn was badly pockmarked. They had dug randomly throughout the grass, and some of the holes barely broke the turf before being abandoned. Leaning tiredly on the handle of her shovel, Sidney looked at the ruined yard and thought, *This is a lost cause.* Despite all their efforts, there remained so much square footage still untouched.

"Let's go in," she said tiredly. "After a hot bath I bet we'll feel much better."

Phoebe, normally a most talkative child, nodded without a word. She dropped her spade and headed toward the house.

By the time dinner was over, Phoebe had regained some energy while Sidney was spent. They sat on the sofa, Sidney rubbing her sore biceps and trying to stay awake.

"I think your grandfather must have been kind of like my dad," Phoebe said. "What was he like?"

"Did all that digging get you thinking about my grandfather?" Sidney stifled a yawn. "Well, he was a great man, in my opinion. We loved my grandmother, of course, but my mother and I especially loved my grandfather. In fact, she named me after him. I had great respect for him. That's why when he asked me, I promised him I would stay and take care of my mother."

"Is that why you stayed here? To help your mother?" Phoebe asked. "Why you never got married and had kids?"

Maybe it was as simple as that, Sidney thought, taken aback. It certainly wasn't complicated, the oath she had sworn to her grandfather. Most people couldn't understand why someone would make, let alone keep, a deathbed promise, she thought. But it was sacred, that kind of promise. People didn't know. And in the end, did it matter what they thought?

Phoebe, impatient, broke into Sidney's ruminations. "So your grandfather asked you to take care of your mom?"

"Yes, he was very sick. But he didn't want to die in a hospital, so he was here at home. My mother was caring for him."

Sidney tucked her hands under her arms, remembering. "I have to say that I was no help to Agatha. Death might be part of life, but I was only a teenager, and I couldn't face it. Most of the time, I was downstairs watching television. Game shows, sitcoms, anything, but mostly old movies. I saw every movie on TV that summer. Now I can't even hear the titles of some of those movies without thinking of my grandfather."

Sidney paused and Phoebe waited silently.

"One night—it must have been after midnight—I was heading from the bathroom back downstairs to watch the rest of a Jimmy Stewart movie. I passed the front bedroom where my grandfather lay dying."

"The front bedroom I sleep in?" Phoebe asked, alarmed.

Sidney hesitated and considered telling the truth. "No, the other room," she said. "There was no way Grandfather could have seen me. I'm surprised he was even awake or aware at that point. But he knew I was there. He called my name, like this: 'Sidney, Sidney.' I was a little scared, but I went in."

"Why were you afraid? Was he a ghost already?" Phoebe's eyes were wide.

"No, not a ghost. But he didn't seem like Grandfather anymore either. Anyway, I went into his room. It felt like it was freezing in there. I think I said to Grandfather something like, 'Aren't you cold?' But he didn't answer. He didn't even act like he heard me. He just looked at me really intently. Even though he was so sick, his eyes were still piercing." Sidney stopped, remembering the scene.

"He said, 'Sidney, promise me that you'll take care of your mother.' So I said it as solemnly as I could, 'I will.' He must not have thought that was good enough because then he practically shouted, 'Promise me!' Where he got the energy, I don't know. It scared me half out of my wits. So I said, 'I promise. Cross my heart, I promise.' I didn't want to say cross my heart and hope to die, but you see why it was such an important thing."

Sidney stopped. Phoebe looked frightened. Sidney hadn't meant to scare her, so she hurriedly wrapped up the story.

"That's why I felt a sense of responsibility with my mother. Until the very end, I took care of her." Sidney couldn't help wondering, not for the first time, if her grandfather would have approved of how she had handled things or whether he would have faulted her somehow. Maybe he would have said, *Good Lord, Sidney, I didn't mean for you to sacrifice your entire life for your mother.*

"Maybe," Phoebe said, as if reading her thoughts, "now is the time to do all the things you want to do."

Sidney rose and busied herself plumping up the single, threadbare throw pillow and arranging it in its spot on the hard sofa, as she did every night before going to bed. "I know it's not that late, but we're both very tired. Let's get to bed. I do have to go to work in the morning."

"But it's still light out," Phoebe started to protest but then saw the look on Sidney's face. "Okay," she agreed.

What a good kid, Sidney thought for what must have been the hundredth time. Why would any parent abandon this child? Sidney watched Phoebe climb the stairs and then turned toward the kitchen. Since Phoebe had arrived, Sidney had gotten into the habit of making one last nightly check to make sure everything was locked up. Their security, Phoebe's mostly, was important. At the staircase. she was accosted by Phoebe, who had run back down to envelope her in a bear hug. A surprisingly tight one, considering the girl's spindly arms.

"Okay," she muttered, awkwardly patting Phoebe's back. "Let's get a good night's sleep, and—"

The ring of the doorbell was coupled with a sharp rap on the front door, only a few feet from where Sidney and Phoebe stood, and it jolted them. Heart pounding, Sidney went to the door and tilted her head to listen. Another loud pounding caused her to jump back. She drew a shaky breath, and after a bit, found the courage to ask in a quavering voice, "Who is it?"

"Sidney?" boomed a voice that sounded as if no walls or door separated them. "Open up. It's your dad."

Thirteen

Nicholas Baker arrived early for yet another Poppy Press "leadership" meeting. The meeting was mandatory. Not that Nicholas had much of a choice, even with meetings billed as optional. As the president's assistant, he had zero status and was expected to do as he was told.

Nicholas sat in the furthest corner of the conference room, as far away as he could get from the people gathering around the long, shiny table. He would attempt to blend into the shadows in the corner, he thought. Not much chance of this particular group acknowledging or even noticing him, he realized as he studied the others. They were trying to avoid small talk even with each other, so they wouldn't be inclined to engage him in conversation.

Just in case anyone might glance in his direction, Nicholas arranged his face into a stony expression, one that could be interpreted as bored. He definitely didn't want to appear interested. It might lead to them drawing him into the discussion. Worse, it could be a sign that he was party to what they would be doing. Nicholas refused to implicitly endorse any of these activities—whatever it was that Ayers had cooked up and would demand of his "leaders," as he liked to call them when he wanted them to do his dirty work.

Ostensibly, Ayers had been brought in to rebuild Poppy Press. Nicholas believed that Ayers saw it as an opportunity either to make the company successful, which appeared immediately doubtful, or to move a failing business off the books. In either case, it was a means for Ayers to make a name for himself with the board of directors. In his mind, he would become their Mr. Fix-it, the guy with a keen business sense who generated profits and shagged off losses.

Ayers was well on his way to doing just that with Poppy Press when Harry started messing with things. The man had done nothing but screw up his plans, according to Ayers, who ranted about this to Nicholas almost daily.

At first, Ayers's plan to put the Press into bankruptcy seemed, to Nicholas, a logical way to proceed. The Press was not in good shape financially. Barely any print jobs were coming in. Bankruptcy would theoretically allow Poppy Press to recover from debt and hopefully emerge a stronger company. Okay, that made sense. What was troubling was Ayers's incessant tinkering with the plan and his crazy ideas to "save money," which he believed would make them look good both to the bankruptcy court and to New York. Then there was the increasing obsession to purge the Press of as many employees as possible. This seemed really disturbing. It made Nicholas physically ill. He couldn't even see how it made business sense. Would throwing half the staff out of work accomplish anything?

Ayers swept into the conference room and everyone automatically sat at attention. He took the seat at the head of the table and, with a flourish, pulled out a pair of reading glasses, opened a leather portfolio, and studied the papers inside. Still silent, he handed several papers to Candace from Accounting, who was to his right, and nodded for her to distribute them. Candace, irritated, looked like she wanted to comment, but she settled for shoving the wad to the next person.

"You could get up and pass these around like a good girl," Ayers observed without looking up. Candace muttered under her breath.

"All right," Ayers announced, rubbing his hands together. "Let's get started, shall we? Who wants to go first?"

The group, who had been reading the papers with dismay, fidgeted uncomfortably until Harry Corcoran spoke up.

"Perhaps, first, you could explain what this is." Harry held up his paper. *He's actually smiling*, Nicholas thought, watching in amazement.

Ayers was not amused. "Obviously," he said acerbically, "it's a list of employees, broken down by department. You can see it, can't you? Name, department, and the names of those in your reporting chain?" He threw Harry a look over his glasses. "Or do I have to spell it out for you?"

"That won't be necessary," Harry responded evenly. "Yes, we can see that it's a list of employees. What we're wondering is, what do you expect us to do with it?"

The question was innocuous enough, Nicholas thought, but the effect—as he might have guessed—was volatile. Ayers's face turned an unpleasant purplish-red color, and his hands formed trembling fists. Nothing came out of his mouth initially, but when the words came it was as if his rage had expelled them.

"What am I expecting? What do I expect? I EXPECT," the president bellowed down the length of the conference table, "that we would have a little COOPERATION HERE, and that you people would give up some names that we can CUT from the payroll. Or haven't you noticed that this company is in bad financial shape? If we don't do something,we're all going to go down."

Fuming, Ayers scowled at the others as they recoiled. "You're a bunch of babies. I know what you're all thinking. 'How can I save so-and-so's job? I don't want to be the one to put someone out of work. Joe Schmo has six kids.' You all need to grow a spine."

There was a good thirty seconds of silence, finally broken by Ayers.

"Come on, come on. Let's hear it. Who's next on the chopping block?" Silence again. "Let's go!" Ayers exhorted. "Give up some names, or I will personally make sure each of you is the next one to lose a job."

The vice president in charge of pressroom operations, who bore the unlikely name of Buddy, cleared his throat. "I suppose we could spare Joe B. and Fred from second shift."

"See!" Ayers's eyes were dark pools, terrible to behold. "That wasn't so hard, was it? Even for a bunch of wimps. They're on second shift? Everyone on second shift goes. Next."

Buddy hesitated. "Do we shut down the second-shift operations then?"

Ayers sighed heavily and rolled his eyes to the ceiling. "No, you moron. Not if there's work for a second shift. What the hell do you think? The first-shift crew will just have to put in any additional work until everything is done. And I don't want to hear the unions complaining about overtime. Tell them they're damn lucky to have jobs. Next!"

Buddy looked like he wished he could disappear from the room. The rest were equally uncomfortable, Nicholas thought. Only Harry had a ghost of a smile on his face.

"Let's go! We need that list. Or do I have to start naming names? You don't want that, because the names might be yours." Ayers jumped up and began to pace in the small section behind the table. He looked like a deranged cheerleader, Nicholas thought. *Maybe today is the day that the bastard finally has a stroke. At least that would put me out of my misery.*

Candace spoke up. "Harry." It was spoken softly but took everyone by surprise. Even Harry seemed startled. Candace, clearly pleased by the reaction, suppressed a smile.

"Don't you have that woman in your group—Sidney, I think her name is? No one seems to know exactly what role she plays, except perhaps to be your little errand girl. I would say she qualifies as dead wood, wouldn't you?"

Candace looked around, now unabashedly wearing a satisfied cat smile. The group might detest Ayers, Nicholas thought, but people weren't necessarily falling in line behind Harry either.

Harry leaned back and tapped a pen against the legal pad on his lap.

"A woman named Sidney?" Ayers interrupted. "Whatever. How much value could she possibly bring anyway?"

Someone gasped and quickly turned it into a cough. Harry ignored it all and turned to Candace.

"Thank you for your thoughtfulness in bringing this up, Candace." His voice was milkshake smooth. "We have to be team players, I agree. But you might not know that Sidney O'Neill plays a very special role at Poppy Press." He paused for dramatic effect.

It worked. Ayers stopped and looked at Harry expectantly.

"Such as?" Candace asked. "As far as I know, she's a proofreader. How essential is she, especially anymore?"

"Ah, Sidney, the heart and soul of this place," Harry continued, undeterred. "Take her out of the mix, and the Press would fall apart. She's here early in the morning until late at night. She's given us sales leads. Who would have guessed that she had such a keen eye for that? Personally responsible for thousands of dollars of business. Never complains. Epitomizes the most valuable qualities you could ask for in an employee. Yes, removing Sidney would be like removing the Rock of Gibraltar."

Ayers sat down heavily. The room held its breath, waiting for another explosion. "So what? Put this Sidney person on the list." His words, however, were somewhat subdued, for Ayers.

"By the way," he said as he ripped a blank piece of paper from the pad in front of him, crumpled it, and expertly hooked it over several heads into the wastebasket in the far corner, "the list is not for layoffs. Repeat, not for layoffs. No, we're not going to give them the easy way out, so they can sit there and collect unemployment. Nope," he said quite cheerfully, "instead, you're going to have to fire them. Shouldn't be too difficult. There's something you can get on everyone. Even this Sidney person, who Harry apparently thinks is Joan of Arc."

Harry caught the assistant looking at him and gave Nicholas a broad wink.

A grueling two hours and twenty-seven names later, it was over. Numb, the managers filed out of the room in silence. Ayers shoved the list of those to be fired at Nicholas as he passed, and Nicholas clutched at the papers, following Harry out the door. They fell into step together, moving down the corridor, until finally Nicholas spoke. He had to ask Harry the question that was nagging at him. "Did you mean all that stuff about that woman—you know, Sidney? Was all that true?"

Harry snorted. "Could be, could be. I have no idea, to tell you the truth. I barely know her. She was added to my group recently. She probably has no business being in the sales group at all, but you have to work with what you get."

He glanced at Nicholas. "Oh, don't look so disappointed. I was testing. Testing to see if anyone in that room had a heart. Or a backbone." Harry turned down a corridor and said over his shoulder. "As you can see, no one did." He strode off, whistling.

Nicholas took his time returning to the executive offices. When he got to his desk, he looked through the sheaf of papers in his hand at the list of employees to be fired.

Yanking open his middle desk drawer, he rummaged through a collection of pens, stray paper clips, and rubber bands until he found it, the thick black marker. He uncapped it, and with a flourish, over and over again, Nicholas blacked out the name of Sidney O'Neill from the hit list until there was no evidence of her name, until he felt human again.

"They're putting a list together. All the ones who are the next to go," Helen Ebney pronounced to the Lunch Ladies, her head bobbing for emphasis. "I have it on good authority." A few women rolled their eyes. Helen was the girlfriend of a foreman who unsurprisingly was the source of her information. That fact managed to give Helen's news far less authority than Carla's.

Sidney, in her usual seat in the corner, tried not to listen. She tried instead to let Helen's voice blend with the other cafeteria sounds, hoping it all would become white noise. On this day in particular, she didn't need any Poppy Press drama. She watched the patch of sky that was visible through the upper window. It was her favorite spot, her glimpse of heaven. Today, though, the sky was a disappointing, dull gray, with little to differentiate it from the equally dreary walls of the lunchroom.

"Mark my words. They're putting a list together," Helen said, her voice growing louder with frustration as she realized that the Lunch Ladies weren't sufficiently impressed. She hoisted herself from the table. Not nearly as heavy as Carla, she nonetheless was plump and tended to wear clothing several sizes too small. She headed back to the food station, a sausage in her tight jacket.

"So they have a list. So what?" Carla didn't miss a beat. In the moments it took Helen to shuffle out of earshot, Carla managed to steer the conversation back under her control.

"Who do you think would be the first to go? I'll bet it's anyone over a certain age," Betsy offered darkly. Betsy was sixty-four but looked older, with wispy, white hair.

"Nah, they'll get rid of whole groups, like the people in Fulfillment," somebody said from the other end of the table.

"Yeah, and how about the mailroom? They could stand to be more efficient."

They took turns guessing possible victims. Even before this latest rumor, it had become a game for them, speculating who might get a pink slip. Sidney had long ago noticed that they always managed to exclude themselves.

Rigid, avoiding eye contact with her coworkers, Sidney tried to mentally separate herself from the group and their pointless exercise. But she couldn't block out their voices. She couldn't avoid hearing the fear surfacing amid the false bravado. It seemed that the more apprehensive they became that they would be next in the unemployment line, the more they relished this pretense of naming victims.

Sidney wanted to scream in frustration. She wanted to climb on the table top, look down at them with contempt, and shriek, *Why sit around and let them humiliate you? End this awful waiting! Get it over with! QUIT!*

But that was fantastical thinking. She couldn't imagine dispensing even a mild scolding, and it would be the height of hypocrisy if she did. None of them, including Sidney, had any plans to voluntarily quit. Each person was desperately holding onto the hope that something would happen, anything that would turn the company's fortunes for the better. Maybe Harry would pull off a miracle, or Charlie Post would come to their rescue. Their jobs would be saved, and they could continue to keep their families fed and their mortgages paid.

Sidney observed the women around the table. Most looked careworn, ready to give up. Still, quitting didn't seem an option. Perhaps they would be laid off, which would make them eligible for unemployment benefits. An employee who quit or was fired, everyone repeatedly noted, could not collect unemployment. This had become a mantra around the Press.

"This is all very discouraging," blurted Helen, who had returned and was bent over her dessert. She suddenly threw her spoon on the table and burst into tears.

As the other women spoke soothingly and tried to comfort Helen, Sidney twisted further in her seat until she was nearly facing the wall. She found this kind of scene intensely uncomfortable. Without even looking around the lunchroom, she knew everyone was watching their table. Just then, a pitiful sob escaped from Helen. Sidney felt the flush on her face deepen.

"Stop it!"

The command emerged from Sidney, full-throated and louder than the women had ever heard from her before. Everyone turned. Even Helen's pinched-looking face peeked out from someone's bosom.

"We're all in the same boat, Helen. You need to accept and deal with it. Or quit."

It could have been Sidney's imagination, but the others seemed to fall away. It became a confrontation between the two of them, with Helen's face contorting in anger.

"You have a hell of a nerve talking to me like that. You know why? You know that list they're working up? I have it *on good authority* that you're on that list, Sidney. You. Out of all of us here at this table, it's just you they're getting rid of. Like tomorrow. It's happening tomorrow. Let's see how much *you* accept it."

Struggling to her feet, Helen managed to retain some dignity by flouncing her hair as she left. One by one, the other women drifted away.

The shock that kept Sidney frozen to her seat as Helen's words rained down on her started to wear off as the lunchroom emptied. She could feel tears stinging her eyes and blinked them back. She needed to get a grip, she thought, gazing down at her hands.

When at last she dared to look up, she was alone. Everyone had left, and she was grateful for that. She needed a few moments alone to collect herself and digest what she had just heard. There was no point in returning to her desk and pretending to work. There wasn't any work to be done. And why bother, she thought, suppressing a shiver, when she was about to be let go? That is, if Helen was to be believed.

But in that moment, sitting in the vacant lunchroom and listening to muffled sounds of activity in the building, she knew it was true. She was the one who had to face facts.

Rationally, she had been aware of the distinct possibility that she might lose her job. Of course, she had known that. She was always reminding herself of that possibility. It was just, she thought, studying the familiar outlines of the high window, that she hadn't expected the fates to be quite so cruel. To have your mother die and then to have to fight for your house, not to mention taking care of a young runaway. Then to lose your job on top of all that?

It was a lot, more than most people could handle, and Sidney had never been that strong of a person.

If she were to voice these grievances to others, she could imagine them saying, "Oh, come on, it can't be that bad." That's what people always said when it wasn't happening to them. But this time, it was that bad.

She closed her eyes and prayed. *God, please don't do this to me.*

"It can't be that bad, is it?"

Sidney jumped and stared at J.T. as he dropped into the seat opposite her. She certainly would never mistake J.T. for God, but he had the most disconcerting knack of showing up at critical moments, as if he had a sixth sense, inside knowledge, or something.

She gave an imperceptible sigh and decided that she might as well confide in him. He probably already knew.

"My name is on the list of people who are the next ones to be laid off or fired. Whatever. I just found out."

J.T. didn't react. He simply gazed back, unblinking.

She gave him a closer look. Even in the dim light, he appeared hollow-eyed and disheveled. He looked as bad, maybe even worse, than he had the last time she saw him, when she thought he was developing some serious mental issues. His appearance was so worrisome that it managed to distract her from her own problems.

"You look terrible," she said bluntly. "Where have you been? I haven't seen you around."

J.T. dismissed the questions with a weak wave of his hand. Scanning the surroundings, he nodded a few times as if his suspicions were confirmed.

"Don't worry about where I've been," he responded after a long pause, suddenly agitated. "Who wants to know? Who's asking?"

He leaned over the table, his face inches from hers. Sidney wanted to jump up and escape, but she couldn't move. He wasn't touching her, but it was almost as if his hands were physically around her throat. For the first time, she was afraid of him.

Then a shadow crossed J.T.'s face. He spoke, his voice calmer, but Sidney was still unnerved.

"Look, if anyone asks about me, tell them you don't know. And you don't know, okay? That's why I haven't told you everything because it's better that way. Safer. They can't get anything out of you.

"I will tell you this much," he said, his eyes narrowing. "But first you have to swear you won't repeat it. Swear it! All right." His voice dropped to a whisper. Sidney had to lean forward to hear. "Ayers and those New York people? Anyone in charge of this disaster? The ones who did what they did to my brother? They got rid of him, and now you say they're trying to get rid of you? Don't worry. They're going to pay."

Sidney's mouth started to form the word "How?" but instead she managed to convert it to a simple thanks. That seemed to placate him. She watched him turn to leave, and wondered about his plans. How bad or dangerous could they be? Probably very bad, she answered her own question as J.T. let the door slam. She debated whether she should let someone in authority know what he might do.

I'm about to get fired, and yet I'm thinking of blowing the whistle? On somebody who's supposedly my friend? She laughed out loud. *They wouldn't believe me anyway.*

An even bigger question was, why should she care what happened to the Press? Management was not going to save her job, so why should she do anything to help them? It might be petty, but she had to start thinking of herself. Herself and Phoebe. Lately she automatically included Phoebe in everything.

If Sidney lost her job, her situation and Phoebe's would only grow worse. It was a shame that they had not yet been able to locate the insurance money. Sidney was beginning to believe that if Agatha had buried the money, she might have dug it up again at some later point. It was possible that Agatha had found that she needed the money, even if she had originally intended to save it for Sidney. That is, if she ever buried it in the back yard in the first place. If there ever was any money. Some days, Sidney didn't know what to believe.

The trouble was there were too many competing problems to worry about. For instance, Sidney's father. He was a big problem, one that was only getting bigger. After the warning from Mr. Smithson, she should have expected her father to make an appearance sooner or later. But she hadn't guessed that he would have had the nerve to show up at the house as he did, showing a level of audacity that even Agatha, who had despised the man, would have considered breathtaking.

Sidney frowned as she recalled the incident. Why had she let him in? That was a mistake, although she had had no choice. He had known she was there, cowering in the vestibule.

"Open up! Open this door!" he kept bellowing after Sidney's timid, wavering inquiry gave them away. Although she knew that he had to be in his eighties, the blustering sounds he made were nothing like that of a frail, old man.

His tirade built into a crescendo. Sidney stood by the door, head down and eyes shut, willing this awful man to leave. She felt rather than saw Phoebe's wide-eyed gaze from behind her. Then, the noise subsided. Sidney breathed again. She was just beginning to wonder if it had been that easy to wait him out when the first kick came.

It reverberated not only through the door but also the entire front wall. "I swear to God, I'll kick this door down if you don't let me in," he yelled. Another loud thump promptly followed.

Sidney gasped and, with shaking fingers, undid the dead bolt. She threw open the door, and her mouth also fell open.

As astonishing as it had been to hear from Mr. Smithson that her father had resurfaced, as difficult as it had been to wrap her mind around the fact that he would come back with the sole purpose of trying to take her house, and as much of a shock as it was to lay eyes on someone who might be her father for the first time at her age—she still wasn't prepared for the sight of him.

This person, whose appearance and personality had always been a mystery, was a very short, bald, wizened old man, with bowed legs and weather-beaten skin. He wore wrinkled cargo pants with the cuffs rolled up and a dirty windbreaker. If she had passed him on the street she would have taken him for a homeless person.

"How long were you going to keep me out there? I'm your father! The proper thing would be to answer the door and invite me in." He glared at her.

Flushing, she was tempted to make a sharp retort about propriety and the role of parents. It was on her lips, ready to come out, but it was neither polite nor how she was raised. *Agatha would have said it*, the thought came. *She would have had no problem sassing back.*

Feeling like a coward, Sidney reluctantly stepped back to let him enter. His bald dome shone in the lamplight as he swept in, as if he were already the homeowner.

With a glance at Phoebe, he growled, "Who's this? My granddaughter?"

"No." Sidney swallowed. "She's, um, she's visiting, that's all." *Why do I have to make excuses to this man?* This was annoying but she knew it was better to account for Phoebe. The last thing they needed was trouble on that score. Sidney felt Phoebe slip behind her and grab the back of her shirt. Sidney thrust a hand behind her in an attempt to shield the girl.

Fortunately, Sidney's father lost interest in Phoebe as he looked about the living room. In the soft lighting of the table lamps, the room looked cozier and less threadbare than it did in full daylight. Nodding in approval, he turned back to Sidney.

"I suppose it would be asking too much to sit down or get something to eat? I'm hungry. And I am your father, after all." Although he said this in a more subdued tone, the undercurrent of arrogance finally released Sidney's coiled anger.

"You're my father? So you say." She nearly spat out the words. "That person has been missing in action for more than fifty years.

He never acted like a father. My guess is he's dead. You must be an imposter."

The man stood before her, impassive, before breaking into loud laughter. Sidney stared. Even Phoebe peeked around to gawk.

"I'm not dead," he said, wiping his eyes. "And I plan on sticking around for a while. I always knew I would outlast your mother. That's why I kept feelers out, people who would let me know the day she finally kicked the bucket."

Sidney groaned softly.

"What's your problem? It's a fact of life, missy. We live, we die. And those who are left on this earth, those who are the rightful heirs, should inherit the property. I'm here for what's owed me."

"Owed you?" It came out as a whisper, but Sidney could feel the anger building into rage. "What is *owed* you?" It erupted in shrill tones. She tried to lunge and probably would have clawed him but for the firm grip that Phoebe had on her shirt, holding her back.

Sidney stood blinking. Just as fast as it came on, the boiling fury subsided. She was exhausted—tired of this whole mess. She pivoted toward the door and, with a weak, limp movement, opened it wide.

"Get out." She said it very quietly. Surprisingly, the old man didn't argue. He waddled on his bowed legs past Sidney and Phoebe. As he stepped outside, he turned and said, "Don't think this is the last you've heard from me."

Sidney wasn't sure, but she thought he might have been opening his mouth to say something further when she slammed the door shut in his face with a satisfying bang.

It had been a few days since this incident with her father—her alleged father, as she insisted on thinking of him—but as she sat in the empty lunchroom, it was still disturbing to remember. She hated to think that she was related to someone so crass. Someone so *mean*. How could her mother have been married to someone like that?

In the end, though, what did it matter whether this guy was or was not Donald O'Neill, her biological father? He had convinced the law firm that he was. And he, along with the events at Poppy Press, seemed bound and determined to wreck any hope that Sidney might continue with her life as normal. She wasn't equipped to handle these sea changes any more than the Lunch Ladies were. But, in a way—and she seriously thought she wasn't being melodramatic in this view—her life as she knew it wasn't only going to change. It was about to fall off a cliff.

Maybe she should help these events along and just end it all, Sidney thought. It wasn't morbid. It was practical. Then, she heard a small interior voice saying, *What about Phoebe? Are you forgetting that she's counting on you?* It was exactly like an old ploy of her mother's to bring up someone worse off to shame her out of self-pity. This time, it only served to make Sidney feel worse. Despite her own troubles, Sidney wanted to help Phoebe. For reasons she couldn't properly identify, this was the one thing she was clinging to—she desperately wanted to help this child, take care of her, maybe even help her find her father.

But in this, too, she was failing, Sidney thought, without caring if she was childishly caving into that self-pity. She couldn't help Phoebe because she couldn't even help herself.

Fourteen

It was the morning after Sidney had learned that she was on the hit list at Poppy Press. That had, surprisingly, not led to insomnia, as she had feared, but instead to a deep, dreamless sleep. At dinner, she had feigned interest while Phoebe chattered, but headed upstairs as soon as the dishes were finished, murmuring to Phoebe that she didn't feel well. That was true. She simply left out the part about imminent unemployment. There would be time enough for that, she thought as she clicked off the light and fell asleep.

Her eyes opened before the alarm went off. She glanced at the clock. It was a few minutes before five. Too early to get up.

Sidney stared into the darkness and tried to picture the day that lay ahead. It probably wouldn't take long before she would be called into the human resources office and then escorted from the building. In humiliating fashion, like the others. She would receive the same "perp walk," as Carla put it—paraded in front of the other employees with a security guard at her side.

At that moment she realized that she had a choice. Why put herself through this degradation? Why go to work at all? It was clear what would happen. She had received quite a gift from the poor, suffering Helen. Maybe all her coworkers had known that Sidney was on the list, but no one had had the guts to tell her. Not even J.T. Helen probably wouldn't have said anything either if Sidney hadn't provoked her.

And there it was, Sidney told herself. Poppy Press could go ahead and put people out of work, claiming this would save the company. They could continue to do it in their own cruel way, acting as if the employees had done something horribly wrong and deserved to be fired. But they could do all that without her. She was done being victimized.

I won't even bother to call in. I simply won't show up. The decision gave Sidney instant satisfaction. Her absence would barely put a dent in their plans, but in one small way, she was getting one over on them, defying management. It was so unlike her to be rebellious, but there were lots of things she was doing lately that were out of character. So what? She felt immeasurably better not acting like herself.

She rolled over, tucked the pillow under her arm, and a moment later, was back asleep.

~

Harry Corcoran was once again at his office at an early hour, much earlier than usual. In recent weeks he had been arriving twenty, thirty, even sixty minutes before his normal start time. He discovered that he liked an early start to the day, especially during this exciting time. Importantly, he could make sure he was a step ahead of Ayers.

Harry was feeling much more positive about things in general, and today he felt exceptionally good about his strategy. After the difficult conference call with the prospective investors, he had managed to smooth things over. Even better, he was close to persuading several of the wealthier investors to put up a significant amount to back his plan. Especially Heppelwhite, whom the others looked to as a leader. With Heppelwhite on board, the others would fall in line. Harry was tantalizingly close to sealing that deal, thanks to the visit he had paid Heppelwhite the previous evening. Harry could still feel the rush of excitement that came to him when he left Heppelwhite's home. He had used every ounce of his charm, and the result—a handshake agreement—was more than gratifying. Harry knew he had won.

It was a thrill, Harry thought with a satisfied smile, knowing that he was on the brink of closing this deal. Crucially, he had also convinced Heppelwhite to cancel the meeting with Ayers. That meeting seemed off for the moment, which was a relief. Nothing good would have come from it. Not only did Ayers have all the finesse of a raging bull, but he was also clueless about the exact details of Harry's proposal.

Ayers knew that Harry was using the white paper to drum up investors, but he was under the impression that any investment would be in shares of stock in the parent company. However, the scheme Harry and Charlie Post had in mind was different: attract enough investment money to buy back Poppy Press from New York.

No, Ayers would not be at all happy about that idea, Harry thought as he arranged his suit jacket on a hanger and hung it on the other side of his office door. In a way, he was looking forward to the moment Ayers learned that New York was out, and that Harry and Charlie Post were back in.

It was ironic that the white paper, which Ayers so critical of, had turned out to be a key part of the strategy, opening doors for Harry and Charlie.

I'm glad I wrote it, Harry thought, opening the folder on his desk where he kept copies of the paper. He paged through it again. His original intention had been to encourage an understanding, an *appreciation* of printing, especially the value of an investment in printing. He used the story of Gutenberg and his invention of the printing press to show the marvel of the printed word, and how it continued into the digital age. It was a risk, he had to admit.

He had no idea how it would be received. But it ended up a success, as far as he was concerned, a way to set the table for his sales pitch.

It was all worth it, even if Ayers never missed an opportunity to poke fun at Harry. What did it matter if Ayers belittled it? Harry would get the last laugh.

He flipped through the paper to the final section, the part that had been written by Charlie Post that was a perfect response to Ayers. Altogether, it was a perfect ending.

An Ending (or Beginning) Note from Charlie Post

This white paper has used the story of Gutenberg to show why printing, the printed word, is fundamental to our society. As this paper has shown, although Gutenberg may have been the genius who founded the "secret art" of printing, he received no credit for it in his lifetime. In fact, he didn't have an easy time of it at all. He was tossed about by events. He lost business partners to the plague. He spent his family's fortune on developing his invention. And when he gave the world his crowning achievement—the 42-Line Bible—he lost it all in a lawsuit. Late in life he was even dispossessed, forced out of his printing operations and his hometown. It must have seemed the end of printing and all that he had worked for.

Yet the story of printing didn't end with Gutenberg and his failures. His invention spread like wildfire. The seeds of his revolution were scattered throughout Europe and have come down through the ages from the fifteenth century to today. It is why we are presenting this background to show why investing in the continued success of one printer, Poppy Press, is a continuation of this mission.

Why should anyone care about the fortunes of one printing company? There is a lot at stake, including the livelihood of the Poppy Press employees, the value the company brings to the local economy, and the needs of our customers. Yes, the world is communicating in more digital ways, such as through the Internet, but contrary to popular opinion there is still a place for the printed word. There probably always will be.

That's the lesson in Gutenberg's tale. In the same way that people today say "Print is dead," the Dark Ages told Gutenberg "Print will never survive." Both statements are wrong.

It is not an understatement to say that our small printing company is part of a much larger fabric of enlightenment. It is why investing in Poppy Press not only makes good business sense. It is part of an effort to keep print alive and well.

Harry closed the folder and set it carefully at the corner of his desk with a little pat. He then began sorting through the neatly stacked paperwork Antoinette had left for him and opened a file marked "Confidential." His good humor dissipated when he saw its contents. It was Ayers's hit list.

"What a waste of time," Harry muttered. If things went according to plan, there would be so much work that they would have to rehire all the people they let go.

Harry picked up the file and began reading, glancing at the cover memo. It noted that each person on the list should first be notified by their manager before involving Human Resources "in order to make the process easier." Harry laughed aloud. Easier for whom? They were too chicken to tell those on the list that they were about to be fired.

Shaking his head, he glanced down the list, looking for Sidney O'Neill. He might as well get it over with. He read through the names twice. No Sidney.

Harry looked up and stared at the very boring watercolor on the opposite wall. This was very strange, unless…of course, that young guy, Ayers's assistant, Nick. He had seemed pretty upset about the whole thing. Probably still had scruples. Harry recalled that Ayers had left the list in Nick's care. He had likely made his own adjustments and had taken Sidney off the list.

Shrugging, Harry closed the file. It was no skin off his nose. As a matter of fact, it made it easier for him. He had a lot of work still to do, and he could still make use of Sidney.

Harry wandered out to Antoinette's station. She flashed a brilliant smile, as she did every day. She had been his assistant for some time, and he was well aware of her crush on him. He was pretty sure his wife was aware of it as well. His wife's uncanny ability to sense any indiscretion, even the hint of one, was enough to keep his behavior with Antoinette in check.

"Good morning, Toni." He stopped himself from eyeing her body. "Could you fetch Sidney and have her come to my office? I have a few chores for her today."

Antoinette's smile faded for just a moment before she forced it wider. "Sidney isn't here. Normally, she gets in pretty early." She seemed to want to say more.

"Okay. Where do you think she is?" He was more annoyed than curious.

Antoinette scrunched her nose in a way Harry couldn't help thinking was adorable. "Well, that's it. If she was sick, she would have to call in by the start of the work day, and she hasn't called. No one has heard from her." She thought for a moment and added, "Sidney's taken a number of sick days recently, I noticed."

Harry suppressed a sigh. He found unreliable employees tiresome, and he was growing especially tired of the topic of Sidney O'Neill. Some would say that she should be thrown back on the firing list, considering that she didn't care enough to show up for work. But then, he really didn't care either.

"Not much we can do about it, is there, Toni? Why don't you come in then, and we'll get you started on all the things that old Sidney should be doing." He winked at her and retreated to his office.

~~~
~~~

Nicholas Baker was late for work. It was nearly ten o'clock when he reached his desk and—without saying a word to Sondra, who shot him a look—switched on his computer.

It wasn't that he hadn't risen early enough. He had been up before dawn but had once again dragged his feet, finding any excuse to delay going to the office. *What exactly is your problem?* Nicholas scolded himself as he waited for the computer to run through its paces and open its programs. He liked to work. He simply hated this job. And the reason he hated his job was because he hated his boss. He detested Ayers, and that was making it more and more difficult to force himself to work each day.

Ironic, he thought, staring at the computer screen. He was probably the one person at the Press guaranteed a job, and while everyone else was desperate to save theirs, he couldn't care less what happened to his.

Perhaps he should admit that he wasn't all that uncaring about his fate. After all, he hadn't quit. Even though he came into work shockingly late, he always came in, generally after a long argument with the bathroom mirror.

He hadn't always hated his job. He used to love it when he was in the New York office and wasn't working exclusively for Ayers but for a group of executives. Nicholas felt honored when his manager in New York tapped him to join Ayers for this special Poppy Press assignment.

His girlfriend Nancy saw it differently. "It's not surprising that you were plucked for this role. It's not that you don't deserve it," she had said, loyal as always. "It's just, I don't know. Something about the way you describe this guy Ayers. He sounds untrustworthy. Creepy, even."

Nicholas had laughed it off. "How do you know? You've never even met him."

He should have listened to Nancy. Instead, he had signed up for the hitch at Poppy Press, believing that this assignment would be a career builder. Some career, Nicholas thought. He had been miserable for nearly a year, living out of a suitcase during the week and going home on the weekends to see Nancy.

For the first time that morning, Nicholas ventured a look at Ayers's office door. It was closed. That meant, he knew, that Ayers was hard at work figuring out how to make Nicholas and all the Press employees even more unhappy than they already were.

The thing was, Nicholas mused, Ayers believed he was making the right decisions about the Press. He must at least have convinced himself of that, although he tended to gloss over the fact that people might be hurt in the process and lose their livelihoods. Not only did workers' lives fail to figure into Ayers's calculus, but Nicholas believed that it didn't even occur to Ayers to consider them. What mattered to Ayers was Ayers's future, and Ayers's future depended on what happened, one way or another, with Poppy Press.

Nicholas glanced again at Ayers's office and waited for him to burst forth as was his style. Sooner or later, it would happen. It always did. But did he, Nicholas, have to subject himself to it every time?

It was a moment of clarity. There was a resolution for him, a way to come out of this with his psyche and maybe some integrity intact. He could either quit his job—or he could stop Ayers.

~

It was late May, technically still springtime, but unseasonably warm. The afternoon sun beat down with the intensity of summer heat as J.T. waited at the bus stop. It didn't matter whether he stood outside in the blazing sun or moved inside the plexiglass bus shelter where the plastic appeared to waver and was in danger of melting. It was all equally hot, J.T. thought, as he wiped his face with his arm. Yet, he noticed, the elderly man who had settled on the plastic bench inside the bus shelter didn't seem the least bothered by the heat. In fact, the old man wore a shabby, wool sports jacket buttoned up to the neck. J.T. gave him a look of disgust and turned away, again wiping away sweat.

Ordinarily, J.T. tended to perspire easily, but recently he found he was pouring out sweat. It had to be the result of his anxiety. Perhaps "anxiety" was too strong a word, but he couldn't exactly be described as calm. The crazy thoughts that constantly bombarded him didn't help. People assumed he had no awareness of how bizarrely he acted at times. Instead, he was quite aware. He even could observe his own behavior as if from the outside. It made him wonder. Maybe he really was the disturbed man described by the doctor he had been seeing, that shrink his brother and sister-in-law had sent him to. On the other hand, it could be something physical, not mental. Something easily fixed if he only went to another doctor and sought another opinion. But he wouldn't do that. No, he couldn't. Not yet. He had too much to do.

In the meantime, he did what he could on his own to suppress his impulsive behavior. He was always straining to think calmly and logically, but his thoughts remained a jumbled mess. That was probably why he was always sweating. His thoughts created a heat all their own.

J.T. looked down the street, searching in vain for the bus, which was late. Sweat was again beading on his forehead. He kept still, allowing it to drip down his face and neck. Soon it was leaving dark stains at the neckline of his shirt. He hated this feeling of being soiled. He wanted to go home.

Maybe he should go home. The bus stop was only three blocks from his apartment. Easy enough to turn and go back. Forego the whole plan. No one else knew about it, so who would care if it was aborted?

J.T. was tempted to start pacing up and down the sidewalk. But it was important to avoid jostling the important item he was carrying in his backpack. Just thinking about it made the backpack feel weighty and burdensome. It also seemed to radiate even more heat than the sun. He wiped his head one more time.

What in the world was he doing? Now that he was going through with his plan, he couldn't recall the strong desire that propelled him in the first place. It was something important, just out of reach.

One perfectly clear thought floated to the surface. It was a reminder of the consequences if he chickened out. But exactly what consequences? For the life of him, he couldn't remember. He only knew it would be bad.

It had started to happen to him more and more frequently in the past few days—a sense of emerging from a haze of wild thinking and feverish activity, as disorienting as if he had awoken from a coma. It was the feeling he had the previous evening when he had finally completed the device after days of working on it. He had stepped back to admire his handiwork and found himself staring at it as if it were a UFO that had fallen from the sky. His entire vision of the project had vanished. He was not only suddenly uncertain whether this eclectic collection of parts would work the way he needed it to (despite his confidence while building it), but he barely recognized it as his creation.

It had to be the drugs or, rather, the lack of them. He had run out of the medication that the doctor, along with his brother and blasted sister-in-law, had insisted he needed.

His brother's wife had feigned concern about J.T.'s welfare, but he was on to her. "You need help, and we're going to help you," she had told him sweetly. Yeah, they would help him until they wouldn't, J.T. thought bitterly. They were paying for the doctor and the prescriptions until recently, until the point when he needed it the most. Hal had inexplicably turned on him. In that last, terrible phone conversation, Hal, calling from his nice home in North Carolina, purposely picked a fight. When J.T. tried to defend himself (what else could he do? J.T. thought, still disturbed by the uncharacteristic argument), Hal interrupted him to announce that J.T. was no longer his responsibility and that he, Hal, was cutting off all financial support. Going forward, Hal made it clear, J.T. would be on his own. "You're certainly old enough to be on your own, aren't you?" Hal asked into the shocked silence and, without waiting for an answer, hung up with a quiet click.

Hal had refused J.T.'s calls since then and, true to his word, had stopped sending money. J.T. continued taking the meds until his supply petered out. He didn't like how they made him feel, but they did seem to help him think more clearly. Since he had been off them for the better part of the last week, he could see a difference, and maybe it wasn't such a bad thing. It could account for his coming out of this fog. He wondered if the medication had contributed to his frenzy and what he had viewed as his beautiful, crystalline thinking. He thought he had been so brilliant, but maybe, just maybe, those meds were making him as crazy as a loon.

Spent and sweaty, he stood swaying at the bus stop. He no longer thought about returning home. He couldn't say why. Maybe it was lethargy. He continued to wait for the number 53 bus, occasionally wiping his face and scanning the blue, cloudless sky. Another fifteen minutes passed. He began worrying that it might be too hot. Somewhere in his research he thought he read that eighty-two degrees Fahrenheit could be a critical point. He wasn't sure exactly what happened at that temperature, but it was precisely why he wanted to execute his plan before the summer. Yet here he was, standing at a bus stop in May, and it felt like July.

It didn't matter. Regardless of the weather, he had to do something. Events at Poppy Press were getting out of hand.

J.T. scanned the street one more time, but still no bus was in sight. Maybe when he was doing all that research he should have checked the bus schedule. After all, public transportation was supposed to be his escape route. J.T. looked over at the patiently waiting old man, and was about to ask whether he had any knowledge of the bus schedule when the number 53 lumbered up.

As J.T. started to climb on board, he was once again overcome by a wave of panic. He hesitated, his hand on the bus's folding door, one foot raised to step up onto the black rubber-ribbed surface of the main cabin. Despite the heat, he was frozen, unable to make himself move forward. The old man waited behind him, silent.

"Come on!" the bus driver yelled over the rumble of the diesel engine. "I don't got all day."

With a mammoth effort, J.T. pulled himself up and dropped a bus token in the slot. "Excuse me, do you know the temperature outside?" he asked as politely as he could.

"Do you think I'm a weatherman or something?" The driver snapped the door shut, nearly closing it on the old man who was struggling to board. The driver jerked the vehicle sharply from the curb, the momentum throwing J.T. into the front seat. Luckily, J.T. thought as he righted himself, he hadn't been pushed full force against the backpack.

The backpack. He shouldn't lean against it. He carefully shrugged it off his shoulders, trying not to disturb the woman sitting next to him too much. After much effort, he managed to extricate himself from the straps and move the bulky bag to a spot between his knees.

J.T. had barely gotten situated when the bus careened past a slower-moving car and screeched to an abrupt halt. The doors collapsed open, and two men boarded. One was young and looked to be in his twenties, with a shock of shiny dark hair and a demeanor of overwhelming self-assurance. The other was bigger and, despite the warmth, wearing a windbreaker emblazoned with the logo of a local television station. He waved a small, hand-held camera as he hoisted himself up the steps. He stopped and aimed the camera at the bus driver.

J.T. felt a new wave of panic. What was a camera crew doing on the 53 bus? Had they somehow found out about him? The familiar paranoia rushed up, threatening to choke him.

The young man, a reporter, inched closer to the bus driver.

"Good afternoon. We're from Channel Four," he intoned. "How would you like to be the Human Being of the Week?"

The bus driver allowed himself an icy glance at the two, then resumed his studied gaze out the windshield. "Just pay your damn fare and sit down," he said wearily.

The two exchanged glances. The reporter shrugged and motioned to the cameraman, and they took a side-facing seat. Much to J.T.'s consternation, they were directly across from him. He faced forward and tried to avoid watching their every move, even though that was what all the other passengers were doing.

"This is a waste of time," the reporter muttered to the cameraman. He jerked his head slightly to indicate that they should get off at the next stop. Dutifully, the cameraman rose and tried to hang onto a pole as the bus lurched forward.

"Don't go yet." The words came from J.T. before he even realized it.

The Channel Four pair looked in his direction, and J.T. felt he could see himself reflected in them: a pasty guy with clothes dark from perspiration, clinging to a large backpack that was better suited to a camping trip than public transit.

"What's with that thing?" The reporter pointed to the backpack. "It looks pretty serious."

J.T. ignored him. "I know things that are important. Newsworthy things."

"Okay." The reporter gave a small hand signal to the cameraman, who surreptitiously flipped a switch. The blinking red light appeared.

"Yes, at Poppy Press. There's stuff going on."

"Poppy Press? What's that?"

J.T. was exasperated that he needed to explain. Shouldn't the media know this? "Poppy Press. It's the printing place on Copeland Bridge Street," he enunciated as if they were lip reading. "I'm just saying it's kind of important. These New York people—they came in and took over. Now they're driving the place into bankruptcy and ruin. You should look into it. I think they're going to fire everyone."

The reporter raised his eyebrows in a gesture of politeness.

"And it's all the IRS's fault," J.T. added, nodding vigorously.

"Really? Why's that?" The reporter was taken aback.

"It's obvious. The New York people have made arrangements." J.T. leaned toward them. "You see that, don't you?"

The reporter shook his head slowly.

"It might not just be the IRS," J.T. said in a stage whisper. "It could very well be the FBI. Maybe both." He sat back and nodded, pleased with himself. "They think I don't know, that I'm not on to them, but I am aware. Yes, sir, I am."

The cameraman's eyes were wide. He looked at the reporter, who wouldn't meet his gaze, or J.T.'s either. Instead the reporter directed his attention to the back of the driver's head, as if willing him to get to the next stop. As far as he was concerned, the station didn't pay him enough to deal with nut jobs.

Just then, the driver brought the bus to a shuddering stop.

"This is where we get off," the reporter announced and quickly made his way to the exit, the cameraman following on his heels. "Thanks for the tip, buddy," the reporter called as he stepped down to the pavement.

J.T. watched them through the window as the bus pulled away. "Lucky they got that story," he told the rheumy-looking man sitting behind him.

J.T. looked out the window again and decided that he ought to reconsider his plans. It was best to put off this event after all. What did it matter which day he carried it out? It might be wise to delay in case he happened to appear on TV, brought to the small screen by that television crew. Not that he was worried about a television appearance. In fact, he welcomed the idea. It would shine the bright light of publicity on Poppy Press.

Suddenly, he couldn't wait to get back home and check out the news. It would be fine to disassemble his creation and wait another couple of days. In fact, it was a relief. Nothing had felt quite right about this anyway. He needed more planning. Maybe it was a good thing he ran into the Channel Four team.

J.T. stood so he could disembark at the next stop. It wasn't his regular stop, but that was okay. He would take a zig-zag route home, taking two, possibly three buses to throw those IRS agents off his tail.

Fifteen

When Sidney woke for a second time that morning, the sun was already high in the sky. She squinted at the clock. The time was startling: twenty minutes to eleven. She couldn't remember ever sleeping that late, even as a teenager.

She threw off the covers and sat up, feeling dizzy and slightly drugged, probably from too much sleep. "No sense wasting a perfectly good day off from work," she croaked. But still she didn't move. It seemed important to take a moment to plan and think clearly, so that she wouldn't fall into the trap of focusing on the empty days she was facing, long days of worrying about how she would make ends meet. No sense dwelling on the negative.

After a few minutes, though, her thoughts only went in circles. Best to move on with her day—what was left of it—and see how things developed. She rose, hurriedly making the bed and pulling on clothes. She would skip a bath, rather defiantly aware that this was another way she was breaking the rules.

She expected to see Phoebe downstairs in front of the television, but the living room was vacant. Sidney took a cursory tour of the first floor, then climbed the stairs again to check Phoebe's room. She even checked the basement. “Phoebe?” Her call was swallowed up in the still, dark air.

Trying to ignore the little knot of panic (*Phoebe ran away before, so she might do it again*), Sidney stood in the middle of the kitchen, trying to think through her pounding headache. A cup of coffee might clear her head, she reasoned.

As she filled the coffee pot with cold water, she glanced out the window above the sink. Then she looked again more closely, letting the water run unabated. There was Phoebe, hopping about, elfin-like, in the back yard. She was awkwardly holding a shovel that was taller than she was. By using all the weight in her tiny frame, she was jumping on the edge of the shovel in an attempt to break up the earth. Despite her efforts, the blade was barely marring the soil.

Sidney had to give her credit. She was still hunting for Agatha’s buried treasure. While Sidney had been at work, Phoebe must have been spending each day at this task, struggling to dig up the back yard bit by bit.

To what end? Sidney thought. When she had called off the search the previous week she told Phoebe that they had already wasted too much time and energy on it. “I can’t imagine my mother actually digging a hole in the ground,” Sidney had said. “And we can’t excavate this whole place. It’s pointless to keep trying.”

Obviously, she didn’t listen, Sidney thought as she watched Phoebe determinedly digging, her skinny arms shaking as she tried to maneuver the shovel. The sight made Sidney feel a sudden irritation with her mother, even outright anger. *If Agatha had trusted me, if she hadn’t been so stubborn*, she thought, *this could have been taken care of long ago.*

And there was the possibility, of which Sidney was becoming increasingly convinced, that there was no insurance money left. Agatha had probably spent it to keep them afloat. No money, no will. Maybe, in the end, no house either.

Sidney turned off the faucet and set the coffee pot on the counter, feeling guilt for her disloyalty. *Don’t speak ill of the dead,* she could hear her mother saying. She headed to the door to call Phoebe.

Distracted by her own thoughts, she forgot to give any warning. Phoebe, assuming that Sidney was at work, was so startled at the sight of her emerging from the house that she toppled over, theatrically, comically, on the grass.

"I think I just had a heart attack," Phoebe said, face down on the lawn.

"I'm sorry." The sun was strong, leaving Sidney feeling a little faint herself. She sat in the shade of the porch steps.

"I didn't know that you were still looking," she said to Phoebe, who had rolled over to face her.

Phoebe squinted up at her for a moment. "Someday we'll find that money. I just know it."

Sidney sighed. "And someday we might win the lottery." She held out a hand. "Come on, I'll make you lunch."

"Just like that first day when you made me lunch." Phoebe accepted Sidney's hand and scrambled to her feet. Sidney tentatively slipped an arm around Phoebe's bony shoulders, and they climbed the porch steps. "Yes, it is," Sidney said. "Just like the first day."

Over grilled cheese and tomato soup, Sidney related the previous day's events at work, the shock of learning that she was about to be let go, and a halting admission that she lacked the courage to go in and face it. She didn't know why she felt the need to confess it all, but in a way it was a relief to tell someone the unvarnished truth.

"I took the coward's way out. I didn't call. I didn't even pretend that I was sick. I've never done anything like that before." She fiddled with her spoon. "But I never lost my job before, either. It feels so shameful, this business of getting fired."

Phoebe watched Sidney's hand tremble as she stirred the remains of her soup. Phoebe was silent, then suddenly perked up and leaned forward.

"I've been thinking. I want to go out again soon to find my dad. I keep staying here, partly because you're so nice, but also I thought I might help you find the money. I know you say we shouldn't do that, but I wanted to give it one last try. Now, though…" Her voice trailed off, and she looked at Sidney from under her eyelashes. "Well, now, if you don't have to go to work, and you don't want to look for the money, then maybe you should come with me. Easy, huh? We can go to Connecticut together." Her nod began as emphatic but soon became uncertain.

In the lengthening silence, Phoebe's expression of hopefulness turned blank. She finally looked away. Sidney swallowed, wishing that she could tell Phoebe exactly how she felt. That she hated herself for her continued cowardice that was crushing Phoebe's hopes. That a grown woman had more childish fears than a child. Most people in her position (she had no job to go to after all) might have viewed the idea of a journey as a sort of adventure, but for Sidney, it might as well represent certain death.

At the same time, something inside of Sidney was already dying as she realized how bitterly disappointed Phoebe was. Disappointed in *her*, in Sidney. "I'm sorry," Sidney said stiffly. Then she added, "I guess I thought you might want to stay here." She didn't add that she sometimes daydreamed about Phoebe staying for good, them living happily ever after. *How naïve and silly*, she thought. *Of course, Phoebe would want to find her true family.*

Phoebe seemed to read Sidney's thoughts. "I do like it here. I really do. But I have to go and find my dad." Phoebe wouldn't look up, but something in her voice caught at Sidney's heart.

Sidney let her spoon rest neatly against the bowl and dabbed at her mouth with a napkin. Sitting very straight, she folded her hands.

"Phoebe," she said carefully. "I owe you an apology. I said I would take care of you, and I'm doing no such thing. I'm failing."

Phoebe's head popped up, and a range of reactions crossed her face. Slipping off the chair, she threw her arms about Sidney.

"I'm the one who's sorry," she mumbled into Sidney's neck in a voice so low that Sidney wasn't sure she heard it.

Sidney wanted to offer words of comfort but settled for patting Phoebe's shoulder. *I'm not cut out for this parenting stuff*, she thought.

Phoebe raised her head and when she spoke, Sidney couldn't help thinking that she was finding the emotional rollercoaster confusing.

"There is one place we haven't looked."

"Looked for what?"

"The money, silly." Phoebe grabbed Sidney's hand and led her to the kitchen window. She pointed toward the rear of the yard.

Sidney looked and saw the shed. She gazed at it as if she had never seen it before and as if she had not gone in and out of it at least weekly since she had been Phoebe's age. Sidney glanced back, puzzled. "The shed?"

"If your mom didn't *bury* the money, maybe she hid it someplace. Not in the house, maybe, but close by. Like the shed." Phoebe said this proudly, convinced that she had solved the mystery.

Sidney shook her head. "I've been in that shed a million times, cleaned it out, stowed things away there every season. Even if there was a place to hide something, which there isn't, I would have noticed it." She caught Phoebe's crestfallen look and added quickly, "But that doesn't mean we can't check it out. It could be like the purloined letter."

"The what?" Phoebe wrinkled her nose, but her face had brightened. Sidney continued to look out the window and mused, "Well, I suppose it wouldn't hurt to look there. It's not like I have to go to work."

Just then, the sharp ring of the phone interrupted Sidney, sending a jolt through her. It had to be Antoinette, wondering why Sidney hadn't called.

"The purloined letter," Sidney told Phoebe as she took her time moving deliberately toward the phone, "is from an old story about a missing document that everyone kept looking for, and it turned out to be hiding in plain sight." Sidney reached the phone but delayed picking up the receiver for a few seconds despite the insistent ring. Something told her this call could not be good.

When at last she picked up the handset, but before she could say hello, Mrs. Hammond's nearly hysterical voice came piercing across the line, loud enough for Phoebe to hear.

"Sidney? Sidney, listen to me. Thank God you picked up. Listen, listen. There's a man outside your house. He has a gun! He's standing in the street facing your front door, and he's got some kind of gun." There was an infinitesimal pause. "Sidney! Do you hear me?"

Sidney stirred, breaking the shocked, wide-eyed gaze she and Phoebe were locked in. "Yes. Yes, I hear you." She rubbed her eyes. "I—I don't know what to do," she said weakly.

"I'll tell you what to do, you should call the police," Mrs. Hammond screeched.

"Wait, no..." Sidney's eyes swiveled away as she pictured the questions, the explanations that would be required. Most of all, about Phoebe.

"Are you crazy?" Mrs. Hammond's outrage was genuine. "If you don't call 911, I will."

From the corner of her eye, Sidney saw Phoebe heading toward the front of the house. "Phoebe, stop!" Sidney stretched the wall phone's cord as far as it would go, holding onto this lifeline, still trying to reach Phoebe.

"Quick," Sidney called to her. "Lock the back door and put that chair up against it." To Sidney's relief, Phoebe obeyed. Sidney watched her drag a kitchen chair to the door before turning back to the phone. "I'm sorry. This is just terrible."

"Pffft." Mrs. Hammond was slightly calmer. "Who would want to threaten you like this, anyway?" she added, her curiosity getting the better of her.

"I don't know." Sidney stopped. "Wait, what does this person look like? Is he young or old?" She paused. "Bald?"

There was a brief sound of rustling as Mrs. Hammond adjusted her window blinds.

"Well, it's not so easy to get a good look at him..." Mrs. Hammond hesitated. "But he looks to me to be an older man. Not tall, sort of bow-legged. He's yelling something awful out there. I'm not sure what he's saying. All right, he just threw his hat on the ground and is stomping on it. One of those silly fisherman hats. He's very angry, Sidney." She paused. "And, yes, he's bald."

A cold anger spread through Sidney, a fierce determination that she didn't know she had. She would no longer be a victim. But it wasn't just for her own sake. She had Phoebe to protect.

"Mrs. Hammond, please be so kind as to call the police for me. I have someone else I need to call right away."

"Who in the world would you call at a time like this, other than the police?"

Sidney didn't hesitate. "Our lawyer."

Without waiting for a response, Sidney hung up and went straight to the narrow kitchen drawer which served as her junk drawer. She started searching, removing items and placing them methodically on the counter. She knew that she had Mr. Smithson's contact information both at work and in the living room, but she couldn't risk going to the front of the house where Donald O'Neill was. Not just yet. She was hoping that her mother also had kept it in the kitchen.

"What are you doing?" Phoebe whispered. Sidney, intent, didn't respond.

Finally, Sidney pulled an old, stained address book from the drawer and began thumbing through it, grunting as she located the law firm's number. She started to head back to the telephone, then paused to reconsider. Carefully, she placed the address book on the table. Maybe she needed to witness what was happening outside the house with her own eyes before calling Mr. Smithson, she thought.

"Stay here," she commanded Phoebe and disappeared into the dining room.

Sidney hugged the wall and tried to stay out of view of the front windows. At first, all seemed quiet outside. Then it started. Donald O'Neill was yelling a string of obscenities that could be heard as clearly as if he were standing in the middle of the living room.

"Wow," Phoebe breathed into her ear.

Sidney looked over her shoulder. "I thought you were going to wait back there," she whispered.

"I'm scared. Don't you think it's better if we stick together?"

Sidney gave a reluctant nod. "Okay, just keep behind me, and don't go near those windows."

Phoebe kept a hand on Sidney's back as they both crouched low to cross the living room. They reached the windows, and Sidney lifted an edge of the curtains to peer outside.

She had a surprisingly good view of the scene. Donald O'Neill, red-faced and barking, had positioned himself in the street squarely in front of the house. He indeed had a firearm, some sort of pistol, which was shocking to see, despite being warned. From the way he was waving it around, he seemed ready to fire at any moment.

Does he want the house that much that he would kill to get it? She was suddenly quaking. Gone was the steely resolve. Just like that, she was back to mousy, fearful Sidney. She let the curtain drop.

Yet, as afraid as she was, something told her that this was a stunt. Donald O'Neill, or whoever this person really was, might be crazy, but was he crazy enough to kill the person he claimed was his daughter in broad daylight, and in full view of the entire neighborhood? It had to be a ploy to scare her. One thing was for certain, she thought. He was doing a fine job of scaring her.

"SIDNEY, GET OUT HERE RIGHT NOW! I WANT TO TALK TO YOU. DO YOU HEAR ME?"

Sidney and Phoebe watched him march about the street, directing a high-decibel rant toward the house.

"The police are here," Phoebe said quietly.

"Shh, keep down." But Sidney craned her neck to get a view. A half-dozen patrol cars had materialized silently without using lights or sirens to announce their arrival. Sidney could see men exiting the police cars, running to take up positions behind vehicles and houses.

Donald O'Neill had seen them as well. He abruptly halted his rant and turned to face the authorities encircling him. In an astonishing shift from the maniac he had resembled only moments before, he exuded calm. He might have come off as perfectly ordinary had it not been for the gun he still held.

An authoritarian voice sounded through a bullhorn. "Put the gun down on the ground slowly. Your hands up in the air."

He immediately complied, setting his gun on the asphalt. "Look, fellas, I was just trying to…" he was starting to say when a crowd of officers overpowered him. He was on the ground before he could complete the sentence.

Sidney and Phoebe gaped by the window, no longer caring if they were in danger of flying bullets. They watched as two officers helped Donald O'Neill stand and led him handcuffed to the back of a police cruiser.

"It's over, right? He's going to jail?" Phoebe's voice shook.

Sidney looked at the police milling about in front of her house and wondered how to answer. Was everything going to be all right? She had doubts. Somehow this thing didn't feel like it was over. A real parent would comfort a child and tell her everything was okay, she reminded herself. But that would be a lie. She couldn't do that to Phoebe.

Sidney took Phoebe by the shoulders and spoke earnestly. "My guess is that he'll get charged with something. Maybe disorderly conduct or a firearms charge. But whether he'll go to jail and for how long," she hesitated, "I honestly can't say. So all we can do is figure out how to protect ourselves."

Phoebe gave a small nod, and Sidney relaxed her grip. "We also have to find out exactly what rights Donald O'Neill has or doesn't have on this house. He can't possibly be allowed to take it by force. But does he have any rights at all? That's why I'm going to call Mr. Smithson."

The color was starting to return to Phoebe's face. "He was creepy, that guy that night he was here. I was glad when he left."

"Yes, he was. We need to go about this the right way to make sure he stays away from us permanently. Let me think about this for a minute before I call Mr. Smithson." Sidney sat on the sofa, Phoebe sinking down next to her.

Sidney glanced over at Phoebe and had to look away before her emotions overwhelmed her. She needed to get a grip on herself. After all, this girl was not her daughter, not related, even if Sidney felt responsible for her, even loved her as if she were a member of her family. A half-hour later they were still side by side, a silent tableau on the sofa, Phoebe leaning against Sidney, when the doorbell rang.

Sidney rose and again flicked up the edge of the front window curtain. She drew a sharp breath. "It's the police," she whispered. "Go to your room and close the door. Don't come out until I get you."

Phoebe sped silently upstairs. Sidney was counting an extra five seconds when another rapping on the door sounded.

"I'm coming," Sidney called. She didn't know why, as appearances weren't going to count, but she smoothed her hair with her fingers before opening the door.

After a forty-minute interview with the imposing but polite patrol officer, Sidney had an intense headache. It had required all her effort to answer the officer's repeated questions and explain the complex situation involving Donald O'Neill. Granted, it wasn't an easy matter to convey all the family history. Agatha would have been mortified by the entire affair, let alone an officer of the law sitting in their living room asking endless questions, Sidney thought as she muddled through a contorted explanation of the various relationships. As she watched the police officer listening with a small frown, she had the disconcerting sense that she, rather than Donald O'Neill, was the one under suspicion.

She was struggling through a particularly long, meandering response, when the officer looked at the surroundings as if seeing them for the first time. "Tell me, do you live here alone?" he interrupted her.

"What? Alone? Why, yes. At least since my mother died. That wasn't very long ago." Sidney pressed her hands together until they were white. "Maybe you would care to speak with Mr. Smithson, my mother's attorney. I believe I told you about him."

"Yes, you mentioned." The policeman seemed bemused.

"You're sure I can't offer you some coffee or tea?" Sidney asked. It was her third attempt. "A nice glass of water?"

"No, no, I should be going." The policeman hoisted himself from the armchair, leather boots creaking, and headed to the door.

Sidney followed, trying to hide her relief.

"I don't suppose there's any way to keep him away? Donald O'Neill?" she asked as she reached for the door. "This has been pretty scary for…um, for me. Just plain scary." Sidney turned her head to look out on the street.

Busy putting away his notebook, he didn't appear to notice her stutter. "You could come down to the courthouse and file for a protection order. I'm afraid that's the best we can offer."

Sidney nodded and watched him retreat to his car. As he drove away, it hit her. She had been the final interview on the street. The officer had likely paid an identical visit to Mrs. Hammond, as well as to her other neighbors. All of them knew about Phoebe and could easily have mentioned her in passing. However, when asked the direct question whether she lived alone, Sidney had answered with an unequivocal "yes."

Bad answer, Sidney, she told herself. He knew she was lying.

Sidney tried her best to keep calm, but her voice shook as she called through Phoebe's closed bedroom door to tell her that the coast was clear. Phoebe wrenched open the door and started speaking in a rush of words but stopped when she saw Sidney's face.

"What happened? Is your father coming back?"

"How do you know he's my father?" Sidney automatically reminded her. "No, it's not that," she added belatedly.

"What then?"

"I'm afraid I've really messed things up." Sidney mumbled as she headed downstairs.

"How?" Phoebe was close behind.

They reached the kitchen before Sidney responded. She turned to Phoebe. "The policeman asked me if I lived here alone, and I said yes. Why he asked that, I don't know. But I lied. Then, when he left, I realized he had probably already heard about you from interviewing the neighbors. Or maybe even from Donald O'Neill. But the cop must have known I wasn't being truthful, and now they'll probably come looking for you and..." She couldn't finish.

Phoebe was quiet a moment. "Did he use those words, 'live alone'?"

"I think so. Yes."

"Well, you *do* live by yourself. I mean, everyone thinks I'm a relative who's visiting. Okay, so it's a pretty long visit, but I'm a visitor." Phoebe looked at her hopefully. "That could be your answer if they ask about it, right?"

Sidney could actually feel tranquility settling through her. It was remarkable. It *could* work. How this girl, a child, could calm her frazzled nerves that easily, she didn't know, but yes, she thought. She could always claim that she interpreted the officer's question that way, and it didn't occur to her that a visit from a distant relative counted as "living there."

"You are so smart." Sidney impulsively planted a kiss on the top of Phoebe's head. "Okay, now let's get this call to Mr. Smithson over with before I lose my nerve."

Sidney imagined that she would be in control during her phone call with Mr. Smithson. She would ask crisp, pointed questions and demand answers that would make all the problems associated with her inheritance and so-called father disappear. She should have guessed that the call wouldn't follow that script. After the first few minutes she began to wonder if perhaps Mr. Smithson was playing her for a fool.

It wasn't as if talking to Mr. Smithson were an enjoyable thing, even in the best of circumstances, even if she could conjure up the thought of better circumstances. She found him intimidating. But at the moment it was necessary to talk to him because she rather desperately needed some answers. He was the only one who could advise her.

"Sidney!"

Mr. Smithson's unusually loud voice was startling, but she recovered quickly enough. "Yes, sir, I wanted to—"

"No worries, no worries. I know we've been anxious about your locating a will or similar document from your mother. But now, we have other fish to fry, so to speak."

"Actually, I did find something."

"What? You found a will?"

"Not exactly, but—"

Mr. Smithson's interest in her discovery dissipated as if sucked up in a vacuum cleaner. In a brisk tone, he said, "If it's not a will and testament, I'm afraid it does us no good. At this point, I'm not quite certain that even an ironclad will would help you. Now. We must discuss the current situation with Mr. O'Neill."

Sidney swallowed. All her intentions of steering the conversation were gone. She couldn't remember any of the questions she had planned or the points she had wanted to make. "Okay," she said, relenting to his direction.

Later, she decided that it was better that Mr. Smithson had directed things. He was, after all, in possession of critical information and had such a comforting way of conveying it. She could feel the anxiety subsiding, and listened with a serenity she didn't know she possessed, despite the terrifying import of his words. He was so mesmerizing that she didn't wonder until much later why he hadn't made an overture on his own to alert her to the danger, instead of waiting until she called him. It was just Mr. Smithson's way, she supposed.

The gist of what he told Sidney confirmed her worst fears: Donald O'Neill was not going away, and there was more than a slight possibility that he would take possession of the house.

"This is a complicated issue," Mr. Smithson said. "It may come down to whose name is listed on the deed of the house. We believe it would be in your grandfather's name, but we are still researching. We're also consulting with several firms that specialize in these areas of the law, just to be certain. It's due diligence. As you can imagine, Mr. O'Neill is quite impatient."

"And you're sure that this man is my father?" Sidney asked.

"What? Oh, yes, of course. We believe he's shown sufficient proof."

An uncharacteristic anger emboldened Sidney. "Really? Like what? I simply don't understand how someone who shirked all his responsibilities can appear after five decades, and everyone is willing to hand over an inheritance without knowing anything about him." She paused, breathing hard.

"And another thing," she added, "I never laid eyes on him before he showed up here. There are no photos of him that I've ever seen. Who can vouch for him? If he's shown you a marriage certificate, that could be fake!" She was shouting, as Phoebe stood by, wide-eyed.

"You make good points," he conceded swiftly. "I'll tell you what. We will do a DNA test to establish paternity. That will require you to stop by the office tomorrow for a brief moment, for us to collect a swab, and then we'll get one from Mr. O'Neill as well. Does that sound reasonable?"

Sidney mumbled something that could be construed as assent. She wanted to ask why a DNA test hadn't been suggested before, but that would only make her seem peevish. She had the distinct impression that the firm had already decided to pursue this option and that Mr. Smithson was using this to placate her.

"Now, Sidney," Mr. Smithson's voice dropped, conveying grave concern, "you should be aware of something else. More imminent, perhaps, and quite worrisome. About Mr. O'Neill's, shall we say, level of impatience?"

Sidney's eyes swung to Phoebe, who in turn whispered, "What is it?"

"We have explained everything carefully to Mr. O'Neill," Mr. Smithson continued, "but I'm afraid he did not take it well. Particularly the expected timeline for a resolution to this, well, matter. I'm also afraid that he then said something threatening that was directed to you, Sidney. That's what I need to warn you about. He may very well show up."

"He already did." Sidney gave a brief rundown of the day's events.

"Oh, goodness. That's terrible." Mr. Smithson sounded distressed, more so than Sidney expected.

"There may be somewhat of an additional problem," he said hesitantly. "Donald O'Neill made a very specific threat, and I am now extremely concerned that he is unstable enough to make good on it. He said that if you didn't leave the premises, he would come over and flush you out." He added quietly, "Mr. O'Neill threatened to burn the house down."

Sidney sat back hard against the straight-backed chair. "How can this day get any worse?" she addressed the ceiling.

"What is it?" Phoebe repeated, gripping Sidney's arm.

"Let's just try to stay calm," Mr. Smithson said.

"I am calm," Sidney said. Strangely, she was. "Maybe he won't do that. He already showed up here with a gun. That was threatening enough."

Mr. Smithson was doubtful. "It's possible, I suppose, but I am concerned for your safety. Our firm doesn't handle criminal cases, so I wouldn't venture to guess exactly how the incident with Mr. O'Neill waving a gun might ultimately be resolved, but I think you have to consider the possibility that he could be released, even if it's on bail.

"I can also tell you that we will go to court posthaste on your behalf and file a motion for a protective order, and rest assured that we will bring up these threats he's expressed to us. Still," he added gravely, "you must consider the risk of him coming back. It's not safe."

His words poured over Sidney, but she was having difficulty processing what he said. Wild thoughts ping-ponged in her head. Finally, she went back to Mr. Smithson's earlier point, that Donald O'Neill could be a free man again in short order. Despite warning Phoebe of precisely this possibility, Sidney found herself incensed by the idea.

"Released! That can't be right. They took him away in a police car. He was brandishing a gun!" Sidney angrily paced to the corner of the kitchen, as far as the phone cord would allow.

She came face to face with Phoebe. "Is he coming back?" Phoebe whispered. Sidney shook her head and turned back to the phone. "Look, Mr. Smithson, there must be something more we can do. Can't we ensure that the police lock him up?"

"The law seems so unfair sometimes, doesn't it?" He sounded so smug in that moment that Sidney detested him. "As I said," he continued, "we will pursue our options, including a restraining order. Unfortunately, you should be aware that those orders often don't do very much to protect people. There remains a serious safety issue."

He took a long pause. "I'm going to suggest that you leave."

Sidney was stunned. Leave! Donald O'Neill was a menace who had already caused a police incident, threatened to burn down the house, and was harassing her no end—yet *she* had to leave? She clenched the phone.

"No," she said through gritted teeth.

"Now, before you answer, Sidney, I want you to listen," he said, ignoring her answer and launching into a lengthy speech peppered with platitudes. But it worked. Before long his soothing voice had lulled her into the belief that his proposal made sense. It would indeed be logical, as he said, to take every precaution for her personal safety and let the judicial system run its course.

This is a sign, Sidney thought. *God is literally pushing me out the door. I have to drive Phoebe to Connecticut to look for her father.*

Her next thought was: *What will I do for money?* There was the emergency cash she kept in an envelope upstairs, but that probably wouldn't be enough. She had dipped into it several times since Phoebe had arrived. Was there anyone she could borrow from? That would not only be an act of desperation but also out of the question. Who could she possibly ask?

If only they had found the insurance money… Mr. Smithson's voice pierced her thoughts, coming through like another message from heaven. "And if you need some money to finance this trip, the firm can certainly help you with that. We can have that cash available as well when you stop by the office tomorrow."

His dismissal of her thanks was gentle. "I'm just glad you see the sense in this plan," Mr. Smithson said. "Do you have a safe place to go?"

"Yes," Sidney said. "Connecticut. We have people there. Some friends."

She didn't feel any guilt about lying. She wondered if perhaps she was becoming a different person after all.

It was morning of one of their final days in the house. They still had packing to finish but would be ready to go soon. Not as quickly as they had originally thought, when they planned to escape within a day, but it had taken more time than expected to prepare for this journey. For Sidney, it was a journey into the unknown.

Sidney woke before dawn and slipped downstairs for a solitary farewell to her home. She wandered about, running her fingers along the furniture and walls, touching paintings that had hung there since her grandparents' time. It seemed important to touch things, as if she could hold the memory of them in her fingertips.

She went outside into the gray, misty air, and down the walkway. Pivoting on the sidewalk, she craned her neck to look up at the house, much the same way Donald O'Neill had done.

The Victorian was a hulking silhouette against the brightening sky. Sidney studied it with new eyes, trying to memorize every detail as if she didn't already know them by heart. Birdsong sounded from under an eave, joining the other birds waking in the neighborhood. There must be a nest up there, Sidney realized. For some reason, it struck her as inexpressibly sad that birds could continue to make their home there, but she could not.

Once we leave, I might never see the house again, might never again set foot in it. She took a deep breath. She had to face the idea that she could very well be homeless. That was what Mr. Smithson had, in his gentle way, tried to get her to come to grips with when she stopped by his office to pick up the money he had offered.

By rights, the very idea of being homeless and indigent should have stoked anger in her. She should have been outraged that she could actually be forced out of her home.

On the contrary, she wasn't angry. She was worried and frightened, yes, especially for Phoebe. If nothing else, it was safest to leave, and necessary for Phoebe's sake. Sidney suspected—no, *knew*—that despite the efforts of Mr. Smithson's law firm, Donald O'Neill would likely prevail. As difficult as it was to accept, she had accepted it.

She looked at the house with sorrow. It was probably only because she was such a pushover, but she had quickly conceded the battle. Without so much as a struggle, she had become resigned to the sure knowledge that Donald O'Neill would win and that she would have to find another place to live. For that matter, she would also need to find another place to work. Because there was also the fact that she was jobless.

Is anything going right? Sidney silently railed at the quiet house. A moment later, the sun rose over the horizon, throwing an aurora behind the house. The timing seemed to carry import. It could have been another sign, she thought.

No, Phoebe is the sign, Sidney told herself. Phoebe and her mission were keeping Sidney from falling apart and, more than simply distracting her, were giving her a sense of purpose.

As Sidney watched the house brighten in the glow of dawn, she suddenly grasped that in helping Phoebe find her father, she was also giving herself a chance of surviving her own crisis. She felt better, more serene than she had in a long time. Somehow her own problems would resolve, like magic. Somehow, she was suddenly certain of it, everything would work out.

Sidney gave a last nod to the house and went inside.

~

Adele was jubilant when she found Robert's pocket-sized address book. He had left it behind, still stashed in the back of the desk drawer. Perhaps he had forgotten it, or maybe all the contact information he needed was in his phone. Or, more than likely, he just wasn't interested in contacting anyone.

What did it matter? she thought as she tried to squash negative thoughts about Robert and his state of mind. She certainly wouldn't have bothered to try to hunt him down if she weren't so concerned about Phoebe. She still carried so much anger and resentment against him. If it turned out that Phoebe was with her father, it would be a great relief but would make her even more angry. Just thinking about it sent her in circles of rage. *How dare he assume that he could spirit Phoebe away, and I wouldn't care?*

She fumed again and again at the same scenario she had pictured dozens of times.

Adele flipped through the small address book and was gratified to see his aunt and uncle listed in his tiny handwriting. She prepared to call them, mentally running though how she would approach this elderly couple whom she had never met and who probably didn't know she existed. (*Hi, you don't know me, but I'm the soon-to-be-ex-wife of your nephew Robert.*)

Then she caught sight of another entry in the address book. Jay Locke. Could that be Robert's brother? Adele could recall Robert mentioning his brother only once or twice, in passing. But the longer she studied the name, the more convinced she became—this brother whom Robert cared not a whit about was there plain as day, as if they spoke once a week. For all Adele really knew about her husband, perhaps they did.

Adele never knew why Robert and his brother had a falling out. From the rare, random statements Robert had made over the years, she surmised that it might have had something to do with the inheritance from their parents, who were killed in a car wreck when Robert was a teenager. Or maybe that had nothing to do with it. Robert hadn't confided in her. Adele remembered when she once had innocently enough raised the topic of his family, he had reacted angrily. "Leave it alone," he had snapped.

Adele had raised her hands in mock defense. "Okay, okay! Just wondering why you don't speak to your family. I was only asking the question."

"Yeah, well, don't ask again." But the retort was more subdued.

Adele studied the name in the address book and wondered if she would get the same reaction from Robert's brother. *So he gets mad and hangs up. That's the worst that could happen*, she thought.

Before she lost her nerve, she tapped the number into her phone and, with a deep breath, waited for an answer.

—

Jay, it turned out, was warm and effusive (the opposite of Robert, Adele thought). Within the first few minutes of the call, she was congratulating herself on phoning him. Not only had she avoided all the awkward explanations that would likely have occurred with Robert's aunt and uncle, but Jay actually *wanted* to speak with her. Then the conversation took a sudden turn.

"It's so strange that you should call at this particular time," Jay said. "I'm so glad that we finally have a chance to talk, but still…the timing is uncanny. I only just heard from the police two days ago." He stopped. "Oh, forgive me, perhaps you already know?"

"Know what? Is Robert in some kind of trouble?"

No matter how angry she had been with Robert, the news relayed by his brother was like a physical blow. Adele stayed on the line for what felt like an hour, speechless and gripping the phone as Jay talked and talked. She listened, not really hearing much of what he said, and wondered if there would come a time when she would consider this a watershed moment, with all events marked by their occurrence either before this point or after.

~

When Sidney first announced to Phoebe that it was high time that they went to Connecticut and that she would drive them there, she felt uncertain and a little embarrassed. After all, she had made it perfectly clear that, as a notorious homebody, she had no intention of risking life and limb on a foolhardy journey to such a distant location. Now she was flip-flopping, not at all like a responsible adult. But as the words sank in, it took Phoebe only a moment to shift from confusion to pure joy.

"Really?" she cried, jumping up and down, grabbing Sidney's hand to try to get her to jump along. Then Phoebe suddenly stopped. "You know," she said, "I never stopped thinking about my dad and about finding him. I dream about him every night. It's just that traveling by myself…it was so scary before. I don't think I can go on my own again. But if you're with me?" She laughed and this time clutching both of Sidney's hands, swinging her about. "Together we can do anything!"

Without thinking, Sidney wrapped her in a hug. "I'm not sure I can offer much more than my car and my company. It's not like I know what I'm doing when it comes to searching for missing people."

Phoebe laughed hesitantly.

"What I'm trying to say is," Sidney continued, not certain why she felt compelled to tell Phoebe these risks, "I might be the adult, but I'm not all that sure how to go about this. But we're going to do the best we can to find your dad."

She smoothed the hair on the crown of Phoebe's head. "It's funny. I grew up without a father and never felt like I was robbed of anything. I miss my mother every day, though."

"I know. I had Adele, but it's my dad who I miss." Phoebe looked solemn. "Maybe we were just meant to help each other."

As Sidney gave her a tiny pat on the head, she felt a strange, new feeling swelling inside her. Perhaps it was optimism. Perhaps Phoebe's positive nature was rubbing off on her.

But any positivity Sidney had absorbed from Phoebe didn't survive the preparations for the journey. On the last morning, when they were set to leave, she rushed from room to room, her anxieties roaring back. She bit back the feeling that they were far too late, too late to find Phoebe's father or to escape Donald O'Neill. She had to fight off Agatha's voice and kept hearing in her head her mother pointedly remarking how Sidney had never been a brave person, never one to take any sort of risk, and how this adventure was certainly risky, an outlandish idea, really. Agatha's voice, full of concern, but reinforcing doubts. *Please,* Sidney prayed to drown out the voice, *help me to find the courage this time.*

The more the morning wore on, however, the more panicky she felt. By nine o'clock she was in a near frenzy over what to pack.

"We should be on the road by now," she muttered as she pulled out clothes from her dresser.

Phoebe, who had grown skittish since the Donald O'Neill episode, had overheard her. "Why? Are we in danger?"

Distracted, Sidney shook her head. "No, nothing like that." She opened the closet door again. "This is all new for me. This idea of being flexible? I'm never like that." Shutting the door, she sighed. "Maybe it's because I don't know how much to take with us. I keep changing my mind. Maybe we should just bring everything, as much as we can fit in the car. I don't know if it's a good idea to leave anything important here."

Phoebe looked at Sidney as if she had lost her mind. "Do we need that much? Isn't this just for a few days?" Phoebe asked. "After we find my dad, you're coming back, right?"

Sidney scanned the familiar surroundings, taking a mental snapshot. "I hope so."

Phoebe said, "You know what? When we find my father, I'm going to ask him to bring me back here, and then we'll all find that insurance money." She stuck out her hand. "Deal?"

Sidney sighed. "Deal." She let go of Phoebe's hand to fish a tissue from her pocket. She blew her nose loudly. "Okay, we'll pack for a short trip and just have faith that, uh…"

"That we'll have enough underwear?"

Sidney laughed. "Yes, and that everything will work out. We just have to have faith."

Sixteen

The layoffs continued at Poppy Press, at least one or two announced each day. A strange calm settled over the employees, a quiet that suggested that they had accepted their fate. A closer look showed that people were edgy, even more than before. Most of the remaining staff went about their work silently, some fearfully. A brave few tried to band together to support each other. Those still engaged in gossip and rumor-mongering kept it to whispers. No one wanted to hand management a reason to axe them.

At the same time, the underground rumor mill managed to run at full tilt. The most commonly repeated tale was that the whole place would shut down in a few months, perhaps as soon as in a few weeks. No Chapter Eleven, no reorganization, no return to viability. That was all just a smokescreen.

The Lunch Ladies heard these rumors, of course, and discussed them daily. Secretly, Carla had long since grown tired of the intrigue. She was tired of worrying how far and deep the cuts would go and whether she might be among the next ones out of a job. Carla didn't understand why everyone wasn't sick and tired of it all.

"I still say it's got to be John Ellis," Eloise was pronouncing to the group for about the hundredth time. "I mean, the guy just sits there in that broom closet all day. Hiding and reading the newspaper morning, noon, and night."

"Okay, Eloise, you made your point," Carla said. She gave a loud sigh.

Carla normally didn't get impatient, but then she was also used to dominating the conversation, holding court as the others listened. Others conversing, not letting her command the table—that was mutiny, as far as Carla was concerned. She had to put a stop to this.

"As a matter of fact," Carla talked over Eloise, succeeding in getting the group's full attention, "I have it on good authority that the long-awaited massacre, a *mass firing* of many, many people, will happen before the end of the week. *This* week." She sucked her lips into her fleshy cheeks. "I have that from an excellent source," she added. "We're probably all gone. Start making plans, girls."

The table fell into shocked silence. Carla nodded in triumph. By sheer force of personality, she had succeeded in regaining control. Once again, they were listening to her.

Eloise piped up defiantly, her face like stone. "You don't know what's going to happen. You're not management."

"Yeah!" came a muffled cry from the end of the table.

Carla opened her mouth to put Eloise in her place once and for all when a shadow fell across the table.

"Where's Sidney?" J.T. mumbled.

Carla eyed him. He looked bad, she thought. Like death. His baby face was not only paler than usual but actually gaunt. Lines and shadows had suddenly surfaced, along with grayish tufts of stubble, the result of several days of beard growth. His eyes burned red behind his thick glasses.

"Where's Sidney?" he repeated.

Carla blinked. "I have no idea. Apparently she didn't come to work."

Still expressionless, J.T. turned to leave.

"Hey, where are you going?" Carla called. The women watched the lunchroom door bang shut after J.T., then turned as one to Carla.

"With that loony tune, you just never know, do you?" she said, settling in comfortably. "Did I ever tell you the story of him and his brother? I think we have time for one quick story, don't we?"

The rear of the Poppy Press building was not nearly as intimidating as the front. Instead, it was flat-out dreary. There was an oil-stained loading dock with a pull-down metal door covered in graffiti. An empty lot neighbored it on one side, with a cyclone fence bent down in so many spots that it barely served its purpose as a barrier. The street running behind the building was not much more than an alley and seemed just wide enough for a compact car, let alone the trucks that needed to maneuver in and out of the loading dock.

J.T. stood outside the metal door, which he had propped open with a wooden bar to keep from being locked out. He needed a few minutes to get some air, to be free of the building. He breathed deeply, trying to ignore the seedy atmosphere. After weeks of absence, he had once again set foot in the building only an hour before and already felt suffocated by the place. It started with that encounter in the lunchroom. He couldn't abide that woman, Carla, always making snide remarks about his brother.

He only had spoken to her in an attempt to find Sidney. It was probably a terrible idea to tell Sidney his plans, but he liked to confide in her. She listened and didn't pass judgment, and he was no longer quite confident that he was doing the right thing. Sidney was the only one left who would listen to him. The day of action had finally arrived, and he needed somebody to bounce off his ideas, to remind him why he had been so certain to begin with. Someone to keep him from getting cold feet.

Just then the scarred metal door burst open, thrown with such force that it hit the adjacent wall. J.T. leaped out of the way. Gary, one of the pressmen, stepped out and lit a cigarette. A perpetually angry, diminutive man with a head slightly too large for his body, he wasn't one to make small talk. J.T. eyed him warily, but Gary didn't even look his way. After a few drags on the cigarette, though, Gary peered at him through a haze of smoke.

"What are you doing here?" Gary growled as he exhaled. J.T. turned away, coughing.

"Hey!" Gary said sharply. "Look at me when I'm talking to you."

J.T. turned back.

Gary studied him. "You know," he said, "it's hard to keep straight anymore who still works here, who's been let go, and who just walked out on the job. But I could've sworn you were one of the guys who just left. Thought you abandoned your job weeks ago. So I ask again," Gary leaned in, "what are you doing here?"

J.T.'s eyes widened. The employment situation at Poppy Press had been so chaotic lately that he had been certain that no one would be aware of his absence. He thought people would probably assume (if they noticed at all) that he was visiting his brother, or that he was on vacation. That anyone might keep track never occurred to him.

J.T. opened his mouth to respond, but he didn't know what to say. He took a step back.

Gary continued to glare, but to J.T.'s relief, he didn't move closer. Gary flicked his cigarette away with a snort and turned to re-enter the building.

"Why don't you do yourself a favor and stay away from here?" he said over his shoulder. "This place is bad news."

J.T. remained standing there for several minutes after the metal door banged shut. He breathed deeply and pictured himself responding to Gary, coming up with quick retorts, and facing down the confrontation. The anger was good, he thought. Thanks to Gary, he had rediscovered his bravery. He could finish what he started.

No turning back now, he thought and pulled open the door.

In J.T.'s view, it was a positive sign that he was able to retrieve the package from the janitorial closet without encountering anyone. As he made his way up to the executive suite on the fifth floor, the corridors and stairwells were as empty as a Sunday afternoon. Another good sign.

J.T. crept down the hallway, holding the package carefully before him with both hands. He dared to steal only a glance or two at the cardboard box he had taped up and lettered so precisely. He didn't want to misstep now—he was so close to completion. With the culmination of his plan he would finally achieve revenge, not just for himself and his brother, but for everyone at Poppy Press. Ayers would finally pay.

With that thought supplying fresh courage, J.T. reached the imposing frosted-glass entrance to the executive suite. Shrugging, he decided not to knock. *Just barge in*, he told himself as he roughly shifted the box under his arm, before catching himself. It was so important not to be reckless.

He pulled the heavy glass door open and entered.

It was far from his first time in the executive suite, but it seemed strange to him nonetheless. His plan had been to walk straight into the president's office and drop the package on Ayers's desk. He had not only failed to consider the difficulty of gaining access to Ayers's office, but he had forgotten about the various layers of people who would likely stop him, or at least question his actions. He looked about and blinked. He was in the large anteroom that served as a reception area and outer office. A young man with long hair, whom J.T. recognized as Ayers's assistant, rose from a desk to greet him.

"Can I help you?" The assistant looked at the package in J.T.'s arms doubtfully. He nodded at the box. "Maybe you want to bring that down to the mailroom."

His sense of mission was gone. "I'm not supposed to bring this to the mailroom," J.T. said finally. "It has to go, I mean, it must go directly to Mr. Ayers's office. Orders." He swallowed. "Where's Sondra?"

The assistant narrowed his eyes and fixed them on J.T. "Sondra is out today. What's in there anyway?"

"Um..." Despite all his planning, J.T. hadn't prepared for this. Of course, someone might ask what was in the box! He cast about for an excuse, any bit of information he might have overheard, anything that might seem believable. Then he remembered the white paper—Sidney had mentioned this as Harry's latest pet project.

"You know about that white paper?" J.T. was relieved to see a hesitant nod in response. "Well, Mr. Ayers requested his own supply. He wants them stat. That's what I was told, anyway. I'm not exactly on the inside track, if you know what I mean."

The assistant appeared unconvinced.

"Hey, the man wants his order." J.T. shrugged.

Just then the door to Ayers's office flew open and out popped the man himself.

"Let's get a move on," Ayers barked at his assistant as he rushed by. If he noticed J.T. at all, he gave no indication. "Meeting on four in two and a half minutes." He pushed the glass door open. "Now!" he shouted, not looking back.

The assistant, appearing unnerved, grabbed a legal pad and his cell phone. "Just leave that on my desk, and I'll take care of it when I get back," he told J.T. as he followed Ayers.

J.T. took in the suddenly empty surroundings. He couldn't believe his luck. Ayers had left his office door wide open. Tiptoeing in, J.T. placed the package carefully, right smack in the seat of the president's chair.

There, he eyed it with satisfaction. *With any luck, the little bastard will sit right on it and blow his ass to kingdom come.*

The fourth-floor conference room had wood-paneled walls and indirect lighting that was incongruously sophisticated and elegant for Poppy Press. It was generally only used for the clients the company wanted to impress. It wasn't accidental, Harry thought as he leaned back and examined his manicured fingers, that this was where Ayers had called this last-minute meeting. The meeting was small—only Ayers, his assistant Nick, and Harry—so Ayers's office would have been more than sufficient. The sole purpose, however, was for Ayers to establish that he was in charge and that Harry most definitely was not. Therefore, the setting mattered.

Considering the message that Ayers had just conveyed, Harry realized that Ayers had, first, definitely gotten his point across, and, second, all of Harry's plans with Charlie Post were finished. Things had unraveled. But it was still important, even crucial, that Harry keep his cool and not display any of the distress he was feeling. Ayers would immediately pick up on that, like a wolf tracking its prey. But despite Harry's best efforts, Ayers seemed able to read his thoughts.

"So how does that make you feel, big guy?" Ayers goaded him. "Pretty darn bad, I imagine. You thought you were so smart, didn't you? Thought you could pull a fast one even as we were finalizing bankruptcy proceedings. Bankruptcy! Don't you get it? This place is done. And now your investors will know it, too."

Ayers stated—or, rather, threw in Harry's face—that someone had called to tip him off about the "plot," as he put it. Harry couldn't hide his surprise. He had a pretty good idea who had betrayed him, but he had to be sure.

"Tell me," he said evenly, considering his hands as casually as he could, "was it Heppelwhite who called? He mentioned that he wanted to speak with you."

"Heppel-who? No. No, it wasn't." A grin split Ayers's face. "It was your good buddy, Post."

"Charlie?" Harry was incredulous. Then, more stoutly, he said, "That's impossible. Charlie wouldn't do that. He wouldn't even speak with you, given the choice." *Neither would I*, he added in his head.

"Believe what you want," Ayers said, suddenly irritated. "He's the one who made the call."

The room fell silent. Harry stood. There was nothing else to do but go quietly, he thought. The plans he had painstakingly worked out with Charlie were clearly dead and he had no energy to invent new strategy. To what end? He and Charlie Post had made their Hail Mary pass, and it had failed miserably. He was ruined. He stood, went to the door, and opened it, shocked now that Ayers was letting him leave without a final parting shot. Ayers was definitely the kind of guy to kick someone when they were down, Harry thought.

Harry was on the threshold between the conference room and the corridor when it happened. He felt a sharp rush of air and it felt like the building had taken a deep breath. And then a muffled sound. *Boom!* It came from somewhere deep in the building; they felt it more than heard it. It must have originated just over their heads, because all three instinctively looked up. They looked at each other, animosity gone and a collective shock settling in.

Ayers broke the silence first. "What the hell? That felt like some kind of blast."

Harry craned his neck, studying the ceiling. "Maybe. Whatever it was," he said to Ayers, "it must have happened just above us. Aren't we just below your office?"

The three remained where they were for a full minute, silent and listening, waiting for another blast or for some reaction within the building. It was unnervingly quiet. Then they heard a set of footsteps coming down the hall, and Al the foreman appeared in the open doorway. He looked surprisingly calm. "We think there was an explosion in the building. We think…" he said and stopped. It was as if giving voice to what happened made him realize the import of it.

Ayers also seemed to be feeling the full impact of what happened. He opened and closed his mouth wordlessly.

"Call the police and fire departments, and start getting everybody out of the building," Harry ordered Al. "Go now, man!" he added, when Al didn't move. With that, the foreman disappeared.

Ayers's face was all nervous energy. His mouth worked for a few more seconds as the realization hit home. With a harsh whisper, "They're trying to kill me," he lunged for the door. He darted from the room at the exact moment the fire alarm sounded through the building.

Harry and Nick looked at each other, both wondering where Ayers thought that he was going.

J.T. was a bundle of energy. His body twitched and his thoughts raced. *Walk. Don't run*, he reminded himself. *You'll look guilty if you run.* But it was more difficult than he had imagined to keep a measured pace. He pushed the rear door open and rushed out. Defying his own rules, he immediately broke into a jog. Gulping air, he had made it halfway down the block, already out of sight of the building's entrance, before he allowed himself to slow down. Even then, he continued to dart nervous glances to see if anyone had been watching him run like a criminal.

He forced himself to walk as sedately as possible until he neared the end of the alley at a cross street, an area both more exposed and more populated. He snaked his way to the shadow of a large building, stopping to get his bearings and gather his courage.

It's done now, he told himself.

He put his hands on the top of his head, the better to help him remember the next steps he was supposed to take, as if the details he had planned so carefully would fly away if he didn't hold them in. He should have written it all down. He should have…no, wait, it was coming back to him. He was to go to the gas station at the corner of Fifteenth and Oaks, five blocks away. That garage still had a pay phone, one of the few around. He would place an anonymous phone tip to Poppy Press and warn them of the bomb. While he wouldn't shed a tear if the gift he had left blew up in Ayers's face, J.T. didn't want anyone else to get hurt. He was very scrupulous about this part. He only intended to send a message to Ayers and to New York to leave the Press alone.

During the long nights he had spent working on his "present," as he thought of it, he continued to have doubts that the device would even work. After all, he had learned how to make it by watching a video on the Internet. There were no guarantees that it would operate properly. J.T. had also been forced by necessity to substitute some ingredients, such as the Liquid Plumber that the video had called for. Who knew what the end result would bring?

He ought to go, he reminded himself. He took a hesitant step out of the shadows just as sirens began blaring. He pulled back, then poked his head around the fence at the end of the alley as a succession of police cruisers, a fire engine, and an ambulance came racing past.

J.T. was horrified to see that they were heading toward the Poppy Press building. That could only mean one thing. Though he hadn't heard the blast, it was clear that the bomb had already exploded.

He stood stock still, trying to think. On the one hand, it astounded him that it had worked. Would anyone guess he was behind it? The thought was surprisingly calming, and even allowed him a certain measure of pride. He had actually constructed a bomb! He wished he could tell his brother. Maybe, just once, he would be able to impress Hal.

Ayers at last managed to reach the exit of that godforsaken building, but there he encountered a tangled knot of Poppy Press employees taking their good, sweet time to march outside. As if there were all the time in the world, he thought bitterly. As if this weren't an emergency. He wanted to scream at them to move.

He shouldered his way through the crowd like a football player fighting for yards, ignoring the grumbling employees. Then he was outside, blessedly free, where the sun was shining and a breeze was kicking up. Where life was continuing as normal.

Ayers was walking to retrieve his car to make his final escape when he pulled up short. He stood in the middle of the walkway, allowing the cool air to dry some of the sweat that had soaked his shirt. *What if there's a car bomb? I can't take the chance. I need another way out of here.* He would call his wife. Okay, his ex-wife, and it was unusual, but she would help him. She always did. He reached into his pocket for his mobile phone. It wasn't there. He frantically patted his pockets, checking and re-checking, back in panic mode, unable to breathe. Had they stolen his phone, too? Then he remembered, could clearly picture, the phone sitting on his desk when he set off for the meeting with Corcoran. Well the phone was as good as gone. Ayers touched his throbbing temple.

He needed to calm down. There was more than one way home, and he still had his wallet and credit cards. He could get to the train station—he had done that plenty of times. Perhaps rent a car. He thought he remembered seeing a car rental place on his way to the station.

He set out, lost in thought. Not with his usual confident stride, but he was under duress. He had to think and plan, to keep one step ahead of whoever was trying to kill him. His grimace relaxed into a sickly grin as he moved forward, unaware of his surroundings and no longer caring. He was so wrapped up in his thoughts that he never saw or heard the truck rumbling around the corner, was unaware of the driver slamming on the brakes but unable to stop in time to avoid crushing Ayers as he stepped blindly off the curb and directly into the truck's path.

Seventeen

It was close to noon when Sidney and Phoebe finally drove away from the house. That should still have been plenty of time to make the journey to Connecticut, but it was nonetheless much later than Sidney had wanted to leave. Later by a couple of days.

While Mr. Smithson's warning about Donald O'Neill had been enough to get Sidney to spring into action, and should have been enough to spur them to be out of town within a day or so, there had been much to do—so many details involved in planning the trip and last-minute arrangements to make before they could leave.

Their preparation involved a great deal more than simply plotting a route, although Sidney had spent hours poring over the map of the eastern United States. Certainly, there was more to it than packing, which Sidney felt in the end had been accomplished haphazardly, despite the time and care she took. Although she had assured Phoebe that she would bring only enough for a few days, Sidney not only overpacked her grandfather's ancient suitcase but also spent days filling large trash bags with items she was reluctant to leave behind. Silly things like kitchen utensils. There was absolutely no need to bring them, and it was difficult to fit everything in the trunk of the car, but she couldn't bear to leave any useful item for Donald O'Neill. The entire process had been like snatching up as many treasured mementos as possible just before escaping a flood.

The trip was also necessarily delayed by the visit to Mr. Smithson's office to pick up the cash he had promised. She ended up spending more time than she had intended on unexpected errands because Mr. Smithson convinced her—insisted, really—that she needed to purchase a mobile phone.

"It's just not a good idea to go off like this without a cell phone," he argued, uncharacteristically adamant. "You're not used to traveling. I want you to call me and check in, let me know you're safe. How would you do that without a cell phone?"

"I suppose I could call you from a pay phone," Sidney said.

"A pay phone..." He stopped, looking distressed. "Sidney, I certainly hope I haven't made a mistake by encouraging you to leave. You might not be aware of this, but there aren't many pay phones anymore. You may be hard pressed to find one. People use cell phones."

Sidney was confused. "Really? Isn't there one at that gas station on Main Street?"

Mr. Smithson sighed. "Please allow me to give you the money, and then you can purchase what they call a burner phone. Do it for me. I'll tell you exactly what you need to do."

Sidney had complied, dutifully bringing to the store the instructions that he had written out for her, feeling like a schoolgirl bringing a note from a parent. The transaction went smoothly enough, but when she returned home she pulled the phone out of the bag and wondered if it had been a big waste of money. Placing it on the kitchen table, she stepped back and stared at it, as if it might suddenly come alive.

Phoebe moved in to see what was drawing Sidney's attention and squealed. "You got a cell phone!"

Dumbfounded, Sidney watched Phoebe pick it up and begin to manipulate it. "You know how to use this?" Sidney asked after a few minutes.

"Of course. Everybody does." Phoebe glanced up. "Oh, sorry. You probably don't...But don't worry, I'll teach you."

"That's okay," Sidney said quickly. "I'm happy to put you in charge of the phone."

Phoebe, who was clearly pleased with this arrangement, sat in the passenger seat with the phone cradled on her lap as they set out on their journey. Sidney was tempted to take one last, longing look at the house, but she forced herself to look straight ahead as she put the car in gear. She drove slowly down the street, feeling numb.

Phoebe was prattling about wireless technology before they reached the corner. "Seriously, once you start using a cell phone and see all that it can do, you're going to love it," Phoebe said, oblivious to Sidney's silence. "You can get on the Internet and everything. I mean you don't even have to have a wireless plan if you don't want. You can just use Wi-Fi."

Sidney took advantage of a red light to fish a tissue from her pocket and surreptitiously wiped her nose. She needed to focus, to pay attention to what she was doing. "Y Phi?" she asked.

"Yeah, Wi-Fi. It means wireless access you can pick up in certain spots."

"How do you know all this?" Sidney asked.

Phoebe gazed out the window. "I'm not so smart. A lot of people do this now. All kinds of people, like grandmothers."

Sidney made an involuntary sound. "I guess I'd better get with the program."

"I guess." Phoebe looked at her. "Maybe you ought to think about getting a computer. You know, one with Internet access, not just Wi-Fi. It's a good idea to keep up."

"Keep up with what? We talked about this before. I have a computer at work, and that's quite enough." Glancing over, Sidney caught Phoebe's eye roll. Then it occurred to her that she no longer had a computer at work.

"Well, maybe I do need to join the twenty-first century," she said after a moment.

"Yes!" Phoebe was exultant.

"But," Sidney warned, "I'm only going to think about it. No promises. Right now I'm going to stop at the gas station, fill up the tank, and see if Mr. Ahmazhetti has any other maps. I would feel better with something other than a map of the entire eastern United States."

It wasn't until Sidney was finished pumping gas and was heading into the mini-mart that it struck her that Phoebe had been talking as if it weren't only Sidney who would return home. Phoebe sounded as if she would be back as well.

Maybe Phoebe didn't really believe that they would find her father. Sidney tried not to give herself false hope, but it was tempting to believe that Phoebe might want to stay with her after all. It was a small window into a possible future. *Was that so terrible?* Sidney wondered.

"You know, most people don't use maps anymore. They use GPS," Mr. Ahmazhetti said patiently in response to Sidney's query.

"GPS," Sidney repeated dully. She had heard of it, but it was another term that was a mystery to her. Another technology that she would have to master. This was exhausting.

"Yes," he said, "you can have GPS on your phone or on a device in your car."

Sidney looked at him blankly for a moment. "I do have a cell phone now," she volunteered.

"Excellent, there you go."

"But I would feel a lot better if I had a map. As a back-up plan, you see."

Mr. Ahmazhetti looked at her and then gave a long sigh. "Okay. For you, I will give you the last map I have. It's the one we have pinned on the wall that I keep on hand for those who are lost. However, we can live without it for a little while. I would appreciate it if you would bring it back when you return."

"Of course," Sidney murmured. She watched as Mr. Ahmazhetti retreated into the back office to pull the map down from the bulletin board, and she thought about how everyone seemed so confident that this trip would be brief and smooth. *I can't pretend any such thing*, Sidney thought. *I can't even think about it. If I think too much, I'll get scared.*

After paying for the gas and thanking Mr. Ahmazhetti profusely, she felt more like her normal self. She walked out of the mini-mart and crossed the first gasoline pump island on her way back to the car. It was a very good thing that she had achieved such a calm state of mind, Sidney later thought, because it was at that moment that she encountered the last person she expected to see at her neighborhood service station.

She nearly crashed into J.T. as she stepped off the gas pump island. He must have been running, cutting through the gas station, because he was moving fast. But why would he be running, and why was he in this part of town? She stared at him as she would at any stranger who had nearly knocked her down.

Breathing hard, J.T. stared back. "Sidney? What are you doing here?"

Sidney's eyebrows shot up. "I live around here. What are *you* doing here?"

"I was just—I mean, there was a... Hey, didn't you go to work today?"

Sidney's mouth fell open. "Don't you remember? I was on the layoff list. They fired me. Remember, we talked about it in the lunchroom?"

She couldn't help feeling peeved. The moves to get rid of staff were all that J.T. had gone on about for months, with her faithfully listening to all his crackpot theories and speculation. But once she became one of the victims, J.T. couldn't even recall the conversation.

"Yes, yes, of course." He looked nervously about the gas station.

It suddenly struck Sidney that J.T. appeared even more frenetic than usual. She was on the verge of asking him point blank why he was running through the streets like a maniac, when a tremulous voice behind her caused her to whirl around.

"Sidney? I got worried. You were taking such a long time."

Phoebe looked more vulnerable than ever. A car pulled up slowly behind her, and the driver, impatient that she was in the way, blared his horn. Phoebe stumbled and would have fallen into the car's path if Sidney hadn't grabbed her. "Let's move out of the way," Sidney said, sheltering Phoebe with her arm.

"And who is this young lady?" J.T. asked as Sidney led the way back to her car.

"It's..." Sidney considered trotting out the now oft-repeated lie about Phoebe being a distant relative but decided against it. J.T. didn't need to know the whole story, but there was no sense in lying.

"This is Phoebe," she said simply. "We're on our way to Connecticut to try to find her father. He's been missing."

"Really?" J.T. looked at Sidney and Phoebe, then at the car, and back at them again. Sidney instantly regretted telling J.T. about the trip, but she never would have predicted his response.

"Can I come with you?" he blurted.

"What?" Her hand on the car door, Sidney gaped at J.T. "You can't be serious."

"I am serious." J.T. had recovered some of his confidence. "You're on a mission to assist this child in finding her father. What could be more important? I can help with driving, help with directions, all kinds of things. It could be a long trip, you know."

Sidney hesitated. He knew enough about her, or guessed correctly, that she would be terrified about the prospect of driving to parts unknown. She was a nervous driver on short, familiar routes.

"I can be your chauffeur, so to speak," J.T. continued, undeterred by her lack of a response. "I'll get you to Connecticut, safe and sound. What do you say?"

"I don't know..." Sidney glanced at Phoebe, who also looked uncertain and seemed to be trying to figure out whether this strange person could be trusted.

"Look at it this way." J.T. tried again. "You obviously feel a sense of responsibility toward her. Phoebe, right?" He grinned at Phoebe, making her flinch, then redirected his attention to Sidney with an earnest, pleading look.

Sidney returned his gaze as courageously as she could, but she had the feeling that she had already lost the battle. J.T. seemed to sense that. He pounced.

"You need to understand that the roads you'll take are mostly highway. High speeds, lots of traffic, tough for inexperienced drivers. Now, I'm sure you're a very careful driver, but this is a whole other ballgame. You don't want to have an accident, do you? Especially with little Phoebe in the car."

"No." Sidney was miserable. J.T. was tapping into her fears. What made her think she could pull this off? She drew a long breath. "Do you even have a valid driver's license?"

"Of course, I have a driver's license," he said. "I don't happen to own a vehicle at the moment, but I can assure you that I have a great deal of driving experience." Confidently, he moved toward the car.

"Wait," Sidney said. "We're on our way out of town right now. We've already gotten a late start, so we don't have time to wait for you to get ready."

"Not a problem." J.T. turned slightly to show the knapsack on his back and reached behind him to pat it. "I happen to be all ready to go."

"But how?" Sidney's weak protest was futile.

"You'll see, it will be fine," he said, opening the back door of the car to usher them in. "You both climb in here and sit back. It will be just like a taxi. Now, Sidney, where are your keys?"

Eighteen

I have to get upstairs to the office, to Ayers's office, Nicholas thought as he sprinted down the hall. His long, skinny legs took him to the elevator in just a few strides, despite the need to maneuver around the growing chaos of people streaming in the corridors. The fire alarm continued its relentless screeching. Nicholas punched the elevator call button, then impatiently smacked it a few more times.

"Come on, come on," he muttered, waiting for the light.

If what they had heard—or rather felt—had been an explosion, if it really was some sort of bomb, it was, if nothing else, unbelievable timing. Somehow, someone must have gotten wind of what Ayers had planned for that very day. Ayers had not only gotten the green light to execute the bankruptcy that had been hanging over the Press for so long, but unbeknown to nearly everyone but Nicholas, Ayers was planning to shut the place down. His intention was to throw everyone out of work and put Poppy Press out of business as soon as possible.

Had someone discovered these plans? Maybe this bomb was a desperate attempt to stop or delay them. It could have been Harry—except that he seemed genuinely taken aback in the conference room when Ayers told him his plans. That was just before all hell broke loose. There was no mistaking Harry's disappointment, but if there was one thing Nicholas had learned, it was that Harry was an excellent actor. Maybe he had discovered Ayers's maneuver, his checkmate, ahead of time and had sent that strange man with the package, which could very well have been a bomb.

Nicholas raised both hands to smooth back his shiny hair, then hit the elevator button again.

"Enough of this," he said and headed toward the stairwell. It was only when he pulled open the metal fire door and waded into the crowd that he remembered that the elevators wouldn't be working during a fire alarm. He chided himself. Of course, everyone would be taking the stairs. He tried to find a pathway upstairs, but it was slow going, given the mob heading in the opposite direction.

He had only made it a few steps up the flight when the fire alarm suddenly stopped and the lights went out. There were a few muffled screams. In the blackness, everyone stayed motionless, afraid of falling down the stairs.

Nicholas threw out his arms, trying to find the wall, a railing, anything he could grab, but he only felt the fleshy surfaces of those around him. He attempted to step forward, but his foot found nothing but air, and he almost pitched over. "Hey, careful," someone said in his ear and put a steadying hand on him. The same man said more loudly to the crowd, "Everyone, stand still!"

At the same moment, the emergency lighting flickered back on, and the distant hum of a generator could be heard. With a collective breath, the employees resumed their slow trek.

With great effort, Nicholas pushed through in the opposite direction. It took another ten minutes to work his way upstairs and the full power came back on just as he made it to the fifth floor. He leaned against the exit door's crash bar, nearly falling into what seemed an alternate reality.

The door swung shut behind him, leaving him in bright light and an eerie silence, disconcerting after the dark, crowded stairwell. The vacant surroundings were a little unnerving. Even though he walked down these same empty corridors on his way home on many late nights, long after everyone had left, it now felt different.

He set off toward the executive suite, wondering what he might find. That odd fellow, the one who had shown up with the package that he insisted Ayers had ordered—he must have been the guy, Nicholas thought. The bomber. *I should have questioned him more, or called security, or something,* he thought guiltily.

The lunatic might still be in the building, Nicholas worried as he crept through the area, eyes darting to dark corners. Maybe he would come back to the scene of the crime, he thought, perhaps with a weapon to try to finish off the executives. It did not surprise Nicholas in the least that somebody had decided to take revenge against Ayers and the parent company. Especially Ayers, who delighted in the cruelty of ripping away these people's livelihoods. Maybe the only surprising thing was that it had taken so long for someone to react.

"Whoa. Where do you think you're going, kid?" A burly arm shot out to stop Nicholas just as he was approaching the glass executive-suite doors. Nicholas stepped back involuntarily and looked at the policeman. Despite his lined, tired face, and his fatherly voice, he was sternly blocking Nicholas from entering the offices.

Nicholas motioned to compulsively push his hair off his brow and found that his hair was damp with sweat. He wiped his forehead on the sleeve of his suit jacket, not caring how unprofessional he appeared.

"I work here," he said. "I've got to go in."

"Well, now is not the best time for anyone to go in," the policeman said calmly. "It's been declared a crime scene, and the captain and the fire chief are in there right now. I would say it will be a while."

"Fire chief...was there a fire? We heard there was an explosion. Was anyone hurt?" Nicholas spoke rapidly, trying to look through the glass doors. Everything looked relatively intact on the exterior, but perhaps things were worse than he imagined.

"Take it easy, son." His words were soothing, but the policeman was following Nicholas's gaze with interest. "It doesn't appear, at this time, that anyone was injured." The cop chose his words carefully. "We're having the building evacuated as a precaution. Which is what you should be doing. Evacuating." He squinted at Nicholas. "Tell me why you're here instead."

"I told you. I work in these offices. I'm the assistant to the company president." Nicholas's voice faded as he looked again at the closed doors, searching for shadows of movement behind the beveled glass. "Was it a bomb?"

"Let's just say I can't confirm or deny." The cop pulled a surprisingly large notebook from his pocket and moved closer. "Tell me a bit more about why you think there might have been a bomb."

"I don't know. It's just when we were told it was an explosion...at least, I think...actually, I'm not even sure who told us or what he said." Nicholas felt dizzy, confused, and a little sick.

"Has anyone threatened you or the company recently?"

"No. Not exactly."

Just then the door opened and two men, deep in conversation, emerged. One wore a battered fire coat. They could have been brothers, with the same short stature, gray crewcuts, and beer bellies. They immediately halted their discussion when they spotted Nicholas. They looked at him, obviously expecting an explanation, but Nicholas couldn't speak.

"Who the hell are you?" the man wearing the police uniform said roughly. "And what in God's name are you doing here? Don't you know this is a crime scene? One that you may be managing to contaminate?"

"I haven't touched anything." Nicholas recoiled, holding up his palms for them to see. "Let me introduce myself. Nicholas Baker."

The pair shook his hand briefly. "Captain Lloyd Brubaker," the police officer said, mollified by Nicholas's demeanor. The fire chief stood by quietly.

Brubaker repeated his question. "Okay, what business do you have up here?"

Nicholas still held back, wondering if he should be handling official communications. Ayers wouldn't be happy about it, that was for sure.

"I don't have all day." Brubaker glared.

"Okay, okay." Speaking rapidly, Nicholas started to explain his role, how the Press was in dire financial straits, about Ayers's plans to cut staff, the bad atmosphere, and everything that led up to that day and the explosion. Or what appeared to be an explosion, he added quickly.

"Then there was that strange guy with the package," Nicholas added, almost as an afterthought.

Brubaker's head jerked up from his notebook. "What guy?"

Nicholas related as many details as he could remember about the man, his appearance and what he said. "He didn't seem frightened or nervous or anything," Nicholas said in answer to the captain's questions. "I would say he was just kind of creepy."

He again looked toward the executive suite. "How much damage was there anyway?"

"The damage was contained to the main office. Your boss's office, I suppose. No injuries have been reported at this time. So you're saying you weren't there when the incident occurred?"

There was something about the delicate way Brubaker used the term "incident," in an almost dismissive manner, that made Nicholas lose patience with the entire situation. His joke of a job. The contempt with which Ayers had treated him and everyone at the Press. He wanted to just walk out of there. But he swallowed hard and answered the question.

"I was in a meeting downstairs with Mr. Ayers. We heard something, and someone came in and said it was some sort of explosion."

The two officials exchanged looks. "We're going to have to speak with your boss," Brubaker said. "As part of the investigation, of course. Where can we find him?"

Nicholas was finding it difficult to hide his annoyance with both Brubaker and Ayers. "Good luck with that," he said under his breath.

"What do you mean?" Brubaker demanded.

"I mean that the last time I saw Ayers, he was running out the door like a frightened rabbit. My guess is he's still running. And if you're expecting him to know who his employees are, forget about it. He wouldn't recognize one if he tripped over them. He's been too preoccupied planning layoffs and firings and things." Nicholas shook his head.

They stared at him. "Guess that gives people a reason to hate him, huh?" Brubaker said.

"I guess."

"What about you? You sound pretty sour about the whole thing."

Nicholas was exhausted from his outburst. "Me? No, not me. I have work to do. Can I just go to my office?"

"No, I'm sorry. No one can go in there right now. Instead, it would be best if you could come to the station and give us some more information about this. Help us sort this out."

"But I already answered your questions. I don't have any more information to give."

"In your boss's absence, you could still be very helpful. You could provide some details, that sort of thing." Brubaker was now soothing. "It's all completely voluntary, of course, but we could really use your assistance. Especially if we have trouble locating Ayers."

After repeated rebuffs and more persuasion, Nicholas finally relented. Together, they marched down the now-empty stairwell to the main lobby. There, Nicholas spotted Harry, talking quietly with a small knot of men.

"Hey!" Nicholas called to Harry. "See if you can find Ayers." With that he was whisked through the revolving doors.

Harry watched the doors grow still. "Ayers who?" he said to himself, but as he walked off he left a trail of laughter from the other men.

Inside a small room at the police station, clearly an interrogation room, Nicholas impatiently drummed his fingers on a metal table. Captain Brubaker had left him sitting there for some time, despite promising to return shortly. And even after repeated assurances that this was a voluntary discussion, Nicholas, sitting so long in this hole of a room, didn't feel like much of a volunteer.

I've seen enough cop shows to know he's softening me up by leaving me sitting here, Nicholas thought, his leg going up and down like a jackhammer. *Am I a suspect?* Neither Ayers nor Harry, he knew, would lift a finger to help him. He was on his own.

After a while, fatigue replaced anxiety. He was almost falling asleep when the door opened and Captain Brubaker entered. Nicholas watched warily as Brubaker threw a legal pad on the table and grappled the chair opposite him, seating himself heavily. Nicholas decided that he would not be intimidated. That was exactly what Brubaker wanted.

"Am I under arrest?" Nicholas demanded. "If so, what for?"

Brubaker raised a bushy eyebrow. "Did we tell you that you were under arrest? Did we read you your rights? No, we did not." He tilted his chair back as far as he could, which was only an inch or so in the tiny closet space, and laced his fingers over his belly. "As I've told you, we simply need more information. Information you may have. Don't forget, you were the one who showed up at the scene."

"Why am I cooped up in this room?" Nicholas groused.

"You agreed to come here for a conversation. We're having a conversation. This is the room where we have conversations, and I apologize that it isn't comfier. You can leave as soon as we're done.

Now," Brubaker sat up again and pulled the pad of paper closer, "we have several things to discuss, but first, let's go over exactly what happened. Starting with this person who dropped off the package."

Nicholas sighed and began to relate the encounter once again. He made a concerted effort to include every detail he could remember. Brubaker took notes, asking an occasional question.

"So you don't know the employees well because you're from the parent company in New York, correct?"

"I don't know them at all. I work pretty much exclusively with Mr. Ayers. I know some of the company's management from various meetings I've attended."

"Hmm, yes, we're also questioning the managers about who this 'mailroom' person could be, but it's difficult with only a physical description. I don't suppose Poppy Press has an employee database, with photos, headshots, that sort of thing?"

Nicholas shook his head. "No, nothing like that. This is a shoestring operation on the verge of bankruptcy. The bankruptcy is one big reason why everyone is so upset."

"There are other reasons?"

"Well," Nicholas hesitated. "Mr. Ayers has been cutting staff. It's been pretty drastic, and he had plans to fire, lay off, whatever you want to call it, a lot more people. That plan was supposed to go into effect today."

"Do you think the employees got wind of this plan?"

"Maybe." Nicholas shrugged. He hesitated and added, "I'm sure Ayers started out thinking that it made sense to trim staff, given the financial circumstances. After a while it was like he *enjoyed* it. He was looking into ways to ensure that none of those who were laid off would be able to collect unemployment benefits. Said it would cost the company too much."

Nicholas gave the ceiling an agonized look. "I don't know. Maybe the employees caught on to an important fact."

"What fact?"

"The fact that Ayers is ruthless. He won't stop."

Brubaker's deep-set eyes revealed nothing.

"You should know," Nicholas continued, sounding his most earnest, "I had nothing whatsoever to do with the package or the explosion or whatever it was. The most I did was remove a person's name from a firing list. One person. I felt bad about the way they talked about her, like she was a piece of trash or something. So I took a marker and scratched her name off the list. That was all."

It was difficult to tell whether Brubaker suspected Nicholas of more involvement or not. He said mildly, "If it's getting to you, why not quit?"

Nicholas gave a strangled laugh. "Good question. I've asked myself that many times. I guess I thought I needed the job. Just like everybody else at Poppy Press."

Brubaker waved a hand. "Nonsense, you're young and skilled. No sense being miserable. Anyhow," he said dismissively, "I appreciate your taking the time to give us these details. Before you go, I want to share two important items that have come to our attention. First, this." He dug into his inside jacket pocket, pulled out a crumpled manila envelope, and slipped from it an even more crumpled paper, spreading it out on the table between them.

"This note," Brubaker said, "was discovered in the Poppy Press mailroom a short while ago. We don't know exactly when it was delivered. But it appears to *complement*, let's say, the package in the executive suite."

Nicholas shot him a glance, trying to assess the police officer's motive for showing him this piece of evidence. Then he turned his attention to the paper. It was scrawled with crazy, tilted letters that appeared to be written in red crayon. "Is this crayon? Seriously?"

"Just read it and tell me what you think."

Nicholas looked down obediently. "Watch out, Poppy Press," the note read. "Look what happened to Airs. More to come." It was signed, "From the Mad Bomber 2."

"Well, he misspelled Ayers's name," Nicholas said slowly, studying the words. "What do you think this means, 'From the Mad Bomber 2'? Is it like, from the Mad Bomber also?"

Brubaker snorted. "You're giving this guy too much credit for command of the English language. On the other hand, he could also be intentionally trying to look like he's uneducated to throw us off."

He explained to Nicholas about a fanatic nicknamed the Mad Bomber who terrorized New York in the 1950s and turned out to be a very ordinary, nondescript man. "This case was the one that really started criminal profiling because someone, a psychologist probably, predicted that the Mad Bomber lived with his mother and wore double-breasted suits. And that was exactly what the Mad Bomber did."

Nicholas grunted and looked at the letter again. "Well, it's disturbing, but I'm not quite sure what you're asking me. I would say, though, that he does seem to be gunning for Ayers. A mad bomber after one guy. Look, if you're worried about Ayers's safety, my guess is that he's already back in New York. He's not hanging around for somebody to take another crack at him."

Brubaker's gaze was inscrutable. "Let's have you look at some mug shots before you go. See if you can ID the person who came in the executive offices. But first, let me tell you about one other piece of information that has come to light." He paused.

"Just minutes after we arrived here at the station, we were informed that Mr. Ayers has been found. He was crossing a street near the Poppy Press building and was struck by a vehicle. A dump truck, I believe."

Nicholas said nothing for a full minute, although his mouth tried to form a question. He hated Brubaker for making him ask it. "And how…how is he?"

"He's dead."

Nicholas searched the room for a place to focus on until he could process this news. Ayers, his hated boss, the tyrant, was dead. There was the inevitable sense of relief but also something else. Guilt. Weren't there times he had wished, even prayed, that the guy would just die? Obviously, someone at Poppy Press felt the same way. This couldn't have been a mere chance traffic accident.

Not on top of the explosion. No, if nothing else, this was a series of events set into motion by Ayers himself. If he hadn't been dismantling the company, there probably would never have been a bomb. And if Ayers weren't such a coward, he wouldn't have been running away, running across the street, wading into traffic.

"Ironic," Nicholas whispered to the ceiling.

Shifting his weight so that the plastic chair groaned, Brubaker adjusted his questioning. "Sorry, yes, I'm afraid Mr. Ayers didn't make it. But, as you suggested, perhaps he wouldn't have been the best person to help us figure out which of these apparently disgruntled employees might be suspects in the bombing. We're hoping you can tell us who else in management might be in a position to help."

Nicholas looked at Brubaker. In a subdued voice, he said, "Contact Harry Corcoran. He could probably tell you a lot. More than Ayers, anyway."

"Harry Corcoran, you say? Now you're talking. Why didn't you mention him before?" Brubaker was already scrambling from his chair. The door shut and Nicholas was alone again.

"Because you didn't ask," Nicholas told the door. He sighed and put his head on the table. What he wanted to do was to go home to New York or anywhere, really. Anywhere that wasn't this room or Poppy Press.

Nineteen

"Off we go." Sidney put the car into drive. The announcement was superfluous and, from J.T.'s perspective, probably an insult, considering that they had spent the previous forty minutes arguing over who would take the wheel of Sidney's ancient Chevrolet on its inaugural road trip. J.T. contended that he was the superior driver and more experienced in highway driving, something Sidney couldn't dispute. She certainly couldn't claim that for herself. But she stubbornly fought back, insisting that it was her car and that she was responsible for getting Phoebe safely to Connecticut.

"Don't forget, you're a guest on this trip. You invited yourself. I don't let hitchhikers drive my car." Still flustered, Sidney continued to jab at J.T., even after he had acquiesced and moved to the back seat.

Sidney checked her seat belt and glanced in the rearview mirror at J.T.—he was staring out the window with a sour expression—and then to her side at Phoebe. The girl sat stiffly and avoided Sidney's glance. *I would be wondering about J.T. too if I were in Phoebe's shoes*, she thought. Not for the first time since J.T. had appeared at the gas station, she questioned if she had done the right thing by allowing him to accompany them. But he hadn't given them much of a choice.

Although the journey had just begun and they were still on familiar roads, Sidney sat rigidly behind the steering wheel. She drove even more slowly than usual, and her usual pace was plodding at best. She was nervously anticipating the moment they would reach the interstate highway, a road she would ordinarily never dream of attempting.

The car was silent. Bit by bit Sidney relaxed enough to become aware of, and even enjoy, the glorious spring afternoon enveloping them. Once or twice she dared to tear her eyes from the road long enough to take in the deep green roadside drenched in sunlight.

Either the weather or a sense of adventure eventually softened Phoebe's mood, and she picked up her usual commentary about everything they passed, soon happily bouncing against her seat belt. Her excitement about the trip was contagious. Even J.T. lightened up and began to participate in the conversation.

Sidney allowed herself another look at the passenger seat and in that instant caught sight of Phoebe with the sun glinting on her hair, her face beaming with its own light. For a moment it made Sidney feel free—free of the sad, swampy mess at work, free of Agatha's ghost, free of the burden of what might happen with the house. There was nothing in their lives to focus on but this mission, and even that seemed doable. Connecticut couldn't be that big.

But before long this sunny optimism faded at the same time that thickening clouds created a grayness, blending with the road's monotony. Once again the car grew quiet. When Sidney was able to spare another look, she saw that Phoebe had fallen asleep.

Sidney felt the worry creep back with the disappearance of the sun. They might get hopelessly lost (she had no confidence in her map-reading ability), or they might get in an accident despite her best efforts to drive carefully. There was so much traffic, which was adding to her anxiety.

Just keep your eyes on the road, she reminded herself as she let up on the gas. Vehicles screamed past them.

After long, agonizing minutes of gripping the steering wheel, she started to feel that she needed a break. She spotted a sign for the next exit, only two miles away. Two miles wasn't far. In fact, she realized, they would be on top of the exit any moment. Panicked, she snapped on the turn signal and started braking hard.

"What are you doing?" J.T. yelled in her ear just as a truck's horn blared behind them. Sidney, completely unnerved, slammed on the brake pedal. The truck swerved at the last moment and passed them, the driver leaning angrily on the horn. Sidney awkwardly turned the car onto the exit ramp, which thankfully had a wide shoulder. At last they came to a stop.

Sidney rested her forehead on the steering wheel, trying to control her breathing. After a few minutes she looked around. J.T was staring at her.

"That does it. I'm taking over the driving," he said.

"It's my car," she protested weakly.

It was the same argument she had used at the gas station, but this time J.T. flicked it off.

"You're not used to highway driving." It was an obvious point, and J.T. said it without rancor, but Sidney was wounded by the criticism.

"Think about it," he continued. "It will be getting dark soon. Do you really want to drive the highway at night?"

Sidney hesitated. "All right, you win," she said testily and opened the door.

"I'll sit back there with you," Phoebe said hastily, undoing her seat buckle.

Once they were in the back seat, J.T. made short work of adjusting mirrors, starting the engine, and finding his way back onto the highway. They drove north at a much faster clip.

After a while, relief replaced Sidney's petulance. While huge responsibilities continued to weigh on her, driving through metropolitan New York didn't need to be one of them. She also had to admit that J.T. was indeed a good driver. She leaned back against the seat, closed her eyes, and let the tension seep out of her.

"Tell me again why you want to go to Connecticut?" she asked J.T. languorously.

"Oh! Well, I want to visit my brother's wife's family. His in-laws. That's where she's from originally, you know."

Sidney didn't know but decided to drop it. It was extremely unlikely that J.T. would be visiting relatives of his sister-in-law, even if he got along well with her, and Sidney knew that he detested her. J.T. had complained innumerable times about her meanness, bordering on cruelty. J.T. believed that she was the sole reason Hal had cut him off. Sidney knew all this, but it seemed pointless to call J.T. out on it.

What am I doing? Sidney thought, suddenly veering back to panic. *Here I am in the back seat of my own car, letting someone who I really don't know all that well drive me to a place where I don't know a soul on what is undoubtedly a wild-goose chase.* This was not who she was, not who she had ever been. She was the type of person who lived in the shadow of others, who never took risks. Why did she think she could be bold enough to attempt this adventure? She pressed her hands together to stop them from trembling.

The song on the radio ended, and a news announcer's stern voice replaced it. "At this hour, police are searching for a missing—"

J.T. reached over and switched off the radio.

"Why did you do that?" Sidney cried. This was dreadful. Were they finally on the hunt for Phoebe? "A missing eleven-year-old girl," was how she imagined the broadcaster's sentence ending.

"You shouldn't have anything distract you from your driving." Perhaps to prove his point, J.T. kept his attention riveted to the road.

"Nonsense. Everybody can listen and drive at the same time. That's why they put radios in cars." Sidney knew she sounded both querulous and hypocritical, considering her own poor driving skills.

Maddeningly, J.T. ignored her. Sidney sunk down. She again clutched her hands together, this time to pray, until she felt Phoebe gently trying to pry them apart. Sidney let her hand go limp and Phoebe took it, cupping it in her own. Sidney looked at her.

"Don't worry. We're fine." Phoebe's words were barely audible, but they gave Sidney heart.

Sidney turned away, looked at the landscape rushing past the car window, watched giant streetlamps appear and disappear. A fragment of an old song played at the edge of her mind. Something about going clear. Or was that from the Bible? It didn't matter. She couldn't stop thinking of the phrase, and she wondered why. *Because*, she answered herself, *it's what we're doing. We're escaping.*

~

To Adele, the preparations to travel to Connecticut seemed to take forever. But when a person has become an anxiety-ridden, quivering mass of emotion, as she had, obstacles and roadblocks emerged everywhere. Or they appeared to, she thought. In reality, Adele had made all sorts of arrangements at breakneck speed, including contacting Robert's relatives in Connecticut, flying her mother to the East Coast to stay with Bobby, and arranging to take off from work. All to travel north, in the hope of learning whether Phoebe had managed to make her way there. Adele prayed that she might discover some clues about Phoebe, maybe even find her and bring her back. That hope drove Adele to move at this rapid pace and also caused her to berate herself for not acting sooner.

Why didn't I think of calling Robert's relatives before? Adele thought, not for the first time, as she drove through New Jersey. She was driving as fast as she dared, her own way of making up for lost time.

To distract herself, she thought back, as she had many times over the previous days, to her conversation with Jay. That talk, she realized once again, had been oddly comforting despite the circumstances. At the same time, it had been devastating. There was, of course, the terrible news about Robert's death. There was that. But it also reset all of Adele's alarm bells about Phoebe, who had not surfaced in Connecticut. At least, she hadn't contacted Robert's family.

"I was hoping that perhaps you heard from Phoebe. That she made her way up there..." Adele's voice caught.

"Listen. Why don't you come up here to Connecticut?" Jay had a false cheeriness that Adele knew was well intentioned. "I think you deserve to hear, in person, what happened to Robert, at least as much as we could piece together. It might help you come to grips with it. Perhaps." He paused.

"Give it some thought," he added hastily, as if concerned that he had been too negative. "It's always possible that Phoebe could make her way up here. Who knows? We might get lucky."

"Lord knows we need some luck." But Adele already knew that she would go. The idea of taking action—rather than cowering, worrying, and searching within the limited radius of their home—had a lot of appeal. Going to Connecticut could even be, as Jay suggested, the answer to her prayers.

Adele's upper back and arms cramped as she hunched over the steering wheel. She forced herself to sit straight and loosen her grip. She glanced at the speedometer. Seventy-two. Too fast.

Breathe deep and think about something else.

That was a joke, Adele reflected bitterly. But she could feel herself calming. It was something a mom might say; in fact, it was exactly what her mother would say to her in this situation. Thank goodness for her mother. On hearing about Robert, she hadn't hesitated to offer help while Adele made the journey to Connecticut. "Go do what you need to do," her mother had said. "I'll take care of Bobby, so you have one less thing to worry about."

It *was* comforting, especially amid the turmoil and emotion surrounding Robert's death. Really, it wasn't much different from all the turmoil that had followed Robert throughout their marriage and apparently his entire life. Turmoil that always seemed of his own making.

So many times, especially during these last few years, she fantasized how much easier her life would have been without Robert. But then he walked out, leaving her feeling abandoned, hurt, and angry, and that was worse. It was like his very absence created more chaos. It certainly did for Phoebe, who ran away to try to find him. In turn, that just caused more heartache. Adele shook her head. *What a mess you created, Robert*, she thought.

If only I could find Phoebe, I would convince her that she is my daughter, the same as if she were my flesh and blood. All I need is a chance to talk to her, to explain about her father, and show her that we're a family, she, Bobby, and me. We can pick up the pieces and move on.

Adele drove and drove, her lips moving in silent prayer.

~

It had grown dark, and still Sidney's Chevrolet continued north, mile after mile without seeming to make much progress. *But how would we know?* Sidney thought, looking out the rear passenger window at the unfamiliar landscape. She knew that they were still in New Jersey, but beyond that, she had no point of reference, never having traveled outside Pennsylvania.

She looked at the back of J.T.'s head. He appeared completely comfortable behind the wheel, as if he drove the New Jersey Turnpike every day. Just then J.T. shifted in his seat, and his body odor, pronounced when he first climbed into the car, came wafting to the back seat. Sidney cracked her window and noisy air rushed in. She looked at Phoebe, who was leaning her head against the opposite window, her eyes shut. Whether she was asleep or pretending to be, Sidney wasn't sure.

"Where exactly are we going?"

Sidney jumped. She wasn't expecting J.T.'s question, although she should have.

"You mean, where in Connecticut? I'm not exactly sure."

"You planned this big trip, and you don't know where you're going?" She could see him eyeing her in the rearview mirror.

Sidney threw a nervous glance over her shoulder. In the rear window, shockingly huge headlights of a truck seemed to loom inches behind them. The car was starting to slow, or perhaps Sidney imagined that, as she gasped. At last, at the exact same time Phoebe made a whimpering cry, Sidney found her voice.

"J.T.!"

"What are you doing?" Phoebe screamed. "I thought you would make us safe!"

A deep horn blared, drowning out Sidney's and Phoebe's shrieks. The truck's impatient horn may have been the catalyst that caused J.T. to jerk the car to the right, off the road, narrowly avoiding the tractor-trailers hemming him in. Sidney clutched Phoebe until they rolled to a stop on the gravel shoulder of the highway.

They were silent for a full minute.

"Can we get off this highway? I feel sick." Phoebe did appear sallow, even in the little amount of light coming in from the highway fixtures. Sidney watched her, debating whether to open the door to allow Phoebe to get out. But that seemed dangerous.

J.T. turned. He looked a bit pale himself, yet when he spoke he sounded perfectly reasonable. "Can you hold out for one more mile? There was a sign for a rest stop. I think it's just up ahead." He actually winked at them, then focused on Phoebe. "Hey, did you yell out something about being 'safe'? What did you mean by that?"

"Nothing," Phoebe muttered and looked away, but not before Sidney caught a trace of fear. Phoebe, who had bravely traveled on her own for miles and miles, was afraid of J.T., she realized. This was her fault, Sidney thought, for allowing him to join them.

Sidney lashed out at J.T. "Don't you worry about it," she snapped. "It's none of your business. Let's not forget that this is my car, and this is our trip. You, sir, are a guest. *Merely* a guest. Now," she waved toward the windshield, "let's get moving."

J.T. glowered and muttered something under his breath as he put the car in drive.

So he thinks I'm a bitch, Sidney thought, looking out the window and considering how everyone, not least of all Agatha, would be shocked at her behavior. *So what? Better that than a doormat.*

She smiled at her reflection in the glass. *Welcome to the new Sidney*, she told herself.

"Hey, what do you say we get something to eat?" J.T.'s buoyant mood had inexplicably returned as they piled out of the car and headed to the brightly lit rest stop building. "I could go for a hamburger," he added when the others didn't respond.

"The reason we're stopping is because Phoebe isn't feeling well," Sidney said sharply. She was still annoyed. The entire trip was out of control. She never should have allowed J.T. to come along, no matter how horribly deficient her driving skills were. They would have managed.

"Maybe eating would make me feel better," Phoebe said in a small voice.

"See?" J.T. said with more than a little pettiness. Sidney ignored him.

After they had placed their orders in the large fast-food area and headed back to the car with their paper sacks, they all seemed to have gotten a second wind. *Maybe J.T. will even behave himself for the rest of the trip*, Sidney thought as she climbed into the back seat.

Darkness had fallen by the time they pulled onto the highway again. She wouldn't have admitted it out loud, but Sidney was once again grateful that J.T. was driving. They were skirting New York City. Sidney held her breath as they drove the long span of a bridge across the Hudson River. "Are we in Connecticut?" she asked when they finally reached the other side, aware that she sounded like a child pestering a parent.

"Still New York," J.T. grunted, concentrating on the road.

Within minutes they were on a much quieter roadway, crossing some invisible sound barrier that separated them from the intensity of New York. "Now we're in Connecticut," J.T. announced.

Joyful, Sidney reached for Phoebe's hand. It was unexpectedly overwhelming—as if Sidney were the one who had traveled on foot for days on end, regardless of the peril, to search for her missing father. All she had done was help with this last leg of the journey, but she felt like someone reaching the end of a lifelong search. She looked at Phoebe. The girl looked beatific.

"We're going to find him. We're really going to find him," Phoebe whispered.

They sat, gripping hands and peering out the car windows into the darkness, feeling that they were on the brink of reaching their near-mythical destination that, while only a few hundred miles from home, felt like a world away.

J.T. broke the silence. "Connecticut might not be the biggest state in the Union, but it's big enough if you're looking for someone. Do we know what town we're supposed to be heading to?"

Sidney felt her stomach knot again. He had already asked that perfectly reasonable question, but she had ignored it. Nor had she addressed it in all her travel planning. She had been so focused on getting to the state that she had given almost no thought to what they would do once they actually reached it. Then a thought occurred to her. She asked Phoebe, "Do you have that postcard your father sent from Connecticut? The postmark will tell us what town."

Phoebe automatically reached for her backpack, but her hand stopped midway. "I didn't bring it," she said, stricken.

Sidney pursed her lips. After a moment she pulled from her handbag the map of the eastern United States. "I knew this would come in handy," she said, unfolding it and squinting at the unfamiliar roads and names under the weak dome light J.T. had flipped on. She located Connecticut but couldn't get her bearings.

"Is there a place like a color?" Phoebe's voice floated past her.

Sidney squinted and ran her finger down the tiny print of the legend of street names, with town names in larger boldface. "Orange?" Sidney said. "There is an Orange, Connecticut."

"That's it," Phoebe sank back on the seat, satisfied. "That was what was on the postcard from my dad."

Sidney was grateful to leave the details of finding Orange, Connecticut, to J.T. Before long they exited the highway and were making their way to a well-lit road. It seemed as though they had reached their destination, but still they drove for miles, passing strip malls and businesses already closed for the evening. Pulling into a nearly deserted parking lot, they voted after a brief discussion to get a motel room for the night and resume their search in the morning.

"Door to door, if we have to," J.T. said. He was euphoric, perhaps feeling Sidney's and Phoebe's exhilaration. In that moment, in the near-vacant parking lot, they were bound together by an aura of invincibility. Nothing could stop them.

Those good feelings had nearly all drained away by the time they found and had gotten settled in at a motel. Sidney was spent, and had trouble keeping her eyes open during the last push to search for a motel, even though she knew that it was difficult for J.T. to drive and scan their surroundings at the same time. In the end it was Phoebe who spotted the anonymous-looking EconoLodge they had driven past twice before.

When they were finally installed in a room, and J.T. had been sent with money and instructions to find a convenience store for some snacks, Sidney flopped on the bed and threw an arm over her eyes. It felt like years had passed since they had left that morning. Her body clamored for sleep, but worrying about Phoebe kept her awake. Sighing, she pulled herself to a seated position and watched Phoebe switch TV channels with the remote control. Images flashed on the screen and quickly changed, as Phoebe, despite her expertise with television, couldn't find anything to hold her attention.

The room and furnishings were nondescript at best, with a rough, stained carpet and a deeply scarred dresser on which the television rested. In addition to the double bed that Sidney and Phoebe would share, a cot was folded up in the corner for J.T. The walls were bare except for two pictures, one a bad seascape of an angry sea and a dark sky slashed with white, prowling seagulls, and the other a cross-stitched sampler. They hardly seemed standard motel issue, even to Sidney who had never stayed in a motel before in her life. She rose to take a closer look at the sampler.

Try to today laugh a little, love much, listen well.

You may then find what you seek.

Odd, Sidney thought. It was like a proverb, originally in another language, that had failed to translate well. Why not say, "Today, try to laugh"? In any case, it was a mystery why anyone would have gone to the trouble to painstakingly stitch this for strangers to ponder in a motel room.

"What's that?" Phoebe asked at her elbow.

"Some kind of saying, I guess." They studied it in silence.

"It's a good sign," Phoebe pronounced finally.

J.T. came in loaded with plastic bags. "Dinner," he announced curtly, his good mood long gone.

They divvied up the food. J.T.'s idea of snacks were mostly chips and Styrofoam-like cheese curls, which made Sidney wish she had been more specific. She sat propped up against the pillows of the double bed as Phoebe perched on its lower edge, munching away as she watched TV, having found something to absorb her. J.T. sat in the single straight-backed chair. He talked as he ate, without regard if anyone were listening. Despite her fatigue, Sidney fell into her old habit of serving as his audience. She willed her eyelids to stay open as she listened.

Before long J.T. was back to his usual rant, railing about Poppy Press and the hated New York management. Sidney plucked at the bedspread and thought how easily she had become disconnected from the Press. *I used to think about it so much and I used to worry*, she thought. *Now I don't really care.* It was probably selfish, but she didn't want to hear about the Press and its troubles. It only reminded her how she had been kicked aside like a piece of trash.

Nonetheless, she sat, saying nothing and listening politely. *How would J.T. react if I suddenly told him to shut up, that I didn't want to hear this anymore?* The thought brought a faint smile to her lips.

"They've been planning the biggest, baddest set of layoffs. Most of the company was going to get pink slips," J.T. was saying. "This was the worst. The absolute worst. So I had to do something to stop them."

Sidney's head snapped up. This was similar to statements he had frequently made in their endless conversations at work, but the way he said it in the dim motel room was somehow different, more sinister. "What do you mean, stop them?"

"And stop them I did." J.T. was triumphant.

"Exactly how did you stop them?" Sidney felt growing irritation along with rising worry. She thought back to J.T.'s sudden arrival at the gas station. Maybe there was much more to it than he had let on. The idea that it was pure coincidence that he had been in that part of town had been nagging at her, as it had bothered her how anxious he had been to leave and his strange insistence on accompanying them.

In a flash of understanding, Sidney knew that J.T. had done something terrible, yet something he was inordinately proud of and was dying to brag about.

"Okay, I'll tell you." J.T.'s sigh was like a hiss. "No one was stepping up and doing anything, especially about Ayers or the other New York people. Well, really, about Ayers. He's the guy who had to go. So *I* acted. *I* built a bomb, just a small bomb, and *I* brought it to his office and left it on his chair."

Sidney was in shock. Phoebe swung around to face him. J.T. looked from one to the other with an odd combination of nervousness and defiance.

"Somebody had to stand up to them," he repeated defensively.

"You blew up Poppy Press? I can't believe this. I can't..." Sidney couldn't catch her breath.

"I didn't blow up the entire building. Just Ayers's office. Everyone else got out safely. I'm pretty sure about that."

"Oh, dear God."

In the stony silence that followed, Phoebe sat rigidly on the edge of the mattress, her gaze darting back and forth between J.T., whose round face had hardened into defiance, and Sidney, who looked gray and slack. But when Sidney spoke, she was composed.

"How did you learn how to build a bomb?"

"The Internet." J.T. was equally cool. "It's really not a big deal," he added as an afterthought.

"Not a big deal…" Sidney's voice trailed into a sound of disgust. She looked at J.T. as if he were a stranger. Maybe he was. All those times she had sat and listened to his crazy talk at Poppy Press, she had assumed that he was completely harmless. How could she have miscalculated so badly?

"Look," she said, "it's one thing to be upset with the company. Maybe there was even something productive that could have been done through the unions, or bankruptcy court, or Harry Corcoran. But a bomb? Violence? What were you thinking, for God's sake?"

J.T.'s face turned an ugly reddish color, his eyes tiny slits. "Don't you dare. Don't you EVER dare lecture me! Don't you question what I'm doing!" Then he stopped, panting, his outburst over as suddenly as it had started.

Phoebe shrank back, but Sidney was not intimidated. Strange, she thought. She had her own well of previously unforeseen deep anger that was bubbling over more and more. And at this point she was angrier at J.T. than she had ever been at anyone.

How dare I question him? That's rich. Sidney thought back to how J.T. pretended to care about getting them to Connecticut. Pretending to care about Phoebe when he was only trying to flee. Her heart sank at the realization that they had helped a fugitive escape.

"J.T." Her voice took on a terrible coldness. "I want my car keys back. Now. Then you need to leave." She held out her hand for the keys.

The three of them were a silent tableau. J.T. stood with clenched fists and a look of pure hatred. Sidney sat as straight as she could on the bed, chin up, defiant. Phoebe was still at the foot of the bed, fear moving across her face. It was hitting home that they were stuck in uncomfortably close quarters with a dangerous man.

J.T. broke the spell. "So you're going to throw me out?" he spat out. "Really? We're a hundred fifty, two hundred miles from home. I have no money. But you'll throw me out on the street?"

Sidney pressed her lips into a thin line.

"Fine." With shaking fingers, J.T. dug the car keys from the pocket of his dirty jeans and threw them toward Sidney with a violent twist of his arm. They struck her in the side of her head, knocking her glasses off. She recovered quickly, fumbling for the keys before he could change his mind.

"Sidney, you're bleeding!" Phoebe whispered, touching her own face.

Sidney felt her forehead and looked down at her bloody fingers, then directed another cold stare at J.T. "I don't care if we're in the middle of nowhere. I never want to see you again." She reached for a tissue box on the nightstand. She had dabbed most of the blood from her face before she noticed J.T. still standing in the same spot. "Get out," she said wearily.

He looked to be in shock, but at Sidney's directive, he blinked and began a slow pivot toward the door. As he turned, he came face to face with Phoebe, who was watching him, fascinated.

"All right, I'm going," he said. Then, in a surprisingly lithe move, he lunged and snatched up Phoebe.

As J.T. held Phoebe in a headlock, gripping her with the crook of his arm, Sidney watched gaping. She couldn't think, couldn't fathom these events. They were happening too quickly. One minute he was leaving, and the next he was holding them hostage.

"Do what I say," he said in a harsh voice that was unrecognizable, "or I'll snap her neck."

Twenty

By the time Adele reached her destination, a town just outside New Haven, she was frazzled, over-caffeinated, and still without a definitive plan. What exactly did she expect to gain from this journey? She didn't know. She drove aimlessly until a sign for a well-known hotel chain caught her eye. She pulled into the parking lot. Jay had provided his address and encouraged her, almost begged her, to stay with his family, but the idea made her uncomfortable. She couldn't simply show up on his doorstep, no matter how nice he had been on the phone. She would check into the hotel, call her mother to check on Bobby, and then crash. Time enough to get in touch with Jay in the morning.

But she changed her mind and called Jay a few hours later.

"Don't stay at a hotel. Come here, instead," he said again. "We've got plenty of room."

"I don't want to put you and your wife to any trouble."

"It's no trouble, honestly." Jay paused and changed tactics, to Adele's relief. "Well then, how about we take you to breakfast in the morning. It's the least we can do. Lisa and I want to go over everything with you, okay? Maybe at the same time we can convince you to stay with us. You're family." He gave her directions to a local diner.

"I can't tell you how much I appreciate your kindness." Adele was embarrassed at her shaking voice.

"I can't say I know what you're going through, but I can imagine. Nothing short of torture most likely. Robert leaving like that, your daughter disappearing. Then, this terrible news of Robert. Taking his own life like that."

Adele had to bite her lip. She didn't know how to respond to the litany. It was true enough.

In the awkward silence that followed, Jay cleared his throat. "I know this sounds like prying, but I have to ask you something. What reason did Robert give for leaving? I want to make sure you're aware of," he coughed a little, "of the truth."

Adele had promised herself that she would keep her emotions in check, but they managed to surge before she could stop herself from snapping a rejoinder. "If you mean, did Robert tell me that he was gay? Did he rub in my face about why he left? Yes, I know that truth. And Robert was—well, let's say he was defiant about it."

"Wow." Jay said it quietly but seemed taken aback. He may have heard a different version of events, Adele thought. "Okay," he continued after a beat, "so you know that Robert came to Connecticut because of someone. It's a person Robert knew from school and, I gather, had been in contact with for quite some time. It seems their relationship had developed in recent years when this person was working in Pennsylvania, very close to where you live."

"How do you know this? I thought Robert didn't keep in touch with you."

"He didn't. I got this information from Stuart—the person Robert was, um, with. He was the one who tracked us down as Robert's next of kin. Stuart was very distraught when Robert died. It's understandable. He believes Robert committed suicide because of him. Stuart was trying to end the relationship."

"Understandable." Adele knew it sounded cruel but was beyond attempting to hide the bitterness.

"I know, I know." Jay was flustered, which made her suddenly regret not curbing her sharp tongue. Robert's sins were his own and his brother wasn't accountable. She was also beginning to regret her impulsive choice to come to Connecticut. The real reason, the only reason she made this trek was the wildly improbable hope of finding Phoebe. Now Adele realized how foolish that hope had been. It was already becoming clear that there was no sign of Phoebe. Just a disengaged family struggling to understand Robert's sad tale, a few remaining relatives who expected Adele to join in the group mourning. As if she could mourn Robert, who had betrayed her in the worst way possible and then abandoned his children to boot.

"Let's talk about it in the morning over coffee," Jay said. "I'll show you the letter Robert wrote."

Adele willed herself to stay on the line and not drop the phone and run back to the car to drive home. "Okay, I'll be there," she promised.

~

When Sidney woke early the next morning, she felt disoriented. It wasn't because the memory of J.T. going crazy and holding Phoebe and her hostage had somehow slipped away in her fitful sleep. No, she remembered that all too well. She was foggy only because she had been dreaming once again, and this time quite vividly, of her mother.

In the dream, Agatha had looked as she had near the end of her life, dark spots showing through her thin, white hair, a disconcerting split in the cartilage of her nose. She was wheelchair-bound, with swollen legs that splayed her feet out at grotesque angles. Sidney dreamed she was struggling to maneuver Agatha's wheelchair toward her bedroom. "No, no, no!" Agatha had screamed, dragging her swollen feet to stop the chair. "I don't want that! You never know what I want!" This upset Sidney, but she continued to push the wheelchair with all her strength. With her mother's gasp came the realization that they were at the top of the stairs, and Agatha was on the verge of pitching forward. Then, there went the wheelchair, tumbling in acrobatic circles down the steps. Sidney could see Agatha's terrified look and tried to grab a limb, a wheel, anything. She clutched only air.

Sidney gasped and struggled to sit up. Rubbing her stiff neck, she looked across the room and saw J.T. still sleeping, sprawled halfway across the cot, his legs dangling to the floor. Phoebe was just as J.T. had arranged her, still with her wrists tied in strips of bedsheets to a metal bar at the opposite end of the cot. She had drawn up her legs and was curled in a ball like a kitten, asleep.

Daylight was beginning to brighten the edges of the window draperies. The endless night might finally be over, Sidney thought, but she was no closer to coming up with a way out of their predicament. When they had started out, what seemed like a million years ago, she had anticipated a long, stressful journey. But how could she have predicted J.T. and his erratic, psychotic behavior? Granted, he didn't seem to have a weapon—at least he wasn't brandishing one—but Sidney knew that he was easily capable of overpowering the two of them. He had threatened to hurt Phoebe. She wasn't sure, though, why he had relinquished the car keys, or why he hadn't taken them from her again to escape, maybe taking Phoebe as hostage. That would have been a nightmare, Sidney thought, shivering. She felt for the keys in her pants pocket. Thank God, they were still there.

What was J.T.'s plan? she wondered. It was possible that he didn't even have one. That meant it was up to her to resolve this and figure a way out of their situation, stuck in this motel room with no clear means of escape.

Her mind once again going in circles at top speed, she tried to think of some way to convince J.T. to set them free, to go away and leave them alone, just as she had pondered for hours, curled up on the bed and clutching her purse, before falling asleep. She had meant to keep watch all night, but exhaustion had won out.

It was curious, though. Their situation was desperate, and even the bravest person might lose their nerve, let alone someone as timid and fearful as Sidney. Yet she felt perfectly calm and in control. Something told her that she had the upper hand. She was very familiar with J.T., and that was an advantage. It was simply going to be a matter of figuring out the right way to appeal to him, the old J.T., the one she knew from the Press.

"Phoebe?" Sidney whispered.

Phoebe stirred.

"Are you okay?" Sidney saw Phoebe's head lift up from the cot and nod.

As if on cue, J.T.'s eyes fluttered open. He struggled to sit up.

"Hey!" He most likely meant it to sound threatening, but it came out as a groggy croak.

Sidney took a breath and spoke with as much authority as she could muster. "I'm not even going to say good morning, J.T., because we need to have a serious talk. But first, Phoebe and I are going to go get some coffee. Then we'll have that reasonable conversation. Is that clear?"

J.T. stopped massaging his face in mid-stroke. "Weren't you paying attention last night? I *told* you, you aren't going anywhere. Certainly not without me." He glared. "You must be crazy or something to think I'm just going to let you take this kid and walk out of here."

The old Sidney would have retreated. But this time Sidney simply felt rage, rage at the condescension, at the disdain he showed them, and especially at the thought of J.T. or anyone mistreating Phoebe. Sidney looked at Phoebe's hands tied to the cot and then back at her own hands curling into fists.

"*I* must be crazy? *Me*?" she sputtered, red-faced. "You're the one completely off your rocker. What a brilliant idea to plant a bomb at the Press. A bomb, of all things! You're the one out of your mind, not me."

J.T. also flushed. "Yeah, well, there's a method to my madness. I'm winning this battle. That explosive was intended to send a message. A message to New York. It wasn't supposed to hurt people."

"Oh, of course! Why did I imagine a bomb would somehow hurt people?"

Sidney and J.T. fumed at each other across the small span between the beds. J.T. opened his mouth to retort but was interrupted by Phoebe, who had been watching them warily.

"Excuse me, I need to go to the bathroom," she whispered.

J.T. glanced at her with annoyance.

"Please," Phoebe said. "I really have to go bad."

"Oh, come on," Sidney snapped at J.T. "She has to go."

With a sniff, J.T. untied the bedsheet knots, and waved an arm toward the bathroom. Phoebe scampered off the bed and shut the bathroom door silently.

"You don't know that anyone got hurt," J.T. continued his tirade. "You didn't know anything about the whole event until I told you. Now you want to turn me in to the police. That's why you were telling me to leave. I'm onto you and your scheme."

"Don't be ridiculous." Drawing herself as straight as possible, Sidney stood over J.T. But she was trembling so much, she thought her legs would give way. "If I was going to turn you in, then why would I want you to leave? How would the police know where you are?"

"You were going to call the cops and tell them what I did," J.T. repeated stubbornly. "Anyway, everyone got out of Poppy Press just fine."

"How do *you* know that?"

Inside the bathroom, Phoebe locked the door and stood listening to their bickering for a moment. She turned on the faucet full force, hoping that the sound of the water would be loud enough. From the pocket of her jeans, she pulled out the cell phone, the only means of communication they had, the phone that Sidney had placed her in charge of.

Phoebe knew what to do. She dialed 911.

~

Jay had provided simple but clear directions to the restaurant where they were to meet for breakfast, and Adele had no trouble finding the diner, one that looked like a shiny, refurbished railroad car.

Adele was early, but when she pulled open the door and looked down the row of booths, she caught sight of a tall, sandy-haired man standing and waving to her. As she moved closer, she saw that he bore a vague resemblance to Robert. When he spoke, there was no question. It might have been Robert speaking.

"You must be Adele. Welcome, welcome." He ignored her outstretched hand and enveloped her in a bear hug. "I want you to meet my wife, Lisa," he said when he came up for air and stepped back to reveal a woman sitting in the booth. She gave Adele a warm smile. Adele slid in the opposite bench seat, and they sat looking at each other. Adele thought how odd it was that this moment didn't feel strange. They could have been old friends meeting up after many years.

Jay read her thoughts, nodded. "It's been quite a journey to get to this point, hasn't it?"

Adele hesitated. "Would it help if I filled in some gaps?" she asked, immediately regretting the offer. But their nods of agreement came so quickly, she had no choice but to spend breakfast giving a halting description of her relationship with Robert, beginning with how they had met when he was a struggling single parent in the wake of the death of Phoebe's mother. Adele confessed that she had cast aside doubts that Robert had married her primarily to help raise Phoebe. "Maybe there was a tiny bit of that in the beginning, but it became real. There were definitely some good times." She looked across the restaurant, blinking back tears. "I guess it was after Bobby was born that Robert just lost interest. He became, shall we say, very distant."

She dropped her eyes to examine her coffee cup, unable to continue. It was a mistake to discuss these personal, intimate things with strangers. Even those who were supposedly family.

Jay broke into her thoughts. "It sounds like Robert realized at some point that he was gay. Is that right?"

The words came out of Adele before she could stop them. "I guess so, but he didn't bother to tell me. At least at the time." Their expression at her outburst made her bite her lip in embarrassment.

"Look," she said, as controlled as she could manage, "I knew something wasn't right in our marriage, but I didn't even guess that. Stupid, huh?" She tried to laugh. "Please, it's important to me that you know I'm not angry at him for who he was. His life, his choices. I get that. It definitely hurt a lot, just as it would hurt if he left me for anyone. What I am upset about is the way he abandoned us. He left his kids, left us as a family, and, of course, left me to pick up the pieces. Then he goes and kills himself?" She shook her head. "I'm angry, really angry about that."

Lisa darted a glance at her husband, but Jay kept a determined gaze on Adele. He drew an envelope from his pocket and slid it across the table. "This is Robert's farewell note. Would you like to read it?" He cleared his throat. "Fair warning, it's addressed to Stuart, but Stuart wanted you to have an opportunity to read it. If you would like to, that is."

Adele put both palms on the table and stared at the envelope for a long moment before sitting back and shaking her head. "No. I don't even want to know." After a moment, she added, "Maybe you could tell me if he said anything about the kids. That might be nice to tell them some day."

Jay hesitated, but Lisa broke in. "I really believe, Adele, that you would be making a mistake if you don't read this letter. As difficult as it must be, you owe it to yourself." She reached across the table and took Adele's hand. "It does have a message for you and the kids. For Phoebe."

Adele looked at them, uncertain, still gripping the table. She felt as if she had lost her moorings. Her anger with Robert was washing away, and she wanted to get it back, to hold onto it, afraid she would be washed away with it. What they were saying was probably true. In any case, it was entirely possible that Robert would express concern about Phoebe, even in the nightmarish hell he must have been going through. He loved Phoebe, even if he had stopped loving everyone else, including his wife.

Adele blinked, suddenly aware that she must look like she was having some kind of seizure. It was clearly making the couple uncomfortable. Lisa patted her hand weakly, trying to hold a smile that kept fading to a worried frown.

"Okay," Adele murmured. Jay and Lisa sat back, relieved. *Why is this so important to them?* Adele thought, irritated. She scooped up the plain, white envelope and pulled out the pages. Robert's distinctive handwriting was unmistakable.

Although she had been Robert's wife, Adele was at first mortified to read such an intensely personal communication to a loved one, from Robert to Stuart. It felt voyeuristic. She was about to stuff the papers back in the envelope when the words "AIDS" and "HIV" caught her eye. She read quickly. Apparently, Robert had tested HIV-positive, but Stuart had not. (*What does that mean for me?* Adele thought, shocked. *How long had he known about this and didn't say anything?*) Stuart had promptly ended the relationship, moving to Connecticut for a fresh start. That left Robert devastated, he told Stuart in the letter. He had figured that if he was just so very careful, if he took every precaution not to spread the disease, he could make things right, Robert wrote. But he had failed to predict how this would undo their relationship. Worse—with his being so focused on trying to get Stuart back, planning to leave everything and follow him to Connecticut—Robert had ignored his own health crisis. He was diagnosed with AIDS.

I guess you could say I'm an idiot for not addressing this when so many people are living with HIV these days, Robert wrote. *Okay, I'm an idiot. I waited too long. It's true I could find treatment, but it's all too expensive. Especially since I already quit my job and no longer have health insurance. I certainly don't want to put this burden on you—although I have to confess that I was cowardly enough that I was going to ask your help. You know, when I called you? You wouldn't speak to me, and it's actually better that way. There's no way out. No matter how I look at it, I would end up being a drain on everyone, especially my family. The family I betrayed in the worst way possible. So I came home to Connecticut, to be near you, even if you wouldn't see me. In a way, it's comforting because this is where I grew up. And this is where I'll die. Seems fitting.*

Tell Adele and the kids I'm sorry. That doesn't begin to cut it, I know. Not when I've failed them the way that I have. I wish I could say there's a big life insurance policy stashed somewhere, but there isn't. All I have left to offer is to take myself out of the equation. To end this now, so I'm not a burden, not a financial drain. So that I don't cause any more pain. I'm sorry about all the pain.

Just a last message to my family. Bobby, be good, and listen to your mother. Phoebe—what can I say, Phoebe. I'm going to miss you, my darling girl.

I love you all.

Adele put the letter down and felt her face crumble. Tears spilled out, her shoulders shook. It wasn't grief that set her crying uncontrollably. It wasn't even fear that he might have infected her with the virus—it had been so long since they had been together that she doubted it, but of course she would have to make certain anyway. And it wasn't the sadness over her lost marriage or the unspeakable wrath at what Robert had done to her and how he had betrayed them all, as he rightly described.

No, it was this message to Phoebe. It tripped an invisible wire for Adele. It meant facing the realization that this was what had been keeping her awake at night, sending her into the streets to search, compelling her to hound the authorities, and finally leading her to make this desperate trip to Connecticut. She longed to find Phoebe, not out of duty or even out of guilt. Phoebe must be found because Phoebe was her child, just as much as Bobby was. Now Adele had to (wanted to!) act as both parents to Phoebe now that Robert was gone. Adele wanted her daughter back.

Adele looked at Jay and Lisa. Their faces reflected her agony.

Jay said gently, hesitantly, "More than anything, I wish this could have worked out differently. I wish Robert would have contacted me for help. But he didn't. And believe me, we didn't want to show you this letter to be cruel. In addition to the information that you deserved to know, we just felt that Robert, in his own way, was saying why he did this. It was, really, for you and the kids."

Adele covered her face and sat very still.

"You know what's bad?" she asked, her voice thick. "All of this is proof that Phoebe never did find Robert. She's lost. I may never find her, and it's my fault. All my fault."

"How—?" Jay started to say when his cell phone buzzed. He pressed a button and held the phone to his ear without speaking. Then his expression changed. Still without a word to the caller, he laid the phone on the table, his look so intense that Adele stopped crying.

"That was the local police department. There's been an inquiry about Robert. And I suppose I'm listed as next of kin, so naturally..."

"My love," Lisa interrupted, "please just tell us."

"It's Phoebe," he said. He looked at Adele's red-rimmed eyes, at the mascara running in ghastly rivers down her face. "Phoebe's at the police headquarters, right here in Connecticut. She's fine. She's okay. She's looking for her father."

Twenty-one

On her first day back at work, Sidney felt as uncertain as if it were her very first day there, as if she hadn't walked into the same lobby day after day, year after year. After such a short amount of time, it wasn't that she had suddenly become unfamiliar with the routine or her coworkers. No, she was simply at a loss about the sort of reception she might receive. If nothing else, there was the embarrassment of having been naïve enough to believe the rumor mill and the word of the Lunch Ladies that she would be let go. Instead of waiting for the hammer to fall—and, more importantly, waiting to see if there was any truth to the prediction—she had just failed to show up. Not just for a day or two, but for a couple of weeks.

After Sidney returned from Connecticut it didn't take long for her to realize that she needed employment. She made some half-hearted, futile attempts at a job search but quickly assessed that she had few prospects. So she summoned the courage to call Antoinette, ready to grovel and humbly ask for her job back. After several minutes of a hesitant, one-sided conversation that rapidly deteriorated into Sidney pleading for another chance, Antoinette broke in.

"Sidney, what are you talking about? You haven't been fired or laid off. You still have a job here."

Sidney listened in wonder as Antoinette explained how the bombing had distracted everyone at the Press from focusing on things as mundane as attendance records. In fact, Antoinette believed that no one had noticed Sidney's absence except herself. Even Harry had been too busy to ask about Sidney's whereabouts.

"What were you thinking, though?" Antoinette demanded. "I was so worried. It's not like you not to call. I tried to reach you so many times. Then eventually I heard something about you taking with that guy who planted the bomb? That just blew me away. Seriously, have you lost your mind?"

"I may have finally found it," Sidney said ruefully. "I don't know why I ever listened to J.T. I guess it was because people didn't give him a chance, or maybe I felt sorry for him. But if I had any clue what he was planning? A bomb?" Her voice dropped. "I feel so guilty. Maybe I could have stopped him."

Antoinette's tone softened. "Look, you can't be responsible for his actions. The important thing is, no one got hurt. Fortunately, he wasn't such a good bomb maker. Anyway," she added brightly, "there's good news. Harry is now running Poppy Press! He's turning the company around."

"Really? What happened to Mr. Ayers and the New York people? The bankruptcy and all?"

"Vince Ayers is dead. He got hit by a truck the day of the bombing."

Sidney drew in a breath sharply.

"Sidney, listen to me." Antoinette was firm. "Ayers caused his own death by running away. He literally ran across the street. And when you think about it, Ayers started this whole series of events.

"What you need to do, young lady," she continued, "is to get yourself back to work. Harry's got lots of ideas and I can tell you it's going to be all hands on deck."

Settling in at her desk on that first day and looking around at the once again busy office, Sidney had to admit that Antoinette was right. Everything about the Press was lighter and freer without Ayers and his regime weighing it down. The place was bustling again. The old Poppy Press was back.

At noon Sidney went to the lunchroom but hesitated before entering. Antoinette, with her more sanguine views, might not have held Sidney complicit in J.T.'s crazy schemes, but who knew how Carla and the Lunch Ladies felt? How would they treat her? After several deep breaths she pushed the door open.

Carla was holding court as usual. Sidney slipped into her regular seat at the far end of the table.

"Welcome back, Sidney," Carla said smoothly, barely interrupting her tale, and seemingly unfazed by Sidney's absence. Listening as she unwrapped her sandwich, Sidney recognized Carla's narrative as the story of the bombing. As usual, Carla seemed to be in possession of quite a few details.

Sidney stopped in mid-chew. From Carla's story, Sidney realized that it must have been common knowledge that J.T. had "escaped" with her. Antoinette had mentioned it, after all. She continued listening, fearful that Carla somehow knew everything: J.T. hitching a ride with her, the journey to Connecticut, the motel room, everything. About Phoebe. Sidney tried to swallow.

Carla was well into the manhunt portion of the story. "It was obvious to me, if anyone had bothered to inquire," she said with more than a trace of indignation, "that J.T. was a very strong suspect. The man had issues. Didn't we all see that?" She looked about the table for affirmation, and the women nodded in unison.

"But the police were asking all the wrong people all the wrong questions, until they found the note. It was a letter, actually, sent by the bomber. I have it on good authority, mind you, directly from the guys in the mailroom, that this note was signed, the 'Mad Bomber.' How about that! Of course, the mailroom turned the note over to the police straight away. It was a break in the case because the mailroom guys always heard J.T. going on about this Mad Bomber, the real one. I never heard of him, but J.T. would always talk about how much he admired this bomber. Kind of obsessed, he was."

Sidney stiffened, waiting for Carla to demand to know if J.T. had shared his fascination for the Mad Bomber with her. He had never mentioned it to Sidney, but Carla wouldn't believe that.

But Carla didn't even glance at Sidney's end of the table and was instead focused on opening a Little Debbie snack cake. "So there was the Mad Bomber letter," Carla said with her mouth full. "Then there was also the fact that Gary—you know Gary, the pressman?—reported that he had run into J.T. on the day of the bombing. Gary said he was acting very suspicious." She gave a dismissive shrug.

"I'm not saying what happened was a *good* thing, but the end result is that we have the old Press back. Don't we, girls?" Carla's grin was so wide that her eyes dissolved into small slits.

And that was it. It was as if the entire affair were merely one of Carla's beloved soaps. Switching seamlessly to another topic, Carla said nothing more about the bombing or J.T. Perhaps she didn't know the full story. Whatever the reason, Sidney was relieved.

It wasn't only her job that had returned to normalcy. By some miracle, Sidney had also retained possession of her home.

She had been walking out of the police headquarters in Connecticut, still more than a little in shock, when her cell phone rang. For a heart-wrenching moment she thought it was Phoebe calling. Maybe she had changed her mind. Maybe she needed her help, Sidney thought as she struggled to pull the phone from her purse.

"Sidney?" said an instantly recognizable male voice.

Sidney hid her disappointment. "Mr. Smithson, I was going to call you."

"Sidney, listen. It's very important." Perhaps it was the connection, but Mr. Smithson's voice sounded shaky. "It's your father. He's passed away."

She felt dizzy. "You mean Donald O'Neill? He's dead?"

"Yes, he had a massive heart attack."

She struggled for an appropriate comment, if only because Mr. Smithson seemed to be waiting for a response. She wasn't feeling any particular sort of emotion. Was she supposed to feel bad that he was dead? Regret, perhaps? The most she felt was a mild relief. At least she didn't have to hear about him any longer.

"Well, he was pretty old," she said finally.

"Don't you see?" Mr. Smithson asked, exasperated. "That whole affair with the estate and the house—all that nonsense is over. His claim is gone because he's gone."

Sidney stood stock still. It all made sense. "Yes. Yes, of course." Clutching the phone, she began to walk at a brisk pace toward her car, which the police had been kind enough to transport from the motel to the police station parking lot.

"Sorry, it's been a rough few days. Look, I'm in Connecticut right now, but I'll call you when I get back." She stopped and looked at the cell phone, puzzled. "Can you please tell me how to hang up one of these contraptions?"

Overall, Sidney's life resumed its earlier routine. "Back to normal," she would think. Of course, it hadn't reverted completely. She came home each evening from work to an empty house. Agatha was still gone.

Not having her mother was sad, but the real hole in her life was the one that Phoebe had left. Sidney missed Phoebe terribly, in an aching way that left her feeling guilty. It didn't seem quite right that she suffered far more from the absence of an eleven-year-old who had broken into her home than from the loss of her own mother. Phoebe remained the single biggest reminder for Sidney that life could never go back to normal. It had changed forever.

She found herself replaying recent events in her mind, torturing herself with regret. How she had handled things. How she had let herself be fooled by J.T.'s many lies. How naïve she had been. She questioned why she had refused to act, why she and

Phoebe hadn't fled the instant J.T. admitted to the bombing. Any rational adult would have escaped immediately, she thought. Instead, she had been, as always, too timid. *If it hadn't been for Phoebe's bathroom call to 911*, she chided herself, *who knows what would have happened?* Thank goodness the eleven-year-old had her wits about her.

After the police stormed the room, literally breaking down the door to rescue them, and after they had placed J.T. under arrest and it was all over, she and Phoebe sat in the police station in a daze, waiting for someone to give them information, or perhaps some sort of direction. An idea of what to do. Sidney looked stricken, as Phoebe occasionally would lean over to say something comforting. "It's okay. You were just trying to help me find my dad," she whispered. Sidney nodded, but she didn't believe it. It was her fault. She was to blame.

A police officer beckoned them into a conference room. Sidney felt a resignation, knowing that this time she would have to tell the whole truth and nothing but the truth.

In the ensuing discussion, Sidney did come clean. She told about J.T. admitting to setting off the bomb at Poppy Press and how he fooled her into joining them for the trip to Connecticut, even though she should have known better. She confessed about Phoebe. Reddening with shame, she acknowledged that she had been keeping Phoebe in her home instead of calling her stepmother or the authorities. She explained that they had been on their way to Orange, Connecticut, to try to find Phoebe's father, and yes, she had been traveling with the girl without any kind of parental permission.

Sidney talked for what seemed hours. When she finished, she looked up, expecting to see someone in front of her with handcuffs. To her amazement, the man who had been impassively taking her statement merely excused himself and left Sidney and Phoebe to sit together at the small table and consider their surroundings.

"How about a Coke?" A female officer, who had sat as a silent witness during Sidney's statement, rose and smiled at them. "I'll be right back."

"See?" Phoebe whispered as the door shut. "They're nice."

Sidney agreed that the police were indeed nice.

The investigating officer proved this point when he returned to the room by announcing that they were not going to press any charges against Sidney, although she was warned that she might be required to come back and give testimony in J.T.'s case. He then asked a few more questions, directed at Phoebe about her father. He requested the exact spelling of her father's name and inquired about his date of birth. In a matter-of-fact tone, the officer asked them to wait a little longer while he did "a little more checking." Sidney was prepared for a long siege, but after a brief spell, the officer opened the door and announced that the family of Robert Locke had arrived.

It was shocking for Sidney to witness the reunion between Phoebe and her stepmother—the same stepmother who, as Sidney had convinced herself, had to be uncaring and hateful. Instead, Phoebe and this stranger clung to each other, weeping in obvious, genuine love. Sidney stood by awkwardly. A man peeled away from the small group and introduced himself to Sidney as Jay, Robert Locke's brother and Phoebe's uncle. He pointed out his wife, who looked equally drained, and then nodded toward the woman who was still clutching Phoebe. "That's Adele," he murmured. "Robert's wife and Phoebe's mom. Well, technically, stepmom."

Sidney looked at them and nodded. "I know," she said.

At that moment Phoebe raised her head and asked, "Where's my dad? Is he okay?" That led to a flurry of activity. Jay politely asked the police officer to escort Sidney from the room to give them some privacy. After that, Sidney didn't see Phoebe again. Not really. From her vantage point in the waiting room where the officer had deposited her, she couldn't hear any specific words, just voices rising and falling with a steady undercurrent from Jay's deep baritone. Sidney thought she heard Phoebe give a high-pitched wail. They finally exited the room as a group and rushed from the building, the adults flanking Phoebe, protecting her so she couldn't be seen.

Sidney sat there waiting for more than an hour.

At last the nice female officer emerged from another door. She gave a start when she saw Sidney. "I'm so sorry. Somebody should have told you that you were free to go." When Sidney didn't move, the woman approached her. "Oh, goodness, I'll bet you can't go anywhere because your car isn't here. Let me help you get your vehicle."

Sidney slowly held her hand up as if shielding her eyes from a blinding light. "I know," she hesitated, then started again, "I know it really isn't my business, but can you please tell me what happened? What happened to Robert Locke? Where is he? We came so far to find him."

As the officer looked at her, Sidney studied her as well, noting how young and pretty she was, and how that seemed slightly out of place in a law enforcement role, despite her flawless uniform and dark hair severely pulled back into a tight bun. She appeared torn between sympathy and some code of silence. Sympathy won out.

"Well, you obviously took good care of that little girl. You brought her all the way here to find her father, so you deserve to know." The officer paused, still reluctant to reveal the information. Suddenly she blurted, "I'm afraid Robert Locke is deceased. When Phoebe told us her father's name, we ran a check on it and discovered, well, what happened. Luckily, we were able to reach his brother, who was listed as next of kin."

Sidney's head filled with an incredible noise, and she had trouble hearing anything past the word "deceased." Phoebe's father was dead. It was a twisted end to such a hopeful journey.

Her heart broke at the thought of what Phoebe would be suffering. Even amid that, Sidney couldn't help fanning her own faint hope. Maybe, just maybe, Phoebe would choose to stay with her after all. Maybe things could go back to how they were before this terrible news. Then she saw again Phoebe and her stepmother reuniting, clinging to each other as only a parent and child would.

Sidney looked past the woman before her, the nameless officer still talking. About what, Sidney couldn't fathom. She could only think: It was time to face facts. Phoebe walking out that door with her family—her real family—was Phoebe walking out of Sidney's life for good.

~

Nearly nine months later, having left work a little before her usual quitting time, Sidney was unabashedly light-hearted as she drove home. It was not only because it was spring again, or that the sun was setting in a particularly beautiful golden light, or that a weekend stretched ahead. She was excited, joyful really, because Phoebe was coming to dinner. Adele was bringing Phoebe, along with her brother Bobby.

When Adele had phoned the week before to arrange a meeting, Sidney at first was taken aback, wondering what her motive might be. Would Adele use it as an opportunity to confront her, the anger finally having gotten to her? Or was she simply suggesting a visit to properly close the loop? It was hard to know. Sidney had heard nothing from the family since the day they had walked out of the police station with the grieving Phoebe. *But why should they communicate with someone they likely saw as a kidnapper?* Sidney asked herself.

Just before the end of the call, however, Adele mentioned off-handedly that it had been Phoebe's idea to get back in touch with Sidney.

Sidney's heart had jumped. Since then the notion that Phoebe had wanted to see her had so taken hold that she held onto and cherished this idea as she prepared for their visit. Adele had said that they would just "pop in," but Sidney was insistent, almost pleading. They should come to dinner. She couldn't stand the thought of a brief visit, of Phoebe stopping by and then suddenly gone. *Phoebe wants to see me*, she would think, followed by, *Remember, she's not your daughter. Not your family.*

In spite of trying to hold back any untoward enthusiasm, she couldn't stop it from bubbling over as the day approached. She felt genuinely happy as she unlocked the door of her beloved Victorian and deposited bags of groceries on the kitchen table. *Life is good*, she thought, surveying the kitchen. It was as spotless as it had been in Agatha's time. And most important, it was her kitchen.

Sidney hummed as she made the last-minute preparations. Then the doorbell rang, and suddenly there they were, piling into the house—Bobby shy and hanging back behind his mother, Adele a little apprehensive but with a tight smile, and Phoebe enveloping Sidney in a long, hard embrace.

Sidney broke away and, with an arm still around Phoebe, told Bobby, "I hope you like hot dogs because I thought we would have a cookout." She gave them both a smile.

"He loves hot dogs. How did you know?" Adele shot a glance at Phoebe.

"Just a lucky guess." Sidney shepherded them out the back door. "Come this way. I have the grill going outside, and because it's so nice out, I thought we would eat on the back porch."

The relaxed atmosphere of eating in the warm air, at the glass-topped table that Sidney had covered with a festive, red-checked tablecloth, made the evening go smoother than it might have in the formal dining room. Conversation was also easier than Sidney had expected, even when they started discussing all that had happened on the road trip to Connecticut. Sidney told them about the bomb that J.T. had planted at Poppy Press and the company's recovery in the aftermath.

"The thing is, J.T. really did believe that he was saving the company. He had a crazy way of going about it, and I was a fool to listen to his ranting and raving to begin with. But," Sidney reflected, "he thought he was doing the right thing."

"What's going to happen to him?" Adele asked.

"He pleaded guilty to everything, thank God, so there's not going to be any trial. That means no testimony is required. He hasn't been sentenced yet, but I hope the judge will get him the psychological help he needs."

They sat silently for a moment. Phoebe said, "Some of it was pretty exciting. Remember when we were searching for your mom's will? And how about the time your dad was yelling in the middle of the street, and the police had to come get him?"

"I could have stood a little less excitement," Sidney said as she rolled her eyes. The others laughed, recognizing Sidney's imitation of Phoebe's signature mannerism. Phoebe chuckled, too, and then broke in.

"Hey, Sidney, do you have a flashlight? Let's check out the shed. We were going to look there for the money, remember?" Phoebe started to tell Adele about Sidney's mother leaving a note that she had buried Sidney's inheritance somewhere in the back yard.

"I don't understand. Why wouldn't it be in the house? She buried it?" Adele asked. "Have you searched the house?"

"Yes!" Phoebe and Sidney said simultaneously.

"Did you say buried treasure?" Bobby, who had been paying little attention, was instantly intrigued.

"I can explain," Sidney said. "We were searching for a will that might have been left by my mother. This was when the ownership of the house was, let's say, in dispute. We didn't find a will, but we did discover that letter from my mother, so we dug up half the lawn before I realized that I couldn't picture my mother digging in the dirt."

"So let's search the shed. We never got a chance to look in there. Not to really look," Phoebe persisted.

Sidney couldn't refuse her. She rose. "Okay, I'll get a flashlight."

"Get all the flashlights you've got," Phoebe called after her.

Dusk had fallen, so the flashlights were necessary to navigate the back yard, although Bobby ran headlong after the fireflies dotting the lawn, trying to catch them. At the shed Phoebe trained her light on the padlock so Sidney could unbolt it and throw open the doors. They stood at the entrance, the beams of their flashlights moving and intertwining. The shed was neatly organized, but gardening tools and equipment crowded most of the space.

"I don't know where to start," Sidney said.

Adele was already inside and gingerly snaking her way past the equipment. Phoebe followed. Sidney watched, feeling a bit helpless, as they carefully searched shelves and shifted items.

"Hey," Phoebe spoke up, "is that a cabinet behind this big ladder?" She pointed her flashlight at a rough, wooden cupboard partially visible behind the ladder leaning against it.

Together, Sidney and Adele were able to move things to reach the cupboard. Its door had a crack along the top, and even in the faint light they could see that it was covered in dirt and dust. As many times as Sidney had been in the shed, she couldn't remember storing anything in this cabinet, or even looking inside. It was just always there.

"This is a first," Sidney said. "I don't believe I ever opened this before."

They held their collective breath as she pulled open the cupboard door. It gave a horrid creak, and something fluttered and flew past them and out of the shed.

"I hope that wasn't a bat." Adele's voice shook a bit.

"Too small. Maybe a large moth," Sidney said, but she was cautious as she opened the door wider and used her flashlight to examine the interior. She saw that the shelving inside the cupboard had been removed to make room for a large object. This was covered with filthy, moth-eaten fabric that at one time must have been a small blanket. Sidney pulled it off with the tips of her fingers, revealing a dusty, satchel-like briefcase. They eyed it in wonder.

"I almost hate to touch it. It's so disgustingly dirty," Sidney said.

"Let's just get it in the house," Adele said.

It took both Sidney and Adele to carry the heavy case. Sidney spread newspaper over the kitchen table, and then ran upstairs to retrieve the little key that had accompanied the letter from Agatha. Just as Sidney hoped, the key opened the latch on the satchel. She peered inside. With a startled glance at the others, she carefully reached inside and began pulling out plastic bags of money. It was a lot, what must have been thousands of dollars in currency, as well as stock and bond certificates. There was also some jewelry, which appeared to be gold.

"Well, this didn't come as the result of a life insurance payout," Adele said.

Sidney shook her head and looked at the riches spread out on the table as if they were things from another planet. Her mother had somehow managed to hoard a good part of her grandfather's inheritance. And had saved it for her.

"This means, I think, that you won't have to worry about money anymore," Adele said. "Is there someone, a professional, who can help you with this? Someone you trust?"

"Yes, Mr. Smithson, our attorney," Sidney said faintly, still staring at the table.

Phoebe stood at her side. "I'm glad we looked in the shed."

Sidney responded by putting her arm around Phoebe.

Adele looked at them with an odd expression. "Well," she announced briskly, "it's getting late, and we should be going. Can we help you clear away the dinner dishes?"

"No, no, I've got it." Sidney's voice was robotic. But they all continued to stand around the table, reluctant to break the spell.

Phoebe said, "Why didn't your mother tell you where this money was? It seems like that would have been the easy thing to do rather than hoping you found that letter."

Sidney roused herself. "I think she probably always meant to tell me, but she knew that I would want to use this money to take care of her while she was alive. She wanted it for me, after she was gone, you see. That would be like her." She thought for a moment. "Also, my mother probably always thought there would be more time, but there wasn't. She had a stroke near the end and couldn't speak. Then it was too late. It was all locked in her head."

"That's so sad." Phoebe looked about to cry.

Sidney smiled at her. "Don't worry. You probably made my mother very happy tonight by finding what she didn't have a chance to tell me about."

"Come on, Phoebe, we've got to get going," Adele said. "Where's your brother?"

"Phoebe," Sidney said, "why don't you find Bobby and give him a proper tour before you go?"

Phoebe headed out to the front of the house, and Sidney turned to Adele. "I'd like to talk with you about something. I was planning to ask if maybe we could do this again. I really miss Phoebe and would love to see her more frequently. If that's possible."

Adele started to speak, but Sidney held up her hand. "Before you answer, let me say what I need to say, considering what happened tonight. I mean, look at this." She waved at the table. "This is more money than I'll ever need, no matter how old I live. I don't have any family. Let me help you out. I can help Phoebe and Bobby and you."

Adele stared at her. "I couldn't possibly." Her tone indicated she was not open to discussion, but Sidney, warming to the idea, ignored her.

"Think about it. You're raising two kids by yourself. But more importantly, just think about the series of events that led to this moment. I don't think it was coincidence that Phoebe ended up in my basement. You and I, we might not be connected by blood, but I think we are connected by fate. And most of all, we both just want to help these children."

"Why would you do that for us? What would you get out of it?"

"A family. I would get a family."

Phoebe had come up behind them and was looking at them quizzically. Sidney wondered how much she had heard.

"Are we going or not?" Bobby asked from behind his sister.

"We're going," Adele said. Holding out her hands to both children, she led the way out of the house and toward her car. Sidney trailed behind.

Once the kids were buckled in, Adele paused at the driver's door and looked across at Sidney. "You don't have to pay us to be a family," she said.

In the darkness, Sidney flushed. She was a pathetic, old lady. "That isn't what I meant. I just want to help."

There was a silence. When Adele at last responded, it was a softer tone, Sidney thought. Perhaps it was her imagination.

"We'll see," Adele said as she climbed behind the wheel. She started the car, and as they pulled away, Phoebe turned to wave goodbye, impulsively sticking her head out the open window. "I love you!" she called to Sidney. The words rang in the empty street.

For many minutes after they left, Sidney stood there, her hand raised in response, while a fragment of a hymn from church, Psalm 63, filled her ears.

My soul clings fast to you; your right hand holds me firm.

In the shadow of your wings, I shout for joy.

Sidney could see a clear vision in her mind's eye—Phoebe flying strong and free. And no matter what happened, she thought as she turned to go into the house, that was a comfort. *Yes,* she thought, *finally, I can shout for joy.*

Afterword

Like many authors who try to write around the edges of life—in predawn hours, nights and weekends, stealing time on vacations and holidays—I've brought, and maybe at times dragged, this story along a very long journey indeed. It was a story that was shelved for a long time, but eventually needed to be told. So, it was revised and rewritten, developed and re-developed. At last with the help of others, it became, I think, a better story. Still, the basic tale remained the same, a patchwork of different inspirations.

A news item from many years ago captured my imagination. It was the report of a young boy who took a Greyhound bus on his own, relying on the kindness of strangers as he traveled up the East Coast in search of the father who abandoned his family. Sidney and Agatha were inspired by neighbors we once had, a mother and daughter who both passed away too soon. I often thought, as I listened to the elderly Mary's memorable stories of the past while we ate our post-church services dinner at Pizza Hut, that no matter how many years one has on this earth, it never seems quite enough.

And finally, the workplace element of Poppy Press. That was rooted in one particularly dreadful year, the lowest point of my life. I was a single mother, desperately seeking employment to support my children, and thought I had finally caught a break by landing what seemed to be a great job. That bubble burst on my very first day of work, when my new boss blamed me for the sudden, sharp dive in the stock market the day before, scolding me for "bringing bad luck" and causing him financial losses. It wasn't just a bad boss situation; the company filed for bankruptcy within a fortnight, leaving the employees, including me, scrambling. I did find other employment but this experience showed me how work can sometimes overpower our lives.

There are many people who have been instrumental in making this book a reality and I am truly grateful to these and so many others: Rachel Caldwell, Jesse Coleman, Larry Massaro, Joanne Bowes, Jim Callahan, and Dan Callahan (thank you, Dan, for the encouragement that always kept me going), And, of course, my love and gratitude to Jack, who has been unflagging in his support and belief in me these many years.

Made in the USA
Lexington, KY
24 October 2019